A BRAD STEPHENS NOVEL

BREAKFAST BALL

The 1st Hole

J.A. MALONEY

Breakfast Ball
The 1st Hole
J.A. Maloney

Copyright © 2013 J. A. Maloney

JMPublishing
217 E. Anapamu St., Santa Barbara, Ca. 93101
Visit our website at www.jamaloney.com.

Library of Congress: Filed

ISBN-13: 978-0-9895848-0-7

Printed in the United States of America

Book Design by KarrieRoss.com
Editing by Robin Micheli

First Edition: July 2013

Breakfast ball v: a colloquial expression used amongst recreational golfers to describe the taking of a second shot without penalty. As in, "That one is out of bounds and you're not warmed up yet...take a breakfast ball."
2. Also known as "taking a Mulligan".

DEDICATION

This book is dedicated to:

Anybody who has tried, but just can't hit that stupid, little golf ball straight...

Or, anybody adversely affected by this crappy recession...

Or, anybody who has tried to modify their current mortgage or to refinance in the 'new normal' economy.

You are not alone.

You deserve to take a *Breakfast Ball*.

BREAKFAST
BALL

THE HOME STOOD SILENT AT THE end of the darkened cul-de-sac.

A large lawn dissected by a flagstone walkway ran from the sidewalk to the front of the light brown house. The house was flanked by juniper bushes, making it look more regal than it truly was.

In the back was a small, immaculately groomed putting green, complete with sand trap, chipping area and a commemorative U.S. Open flag. He knew it was there because he'd been watching the house for several days.

He knew that the owners often kept the back door unlocked too.

Earlier in the day, he had used a silenced pistol to shoot out the bulb in the street lamp closest to the house. He had placed a small rock in the middle of the broken glass on the ground. He then did the same thing to two other streetlights. The police would assume it was teenager vandalism.

Now all the light and movement in the house was highlighted with sharp clarity.

Perfect.

A slight breeze blew from the east. The palm fronds on the tree he stood against rustled slightly above him.

At precisely 7:45, same as the last three nights, the garage door opened and a blue Lexus sedan backed out onto the street. The woman driving reversed, braked and then accelerated toward the main street. He knew from recent observation that she was headed for her shift at a homeless mission downtown. She'd be gone at least three hours.

Perfect.

His eyes darted left and right, checking the windows in neighboring houses. No obvious watchers. No busybodies.

Perfect.

He walked towards the garage, stepped into the shadows at the side of the house, and pulled a dark ski mask from his back pocket. He slipped it over his face, then retrieved black leather gloves from his front pocket and fit them over his hands. He reached behind a bush and grabbed some rope he had hidden earlier in the day, hoisted it over his shoulder and walked quietly to the back of the house.

There was noise. It was coming from the study; it would either be a ball game or the Golf Channel. The only person in the house would be there, likely drunk on over-priced Scotch and dead to the world by now.

Soon. Just dead.

He reached the back entrance and tried the door knob. It turned quickly and quietly. No need for his lock-picking tool.

Perfect.

Slowly closing the door behind him, he saw the kitchen ahead, lit only by the faint light thrown off by LED displays. He detected a smell, sweet but antiseptic, and for a moment he was back, a child in the Kentucky hills. His mother had used Lysol to overpower the rancid scent of booze and failure in his home.

Maybe this woman was trying to mask the odor as well? He put it out of his mind.

He made his way through the kitchen, down a short hall and rounded a corner to the study. From behind he could see his target sitting straight up in a large leather chair, his right hand holding a remote control and his left wrapped around a glass of scotch balanced on the arm of the chair.

Damn! Was his target awake? If so, he'd have to come back tomorrow night. He moved closer. The man was facing the TV, where a golfer in yellow pants was lining up a putt. As he stepped closer, he could see that the man's eyes were closed. His target was snoring lightly.

Passed out.

Perfect.

He knew the ceiling in the study provided a perfect, sturdy main beam. He tossed the rope over it, grabbed the open knot and slipped it over the man's head. A snore erupted into a snort, but that was his only reaction. The guy didn't even move when the knot was cinched tight around his neck.

He threw the end of the rope under the heavy couch nearby and looped it around its leg, painstakingly tying the knot. He tried it several times until he was sure it would hold. He grasped the rope and slowly—with effort that took his breath—began hoisting the man out of his chair. Once the body was suspended well above the chair, he yanked as hard as he could.

It flew skyward instantly, startling both him and the target. Now the man was awake, his eyes pinballs in their sockets, his legs kicking frantically. The man grasped at the knot and tried to scream but nothing came out of his mouth.

The man's eyes focused on him for a brief moment as if pleading for help; as if begging for an explanation.

The killer looked away and surveyed the study. Lining the walls was golf memorabilia, golf trophies and photos with famous golfers. "Okay, I get it, you liked golf buddy," he said under his breath.

When he turned back, the body was still, the eyes open, the tongue protruding. The killer reached into his left back pocket for a small mirror, held it in front of the man's nose and mouth. No fog. His target was dead.

Perfect.

God, what an awful way to die, he thought. But, really, was there a *good* way to die?

He snapped himself back; still work to be done. He went back into the hallway, thru the kitchen and thru a door to retrieve the six-foot ladder he had seen in the garage.

Back in the study, he set the ladder close to the body that now twirled, ever so slightly. He spread the ladder's aluminum legs, and then knocked it down.

Did it look like the man had kicked it out from under his feet? He adjusted it a bit. That's it; that's what it would look like.

Perfect.

He walked toward the desk in the corner of the room.

Unlocked doors, a target who was drunk as a skunk every night, and now, no password protection on his personal computer…He'd gotten lucky. It was a killer's dream scenario.

Perfect.

He started up the computer, called up a Word doc and typed what he'd been told: I'm sorry. I love y'all. I just can't take the losses.

He had no idea what the words meant.

He punched 'print' but nothing happened. What the…? He realized he had to turn on the printer, which started up noisily.

He printed the note, folded the paper into quarters and crossed the study, avoiding the sight of the swinging corpse as he walked by. Wishing to get away from the dangling man, he quickened his pace and headed towards the door.

He stopped. *Shit.* He almost forgot something.

No ignoring the body now. He went back to it. Pulling it toward him with his left hand and reaching around it with his right, he thrust the paper into the man's front pocket.

He left the house, closing the door behind him. After a few steps, he pulled off his gloves and ski mask. He was shaking some, but not much.

Considering.

He strode to the front of the driveway, retrieved from his jacket a cigarette and a cheap lighter. The lighter had a slogan imprinted on its face: Visit Beautiful Orlando. One of the Safest Places on Earth.

Before he lit the cigarette he had one more thing to do. He opened his cell phone and dialed the number he had been given. "It's done," he said.

"Good job," came the response on the other end.

"I'll be back soon."

"Alright."

There was a pause and then the voice on the other end said, "And, Curly, God Bless." The line went dead.

He looked at the lighter again and managed a small chuckle. He lit the cigarette and strolled down the street.

It *was* a nice area. But for the dead body in the study, it probably was a safe neighborhood, generally speaking.

Probably a *perfect* place to raise the kids.

2

Brad Stephens watched the sun rise from the comfort of his spacious home office.

He was a light sleeper these days. The recession was part of it, he supposed. His personal financial fiasco, however was really the root cause.

He knew.

Most mornings he liked to get a cup of coffee and take the newspaper into his office. He'd read the Wall Street Journal while watching TV and sipping coffee.

Multi-tasking the American way.

Today, he flopped his 6'2" frame into his deep brown, leather, swivel chair, stretched his long legs out, rested his bare feet on an adjacent chair, arranged support for his perpetually aching lower back and clicked on the TV.

It was a bright Thursday morning, and the streaming sun made the TV difficult to view. But once his eyes adjusted, he had no trouble seeing the female anchor on screen—a tan woman with large breasts and platinum blonde hair.

She was conducting an interview with some typical titan of the business world. The guy was wearing a gray suit, white shirt, red tie, and was expressing his 'sincere' dismay at the depths of the recession.

Same old crap.

"Excuse me," the interviewer said, suddenly turning towards the camera. "We have breaking news. James Aderly, former CEO of Green Ship Mortgage, was found dead this morning in what officials are saying is an apparent suicide. Green Ship Mortgage was one of the nation's leading subprime mortgage lenders in the period leading up to the mortgage crisis. Mr. Aderly was due to testify before Congress next month about the actions of his firm. We will bring you more details as we get them."

The anchor returned to her guest as if nothing had happened. She smiled and asked him to continue with his 'brilliant' insights.

Talking head.

A wonder more guys hadn't committed suicide in this screwed-up economy, Brad thought, while taking a sip of his coffee.

He opened the Journal, looked at the front page headline and muttered, "No shit," as he read on. SUBPRIME LOANS CONTINUE TO WEIGH DOWN FINANCIAL MARKETS.

Great. His profession was all over the news.

Again.

Residential mortgage lending—the industry that he unwittingly helped build over the past thirty years—used to be an honorable profession; one he enjoyed and one he was very good at.

Now this crap!

The article went on to describe how foreclosures were undermining the value of real estate and pulling down the market. Subprime loans were to blame. Criminal charges were being considered.

Well, he thought grimly, with Mr. Aderly's suicide, there probably was one less criminal to worry about.

"Fuck this business; fuck this recession," he said quietly to himself. And while we're at it, he thought, fuck subprime loans.

Not that he was bitter or anything.

Subprime. The name implied 'below desired quality,' but greedy investors on Wall Street and worldwide had sought them with insatiable desire.

As secured loans as opposed to unsecured loans like a credit card, they were made to inferior borrowers who either purchased or refinanced real estate between 1995 and 2007. The loans pulled in much higher profits than normal 'prime' loans. The theory being, risk equals higher yield.

Well, how'd that work out?

What average people didn't understand is that the fun just started when the loan was made. Lenders and Wall Street 'experts' would chop up the principal owed into little pieces called CDOs, Collateralized Debt Obligations. They would sell them and then the paper would get resold again and again—all the while raking up-front profits back into the lenders' coffers.

Risky?

Only if you were the borrower or the eventual purchaser of the CDO.

Wall St. convinced investors that the loans were secured by U.S. real estate, which, as everyone knew, would always go up in value, never down.

Oops!

Guess who was holding the bag when the gigantic Ponzi scheme crumbled? Not the banks; not Wall Street; not the poor schmucks who took the loans and got foreclosed on. The victims were the investors who had bought into the high yield bullshit.

And...the entire U.S. economy.

And, as it turns out, the entire world's economy.

Brad's own personal economy would've taken a dive no matter what. Mortgages were his business; the commissions they paid were his only source of income.

Let's face it; he was a one trick pony. And the trick had taken a tragic turn for the worse.

Overnight, seemingly, lenders stopped lending and borrowers stopped borrowing.

A credit freeze, they call it.

'Cold Turkey' is what drug addicts call it.

And, unfortunately, Americans had become addicted to cheap, easy credit. The cure was not going to be fun.

In retrospect even if income hadn't been an issue, Brad would've been screwed anyway. That god dammed Truckee investment!

He told himself, as he did every day, to shake it off. Don't dwell on it. Too depressing. Still, some days he wanted to lie in bed all day and suck his thumb like a little baby.

But he still had to make a living—even if the mortgage business was now, officially, the 'shits', over-regulated, under-compensated and one constant pain in the ass. He had to persevere. It was his only option.

He tossed the business section across the desk and picked up the entertainment section. Jennifer Aniston was getting married again.

No subprime drama there.

His cell rang; the number was familiar.

"John boy, how you doing?"

"Great! I'm hitting it solid and my putting is really coming around." His pal John Linden, pro golfer and current U.S. Open champ, always responded to that type of question according to how well his game was going. His game was his life. And vice-versa.

"Oh yeah? Great, that's what I want to hear."

"Thank God for the Claw grip. You know old timers say that their careers would've lasted another ten years if they'd known about the Claw." Brad knew Linden was in love with the Claw, even if some golfers found the grip highly unorthodox—the top hand is placed around the butt of the club and the other pushes the handle. It looks funny; no doubt about it, but it worked miracles for those with the 'yips'.

These days Linden was on a mission, proselytizing about the Claw; he was convinced it had changed his game. Brad couldn't disagree. Hell, it had changed his own game.

But even before the Claw, Brad always admired Linden's beautiful, flowing swing. From the time they met at a Pro-Am several years earlier, Brad had enjoyed watching in awe as John unleashed one powerful drive after another.

"How's it out there in beautiful Santa Barbara?" Linden asked.

"Can't complain. Well, I could, but nobody would listen and few would care."

"Your finances getting any better?"

"Not really. Business is sketchy and I've got a ton of debt."

"Like most Americans."

"Yep. Like most Americans," Brad agreed, and then added, "But I'm trying to modify the loan on the house and I'm advertising like mad, so who knows? Maybe things will pick up."

"I've heard from a few friends about that modification deal. They say it doesn't work worth a shit."

Brad nodded and smiled. "They're right, but you got to try if you can't sell or can't refinance. My bank has made up all sorts of excuses for not modifying me, but I keep at it."

"Speaking of houses," Linden said, changing the subject quickly. "That's the main reason I'm calling. I've decided to make Montecito my new home base. I want to buy a house out there. And I want you to represent me on the purchase. It will probably mean a *big* loan."

"Wow. That's great!" Brad's voice raised a few decibels. He winced; he didn't want to act overly enthused.

It was a guy thing.

Play it cool even though he relished the notion of having Linden as a neighbor and, of course, the prospect of making a substantial commission was very exciting. He couldn't let his buddy know.

"I'd love to represent you as long as you aren't going to get too picky and turn into one of those 'Everything has got to be perfect' buyers," Brad said, trying to take the enthusiasm—he hoped it wasn't desperation—down a notch. "I've dealt with a few of those before. I'd rather stick needles in my eyes than put up with that crap."

"Naw, I won't be a pain in the ass. I'm too busy on the tour. Besides, you know I'm easy to get along with. You do all the leg work. Find something *we'd* like.

You can coordinate financial statements and such with Art. You remember him, my manager at IFPG, Art Smalley?"

"Sure. How can I forget the day we played him and that young pro Tyler Powell and kicked their asses? Nice guy." He smiled at the thought.

Something occurred to Brad. He didn't want to raise any negatives that could sour the deal, but Linden was his friend first and foremost. "You know, are you sure about the logistics?"

"What logistics?"

"Well, Freddie used to live out here but decided traveling to and from was tough."

"I'm not worried about travel. Besides, I've never been a big fan of Orlando, and I've always loved it out there. There must be a reason so many business big shots and Hollywood honchos live in Montecito—don't you think?"

On the other end, Brad silently nodded. "Of course there is," he said. "It's a great place to live and raise kids."

"My point exactly. These people could live anywhere in the world but they choose Montecito. That says a lot to me."

True. The Santa Barbara area *was* gorgeous.

Nestled between the Pacific Ocean and the Gibraltar Mountains, sunny 300 days a year the coastal paradise located in the southern part of Central California was known as the Riviera of the U.S.

A very reasonable nickname, Brad thought.

And Montecito, the small, wealthy enclave that bordered it to the southwest, with hills rising from the ocean studded with Craftsman cottages and bougainvillea -splashed mansions, was beyond spectacular.

And the best part; the place was one of a kind.

"All right then. Let's do it. Lord knows I could use the income. But now I'll ask the sixty-four-million dollar question: Who is we?"

Brad could practically hear Linden grinning. "I think I've met the next Mrs. John Linden," he said proudly.

"Careful there partner. You remember the last time this happened. The name Connie ring a bell?"

"I know. I know. But Fabiola is different. She likes to travel, she likes golf! She's from Mexico originally, but she lives here now. Connie wanted to settle down and have kids. Hell, she wanted me to become a local teaching pro. Can you imagine that…me a teaching pro?"

"Nope. You're a wanderer. Not a nester."

"That's right. And by the way, I'm a lover, not a fighter, too." He paused letting his joke set in. Then he continued. "Brad, Fabby is hot—really hot! And, apparently, the fact that I'm 20 years older than she is doesn't seem to bother her one bit in the sack. Hell, she told me she prefers older men!"

"Well, there's that."

Linden paused. "Hey, hold on, someone's trying to call me." Brad waited for a minute, another minute more. Then his friend came back on the line.

"I can't believe it." The usual swagger had gone from Linden's demeanor.

"Believe what? What happened?"

"That was a buddy of mine on the tour." Linden's voice grew shaky.

"What is it, John?"

"My manager at IFPG, Art Smalley, is dead."

"DEAD?" BRAD SAID, NOT KNOWING how else to respond to such startling news.

He had only met Art Smalley a handful of times, but still, he was shocked. Who wouldn't be? And then he remembered that Smalley was younger than he, which was not a comforting thought. "How? *Shit.* We were just talking about him."

"I know, spooky, huh? My friend says he hanged himself. In his own house." Linden, who playing pros secretly called 'flappy' because of his motor mouth while playing, seemed at a loss for words. "I just can't believe it." Brad could almost hear his friend shake his head and could envision him running his empty hand over the front of his face.

"Had he been depressed?" Brad asked, groping for an immediate reason—trying to make sense of the senseless.

"No, that's the thing. He seemed happy. He was planning to take his wife on a cruise. There was nothing obviously wrong." He paused as if pondering whether he should reveal the next piece of information.

After a moment, he continued. "Well, I mean, lately the guy had been hitting the sauce a lot I think. He had a little problem there. But he just wasn't the kind of guy.... This doesn't make sense."

Brad rotated his seat away from the phone and turned towards the window. It was one of those clear days when he could see past the green of his lawn, down the hills to the coastal scrub which gave way to the ocean. Sail boats danced in the distance. He sighed. "I'm sorry. I know you two were tight."

"Yeah..." Linden was silent for a moment. "Well, what I was going to say is that we're coming out there soon. I thought I'd send Fabby out ahead of me, maybe the two of you could look at some houses."

"Sure, that's fine. She can stay here, I'm sure Mel wouldn't mind."

"That's great. Fabby's really excited about buying a house."

"You know," Brad said gently, "I'll still need to get your paperwork, tax returns, simple stuff like that."

"Right. I guess I'll need to call IFPG and authorize access. I don't know who will be handling my account now." He paused. "I just, I can't...I mean suicide. No way."

"I'm really sorry, buddy. Let me know if there's anything else I can do."

"Listen, helping me out with the house—and taking care of Fabby—is plenty. Thanks." Brad could swear he heard Linden sniffle.

"Listen, Brad, I'll text you her details."

He hung up without saying good-bye.

BRAD SPENT THE AFTERNOON HITTING golf balls at the local range, his thoughts drifting from the death of Linden's manager to expectations of finding John a nice home and, who knows, maybe experiencing some financial salvation himself.

He'd wanted to tell his wife, Mel, immediately about the nice plum that just landed in their laps, but she was out with a friend so he decided to chip and putt for a while. The little driving range bordering the ocean was quite a step down from his old country club, but at this stage of his economic life any golf was good golf, he supposed.

When his finances took a dive after Truckee, he'd given up his country club membership and sold his nice car. He didn't expect anyone to feel sorry for him, he was, after all, still hanging in there, but losses are relative.

They hurt.

Period.

End of story.

The drive back home took him north and east through the roads of Montecito, past stone walls and security gates that led to hidden estates. Montecito's real estate market had suffered in the recession; it wasn't immune, hell no place was. When the tide goes out and all that he supposed.

He drove this way all the time to and from his office, but for once, he really paid attention. He would have to get to know the area better if he was to find Linden the right house.

The scent of late afternoon eucalyptus hung in the air like exotic perfume as he made his way thru the winding roads.

Settled in 1769 by Father Junipero Serra, Montecito, California, is a ten square mile area filled with world class shopping, incredible restaurants, and magnificent estates occupied by some of the world's richest people.

Occupied initially by Chumash Indians and Spanish laborers, the area whose name translates literally to 'little woods', prospered and grew during the early 1800's. Its local hot springs and mineral waters attracted visitors afflicted by gout and respiratory ailments. However, by the middle of the century it had become known as a hangout for robbers and thieves—the many trees and rugged terrain providing excellent cover for their illegal activities.

Today, Montecito is inhabited by wealthy retirees, Hollywood celebrities (think, Oprah), business moguls, and upper class trust fund babies. The land of 'little woods' had become the land of 'big moola'.

Montecito and its surrounding environs—all of Santa Barbara, really—was a small enough community that its residents often encountered flamboyant characters who had become local lore. Elsie Reebottom was one of them.

An elderly woman, she was known for matching her outfits to the color of the vintage Cadillac she drove that day. She had seven Caddies, her "Seven-day fleet," she called them, and today's was pale blue. A 1975 model.

She pulled out from the gas station right in front of Brad. *Shit.* He braked and slowed down, settling in behind her as she putt-putted along for almost a mile.

When he saw his opening, he sped past, glancing at the old lady. Today, she donned a pale blue wig, pointed blue sunglasses and a matching blue hat. Quite sporty…if it were 1960. He gave a little wave.

She raised her middle finger.

Brad laughed out loud. "Good for her." Still some life left in the old gal. Linden would like living in Montecito.

He sped ahead passing his good friend Steve Zindo's mansion. He gave a small wave at the property as he passed and smiled. Zindo was a quirky, retired multi-millionaire whose answer to this recession was to pound his chest like a gorilla and say, "You're the master of your destiny. You're like a gorilla. Take charge of your future."

Words. Somehow they helped.

Brad chuckled, remembering the time he and Zindo had consumed too much red wine. "Brad," Zindo had said. "Don't feel so bad, buddy. Everybody has a turd floating in the water. Let's compare problems. You go first."

And Brad had, telling him about the Truckee deal and how he had lost all of his retirement and how he had considered suicide during the process.

Zindo had smiled. Not in a funny, ha-ha, way, but in an empathetic manner. "That's good and I know it hurts. Fuck Truckee." Zindo had paused and had taken a big swig of red wine. "Okay, okay, okay…I'm not trying to brag but I think I can out-do you."

"Bring it on," Brad had said as if it were an athletic competition.

"Okay. I've got a hotel built in Louisiana…and its sinking. Going to cost me a fortune to fix it."

"Holy shit! You got me," Brad had said.

"Not really. The point is we all got problems." Zindo had poured more wine for both of them and then said, "Now pound your chest like a gorilla….."

Brad smiled again and then punched the accelerator. He was anxious to give Mel the good news.

"Hey, there you are. I'm just taking salmon out of the freezer," Mel said as he entered his house.

Brad suppressed a groan. He loved Mel. They'd been college sweethearts, now married 30 years and still going strong. She still looked great—five-six, long, blondish hair, lithe body, and a smile that could fill up a room. Mary Tyler Moore had nothing on Mel.

Cooking, however, had never been her strong suit. Some people fake orgasms. Brad faked delight in Mel's culinary offerings.

"I got this really cool way to fix the salmon from the Food Channel!" she said, so excited it almost broke his heart. "I'm dying to try it!"

"How 'bout I barbecue tonight?" he said. "It's such a nice evening and I don't want you to be inside cooking."

"Okay," she said; no suspicion of his ulterior motives detectable in her voice. "We can do the recipe another night."

Phew! Dodged a bullet, he thought. He poured himself a stiff Jack Daniels and soda. He allowed himself two drinks a night. Ever since the economy tanked, those drinks had gotten stiffer. Still only two. But, in truth, they were strong enough to be three…or four…depending on what you considered "a drink."

Brad passed the hallway mirror and shot himself a quick glance, a habit that tended to drive Mel crazy. Like Mel, he had aged well. His body was lean. The gut hung over the belt a bit, but whose didn't at his age? Mel said it was good for snuggling.

His brown hair was now showing signs of gray. The short beard he kept neatly manicured was gray now, too. His friends, using an indiscriminate foreign accent, liked to tease him about being "The Most Interesting Man in the World," referring to a popular beer commercial.

Lately, every time he glanced at his checkbook he felt more like "The Most Stupid Man in the World." Maybe it was time to shave the beard? He decided to ask Mel about it when he got a chance.

He headed out to the patio. He loved this place, with its views of the ocean to the southwest, the mountains to the north and the fruit and oak trees that surrounded the house. It was a good property. He hoped he could keep it. That was something to drink to.

Ah. That first sip was always the best, smooth and warm, yet refreshing. He'd long ago learned to stick with whisky. Beer gave him a headache. Vodka made him crazy. And tequila—don't even ask about tequila! He almost lost both eyebrows due to that Devil's drink.

Golfers prank.

Mel sat down next to him on the patio, glass of white wine in hand. "How was your day?"

"Well, as a matter of fact, it was quite interesting."

"Good interesting or *bad* interesting?" She had had a lot of bad news recently. She had learned to be discerning.

"Good...I think." He paused and took a sip of his drink. "John Linden called and asked me to represent him in finding a new home in Montecito. It means a large commission on the real estate side and a decent commission on the loan side as well." He beamed at his wife. "This one deal could solve a lot of our immediate debt problems."

Mel's eyes grew wide. "So maybe I can hang on to my house?"

"Maybe. It's definitely a step in the right direction. I'm pretty confident it's going to work out. But as you know, it ain't over till the 'fat lady sings'."

She grinned. Took a sip of her wine and patted Brad on the knee. "I know. But hope gives me some comfort."

Their financial setbacks hadn't been pleasant or easy. But throughout, he and Mel's relationship had remained intact. If they had to make further changes, it would be painful, but Brad knew as long as the two of them could hold it together, everything would be okay.

"John has a new girlfriend. She's the one who wants the house. He thinks she could be the next Mrs. John Linden."

"More like the next future ex-Mrs. John Linden, don't you mean?" Mel's humor was dry, her instincts usually right on.

"Could be. He doesn't have a good track record, does he? But this one is special...so he says. John's crazy about her. Her name is Fabiola."

"Fabiola! What the hell kind of name is Fabiola? Is it the female version of Fabio?"

Brad smiled. "John says she's a real Latin bombshell who enjoys having wild, animal sex."

"Animal sex?" Mel shot him a bemused look. "Where did you come up with that?"

"Don't know. It's just an expression. Seemed appropriate for this specific conversation. In the future I'll be sure to use something more formal like, 'She enjoys riding the one-eyed squirrel' or 'She likes doing the horizontal bop'"

"No that's okay. You can stick with animal sex. It's more juvenile, just like you and John." She unleashed her unfettered, contagious laugh.

Her eyes—those translucent green eyes—still sparkle, Brad thought. Mel laughed and smiled like she did when they were young. Lately, she didn't have much to laugh about. He was trying desperately to change that.

Mel went inside to refill her glass. Brad gazed at the sunset, a golden highway stretched as far west as the eye could see. He could spot deer frolicking in the canyon below.

He'd been blessed. He still owned his home, had a great-looking wife, wonderful kids, his health and good friends.

He might be broke, but he wasn't *broken*.

Along the way, he had even developed a decent game of golf, which actually mimicked life, when you thought about it. If you hit a bad shot, then you'd have another chance to hit a good one. The game of golf—like life—was impossible to perfect, but the pursuit of perfection was what made it interesting. Even when you hit it into the rough, he had to remind himself.

He suddenly thought about Art Smalley. And James Aderly, the subprime mortgage guy. Both took their own lives. It seemed pretty clear to Brad what Aderly had been troubled by: the subprime mortgage meltdown.

But what would have bothered Smalley so much that he was driven to kill himself? He pondered this as he watched Mel walk towards him, full glass of wine in one hand, bottle in the other. Was she going to drink the whole bottle? He hoped so. She tended to get amorous filled with that much wine.

A few minutes later, the sun began to set. Mel poured another glass of wine and stared at him. "What a strange night this is," she said, her eyes slightly glassy from the wine. "Linden moving into town, his manager committing suicide, you getting a chance to make some big commissions and all this talk about 'Animal Sex'. Must be a full moon."

"Must be."

She grinned. "Maybe we'll just skip dinner tonight," she said, grabbing his hand gently and leading him towards their bedroom.

5

THE NEXT DAY, FRIDAY, SEVERAL thousand miles east of Santa Barbara, the rising sun exposed a crisp, vibrant, Georgia morning.

It was early April and the ground in the foothills was just now beginning to thaw. Loud snoring could be heard coming from the white tents pitched along the river bank. Coffee pots hung over open fire pits and a guy dressed in cook's garb began scrambling a massive batch of eggs.

"Looks like we're going to have one hum dinger of a day, sir," said the cook to the tall and regal looking man who approached him.

"Be sure to feed them well, Clem. I've got a busy day planned for the men."

The man stood six foot two and weighed one hundred and eighty pounds. His muscle lean, his long face tan and clean shaven. He wasn't handsome in the traditional sense, but you could see in his eyes a depth of understanding that softened the crags and crevices in his face.

He was dressed in what was typical daily wear for him: military fatigues, calf-high boots, and a red hat he had personally designed. It had a picture of a hawk flying upward—towards Heaven. Rather than a mouse or rabbit in its bill, the hawk carried an AK47.

Nice touch; he was proud of it.

He was also proud of the group now camped around him. Ten able bodied men, training for events yet to unfold.

The son of a traveling evangelical minister, he had followed his father's lead a few years before the recession hit. As it became harder and harder to secure full time work, he turned to preaching more enthusiastically. Soon he found he could raise small amounts of money by passing the plate at carnivals or revival meetings. Then, almost as having an epiphany, he discovered that other unemployed, white men would actually follow his commands.

He preached against the ills of Satan; the ills of society; and, most importantly, the ills of the Federal Government.

And, surprisingly, they listened.

He now had these men following him. They called him commander and he treated them like soldiers— his soldiers. His pride in this accomplishment knew no bounds.

The 'men' were a group of rag tag volunteers; some believed absolutely in the commander's vision, some worked solely for the chance at a big pay day, and others were just confused, bored and otherwise unemployed. Whatever the case, the men appeared ready to perform whatever duties the commander had planned for them.

The two professional mercenaries in the squad were in charge of the daily military exercises. They made it known consistently that they were motivated by the money the commander had promised them. They had no loyalty to the commander—he knew it and they made it obvious that they didn't buy in to his fundamental religious views. But they would tolerate the nonsense as long as they got paid.

The religious followers—and there were several in the unit—would be the ones to carry out the difficult missions. The mercenaries would probably run if the going got tough.

The cook, a middle-aged guy with a scraggly gray beard, large beer belly, and forearms that looked like Popeye after he swallowed spinach, blew on the amber coals and responded to the commander's request. "You bet. I'll be sure to make extra bacon today."

"Good, they'll need it."

Shots rang out from the clearing in the woods. Several men had awoken early that morning. They had waited anxiously for the first rays of light. Once they could see the cardboard cut-out targets nearly 50 yards away, they opened fire with their modified assault weapons.

Let them have their fun, he thought. The time was quickly approaching when several of them might be required to make the ultimate sacrifice.

Thanking the cook once again for keeping the men full and fit, he turned and began walking towards his tent. Suddenly, his cell phone rang. Same number as the other day. He answered it quickly.

"Good morning," he said pleasantly, yet assertively.

"Good morning, commander," the voice replied, quietly—almost in a whisper.

What was it with this guy's voice? Perhaps he'd strained his vocal chords? Or, maybe he just spoke quietly?

The voice on the other end continued. "Your man performed admirably in Orlando. The police have determined it was a suicide and the case has been officially closed. Well done."

"Thank you, sir," he responded, voice swelling with pride. Praise from this man had been few and far between.

And now, hard won.

"I may have a few other tasks for you, commander. Will you be up to the challenge?"

He paused. Was this the right time to ask his bene-factor the question that had been burning at him since he read the article? He shrugged. No better time than the present. The 'whisperer' was actually happy with him and his group. Might as well take advantage of the situation. "Of course we are. Your financial contributions have been greatly appreciated. My men are becoming better trained as we speak."

"Good. That is what we intended," the soft voice whispered.

"But, there is something else."

"Yes."

"I have a mission for one of my men. It won't take too much planning and it shouldn't interfere with our work for you, but........it is something I *have* to do." His voice trailed off as he once again glanced around the compound.

The 'whisperer' said nothing.

"Are you there?"

After a long pause, the man said, "I know about your mother, David. I'm sorry for what they did to her." The caller exhaled. "But you must be careful as you carry out your personal vendetta. Your group can accomplish great things, but they need their leader."

"I understand." How did the whispering man know about his mother?

"Good, I'm glad we're on the same page. Now what is it you propose?"

Satisfied that he had the upper hand, he went on to explain that he had read an article about an upcoming dinner to be held at Johnny's restaurant in Washington D.C.. The sponsor was a national mortgage banking association. Some local and national politicians would be there. Apparently, the group was attempting to buy legislative influence before Congressional hearings looking into the mortgage meltdown were held.

"Sounds risky to me, but do what you must do, just do not allow your group to be destroyed. My goals— *our* goals—are much bigger than the death of a few bad men."

"Thank you, sir. I will only dispatch one man—just like I did in Orlando—and he will use the utmost caution."

"All right. Take out a few politicians at the dinner while you're at it. We support your hatred of the government. I will call you again very soon. In the meantime, continue to train those men." And then, as an afterthought, the 'whisperer' added, "Good luck on your mission. I'm sure your mother will rest more comfortably when you are through." He hung up.

He nodded. Yes, his mother would. He would. And, to be honest, the world would.

Bankers had destroyed the economy. It was time some of them paid. And, he had to admit, he liked the idea of taking out a few cheating politicians as well.

He turned and glanced at his men again. He took another deep breath, tasting the air as if it were a fine wine. He sighed. He and his men were up to any challenge. First, though, he had to prepare for the small, upcoming mission.

He smiled to himself, began to walk briskly and then stopped. He raised his hands skyward and said quietly, "Thank you lord, this is going to be a glorious day."

"Truly glorious."

6

THINGS HAD BEEN GOING WELL for pro golfer, John Linden.

He was playing great golf. Top ten on the money list; top twenty in driving accuracy; top five in greens in regulation; and, this was really the crème de crème....top 50 in putting. He had never even sniffed the top 100 in putting! The 'claw grip', or in his case, the abbreviated saw, was really paying dividends. Physically, he had never been stronger. He had won the U.S. Open by six strokes and was now universally acclaimed as one of the top golfers in the world.

If all that wasn't enough, he was getting laid regularly and, unlike most of his friends, didn't need the little blue pill to perform in the sack.

But, the 'suicide' of Art Smalley had thrown him for a loop.

He didn't believe for one minute that Art would commit suicide. It just wasn't something he'd do—at least, not the Art Smalley he knew.

The son of a working class family, Linden had grown up in a modest neighborhood in St. Louis. His parents had been extremely frugal and although their son never went hungry, he had never enjoyed the benefits that come with extra discretionary income. Unlike many of his contemporaries who had been raised in country club settings and had started golf young, John Linden hadn't picked up a club until his late teens.

When he turned pro, he immediately turned over all of his financial affairs to Art Smalley at Investments for Professional Golfers—IFPG for short. Recently, his coffers had been filled by his victory in the U.S. Open and by various endorsement deals.

"You're loaded with money, kid. Just go out and play golf. I'll make sure that your money grows; you worry about making those 15 foot putts," Art had said to him recently.

"No worries, bruddah, I got the 'claw grip'. They all go in nowadays."

"You have no idea how good that is to hear," Smalley had said. Linden had detected a certain anxiety in his manager's voice at the time. Probably stressed with work and family, he had concluded.

Nothing to lead to suicide, though.

Linden knew it was a recession. Not just any recession; but the Mother of All Recessions. Unemployment was sky high. Credit was tight. Here he was playing a silly game—chasing a little white ball around with a stick—and he was loaded. Not a financial care in the world.

Did he feel guilty? Not really. He worked hard. He hadn't been born with a silver spoon. Could he help it if he had superior eye/hand coordination combined with nasty fast-twitch fibers?

Let's face it, the American public paid good money to actors and athletes—in good times and in bad. Maybe, just maybe, his exploits on the course brought joy to viewers; providing them with escape from their daily economic woes.

When justified this way he was proud of what he did for a living. He brought joy. And…he got paid a lot of money. Despite the economic downturn, America was still the land of opportunity.

John Linden was living proof.

Still he felt tiny pangs of guilt from time to time. Was this move to Montecito too ostentatious? Would his buddies in St. Louis and Orlando still respect him? He shook off the doubts and remembered that Fabby wanted this house and *he* wanted Fabby. Besides, Brad would make good money, and he had assumed, Art Smalley would support his decision.

Now Art was dead.

He'd have to get past his manager's death and focus on making his soon-to-be fiancée happy. But it was hard. Sitting on his couch, watching a replay of his victory at the Open on the Golf Channel, he waited for a commercial break and then picked up his cell phone and called Fabiola; it was time to tell her about Art and Brad and his plans to have her visit Santa Barbara.

7

"HE'S REALLY SHOOK UP ABOUT Art's death," Brad told his long-time assistant, Stefanie Ramirez, Friday afternoon as they sat down for lunch at Ronnie's Grill, a downtown restaurant specializing in seafood and beer.

The floors of the popular restaurant were covered with sawdust and day old peanut shells—a local custom. The walls were filled with typical seafood paraphernalia: old buoys, webbed nets, fishing rods and, of course, the mandatory stuffed marlin. It was classic Coastal California and Brad loved it.

"John Linden doesn't seem like the touchy feely kind of guy to me," Stefanie said, placing a napkin on her lap and picking up a well-worn menu.

"He's not. But he had developed a very close relationship with Art. In some ways, Art was like a big brother. Not a buddy, really, from what John says, but the kind of guy he could go to with professional and personal problems."

"He can always go to you," Stefanie said, while browsing the menu.

"I know, but it was different with Art. IFPG really knows the golfing world and Art Smalley was the best manager they had."

"And now he's dead. What is John going to do?"

Brad shrugged. "I don't know, but I'm sure he'll figure it out."

He frowned as he watched an obviously drunk patron rise from his bar stool and stumble towards the restroom. "Geez, it's only noon and that guy's drunk as a skunk."

Stefanie turned her head and watched as the man fumbled with the restroom's doorknob. "Don't be too judgmental, Brad, I have a feeling this recession has created a lot of noon-time drinkers."

"Yeah, I guess that's true," Brad said, shaking his head and grimacing. "It's a shame."

They sat in silence for a few moments. Finally, Brad broke the quiet by suggesting they order. "Lunch is on me. You can have anything you want except the lobster salad; we haven't made the commission off Linden yet," he joked.

Predictably, he supposed, she ordered the lobster salad; he, the snapper Veracruz. They split a bottle of Foxen Chardonnay.

In the middle of her meal, Stefanie put down her fork and smiled. "Do you remember the first time we had lunch together?"

He thought for a moment and then shook his head. "Stef, it's been twenty five years. We must've had lunch hundreds of times."

"Well, I remember because one of our competitors saw us eating together. I never told you this, but she called my husband, Tommy, and told him we were having an affair."

"Really? What did Tommy do?"

Slightly blushing, she stared across the table. "He was pissed at first. He calmed down once I told him you were married with two little kids."

"Who was the competitor?"

"I can picture her, but can't remember her name. Judy or Janie…something?"

Brad grinned and said, "I'll bet it was Judy Persons with Quantify Mortgage. She always hated me. We butted heads a few times."

"Yes, that's it. I wonder whatever happened to her?"

"I heard she died a few years ago. Cancer, I think."

"She's gone and here we are twenty five years later having lunch again."

"Yep, here we are."

"Who would've thunk it?" she said sarcastically.

Brad took a sip of his wine and stared at his longtime assistant. At forty two, she still cut quite a figure. "You never did tell me why you gave up modeling and, eventually, got into this screwed up business?"

Smiling, she placed both hands below her ample breasts, raised them and replied, "I committed the ultimate sin in the modeling world; I grew boobs."

"Shame on you," he said with a wry grin. "But that doesn't answer the question of how you ended up working with me?"

"I was working for the County, remember? It was really boring. One day I decided to find a more exciting profession."

"Any regrets?"

She paused for a moment, maybe contemplating his question, or maybe just appreciating the wine and lobster. "None. We've made a pretty good team. How about you? Do you ever regret giving up law school?"

"Nope. I think I would've been a good lawyer but I don't think I would've enjoyed it." He took another bite of his snapper and then continued. "Most lawyers I know seem unhappy. And they make the worst clients; always throwing their weight around and threatening law suits. I didn't want to be like that."

"I'm glad you chose the mortgage business," she said, reaching across the table and patting his hand, raising her glass in mild salute. "Here's to us," she said.

They clinked glasses.

Changing the subject, Stefanie took a small bite of her salad and asked Brad about John Linden. "Are you going to be able to do John's loan in this tight credit market?"

"I think so. I don't see any reason why not. Smalley's death might make it more difficult to get data quickly, but…." he said with a slight shrug of his shoulders. "He's got good credit, makes solid income, has the down payment and is world renown."

"You know as well as I do, the banks always find *something* wrong these days…." she replied.

He took a sip of wine. It was a nearly perfect day in Santa Barbara. The food was good, the wine excellent and the company exceptional. Things were looking up. He smiled and said, "There will be a few bumps in the road, but we will get it done; we always do." He raised his glass and offered it for another congratulatory toast.

"John invited me up to Bandon Dunes next month for a one day corporate golf outing. I think I'm going to go. It's a great golf course—four courses actually—and we should catch good weather. Maybe it will give us a chance to talk about things."

"What things?"

"I think he needs someone to talk to about Art Smalley's death. I think he's conflicted."

"Conflicted? In what way?"

"He doesn't believe it was a suicide."

"Why?"

Brad shrugged. "Says Smalley was happy the last time he saw him."

"That's not much to go on, wouldn't you agree?"

Brad nodded. He didn't want to admit it but he had considered suicide when his financial world crumbled around him. *Damn Truckee.* It was only momentary and it probably was not sincere, but the thought had crossed his mind one night while making the nine hour drive back home.

Maybe Smalley had hit the financial wall?

Acting as if she had stumbled onto an uncomfortable subject, Stefanie quickly changed gears. "What's a 'corporate' outing?"

"It's what professional golfers do in between regular tournaments," he said, visibly relieved to get back to golf talk. "It gives them a chance to meet their sponsors and to possibly develop new relationships."

"And he invited you to play? How come?"

"We're buddies, why wouldn't he?" he said faking being insulted by the question. "Anyway, I'll be out of the office for a few days, so be prepared. Hopefully, he will be in escrow by then and he and I can talk about the house and the loan status."

"And Smalley?"

"And Smalley...if he wants."

"Where's Bandon Dunes anyway? Is it far? Can you afford to fly there?"

"The course is in Southern Oregon. I'll fly into Eugene and meet John. Then we'll drive over to Bandon. The expense is no big deal; he's picking up the tab."

She smiled, nodded her head and took a sip of wine.

"Eat up," Brad said. "I'm anxious to get back to the office and begin the hard work on John's loan."

"Sounds like a blast," she said rolling her eyes.

"Yeah, ain't life grand?"

8

MORTGAGE LENDING IS PART ART, part science. Brad knew this all too well.

The art, really, is the 'art of the deal'. A lender has product and the borrower needs to be enticed to take the product offered.

Sales yes, but with a twist.

A good lender also has to be part financial advisor, part trader, and part psychologist. Pure sales would eventually fail. Look at Countrywide and the other call-center based lenders of the past.

As he and Stefanie returned to the office, full from lunch and optimistic about Linden's loan, Stefanie nudged Brad and pointed to an office in the corner. Jim Johnson, one of the junior agents in the firm, was pacing around his office, headset placed prominently on his large, bald dome.

"You're a beggar, not a borrower. Now sign the loan documents or stop wasting my time," Johnson screamed at some unsuspecting client. Johnson looked across the hallway and saw Brad and Stefanie. He made a 'thumbs up' gesture.

Brad shook his head and continued walking. "How does he do business?" he asked Stefanie as they came to the reception area.

"They say birds of a feather flock together," Stefanie said. "He seems to attract crass clients who like to be yelled at. What can I say?"

They continued up the stairs and stopped when they got to Brad's corner office. Stefanie thanked him for lunch and returned to her desk. Brad settled in behind his large mahogany desk, checked his messages—both voice and e-mail—and then began the 'scientific' part of loan process.

He took out a notepad and itemized the items need-ed to get Linden approved. He separated the list into "Items provided by IFPG" and "Items from outside sources". Under IFPG, he wrote:

1. Two years' federal tax returns.
2. Two months' bank and asset statements.
3. Year to Date financial reports.
4. Copies of current contracts.

Under outside sources he quickly jotted down: Appraisal, Escrow, Preliminary Title Report, Various Inspections and Insurance.

This was the 'science' of lending. Numbers, due dili-gence, structural reports and…paperwork.

Lord knows the paperwork had quadrupled since the recession. He didn't like it, but he understood it. Too much selling going on in the years leading up to the financial meltdown, not enough analysis.

Fraud, defaults, foreclosures and bankruptcies had been the result. The market had over-compensated—and it wasn't fun—but it was what it was and Brad would just have to play the game by the new rules.

He chuckled remembering a radio interview he had given shortly after the mortgage meltdown.

"Mr. Stephens," the British host had asked in one of those stuck-up, Oxfordian accents. "Who is responsible for this terrible mess?"

Brad hadn't hesitated. "The U.S. Government. Wall Street. Lenders. Investors. Realtors. And, of course, Consumers," he had said while ticking them off one by one on his fingertips.

The host had looked at him quizzically. "Can you narrow it down for our listeners?"

"No, I can't. I realize everybody wants to blame someone specifically, but this was the 'harmonic convergence' of economic events. If any of the participants had acted differently, we might've avoided this meltdown."

"But they didn't," the host said snobbishly.

"No, they didn't"

"And here we are."

Brad remembered sighing before agreeing. "Here we are."

And here *he* was now dealing with an entirely different set of conditions and rules. He picked up the phone to call his friend. It was time to begin collecting the necessary data.

"Hello," Linden said over the sound of a radio in the background and the singing of rubber tires against an asphalt road.

"Turn down your radio. Where are you?"

"Hank and I are on our way to Pebble Beach. I'm going to play a practice round today. The course shouldn't be too crowded for a Friday. They just punched the greens."

"Practice round? For what?"

"The US Open."

Brad chuckled. "The Open isn't for another three months."

"I know. But we had a few days off and it's never too early to begin practicing. Besides, this will put me on the west coast in case you need anything."

"Makes sense, I guess. Well listen, I'm calling because I need to start processing your loan."

"What's processing?"

"It's the collection of data and the presentation to a lender of your financial material."

"I should pass with flying colors; I'm loaded."

Brad sighed. "Well, you aren't going to like all the questions and all the paperwork, buddy. I guarantee it."

"No worries. My guys at IFPG will take care of everything. You just 'show me the money' baby." There was silence on the line for a minute.

"Thinking of Art Smalley, aren't you?"

"Yeah, I'm going to miss that guy. But, hey, life goes on."

"He was a good guy," Brad agreed. But then focusing on the reason he called, he said, "Let's talk about him later when you get a chance."

"Yeah, let's do that," Linden said.

"Anyway the process doesn't work that way. I wish it did. You have to be personally involved in the process or else the bank is going to think that I'm forcing you to finance, or that you're a fictitious person. Or worse, that you're lying."

"No shit!" Brad heard tires screech.

"What was that?"

"Had to swerve to avoid hitting a rabbit. You should see Hank's face, he's as white as a ghost," Linden said, laughing.

Returning to the conversation, Linden said, "So they would really think that I'm not a real person? Don't they watch golf? Everyone knows I'm the U.S. Open Champ."

"I know. I know. Listen, I'll make it as easy on you as I can. I'm sure IFPG will help out. You be prepared for some stupid questions and keep your cell phone on. Okay?"

"Can do, pards. Just tell the lender to be gentle on your ol' buddy before they put the screws to him."

"Okay, as long you understand that it's going to be about as much fun as getting a root canal. And you have to promise not to hold any of it against me. Agreed?"

"Yep. What's the first step?"

"Let's fill out the loan application together while you're driving and then I'll have Stef call IFPG for additional supporting information. Have you contacted them and authorized our inquiries?"

"Left a message."

"I'll have Stef call; maybe your message will be enough."

"Sounds good to me. Anything else I need to do?"

"Sit tight, I'll let you know."

"That's easy. Who knows, this might be fun," he said optimistically.

Brad grimaced, knowing it was *never* easy. And, rarely, was it fun.

9

SHIT HAPPENS.

In golf there are expressions used if you don't like the results of your first swing on the first hole. Most people refer to this as 'taking a mulligan'. When it happens in the early morning, however, avid golfers call this taking a 'Breakfast Ball'.

No harm, no foul. Hit another and, hopefully, have better results.

Technically, it's not legal. Serious golfers would never take a breakfast ball, but it helps amateurs overcome their nerves and leads to a more enjoyable game.

Golf, like life, often comes down to one split second decision. One shot, one result. Once the ball leaves the clubface, it's in Gods' hands. Wind might blow it sideways. Heavy air might knock it down. And, of course, there is always 'rub of the Green'— a seemingly perfect shot that bounces on the grass in a funny way; hits a sprinkler head; comes to rest behind a tree, a rake or a rock.

You're screwed. It is what it is.

Play it where it lies.

It might be different for others, but in his fifty years on this planet, Brad hadn't been offered many breakfast balls. He played life straight up. In retrospect, he could've used a few mulligans between 2001 and 2007.

He, like most people, often pondered past decisions. As he got older, he realized many of his decisions were made in haste, without analyzing all the facts. It was just human nature to be optimistic he thought.

Lately, he took to ranking his past decisions.

Marriage to Mel at such a young age: good decision. She was a great wife and a great mother. Awful cook, but, hey you can't have everything. Children: good decision. Financially painful, but emotionally, fulfilling. They were fine boys; never caused him trouble; seldom needed discipline; were great athletes and, as a bonus, had matured into fun companions.

Mortgage business: bad decision. It had paid the bills and put the kids through college, but overall, it was a stupid business full of hidden trapdoors and landmines. Quitting law school: good decision.

Signing the note and deed—thereby assuming a hundred percent of the liability—on a vacation home in Truckee: bad, very bad, decision.

No Mulligan there. He'd give anything to take a breakfast ball on that one.

Representing Linden on the purchase of the home and the procurement of the loan would be categorized as one of his best decisions. Of that he was sure.

The process of selecting a new home could be fun. The loan should be easy to arrange. John made plenty of money, had substantial investments and, thankfully, his credit report had come back clean.

The commissions earned on this deal alone would pay off a big chunk of the Truckee residual debt. And, best of all, Linden would be around to socialize and golf with more often. With that in mind, he prepared to find his buddy a new house.

Optimism must've been in the air that day. Back at the Georgian camp, Commander David Von Eisenlow, the tall, regal man had just made three decisions.

His first decision: A new name for his troops. Formerly known as "The Sons for Righteous Transition," Von Eisenlow had decided to simplify the name. Henceforth, they would be known as Sons for Sovereign Sacrifice.

Keep it stupid simple. He thought it defined their mission: Sons, for the fact that the group was exclusively male. Sovereign for the fact that they hated the federal government. Sacrifice for the fact that they would sacrifice their lives for their cause.

He hoped.

The second decision involved the sudden influx of money from an anonymous donor. The first time he had called, the 'whisperer' had indicated that his group controlled enormous resources. He said that his group was behind Commander Dave one hundred percent and that he would soon see proof of that support. Well, that day had come.

Von Eisenlow had received a text message the other morning. It simply said, "Money in suitcase by the creek." He had sent his most trusted lieutenant to retrieve it. True enough. Over two hundred thousand dollars in small bills had been delivered.

No more kissing the butts of local supporters. No more begging for funds. His group could now afford new ammunition; significantly better rations; and, most importantly, enhanced reconnaissance information. With his troops ready and chomping at the bit for action, the timing could not have been any better.

The final decision of the day was more difficult. Who would he choose for his upcoming assault? Von Eisenlow possessed no moral qualms about sending a man to his death. He had no patience for cowardice. However, he was a pragmatist. He would need to schmooze the men; this would be a dangerous mission.

It was time to rally the troops.

Standing at a makeshift lectern and thinking that he looked every bit the leader of a mighty cause, he addressed his men. "The time has come for us to take serious action," he said, striking the pulpit with his fist. "Through the grace of God, I have been directed to destroy the U.S. Government. My hope—and absolute belief—is that once we have neutralized certain key politicians, the people will once again experience the joys of freedom."

There was no need to mention his other motivation: the death of his mother and his personal vendetta. The men were primed by the current recession to hate the government and were ready to strike.

They didn't need further motivation.

He surveyed the troops. No negative responses yet. No head shaking. This was good.

The men, ranging in ages from seventeen to forty five, stood huddled together as their commander continued his speech. It was a cold day and some shivered as Von Eisenlow spoke; some shuffled their feet, hoping to create warmth. All wore some form of fatigues and all appeared anxious.

"I will need some of you brave souls to volunteer for upcoming missions. It is likely some of you will lose your earthly life. Fear not, though, as any loss on earth will result in the immediate embrace by God in a far more righteous place! We are his CHOSEN." Again, he pounded the hardwood pulpit with his fist. He stared at his troops and let his words set in.

After a few moments, he continued. "We must strike now while the worlds' economies crumble. We must prepare for the ultimate day of reckoning. This is our destiny. And the time is now!"

Pounding his fist on the wood in front of him, Von Eisenlow emphasized his last point. He glared at the men. He could see some of them shiver. Good, he wanted them to be uncomfortable now. He would provide comfort later.

Without notice or provocation, one of the soldiers, a young man with red hair and matching stubble, raised his hand slowly. The boy couldn't have been older than eighteen and looked to be a hundred and forty pounds, dripping wet.

"Sir. Are you saying that some of us might need to volunteer for suicide missions, sir?"

"Yes, son, that is exactly what I'm saying." He paused and then added, "And remember, it is not just me who is asking you, but our Lord as well." Feeling as if he should justify his statement, he continued.

"Our numbers are too few to launch a massive attack. We need to hit the enemy quick. Hit them hard. Take out their most crucial leaders. Then, and only then, will the masses open their eyes to the divine truth." He pounded the lectern once more.

"Sir, with all due respect, I didn't sign up for no suicide bombing terrorism," the young man said somewhat timidly. He looked around the group for additional support. Finding none, he continued. "I signed up to fight the government. I figured we would hole up in a compound like they did in Waco and invite them sons' of bitches in to our lair. Or blow up buildings," the soldier added. "That kinda shit."

"YOU figured! You! And who the Hell are you, boy? Has God spoken to you? I'll answer for you," Von Eisenlow said facetiously. "No. HE has not! Come forward. Let me see your face. What is your name boy?"

"Sam Howard, Sir."

The gathering grew silent. Was he losing the trust of his men?

The mercenaries would be okay; he could always entice them with cash. He needed their logistical thinking and weapons training. He would pay them a bonus later that day. The rank and file, though, they were his foot soldiers. They were his audience. This was the first time his leadership had been openly challenged.

At first he wasn't sure what to do. Then in a moment of absolute clarity, his father's words came to him: "Sell 'em boy, sell 'em hard."

His father, a traveling evangelist, had raised his young son to follow in his steps. The first lesson he had taught young David was the art of the sale.

"They want to believe son, but when it comes down to it, you really gotta sell 'em. Make a big impression; do something spectacular and make it loud. People like loud."

It was time to sell his soldiers.

"Well Sam Howard, are you telling me that you will not volunteer for a mission if asked? Are you telling me that you are not ready to sacrifice your life for your fellow countrymen and for our lord? Is that what you're telling me, Sam Howard?" he snickered while looming over the soldier.

The boy shrugged slightly and then smiled as if finding new confidence. "Yes sir. That is what I'm telling you. Fighting is one thing. Suicide is another. My momma didn't raise no dummy. At least in a fight, you've got a chance to defeat the enemy and escape with your life intact"

Von Eisenlow surveyed his men. Several were nodding their heads slowly in apparent agreement with Howard. He couldn't lose the men now; he had worked too hard, had come too far. In the beginning, there had been just he and two others. Now, six months later, their numbers had swelled to twelve. Was he going to let a pimple-faced youngster ruin his plans? No, by god, he was not!

Time to make the big sell.

Smiling benevolently like a father scolding a wayward child, and feeling less in control than before, Von Eisenlow said softly, "Then you've missed the point of my teachings and of your training. By all rights, I should punish you for in-sub-ordination." He purposely strung out the last word and let it set in. He smiled again and continued, "But the lord works in mysterious ways. Does he not?"

The commander spread his arms wide and beckoned the young man to approach. In a loud voice he said, "I'm going to give you a second chance, Sam Howard. Our lord has taught us that to err is human, to forgive, divine. You have spoken your words of cowardice and now it is time for healing."

Howard approached the lectern slowly. When he was a few feet away, Von Eisenlow reached out and grabbed him. Arms wrapped around him like a mother welcoming her son home from war, Von Eisenlow pulled the soldier close and whispered in his ear, "You don't know how close you came to death, son." Howard's eyes moved to the German luger Von Eisenlow had pulled from its holster now resting on the lectern. "By all rights, I should have shot you dead. Right there on the spot. And I'm tempted to whip you in front of the men."

The boy winced slightly.

"Don't ever question my authority again. Got it?" Howard nodded. "Do you want to stay with the group, Sam Howard? If not, now is the time to declare your intentions. You are free to leave if you wish," Von Eisenlow whispered. Again, the boy nodded.

"I want to stay commander. I need the money and my family just got evicted from their home. I got nowhere to go."

"Good," Von Eisenlow said. He released Howard from the hug and turned the boy to face the audience.

With arm wrapped around Howard's shoulder, Von Eisenlow addressed the men. "Men, the lord tells us we will face many struggles. Some come from the outside; some come from within. Today, one of us has questioned our mission. He now knows the error of his ways."

He paused, smiled, patted Howard on the back and asked, "Isn't that right, Sam?"

"Yes sir," the boy said, eyes still fixed on the luger.

"Anyone else want to question the Lord's strategy?" Von Eisenlow asked.

Head shakes all around. "Good. Let's proceed to the job at hand," a now confident Von Eisenlow said.

He was again, firmly in control. He released Howard from his grasp, assigned him ten days of kitchen detail and took a deep breath before proceeding. His daddy was right. You gotta sell 'em, he thought proudly.

He moved on to the next item on his agenda: Volunteers. Well, not actual volunteers in the true sense—he had thrown twelve numbers in a hat. The men would each draw a number; 1 thru 12. Other than the one-man assault he had planned on the restaurant in D.C., he didn't yet have a master plan. He was motivated by hate of the federal government; it had ruined the lives of good, god-fearing Americans and it had supported Wall Street and the banking industry. It had caused his mother's death.

And for that, there would be no mercy.

He had yet to devise a master plan. He knew, however, that whatever they did would involve guns, bombs, government buildings, politicians and destruction. His men were ready and, thanks to his new benefactor, they had the money to proceed.

Attacks would be small and tactical at first. If all went right, they would escalate. Volunteers would be chosen based on the numbers they drew.

Along the way, he and his group would perform a few 'tasks' for his benefactor. What harm could it do? His men could use the practice.

"Boys, let us bow our heads in prayer." Von Eisenlow grinned at his minions, proud of himself for re-establishing his authority. Silently, he said to himself, "Now the true believers will take a bullet for me. And the others will fight…as long as I pay them."

10

WHILE LINDEN TUNED UP HIS GAME in Pebble Beach, Brad scoured the multiple listings for Montecito and searched for $3-$4 million homes.

Not surprisingly, there were quite a few.

There was the Tudor, five bedroom, four and a half bath, located on an acre. Pool, cabana, tennis court, expansive landscaping and tremendous view of the mountains—or so the listing boasted. Nicknamed "Casa de Magnifico"—ALL upper end properties had a nickname these days—it was a *bargain*; priced at a mere $3.95 million.

More like "Casa de Mucho Dinero," Brad thought as he thumbed through the pages. John would be traveling six months out of the year. He needed less maintenance. Focus on nice homes, small yards, pool but no pool house.....and, most importantly, adequate space to put in a small putting green and sand trap.

The list grew. There were "Casita Elegante"; "Tranquilo de Oceano"; and "Montanas del Fuego". All lovely homes. All *reasonably* priced.

Using the process of elimination based on price and overall suitability, Brad compiled a list of four strong candidates. Neither "Casita Elegante" nor "Tranquilo de Oceano" made the cut.

"Montanas del Fuego" looked interesting, however. The other three either had no nickname or the listing agents had not yet come up with one. That was okay with Brad because once Linden moved into a new place—any new place—it would invariably become "Casa de Chaos" anyway.

He decided he would go on a Realtor caravan—the process of familiarizing agents with available properties in the area—the following day. His focus would be on the four properties he had circled. Having made that decision, he once again found himself thinking about Linden's loan.

"Stef, did you ever follow up and get actual signatures from John?" Brad asked.

"I thought you were getting them," she replied.

"Nope. Good thing he's my buddy. I can email the forms to him. But we still need the income and asset information from IFPG."

Overjoyed to have a big project going after such a lull in the business, he asked Stef to give IFPG a call and find out who was handling Linden's account now that Smalley was dead. "Have whoever it is send us a PDF of Johns' last two years' tax returns and the last two months' asset statements."

Unlike many processors at the major banks who often just shuffle papers and watch the clock, Stefanie Ramirez actually analyzed data as it came in. Blessed with a solid work ethic and tremendous foresight, she often caught issues in advance which, if left unchecked, could lead to loan denial.

Combined with Brads' understanding of the interest rate market and his expertly honed ability to determine which lender would be the best fit for each borrower, they had created a tremendously successful team over the past twenty five years.

Unfortunately, she had suffered her own financial reversals in recent years (who hadn't?) but she rarely discussed them. She knew Brad had been severely damaged by the recession and was happy that the Linden opportunity had come along. They both would make a good chunk of change.

Confidently, she dialed the number Brad had given her.

"Hello. This is Stefanie Ramirez. We're processing a loan for one of your clients, Mr. John Linden," Stefanie told the receptionist at IFPG. "I understand his personal manager, Art Smalley, died recently." She waited for a response. There was none. She continued. "Can I speak to whoever is handling Mr. Linden's account now please?"

"Who did you say you are, hon? And who are you with?" came the response from the soft southern voice on the other end of the line.

"Stefanie Ramirez; personal assistant to Mr. Brad Stephens. We're with Coastal Care Mortgage, in Santa Barbara, California."

"I see. Well this is very uncomfortable…obviously we're very upset." She hesitated as if she were about to cry.

"I'm very sorry about your loss."

Sighing audibly and voice softening, the receptionist said, "Well, they suspect suicide, you know but I don't believe them. They say he had suffered a bunch of financial losses lately and was despondent."

"It sounds like you knew him well," Stefanie ventured.

The receptionist paused and then really got on a roll.

In a much firmer voice she said, "Mr. Smalley was such a nice man. I never saw him depressed, much less, 'despondent'. I guess lately he *had* seemed pre-occupied," she conceded, but quickly added. "But not bummed. Y'all know what I mean?" She paused for a moment and when Stefanie didn't respond, she continued. "And recently, he looked a little tired—you know, maybe he'd been drinking too much? He took us girls out to lunch once a month and made it a habit to buy fresh flowers for the front desk. His office was always immaculate. It breaks my heart to see the owners and the police go through his stuff. He loved his family and I know he loved his clients. It's awful…just awful," she sniffled as she finally broke down into tears.

"Sounds like a nightmare. Is there anything I can do to help?"

Ignoring Stefanie's offer and continuing her previous thought, she said, "I just can't imagine him hanging himself! It doesn't make sense."

On the other end of the line, Stefanie was somewhat conflicted. It sounded like Art Smalley was a nice man, but her religious upbringing had taught her that suicide was a sin. Fortunately, she didn't know the man and it wasn't her place to cast judgment. As a woman, and a mother, she felt for his wife and children.

"Listen I know it's a tough time for you and your office. I'm deeply sorry. I don't want to add to anyone's burden, but I need to get some financial data on Mr. Linden. Time is of the essence. It's basic information and should be readily accessible. Can you tell me who will be handling Mr. Lindens' account in the future?"

"I don't know. I suppose it could be Arts' assistant, Julie, or it could be assigned to one of the other managers. We really don't have a protocol for this type of thing. I'll leave a message with Julie and I'm sure she'll get back to you when she can. She's awfully upset, as you can well imagine."

"Thanks. You've been very helpful. I'm sorry for your loss. Mr. Smalley sounded like a nice man. I hope his family makes it through this difficult period." Stefanie tried to sound as cajoling as possible. "I look forward to hearing from someone soon." She hung up.

Stefanie was surprised to receive a call from IFPG several hours later. She figured they wouldn't call for at least a day or two.

"Miss Ramirez. I understand you need some financial information on John Linden. Is that correct?" the voice on the other end of the line asked quietly and politely.

"Yes. I need to get some information as soon as is convenient. I'm deeply sorry about your company's loss. I can wait until tomorrow or the next day for the information. I don't want to be a bother," Stefanie said.

"I can help you. My name is Erma, I'm Mr. Ambrook's secretary."

"Mr. Ambrook?"

"Yes, Tyler Ambrook, he'll be handling Mr. Lindens' account in the future. He would have called you back but his voice is weak; he just had some minor surgery."

"Thank you for calling me back so quickly. Let me give you my email address and you can send it through to my secure site."

"Let me speak to Mr. Ambrook first. May I call you tomorrow?"

Startled by the secretary's hesitation, Stefanie said, "Oh, you know what, I bet Mr. Linden hasn't called yet to authorize release of the data."

Erma said, "I really don't know. I'll have to ask Mr. Ambrook about it. Good bye now." The line went dead, leaving Stefanie confused and, quite frankly, concerned.

11

THE 17TH HOLE AT PEBBLE BEACH is a straight shot.

A 175-yard par three. No lakes in front. No baranca to clear.

Other than two sand traps in the front and three in the back, the hole looks to be no trouble at all.

Anyone who's actually played the hole—or watched it being played—knows otherwise.

The 17th can be terrifying. The tiny Green is a postage stamp with deep Green-side bunkers, thick rough and bumps, valleys, trenches, breaks and dips. And while the Pacific Ocean framing the horizon makes for a beautiful sight, it can easily screw up a shot if it is throwing off wind—as it usually does.

John Linden had played the hole many times, but it remained an enigma to him. With wind, he hit a three or four iron; without, he grabbed a five or six. Either way, it should be plenty of club, but always—*always*—he seemed to come up short.

If he stood any chance to repeat his win at this year's Open he'd have to figure out how to remedy this.

He stared at the hole then studied the tee shot. Sunny and barely a breeze. Linden turned to his longtime caddy, Henry Bloom. "Hand me a four iron, Hank. I'm tired of coming up short."

The caddy didn't move a muscle of his 6'6", 250-lb bulk. "It's too much club for you," he answered calmly. "You'll fly the Green and either land in the Pacific or catch the back bunker. Either way, you'll be fucked. Stick with the five and rip it."

"You know, Hank, Nicklaus hit three iron here in '82. And Watson, a two."

The 17th hole became famous—infamous, actually—when Tom Watson chipped in from treacherous rough and went on to beat Jack Nicklaus in the 1982 Open.

"I got news for you, J. You're a good player, but you ain't no Nicklaus. You ain't no Watson either. Play your game and hit enough club to get to the middle of the Green but not enough to bring the ocean into play." Hank handed John a five-iron. "Make a par on this hole and move on."

Mexican music came from Linden's pocket. Cell phones were forbidden on the golf course, but hey, this being a practice round and all, who would complain?

"Mariachi music, big man? Since when do you listen to that shit?" Hank asked.

"Hey, I like Volver, Volver. Besides, since I'm moving out to Southern California, I thought I might as well get used to the music."

"Whatever."

"It's probably Tyler Ambrook returning my call," John said, pulling his phone from his pocket and silencing the music. "Hey, Tyler, thanks for the call.

I need to talk to you about a couple of things. First of all, what's this about Art Smalley? Suicide? I don't buy it."

"Uh, well, hello, John. How are you?" the voice on the other end said.

"Can you speak up, I can barely hear you."

"Sorry, I had a few polyps removed from my throat. I'm in Montana recuperating this weekend. Reception might not be the best." Tyler paused and cleared his throat a few times and then continued, "Yes, well, it's very sad about Art, but yes, the police have ruled it a suicide."

"Bullshit! That doesn't make any sense." Linden tended to yell when he was making a point.

"He told me a few weeks ago he was looking forward to taking his family on a cruise this summer."

"I understand, it's a shock to us all, but he *had* suffered some terrible financial losses recently. In any case, about your account, you told my assistant—"

"Don't you give a shit about Art?" Linden interrupted. Was this guy for real? Someone who'd worked for IFPG for what, twenty-some years, commits suicide and its business as usual?

Linden loved Tyler's old man, Steven—he was a real human being; he'd care about Art—but his son, Tyler, well, the jury was still out on this guy. Steven had handed the reins over a few years ago when he retired. Linden wondered if the old man had made the right decision?

He asked, "Will there be a service?"

"I'll let you know when I know, John, and of course I care about Art. We're a family here at IFPG. Now, what did you need to ask about your financials?"

Linden saw Hank pointing at his watch. OK, might as well get to his second point. "It's not a big deal. I just need you to send some paperwork to my buddy Brad

Stephens in Santa Barbara. I'm going to be buying a house out there and he'll be getting a mortgage for me— handling the whole process for me actually. So he says he needs my tax returns, account statements, things like that. And then of course you'll need to free up the cash for a down payment. He'll give you a call today with the details."

Tyler said nothing.

"Tyler, you there?" John barked.

"So you're buying a house?"

"Yeah, like I just said. So we're cool, then, you can get the stuff to Brad?"

"IFPG usually takes care of our clients' mortgage-lending needs, John, and we can help with the house-hunting, too. I'd rather not share your private financial statements outside the company."

"Brad's my best friend. Don't worry about it. He's dealt with famous people before."

"I don't think that's a good idea. I feel strongly, John, that—"

"Just do it. If there's anything for me to sign, send it over. Brad will be calling." He clicked off the call.

"What was that all about?" Hank asked.

"Those bloodsuckers at IFPG. Don't even care that Art's dead, and they want to keep my real estate business all to themselves."

Hank chuckled. "You're surprised? All they care about is getting a piece of the action on everything you do."

"Yeah, well, fuck 'em. Brad's my buddy, he knows the area, he needs the money. End of story. Let's play." Linden looked down at the five-iron. "You sure this is enough club?"

"It's enough."

He waggled the club a few times and then stopped abruptly. "Oh wait, gotta call Brad and let him know I authorized him calling IFPG."

Hank rolled his eyes. "Okay. Get it done and then, let's play some golf. I still gotta get you to birdie the 18th."

Linden smiled. "Yes you do, big man, yes you do."

== ⊕ ==

"Brad, listen to this," said Stef, her arms crossed as she entered his office. "I just talked to IFPG. Apparently, they're very happy for you to handle the purchase of John's house."

"And?"

"They say they'll be handling the loan, thank you very much."

"That's bullshit! There's no reason why I can't do both. And I'm not going to walk away from the mortgage commission. If John spends $2 million, that's $20,000 to us. No way."

"Well, I talked to the secretary for the man who is now handling John's account. Her name is Erma. She put me off on the first call and then she called me back and told me that they'd be handling the loan."

"What's the guy's name?"

"Tyler Ambrook; he's the president of the company. Son of the founder, Steven Ambrook."

Brad raised an appraising eyebrow. "President of the company?"

"I looked him up on Google," she said with a shrug.

"Call Erma back. Tell her I want to talk to her boss."

"Ooh, I like it when you're riled up. Reminds me of the old days." She flashed another smile and went back to her desk

After a minute, she yelled, "On line three! It's Erma."

Brad put the receiver to his ear. "Hello, this is Brad Stephens at Coastal Care Mortgage. May I speak with Mr. Ambrook?"

"I'm sorry, sir," she replied stiffly. "Mr. Ambrook is not here."

"Well then, how can I reach him? We need to clarify some details about the work I'm doing for John Linden."

"I'm sorry, Mr. Stephens, but Mr. Ambrook is traveling right now; he won't be available until Thursday at the soonest."

"*I'm* sorry, Er...is it Erma? Thursday won't do. My timeframe is much more urgent than that."

"Mr. Stephens, Mr. Ambrook is in Montana this weekend and then beginning Monday will be in Las Vegas, attending a very important equipment convention through Thursday. May I pencil you in for some time after Thursday?"

Damn. He couldn't get started on John's loan until he had that paperwork. And it seemed to him that IFPG wasn't interested in cooperating with him anyway.

What was the problem?

Then he had a thought. "Wow, Erma. What a coincidence! I'm planning to head up to Vegas myself for that convention. I'm looking to replace my clubs." Not true. He was perfectly happy with his clubs, and his balls, and everything else to do with his golf. This was the first he'd heard of any convention. But no reason for Erma—or Ambrook—to know that.

"Uh, well, Mr. Stephens," Erma said, "I don't think...." She paused. "Could you please hold on a moment?"

"Sure thing." Maybe good ol' Erma would get Ambrook on the phone now and spare him the trouble of a hasty trip to Vegas.

After several minutes, Erma returned. "Mr. Stephens, I just spoke with Steven Ambrook, IFPG's founder and Tyler's father. Apparently, I spoke out of turn; we usually don't discuss the whereabouts of our executives. Mr. Ambrook feels it's best if you not try to contact his son at the convention. He'll be quite busy doing business there. We prefer to make an appointment so that Tyler can devote his full attention to you and provide you with everything that you need."

How to play this? "Alright, Erma. I'll have my assistant Stefanie call you to schedule an appointment," he began. "You spoke with her earlier, I believe."

"Yes, I remember," Erma said, clearly becoming perturbed by this conversation.

"But I *will* be heading to Vegas," he continued. "And if I do run into Mr. Ambrook at the convention, of course I'll say hi."

"Mr. Stephens...."

"Bye-bye, Erma, and thanks so much for your help."

12

THE VEGAS SUN ROSE AND STREAMED through the window to wake Brad early Monday morning.

He'd forgotten to close the drapes the night before. When he arrived at the Bellacqua Resort, he'd showered, helped himself to a Jack Daniels and settled into the comfortable bed to watch a movie, but he was asleep well before the ending credits. The suite was beautiful, with a Jacuzzi tub and a view of the lakes. But in the morning, he noticed as he peered through the windows, the city itself sure looked grimy.

A morning in Vegas—without a hangover. What a trip; might as well embrace it.

He threw on his swim trunks and made his way to one of the many pools on the property. By noon the chaise lounges and the Moroccan sun tents would be overflowing, but at 7 a.m. he had the place to himself. He swam a few laps before heading upstairs to dress for his 'appointment' with Tyler Ambrook.

He donned yellow slacks, white Polo shirt and his best blue Armani blazer. Penny loafers without socks, as always. He'd fit right in. Everything else he stuffed into his overnight bag to leave at the bell desk, and checked out, hoping he'd have no trouble locating Ambrook today and wouldn't have to stay another night.

He grabbed a cab to the Las Vegas Convention Center, just off the Strip. He had to fork over $125 for a day-pass, a little steep he thought, but if he got what he came for, it would be worth it.

And it was Vegas, after all.

"Say, I'm going to be meeting someone here," he said to the cashier, an elderly gentleman with tufts of white hair hovering above his ears. "Do you know how I might find out if he's arrived yet?"

"If he registered in advance, then they'll have him checked in right over there." The cashier pointed to his right as he handed Brad his convention badge.

Very official.

"Thanks."

Brad walked a short way to two long tables where four very attractive young women sat overseeing signup sheets and badges.

The dark brunette handling names A-G smiled up at him. "May I help you?"

"Yes," he said, happy to return the smile. "Has Mr. Ambrook of IFPG arrived yet?"

She sifted through the pages in front of her and looked up with another smile. "I'm afraid I don't see him yet."

"Thanks. Do you mind if I come back and inquire again later?"

"Not at all sir."

Might as well check out the wares while he waited.

The vast convention center had been home to gatherings celebrating everything from high-tech electronics to Hollywood porn. Today, it was hosting an elaborate homage to all the myriad ways the modern golfer could part with his cash.

The entire place had been transformed into a mock golf course, with light green artificial turf walkways and dark Greens of real grass; the walkways standing in for fairways, and trees and sand traps dotting the perimeter.

And everywhere, new, shiny toys for the great American golf addict.

No longer was a player encouraged to buy a set of irons that would last him a lifetime. Not when there were so many ways to improve your game! Change your clubs every year—after all, they're being engineered every day to send the ball longer, straighter, higher. Have your swing diagnosed, your angle of descent analyzed. Use the driver that Tiger used, the irons that Ernie hit.

In the multibillion industry that had once been called "the gentleman's game," manufacturers prized endorsements. Brad knew that was why Tyler Ambrook was here—to ensure those endorsement deals got done for his clients.

After about an hour of looking around, Brad returned to the registration desk. Still no Ambrook, so he decided to go out and get some lunch.

When he returned, Ambrook still hadn't signed in. Was the guy trying to avoid him? Did Erma tip him off? He'd have to show up sometime, wouldn't he? The brunette kept smiling, so Brad kept asking.

He'd stopped at every damned booth at least once and tried almost every gadget that promised to change his life and had yet to see anyone who resembled the man in the photo he carried in his back pocket. He spent 45 minutes on the phone with Stef going over pending loans and paperwork for other clients. It was mid-afternoon when the brunette finally informed him that yes, Mr. Ambrook had indeed signed in, about 20 minutes ago.

"You wouldn't happen to know where he was headed?"

"No, sir, but often the agents and managers do business at the Country Club refreshment spots. You might find him at one of those."

"You've been a wonderful help," Brad said, lingering on that smile one last time. Then he was off to find Ambrook.

He found him at one of the bars designed to look like a country club grill at the end of the 18th fairway. Wearing a blue blazer, bright yellow shirt and pink slacks (how could Brad have missed this guy?) Tyler Ambrook stood sipping champagne from a large crystal flute, engaged in animated conversation with two Japanese businessmen.

They all stood at about the same height, about 5'5", Brad guessed. He took a seat at a nearby table, ordered a cup of coffee and waited till they finished their discussion. By that time, Ambrook had downed another glass of champagne and was into his third as Brad approached; he could see he was already a little wobbly.

"Mr. Ambrook," Brad said, approaching with an outstretched hand. "I'm Brad Stephens, John Linden's friend from Santa Barbara." He used the most ingratiating tone he could muster.

"Mr. Stephens." Tyler grabbed his hand and shook it vigorously. "This is quite a surprise."

Tyler Ambrook looked pained, not surprised. But Brad *was* surprised by his voice, small, hoarse and hard to hear. He moved closer so he could hear him better.

"Sorry," said Tyler, pointing to his throat. "I just had some polyps removed. Are you here for the convention?"

"Yeah, thought I'd see what's new. I've been thinking about replacing my clubs. Some pretty cool stuff here. But I knew you'd be here too, so I figured we might as well discuss John's loan. You know, kill two birds with one stone." He gave him a fake smile.

"I don't understand; don't we have a phone conference scheduled for next week to discuss that?"

"Yes, but I really need to get things done more quickly. The process of securing a loan can take weeks. I want to hit the road running, get a good lender and full loan approval in advance. That's how John will get the best price."

"Okay. Consider it done."

"Consider what done?"

"The loan. We'll lend the money internally. No paperwork problems. No red tape."

"Let me get this straight. Are you telling me that IFPG can afford to extend a two million dollar loan to one of its players—and give him a competitive interest rate?"

"Yes I am," said Tyler in his faint, little voice, looking quite pleased with himself. He raised his flute in mock salute and took another sip.

"We've got billions under management. We've been discussing branching out into lending. This is a good start, I think."

Brad was doubtful, but he'd bite. Why not give the guy a little rope? "What terms are you offering?"

"Terms? You want specifics? Okay, this is just between you and me." Tyler leaned in close, as if divulging a secret. "I'd have to check with our finance people, but I would imagine we could extend the funds for, say ten years, and would charge only 7%."

Brad began shaking his head before Tyler had finished speaking. "That's unacceptable for several reasons. Number one, John needs a 30-year amortized loan. Number two, in this economy the rate should either be fixed for 30 years at 5% or he should get an adjustable, fixed for a minimum of five years starting at 3.5%."

Tyler's self-satisfied grin disappeared. "That's impossible. We can't extend a commitment that long or offer a rate that low, either. We'll lose money. We're not a bank, you know."

"Exactly my point. Let me handle the financing. He'll get a better long-term rate from one of the banks I work with. This kind of loan is in their wheelhouse."

Tyler gripped the bar and raised himself to full height, still far from Brad's eye level. "Listen, buddy. I don't know what your game is, but I've been very nice about this up to this point. Now I'm going to tell you…" He burped slightly. "Just stay the fuck out of this. Linden will be treated fairly. We take our client's security very seriously and we're not going to release confidential information to you or to any outside lender. That's it. End of story."

Brad said nothing. He didn't know quite what to make of this little prick.

"Hey, sorry about that," Tyler said, easing back onto his barstool. "I've had a long day. Tell you what, we're both businessmen. You work on commission, right? How about IFPG pays you the same net commission you'd make with an outside lender? You get your cut, every-one's happy."

Brad smiled. Sure would be the easiest twenty grand he'd ever made. But it wouldn't be right. He knew he could get John a better loan. Besides, something about this stunk. Why would Ambrook pay him $20,000 to forget about collecting John's data?

"Sorry, but I owe it to John to get him a better loan," he finally said. "I expect your cooperation. If I fail to get it, I'll have John contact you directly."

Tyler slammed his flute on the bar. "Go fuck yourself, Stephens. Get out of here, and don't try to talk to me again. I'll have security on you so fast it'll make your head spin. John Linden will do what IFPG tells him to do." He turned from the bar, and Brad could just make out his words as he passed: "Piss-ant mortgage geek."

Brad watched him stomp rather unsteadily down the artificial 18th fairway.

That went well.

Brad felt a little unsteady himself. He'd never liked confrontation and now his anger was coming on strong. Tyler Ambrook was not just a little prick but a conniving asshole as well. And he was hiding something.

IFPG didn't need the money it would make on John's loan. And confidentiality—that was bull. If IFPG really cared about that, they could have Brad sign a confiden-tiality agreement and indemnify them. No, this was about something else entirely.

He just didn't know what.

He pulled out his cell and rang John's number. It went straight to voicemail. "John, just saw Tyler Ambrook. He's still refusing to hand over the paperwork. I don't get it but I guess you'll need to talk to IFPG again.

Give me a call later." He pocketed the phone, took a quick look around the convention center one last time and shrugged. "Guess Tyler Ambrook won't be playing golf with me anytime soon," he said to himself.

13

RATHER THAN TAKING A CAB, Brad chose to walk back to the Bellacqua.

The encounter had not been entirely successful, Brad thought as he passed casino after casino along the strip. It was only late afternoon on a Monday but he could still hear the metallic 'ka-chinging' of one armed bandits and smell the lingering odor of stale breath and cheap booze emanating from inside the buildings.

Tyler had not only been uncooperative, but he had tried to bribe Brad as well. What was up with that? The guy was a piece of work; that much was for sure.

He wasn't a micro-manager—he could've never survived in the mortgage business if he was—but Brad was the kind of guy who needed resolution. Unfinished business didn't fit his temperament. Tyler had spoken words; had made a bullshit offer; even appeared contrite at times. In retrospect, it was probably the alcohol talking. But no firm decision had been made. It was clear that Brad needed John's support on this issue. In discussing it with John, he would emphasize that, contrary to what

IFPG would argue, it was in Linden's best interests for Brad to arrange the loan.

IFPG was the worlds' largest professional golf management company. According to the press releases Brad had seen on the internet, they managed over two billion dollars for the players and were averaging an 8% rate of return on funds invested. Even Linden—the non-financial guy he was—knew these statistics. Brad had asked him once in passing, "How is IFPG doing with your dough?" Linden hadn't even hesitated. "8% annual rate of return, pards."

He picked up his pace, passing overweight tourists and sidewalk hacks. He watched a tall guy in a cheap dark suit convince unsuspecting yokels to play 'three card Monty'. He grinned as a heavy-set Elvis impersonator asked him if he wanted a photo with 'the King'.

Shaking his head, he wondered if this five mile stretch of road in the middle of the desert truly represented America…or was it a parody of man's innate greed?

Staring at the massive structures surrounding him, he knew one thing for sure: Vegas was not built on the backs of winners.

Returning to the hotel a few minutes later, he picked up his bag from the bell desk, took a quick leak and began his departure. He had vowed there would be no playing craps on this trip. But as he passed his favorite table in the lobby, he was drawn into the action. What the hell, he thought, just one roll. What could it hurt? The meeting with Ambrook hadn't gone *that* badly. At least he had gotten Tyler's attention. Stirred the pot a little.

He carefully removed two one hundred dollar bills from his money clip and placed them on the 'pass' line. As the stick man pushed the dice towards him, he suddenly felt a slight pang of guilt. He and Mel needed that two hundred bucks. It was hard earned and could buy them groceries for a week.

The dice were upon him before he could remove his bet from the table. Like an alcoholic with a drink placed in front of him, he picked up the dice—fairly certain he was pissing the money away—blew on them a few times and rolled them towards the back wall.

"Winner. Eleven. Pay the line, pay the Field, pay the Yo," the stick man said in a mechanical, nasal voice. Brad grinned. One roll. Two hundred bucks. Not bad. Breathing a sigh of relief, he pocketed his original bet and proceeded to play with casino money. Forty five minutes later, he finally sevened-out, but not before he had made over two thousand dollars.

He collected his winnings, tipped the table men and went to the cage to cash out.

Ten minutes later, the valet brought his car around. The late afternoon weather was warm, but thankfully, much cooler than the day before. The drive home would-n't be half bad. The air conditioning was suspect in the older BMW so he'd have to rely on the outside air from time to time—maybe all the way across the Mojave. He'd take his mind off the drive by listening to a book on CD.

Contemplating his next steps with Ambrook and giddy about his winning roll at the table, Brad didn't notice the red Mercedes that settled in behind him down the strip and on to the I15 South.

The drive out of Las Vegas was straight and nondescript; perfect for listening to a good book on CD. Awful if you hungered for majestic sites or interesting landscape. It was desert. Sand, rocks, tumbleweeds and cactus.

Cell phone reception was surprisingly spotty. Brad tried calling his office twice but couldn't get through. He had just about given up when his phone rang. He recognized Linden's number on the screen.

"Hey John. Thanks for calling back," Brad said.

"No worries, bro. What's up? Where you at?"

"I'm driving back from Vegas."

"What were you doing in Vegas? Did Zindo put an overnight trip together or something?"

"Nope, the trip was about YOU. I'm having some trouble with IFPG. Specifically, Tyler Ambrook. So I came out here to confront him. There's a golf equipment convention going on."

"Yeah, I heard it's bitchin."

"It looked great. I wasn't here for that though." Brad paused as he quickly dropped the phone to his lap, hoping a passing police officer didn't see him talking while driving.

"Brad, you there?" Linden's voice came from Brad's crotch.

"Yeah, I'm here," he said picking the phone out of his crotch. "Had to drop the phone when I saw a cop."

"I understand. I got a ticket a few weeks ago. Cost me two hundred bucks. Now what's the problem with Tyler?"

"He's being an asshole."

"No shit? I told him to cooperate with you. What's he doing now?"

"He wants IFPG to make the new home loan to you. He doesn't want me working on it and he won't provide me with the minor documentation I need."

"Why not?"

"Beats me. We're not talking about a bunch of stuff here: two years' tax returns and two months' asset statements. If you were a normal human being, I could just get them from you directly. I assume you don't get paper copies of taxes and assets. Am I correct?" Brad said more as a statement than as a question.

"You are correct, Sir," John responded doing his best Ed McMahon imitation. "They send me statements from time to time, but I just throw them away. And my taxes? Hell, I haven't seen a tax return for five years. Before, I wasn't making any money so I didn't file. Now, I'm making so much, I just let them handle it."

"That's what I thought. Do you have any idea what you make annually?"

"Eight percent."

"For God's sake, John! You're like a robot. They tell you they make 8% and you go along with the program. Here's the question: 8% of what?"

"Shit, Brad, I don't know. I just know I've got millions and I'm making 8% on my money."

"Okay, we'll talk about that later. I think you need to get more involved with your money—before you lose it all. But the fact is that because you don't have this data, I need their cooperation." Static filled the line. He checked the bars on his phone and could see that he was losing signal. "Anyway John, I'll explain the whole deal to you later. I've got a better loan for you. I need you to call Ambrook and insist that his office cooperate with me. I talked to him out here at the equipment convention. Man to man. He told me to 'kick rocks'. They're trying to rip you off and I won't let that happen."

The signal was growing weaker. One bar and then no bars. He hoped that John had heard that last statement. It was important to him that his buddy knew this wasn't a pissing match over commissions...or seeing whose dick was bigger. This was all about John's best interests.

"You there John? Can you hear me? Shit, I've lost you. If you can hear me, call Ambrook and force him to release the paperwork." (If you can't and I'm talking into thin air—which was often the case with damn cell phones—I hope you caught my gist before I lost you). He pushed the end button and put his phone down.

Before beginning to listen to the book he had brought, his eyes caught several billboards lining the I-15. Gone were the signs advertising instant weight loss and cosmetic surgery. Replacing them were larger, more vibrant signs telling homeowners they could "Short Sell Today; Buy Tomorrow." And, "Got Debt? Dial 1-800-Bankrupt".

An indication of the real estate nightmare Las Vegas was facing? So many foreclosures; so many short sales. Too much 'flipping' and too many subprime loans. He had to shake his head in disgust when, several miles further down the road, he saw a new housing development rising from the desert floor. Who the hell is going to buy those houses? Don't the builders know when to stop?

He inserted the CD into the player and turned up the volume. The book was a Robert Parker Spenser novel; one of his favorites. He settled in for the rest of the long drive home.

Several hours later, he slowed and took the turnoff to his right. The fifty mile stretch of road ahead of him was called the Pear Blossom Highway. A lovely sounding name until you realized what locals called it: Death Highway. A reference to the fact that hundreds of fatalities had occurred over the years on the two lane road. Most of them the result of ill-advised passing.

The road was straight except for various dips and valleys known as whoop-de-doos. These broke up the monotony of the drive and, for the most part, convinced drivers to keep their speed below 60 mph. They also presented a dangerous obstacle to the impatient driver. On-coming traffic was often hidden from view.

Brad was aware of the Pear Blossom legacy. He had driven it many times. He never attempted to pass a slow car or truck. He waited patiently for the slow vehicle turnout and then gunned it past the lumbering turtle.

It was dusk when he took the turnoff and began to head due west. This time of day was especially dangerous as the setting sun could temporarily blind the westward bound driver. Sunglasses and visors helped, but there were times when the sun was just too bright.

Twenty miles into the drive, Spenser was in the middle of one of his classic dialogues with his pal, Hawk, when a red sedan moved out from behind Brad into the eastbound lane and began to pass. As he had dozens of times before, Brad slowed to allow the vehicle to pass.

The sedan pulled alongside him as both cars entered a long stretch of whoop de doos. The driver of the red vehicle—a late model Mercedes—didn't speed up in order to complete the pass. Brad looked over, made a sweeping gesture as if to encourage the driver to finish his maneuver and slowed down even more.

What he saw startled him.

Rather than looking ahead, the driver was staring at Brad. He smiled and then raised his right hand. Brad was no munitions expert, but he was sure the guy was pointing a pistol at him. "What the fuck?" he shouted as if the driver could hear. What was going on? Road rage? What had Brad done to piss this guy off?

The driver pulled the trigger. The passenger window on the red car had been rolled down. The bullet passed through it and hit Brads' window. Shattered glass blew across his lap and a few pieces stung him in the face. Blood trickled in his mouth. Had he been hit by the bullet? Looking in the mirror, he could see that blood was flowing from a small cut on his forehead. Somehow the bullet had missed.

"What the fuck!" he yelled again. He pressed the accelerator and sped up.

The glass probably deflected the shot, Brad thought. Now that the glass was gone the next shot would be clean. Nothing but air between the other driver and him.

He pressed the pedal to the floor, accelerating to eighty and then ninety miles an hour. What if he couldn't outrun this guy? The Mercedes followed him closely. He fought the urge to panic. Taking a deep breath, he focused on the road and yelled at the top of his lungs, "Fuck you! What did I do to you?"

It was moments like this, Brad supposed, that old clichés kicked in. One's life does, in fact, pass before one's eyes. He loved Mel and his kids. He hoped to see them again. He had lived a full life. This was true but there were still places to go and people to see. He wasn't going to go down without a fight. He had to act.

He couldn't swerve. He'd crash into the desert and either die from injuries or, worse, lay there like wounded prey while the hunter took his time finishing the job. He couldn't hit the brakes. At this speed he'd surely spin out—leaving him vulnerable to his attacker. His only option was to punch the accelerator.

The two cars travelled side by side down one mound, up the next. Brad glanced to his left and saw the driver raise the gun. He down shifted the automatic transmission, hoping to pick up some momentary thrust. It worked.

As he sped up, he heard the second shot. This one missed him by inches, the heat of the bullet passing under his chin like a lit candle. He assumed the rapid acceleration had thrown the shooter off. Shaking with fear, he up-shifted to 'drive' and pressed the pedal to the metal. His speedometer hit one hundred ten miles per hour.

The red Mercedes followed him stride for stride. Now he really missed his 2003 Mercedes E500, a casualty of his declining financial fortunes. The car was like a rocket and unlike the older BMW he was now counting on to carry him out of danger, it would have had no problem handling these damn whoop-dee-doos.

And, Brad thought during a moment of absolute clarity, it would've helped had he put new tires on the BMW a few thousand miles ago.

Funny what one thinks about in times of crisis.

As he sped down the backside of one hill, he prepared for the upside of the next. He could see a car coming in the distance. The Mercedes saw it too and drifted back behind him. As soon as the car passed, the Mercedes sped up and pulled alongside once again.

What should he do? He wasn't a stunt driver. He wasn't Steve McQueen in the movie Bullit. That guy could really drive. He was an average driver in an older car. If he pushed it too hard, he could easily fly off the ground as he reached the crest of the hill. Then what? .

He would probably hit the down slope and could, quite possibly, spin out of control if he was going too fast. The other driver had to contend with gravity as well. His car was newer and had a better suspension system. His car could handle the bumps at higher speeds. But could the guy shoot while navigating the ups and downs? That was the sixty four million dollar question.

Both cars cleared the current mogul side by side. Brad snuck a quick peek to his left. He could see the driver smiling. Was he enjoying this?

They raced up the face of the next hill. Brad's speedometer read 100 and then 105.

He was going too fast for the dangerous road, but he had no choice. The glare of the bright, setting sun invaded his windshield—temporarily blinding him. Again, he glanced quickly to his left. The driver had the gun raised and was about to shoot.

This was it, Brad thought, the guy won't miss a third time. He took a deep breath and waited for the fatal shot.

14

HE EXPECTED TO HEAR AN EXPLOSION and then feel the heat of sharp, searing pain.

And then…darkness.

Instead, the sound of metal on metal filled Brads' ears. The smell of burning rubber filled his nostrils.

What the fu…?

He glanced quickly into his rearview mirror. What he saw horrified him.

A big rig semi sat sideways in the middle of the road, smoke and steam coming from the jack-knifed vehicle.

The red Mercedes—what was left of it—was strewn to the side of the road.

It took him a moment to figure out what had happened. But then it hit him. The truck had come over the last hill heading east. The driver of the red Mercedes couldn't see the truck in the afternoon glare. Blinded by the sun; or concentrating on his next shot, he couldn't possibly have seen the truck until it was right on top of him.

They had collided head on.

Brad continued moving but fixed his stare on his rear view mirror. The brand new Mercedes had been pulverized, bits and pieces of the exterior dotting the desert landscape, the chassis wrapped around a nearby Yucca tree; the only remaining wheel still spinning.

He slowed down; almost stopped and contemplated going back to help. Quickly, though, he caught himself. Go back and help a lunatic who might still be trying to kill him?

Fearing that somehow the driver may have escaped the horrible crash, he instead opened his cell phone, saw he had two bars of signal, and dialed 911 to report the accident.

As the dispatcher asked him locational questions, Brad debated whether to file a criminal report as well. Wasn't this just a case of drive-by/road rage? Or, was the guy trying to kill him specifically?

If he reported the driver's actions to the police, Brad was sure he'd have to spend countless hours in Los Angeles answering questions, checking photos, and making sketches. He didn't have time for that stuff, did he? He had to strike on John's loan while the iron was hot.

It wasn't a matter of being scared. He was. And it wasn't that he didn't crave police protection if someone was really trying to kill him. He did. What was it then?

The issue was inconvenience and time management, he convinced himself. He had to make money and he had to make it now. He could always change his mind and report the incident to local police in Santa Barbara.

He hung up without reporting the crime.

Exhaling deeply, he said a silent prayer to a God he wasn't sure really existed, put the car in gear and continued his journey home.

There was a brief period during and after the Truckee financial fiasco that Brad had become numb to the wonderful miracle of life. There had been moments when he actually thought he'd be better off dead. Now, he was sure he wanted to live—more sure than at any time in the previous fifty years.

He only wished it hadn't taken a near fatal episode to reinforce this fact.

Still shaking, he slapped the steering wheel and took a deep, cleansing breath. It was the sweet, fresh breath of life.

It had all happened so fast. One minute, death for him, the next death for the driver of the Mercedes. And what about the big rig? Shouldn't he have tried to help that driver?

He stuck his head out the window to breathe fresh air and to sharpen his senses.

It worked.

For a minute or two.

Five minutes later, he pulled over to the side of the road and puked.

15

"Sounds like a waste of a good Mercedes to me,"
Linden joked as Brad gave him a blow by blow description of the terrifying encounter.

"Fuck You!" Brad responded, deferring to the standard response between buddies. He had called from his cell once he regained his composure. He just had to talk to someone. "The scary thing about it—other than the fact that I was going to die—is that the guy seemed to enjoy the chase. Every time I looked at the son of a bitch, he was smiling. Like he knew the inside joke. It was weird. That's why I think he was a meth-head."

"Yeah. He knew the joke alright—*you* were the punch line. Too bad for him, the asshole didn't get a chance to deliver it," Linden said.

"What a strange experience. I've got no idea what I could've done to piss him off. I don't remember cutting him off. I wasn't talking on my cell. I was listening to a new Spenser CD and out of nowhere this guy pulls along side me with that shit-eating grin, wearing a strange looking hat with some kinda bird on it.

He smiles broadly enough that I can see he chews tobacco and it's obvious he hasn't seen a dentist in quite some time. Then he points a gun at me."

"Is he chasing the bad guy with Hawk?" Linden asked.

"Who?"

"Spenser. Is it one with his sidekick Hawk or one with just him and Susan? I like the ones with Hawk better."

"What the…" an exasperated Brad began.

"Just answer my question," Linden said, cutting him off.

"He's using Hawk as a body guard. Susan and the dog are in it, but they don't play pivotal roles," Brad assured him. Suddenly, he knew what John was doing. Trying to take his mind off the horrible events of the day.

It was working.

Brad had calmed down and had decided that he wasn't going to tell anyone else about the attempted murder—especially Mel. It was a case of road rage; nothing more, nothing less. At this stage in his life, he didn't need the added stress of getting involved with the police. Things were just beginning to pick up in his financial life. He'd be damned if he was going to let this episode sidetrack him.

Financial salvation was, for the first time in years, a potential reality. This decision to not involve the police wasn't a decision made out of some macho code. Brad knew he was no stoic hero. No, it was a practical decision.

It was better to wait and see what happened. He didn't feel good about it—every fiber of his being wanted to report the incident to the police—but it was what it was. He had made his decision.

Besides, the driver was probably dead.

He would get the windows repaired before Mel came home.

"Might not have been road rage, bro," Linden chimed in focusing on the shooting once more. "I mean, you know that you didn't do anything to upset the guy. Right? He takes one shot, but doesn't drive off when he misses. He sticks around and engages you in a high speed chase. Sounds like this guy wanted you dead."

"You really think so? Why would anyone want me dead? I'm a mortgage guy. I'm not in the Mafia. I don't swindle people. I haven't screwed anyone's wife. I just do my thing. Have fun with the family. Play a little golf. Lose all my money. Kick your ass…hey, maybe that's it…you still pissed at me for taking your money last month at Sandpiper?" Brad tried to joke. He paused and then added, "I think he was a crack head, looking for some weird excitement. I was just in the wrong place at the wrong time."

"Dude. All joking aside, I think this might be serious. You should think about going to the police. I'm no Sherlock Holmes, but from what you say, I think this guy was out to get you. I don't think this was a drive-by shooting."

Brad said nothing.

"Let's look at the facts," Linden continued. "One. You didn't cut anybody off while driving. Two. You were minding your own business. You weren't playing loud music or making obscene gestures. Three. The guy was smiling weirdly but you didn't see him ingesting drugs or smoking dope."

"So?" Brad asked.

"So, I would conclude that you've pissed somebody off and they hired this guy to kill you. Either that, or the guy really was a drug-crazed psychotic and was just looking for somebody to kill," Linden said. "Either way, you should go to the police."

"I'll think about it. I'm going to read the L.A. Times in the morning. Let's see if they mention the crash. If the guy's dead—and there's no reason he shouldn't be—I'm inclined to let 'sleeping dogs lie'. If there's any chance he's still alive, I'll go to the police."

"I still think you're crazy, but I'll support your decision. Just promise me you'll go to the police if anything else weird happens."

"Fair enough. I guess it's what Spenser would do, isn't it?"

"Yes it is. And, Brad, I got news for you….you're no Spenser." They both chuckled.

"And John, I'm not trying to be stoic. You know I'm no macho hero. I just don't want the hassle and I don't need any adverse publicity right now. Business is going well; Mel is happy and I want to focus on your deal. Believe me, if I thought I was really in danger, I'd run to the police and spill my guts."

Linden sighed. "Okay, I'll back your play. I'll keep my mouth shut."

"Good." He said it, but he really hoped it was good.

Changing subjects, Linden asked, "Now what do you want me to do about Ambrook and my paperwork?"

"Call him and tell him that *you* are the client and that *you* want me to do the loan and that IFPG should fully cooperate with *my* office. If not, you will call his father and discuss the matter," Brad responded.

"I'm cool with that. I thought I already had this conversation with him. Maybe I should visit him in person. Want to come? We could tee it up with a few of my boys down in Orlando. Play hundred dollar Nassau's. You could probably pay for the whole trip."

"No I can't go anywhere right now. I've got to find you a house and process your loan. I know it doesn't seem like it—'cause I'm such a 'magician'—but these things take time and massive attention to detail. You go see him. Tell the little fucker what's up. Grab your tax returns and asset statements while you're there."

"Is there a tip in it for me?" Linden joked.

"Yep. Here's your tip: When it's breezy, swing it easy," Brad said feeling much better about things now that they were talking about mortgages and not attempted murder.

"Great. Later, buddy. And, hey! Stay out of trouble."

"Later."

Brad hung up the phone and poured himself a stiff bourbon.

When Mel had heard that he would be driving to Vegas Sunday for a meeting Monday, she had decided to visit her folks. They were elderly and enjoyed her company. He was glad she wasn't home. This would give him time to gather his thoughts and get the car fixed.

He sipped his bourbon. It was late. Time to sleep. He had to forget about the shooter. Focus on John's deal. Get on with normal life. Easier said than done. He drained the bourbon and headed for bed.

16

COMMANDER DAVID VON EISENLOW WAS pissed as he gulped a cup of lukewarm coffee Tuesday morning.

Less than twenty four hours earlier, he was higher than a kite. Things had gone well in Orlando. He had proven to the 'whisperer' his men were competent, but now he had two subsequent failures to account for: the restaurant attack in D.C. and the failed hit in California on Monday.

In D.C., his soldier, Marcus Sanford, a five foot five former cotton farmer from Tuscaloosa, had been ready, willing and able to perform the mission. Or so he said.

The commander had given him a sealed envelope with confidential reconnaissance information that the mercenaries had provided. They had isolated the targets and helped with the logistics of the attack.

Nationally recognized mortgage banker, Robert Lewis would be entertaining several politicians at Johnny's restaurant—a popular Washington watering-hole—at precisely seven that evening. The plan was simple: Sanford was to sneak past the parking attendant in the front of the restaurant and then proceed with an assault.

Lewis was the main target but collateral damage was encouraged. When finished, Sanford was to exit out the back door and escape during the confusion or, worse case, turn the gun on himself. What could be easier?

Now here Von Eisenlow was, Wednesday morning, reading accounts of how the operation had gone wrong. The banker was still alive and Sanford was in custody.

Sanford was ill-trained, or perhaps, the most unlucky assassin in America. He didn't sneak past the parking guy as instructed. According to the story in the newspaper, Sanford actually warned the guy—probably a function of coming from the impoverished foothills of Alabama. He felt sorry for the working class attendant.

But this wasn't the *crucial* mistake.

The *crucial* mistake came when his gun jammed. The idiot hadn't checked it before beginning the assault. Now the guy was arrested; he'd probably talk. Von Eisenlow had to move the camp. But where?

While contemplating his options, he re-read on the internet the story the L.A. Times had written about the accident on the Pear Blossom highway. He couldn't be blamed for that, could he? It was a tragic accident. Not his fault. But still…He could feel a headache coming on.

His cell phone rang.

Dispensing with any social niceties, the caller on the other end whispered—almost hissed—angrily, "Your men fucked up yesterday. We won't tolerate failure, Commander. We have provided you with considerable resources." The caller paused, sucked in some air. "This makes me think we may have backed the wrong horse. Please tell me I'm wrong."

"You are wrong, sir. We will prevail! Last night was a fluke. My man had instructions. He followed them to a tee," Von Eisenlow lied. "His gun unexpectedly jammed. It's regretful but I view it as a learning experience. I don't know what happened in California. Next time, my soldiers will be better prepared."

"Make sure they are," the 'whisperer' replied. "I'm disappointed and upset. I can't believe you missed your banker in D.C., and I really can't believe that pain in the ass, Brad Stephens is still alive." He paused, obviously collecting his thoughts and his emotions.

His voice softened. "Listen, commander, I'm a generous man. I'm willing to give you a mulligan on this one. Let's call this fuck up, your personal breakfast ball and get on with life, shall we?"

"Yes, that's kind of you. Shows your Christian charity. These assaults aren't easy you know. We will learn from each of them."

Changing the subject, the caller then asked if Von Eisenlow was moving his men to safer quarters—what with Sanford's capture and all.

"Yes sir. They're packing as we speak. We'll be out of here in a few hours." He wasn't quite sure what a breakfast ball was, but he liked the outcome. He just needed a second chance; he'd prove his value to this strange benefactor.

"And I assume you've got a safe location already designated," the caller said.

He hesitated for a few moments before answering. Would his benefactor think less of him if he told the truth? "No sir. I'm not sure where we're headed. We may disband for a few weeks. All I know is that God will provide. We have come so far, HE wouldn't let us fall victim to the parasites that run this country."

"Shit. I should've known it. You send a moron to kill a senior banker; you jeopardize your whole operation just to get symbolic revenge for the death of your mother; you don't train your soldiers to check their guns in advance; you let him be captured alive; and now, you have no alternative location. Beautiful," the 'whisperer' hissed, anger rising in his voice once again. "Just beautiful."

Von Eisenlow listened intently. He had yet to meet the strange 'whisperer' on the other end of the phone, but the money had rolled in —just as he had said it would. More had been promised. Von Eisenlow had used the money to buy more munitions for the group and a new Hummer vehicle for him and the cook. After all, the commander *had* to travel in style. The men would expect no less of their leader. He still had plenty of cash left over to house the platoon for several months.

As if a sign from the heavens, the caller whispered into the phone. "I thought you might not have a plan B. I was hoping you did; it would've shown me planning and foresight." He paused to let his disappointment settle in. He then continued. "But anyway, in anticipation of this fact, we have arranged for you to have access to a twenty acre ranch just north of Richmond Virginia. I will text you the coordinates. I want you to move your men to this location and sit tight for a few days. Destroy the phone you are currently using. There will be new phones. Continue your plans. Prepare your men better. Time is of the essence. We expect your squad to be prepared to perform a new, larger task by a week from Monday." He hung up.

A week from Monday? *Shit!* That would require a quick move and a massive acceleration of training. Von Eisenlow looked to the heavens and said under his breath, "Hope we can do it."

He turned to the men and said, "Okay, boys, we've got a new location. Quicken the pace. Let's get the hell out of here. The Lord has shown us the way."

17

THE ALARM CLOCK WENT OFF AT PRECISELY 7:11 a.m. every morning.

Brad liked the symmetry. 7&11 were lucky numbers in Craps. 7/11 Grocery Stores in Southern California were called Speedy Marts when Brad was a kid. The memory always brought a smile to his face. Back then he could drink their legacy concoction, a Slurpy, without getting a brain freeze. Today, the thought turned his stomach. And, finally, he had made Eagles—two under par—on holes 7 and 11 at both Pebble Beach and Ballybunion golf courses.

He had slept fitfully Monday night. While somewhat relieved to have discussed the incident with Linden— and outwardly calm the rest of the day—thoughts of death and destruction had returned to his dreams while sleeping.

The dream was vivid. It had startled him awake several hours earlier. A faceless person dressed in a hooded robe chased him through a field, disappeared and then reappeared in the backseat of his car while Brad was trying to start the engine. The faceless figure showed no mercy. It raised a weapon and pulled the trigger...that is when he woke up drenched in sweat.

Brad was no Sigmund Freud. He knew that many psychologists studied dream theory. He wasn't sure why the pursuer had no face. He didn't know the significance of his car not starting. And he wasn't sure why he was in the field to begin with. But it didn't take a Freud to know that the dream wasn't sexual.

It was related to the car chase and his near death experience. It indicated that he could be as cavalier as he wanted while awake, discuss it in a flippant manner with Linden, but once asleep, the incident haunted his subconscious.

And, bottom line, it scared the shit out of him.

This wasn't the first time Brad had experienced sleepless nights and bad dreams. During the Truckee disaster he had tossed and turned. The nightmares were different then, however. Back then, he dreamed of financial destruction and debtor's prison. The phone calls from the bank demanding repayment on a $1.5 million dollar construction loan did nothing to assuage the fears. Quite the contrary, they stoked the fires.

This was different. This wasn't financial. This wasn't dread and frustration. Eventually, he had been able to understand and quantify the financial issues—wrap them neatly in a box and get on with his life. These new nightmares were more serious. These involved life and death. And...questions.

If it wasn't a drugged-out random shooter, then who wanted to kill him? Why? What had he done to deserve the car chase? Did it involve his financial collapse? Did it involve mistaken identity? Did it have anything to do with his kids or family? He was a mortgage guy; a legitimate businessman.

What the hell?

The more he thought about it, the more he came to believe that the dream must be the by-product of his growing belief that the shooting wasn't a random act of violence.

Linden was probably right. Somebody wanted him dead. But who? And he was probably right about going to the police. He'd call them later today or, perhaps, tomorrow.

As he did most days, Brad lay in bed for a few minutes and thought about the upcoming day: Linden's paperwork, loan approval conditions, meeting with a new client at two fifteen, rate sheets to agents and review of any new listings in Montecito. See, he told himself, feeling better about his decision to remain quiet, you're a busy guy; you don't have time to waste with the police. Besides, all of these things would take his mind off the car chase while awake.

He hoped they would consume him while asleep as well.

Shortly thereafter, he got out of bed, showered and set course for the office. It was a foggy morning. Probably because of yesterday's events, Brad drove slower than usual.

Stopping along the way for coffee and a donut, he picked up the morning L.A. Times. Front page story: Semi Truck Crashes Into Sedan. 3 Dead. The story went on to describe another "Pear Blossom Tragedy". The obliterated red Mercedes; the dead driver (good, the son of a bitch had died) and the unfortunate big rig semi.

The crash was blamed on late afternoon sun. However, one of the investigating detectives was quoted as saying: "It would be unusual for both the truck and the Mercedes to be in the same lane unless the Mercedes was passing another vehicle. We'd like to find the driver who was in front of the deceased and talk to him or her. No doubt, this is a tragic accident. But evidence at the scene gives rise to a few questions."

They probably found the shooter's gun, Brad thought. They were right about the passing lane too. Should he pick up the phone and call the officer quoted in the article? Again, he thought about his busy schedule. He had to make hay while the sun shined. He'd call later.

Maybe.

"How'd it go in Vegas?" Stefanie asked ten minutes later when Brad entered the office.

"Okay, I guess. Ambrook didn't back down though. It's clear that John is going to have to get involved. So that's what's happening," Brad fought back the urge to tell her about the shooter.

"Cool. At least we know what the score is. So when should I expect the paperwork?" she asked.

"John's going out to Orlando this week. We should have it all by Friday. In the meantime, I'll try to find him a house and let's focus our attention on our other deals," he said with his normal confident air. He added, "And, Stef, can you find me a good mobile glass guy. Someone threw a rock thru my driver and passenger windows."

Stefanie glanced at him quizzically, "Both windows?"

He took a deep breath, cleared his throat and looked at her. "Yep. Both windows. Glass everywhere.

Not enough damage to file an insurance report, but I should get them fixed today. Okay?"

"Both windows," she said again, shaking her head slowly. "The world is full of crazy people, eh, Brad?"

"Amen to that, Stef...Don't I know." he joked half-heartedly and returned to his paperwork.

Before he attacked the paperwork on his desk, he had a few calls to make. One of them, he especially dreaded. Ever since Truckee, he had been forced to beg his current lenders for either forbearance or loan modification. The process had been demeaning, time consuming, and so far, unrewarding. He reluctantly dialed the 800 number in front of him.

He knew he was probably wasting his time, but he proceeded anyway. This was his tenth call to the loan modification center.

Not for the first time, he wondered about the definition of the word 'insanity': Repeating the same actions over and over with expectations of a different outcome.

If that was the case, yeah, he probably was a little insane.

The voice on the other end was obviously foreign; probably an Indian hourly wage earner sitting in a boiler room in New Delhi or Bombay.

Brad closed his eyes as the dis-embodied voice talked. He imagined a young man in white shirt, dark slacks and plain, black shoes sitting behind a computer screen, earpiece and mouthpiece protruding. The man —or boy actually—would have a four to five page script in front of him. The lines of the script would be color-coded and certain key words would be typed in the margins. When the caller mentioned these words, the boy would read the corresponding line from the script.

"My name is David," the heavily accented voice said. "How may I help you?"

More likely Punjab or Raji, Brad thought. "Well… *David*, I'm calling to check up on the status of my loan modification request."

"Yes sir," came the initial response. "How are you today?"

"I'm fine. Listen, let's cut the fake pleasantries. This is the tenth time I've called this month," Brad said.

"Yes, thank you. So I am to believe you have called to request loan modification. Is that correct?"

Brad took a deep cleansing breath. He knew the loan modification process was bullshit, but he had to try. If he could freeze his mortgage payments at their current level, he might make it to the finish line. The last call he had made a few days earlier sounded promising.

"I'm not calling to request modification; I sent all my paperwork via fax for the eighth time last week. I want to know if the bank has processed it yet," Brad said.

"Yes, I understand. You would like the bank to consider modifying your mortgage loan. Is that correct?"

It was like talking to a machine; this kid had no clue. Hell, he probably didn't even know what a mortgage was. "No I'm not calling to begin the process; I'm calling to check up on the status of my paperwork. Now if you can't help me…*David*…from your post in India, perhaps you could transfer me to someone in the United States."

"Yes, I understand, you would like to discuss loan modification." There was a pause for a moment, the faint sound of papers rustling could be heard in the background. "If you will provide me your loan number, email address and mailing address, I will send you the requirements."

Fighting the impulse to slam the receiver on the table, Brad composed himself and said, "No, you don't understand; I already sent in the paperwork. Please put me in touch with someone in loss mitigation," he demanded.

"That will not be necessary, I can help you."

"No you can't; if you could, you already would have. Now please transfer me to a supervisor…in America."

"That will not be necessary, I am in Dallas," David responded.

"No you're not; don't bullshit me, *David*. You're in India and your name is not David. Now I want to speak to someone in loss mitigation."

The line went dead. He had been disconnected.

Damn! He had been so close to finally talking to a human supervisor. He redialed the 800 number and was put on hold. Stefanie poked her head into his office and asked if he needed anything from the store?

"No, I'm okay," he said. "Thanks for asking."

"Who are you holding for?" she asked, hearing the music coming from his speaker.

"I'm trying to get status on my loan modification request. As usual, the 800 number put me in touch with an idiot in India. I demanded to speak to a supervisor and then the line went dead."

She smiled. "You know the process is a bunch of crap, don't you?"

"Yes."

"You tried to modify the Truckee loan before you went to short sale, didn't you?"

"Yes." He felt like a little boy being scolded by his teacher.

"And now you think they're going to treat you differently on your primary residence? It's the same bank isn't it?"

"Because it is my primary residence, I felt I might get through to somebody in power and make my case; I've been hit pretty hard by this recession, you know."

She came around the desk and opened her arms. "Stand up and give me a hug," she demanded. He did as she requested, felt better, and then sat back down again.

"You know they're just going to give you the run around, but still you call. Why?"

He looked at her with heavy eyes. "I've got to try. Mel loves that house...*I* love that house. The equity in it may end up being my only chance at retirement." He paused, rubbed the bridge of his nose and then continued. "I keep thinking that this nightmare will end and I'll be able to refinance my current loan into something manageable...but it doesn't. My only shot is if I can convince the bank to modify the existing loan."

"I don't think I told you this, but I got a 'trial' modification last year," she said making quote marks in the air. "The deal was that if we made the monthly payments for five months, they would lower the payments permanently."

"That's great," Brad said enthusiastically. "What happened? How low are your payments?"

She frowned. "That's the thing; they gave us the five month period and we made all the payments on time. Then when the five months were up, they cancelled the program and rescinded the offer to modify."

"That's criminal!"

"That's what I thought. So I paid an attorney two hundred bucks to research it. Turns out the lender was within its rights because my loan is not owned by FannieMae."

"That sucks."

"Yes it does," she said sadly. "Anyway, I think you're wasting your...."

Before she could finish her statement, the music stopped and a young woman's voice came on the line. "This is Mary, how may I help you?"

Brad picked up the receiver and demanded to speak to an American supervisor. The girl insisted she was American and that she was handling the call in Dallas. Obviously, she was reading the same script as *David*. Brad pushed her. "Okay, *Mary*, what state is Dallas in?"

Silence. And then the line went dead. Disconnected... again.

Brad shook his head and wondered if, in fact, he had really fallen down the rabbit hole?

18

THE NEW CLIENT, BILL LARSON, sat across from Brad; his short, gray beard framing a tan and pleasant face.

Well qualified, polite and interesting, Larson was the opposite of his agent. Nadia Korsakov.

Nadia—and she spoke about herself in the third person—"Wasn't going to take no BULLSHIT". A Russian immigrant standing five feet tall and weighing well over two hundred pounds, Nadia was a ball buster—with a slightly gray moustache.

Apparently, she—and only she—knew the system was corrupt. In her world, Brad guessed, everyone was corrupt. She made it obvious that mortgage brokers and lawyers couldn't be trusted. She, Nadia, had personally advised her client to visit one of the big three box banks to get his loan. She, Nadia, was there under protest and wanted to make sure that everyone knew it.

The client, Bill Larson, had been referred to Brad by several people at his work. He seemed to like Brad and appeared confident that Brad would do a good job.

Nadia was a different story, however.

As the meeting progressed, it was obvious to Brad that Mr. Larson was embarrassed by Nadia's aggressive attitude. At one point in the conversation, he asked her to go check his car—the meter maids marked the wheels and gave tickets to un-moved vehicles every ninety minutes.

"She really seems to know the market," he said. "I'm sorry she's so negative. She must've had a bad lending experience in the past."

"Unfortunately, it's typical behavior from an agent who hasn't figured out what I do. They don't get that my service is geared to the clients' advantage; not the bank's," Brad stated. "I've found over the past thirty years that real estate agents tend to get very confrontational about things they have no control over."

He continued, "As long as you're comfortable, she can be as negative as she wants. We'll get through this and I'll get you the best loan I can."

"That's what I thought. I just want to get a nice house for my wife and family. Thanks for understanding," Larson said.

With Nadia interrupting repeatedly, the meeting took over two hours. When completed, Brad could only think about heading home. Aggressive agents always gave him a headache.

Mel would be back from visiting her folks and the boys would be coming over for dinner. He grabbed his keys, cell phone and sunglasses and began to leave. Before he made the stairway, Stefanie called to him.

"Brad. Are you leaving for the day? It's only four thirty. We've got work to do."

"Not tonight, Stef. I'm going to spend some time with the wife and kids. We can get caught up on everything else tomorrow."

"Okay. But, while you were in that meeting with that awful woman with the funny accent and awful little moustache—did you notice?—you had a few phone calls. John called. I put him through to voicemail. You might want to listen to it on your way home. Skip from San Diego called. He told you to take the Padres tonight...whatever that means. And someone from the Bellacqua called to congratulate you. What does that mean Brad?"

"I'm not sure," Brad said. "What did they say exactly?"

She scrunched her face trying to remember. "I'm not sure, but I think the man said, Tell Mr. Stephens he got lucky in Vegas." And then as an afterthought, she added, "And he had a very strange, soft voice. Sounded weird."

Brad frowned. What was that, a call from the hotel or a call from the driver of the red Mercedes? But that guy was dead—wasn't he? He forced himself to smile and said, "They probably noticed I won a few bucks at the craps table. You know how they follow up. They want to make sure you enjoyed your stay. Congratulate you on your luck at the tables. That type of thing." He let that last statement hang in the air.

"I wouldn't know. I've never won enough to have anyone follow up with me. How much did you win? Any little bonus in it for your partner?"

"Just enough to pay for the trip, I'm afraid. But these days, that may seem like a lot to any casino. The tables were dead. The only activity seemed to be at the convention center. Next time, I'll try to win more. See you tomorrow." With that he was out the door.

Was there a second meaning to the call? Like congratulations on avoiding death during the road rage? They wouldn't know about that at the casino, would they? It was a silly notion. But, try as he may, he couldn't forget the car chase and the crash. He had to wonder what the hell was going on. He contemplated calling the police immediately. Thinking about the stack of files on his desk, he decided against it.

Maybe if he put out enough positive energy with friends and family, the nightmare he first experienced the night before wouldn't return. He vowed to put on a happy face. He took a deep breath and put the car in gear.

"Is mom cooking tonight?" Brads' oldest son Blake asked as Brad walked through the front door.

"Naw. We're barbequing some steaks. She's making a salad and boiling some corn. You and I are in charge of the hard tack."

"Good. I was over the other day. Had to use your dryer. Ours broke. She was watching the Food Network and was taking notes. That's *never* a good sign," he said with a chuckle.

The boys knew. Their mom was a great person. Wonderful mother. Fantastic wife. But they *knew* about her cooking. Better than anyone. They *knew*.

When they were young, Brad often worked late—missing dinner at home. This left both Blake and his younger brother Scott alone with their mother for dinner in the evenings. Apparently, Mel had found it therapeutic and useful to use the boys as human subjects for her early cooking experiments. This was before the cooking channels hit the airwaves.

Using a respectable and proven cookbook as her guide, Mel had delved into such unique dishes as

Fettuccine Alfredo, Chorizo and Eggs, Half Baked Stuffed Cabbage, and "Angry Fish" with Spaghetti Vongole. The latter a fairly easy Italian dish that only required one essential element—healthy, clean clams. Unfortunately for the boys, the clams Mel chose were several days old.

Later that night, Blake vomited first, his voice echoing through the halls of the home. "Dear God. Let this be the last puke," he prayed. Scott followed shortly thereafter—asking his mother, "Damn Mom, what did you do to us?"

Mel had been remorseful. She vowed never to buy clams from a supermarket again. From now on, all of her fish would come straight off the boat. The good news was her pasta and sauce were wonderful. The boys had said they enjoyed the flavor. She was encouraged. The boys were mortified.

"Dad, you've got to talk to mom. Her cooking is awful! She damn near killed us with those clams! Tell her to warm up pizzas and burritos for us—like all the other moms," Blake had pled.

"Yeah, Dad. We know she means well but you should've tasted the Chicken Cordon Bleu she made last night. Tasted like shoe polish," Scott chimed in.

"I'll see what I can do boys," Brad had assured them. That was when he discovered the successful strategy of barbequing. It wasn't until the boys left home for college that he discovered the mis-direction play with Blockbuster and Taco Bell.

It was an understatement to say that Brad loved his family. They were his entire life. Scott, Blake, Mel and, of course, Rufus the dog.

Family.

The boys, now thirty and twenty seven respectively, had returned to the city of their birth determined to find fortune and fame. Neither famous nor rich...yet...they often ventured to their parents' home for free meals.

Blake, a six foot two, toe-head blonde with blue eyes and a bright smile was his esoteric son. Scott, six foot one, with light brown hair and deep dimples, was more materialistic. Together, they formed a well-balanced team.

Brad hoped they could find their fortunes without their father's financial support. That ship had sailed.

The night was like many others. The boys were jovial, the dog slobbered incessantly and Mel was determined to get the veggies right. Brad had a Jack in his hand while preparing the barbeque.

"So how was Vegas, Dad?" Scott asked. "Did you tag the tables?"

"Not quite. I went there for business and just didn't feel any good 'juju'," Brad explained. "I left before I could piss away my hard earned money." It was only a small lie. No need for anyone to know he had a few extra thousand bucks in his pocket.

"Blake and I are going out there in July for a buddy's bachelor party. You think you can get us comp'd at the Bellaqua?" Scott, who was never shy about seeking a good deal, asked.

"We'll see. Looks like the steaks are almost ready," Brad said hoping to change the subject. "How do you guys want 'em cooked?"

"Make mine medium rare," Scott said.

"I'll take mine well done. Be sure to put plenty of char on the outside," Blake said.

Mel tossed the salad and placed the bowl on the dining room table. Blake asked suspiciously, "Is there anything in the salad we should know about, Mom?"

"I don't know. It's a recipe I saw on Diners, Drive Ins and Dives. Slightly seared watermelon, arugula, goat cheese, pine nuts, and a balsamic reduction. Nothing fancy," she assured them.

It was good. Really good. As bad as Mel was at copying an entrée, she was equally good at making salad.

"Remember this salad, Mom," Scott said. "We can use it when I open my restaurant."

"I will. I can't wait. I've been saving all of my recipes," a happy and confident Mel responded. "You can handle the regular food. I'll come in once a week and cook a special meal. It will be limited. Only five or six servings. You can call it...Momma Mel's Special Meal."

Scott, always the king of diplomacy, mumbled under his breath, only loud enough for Blake to hear, "That will be five or six fewer customers because they'll never come back." He faced his mother and spoke directly to her. "Yeah, well, uh...that sounds great Mom. Let's see what happens. I know, for sure, I'm going to need some good salads. Let's start with that and see where it gets us. Okay?"

Mel seemed satisfied for the time being. They all knew it wouldn't be the last time they discussed her cooking.

The steaks were still on the grill as they finished their salads.

Brad took them off, put them on a large platter and looked at his family from the doorway. They were a fine group. The boys young and virile. Mel, dainty yet strong. How had she given birth to such large boys? They were as close as a family could be in this modern age of transience and uncertainty. Brad would take a bullet for any one of them and he was certain that they, too, would do the same.

Better that they not know about the Pear Blossom Highway chase and shooting—especially Blake. He would take it personally. He'd research it. Make sure the guy was dead. If he wasn't, Blake would go after the guy. In his world, nobody fucked with the Stephens family.

It wouldn't turn out well.

Dessert was served. Apple tarts with vanilla ice cream. They all settled in to watch the last few innings of the Dodger game. Brad would deal with business (and the riddle of the "lucky" call) tomorrow. Tonight, all was right in the world. The air was warm; the jasmine in bloom; the family content; and...Brad Stephens was still playing golf on this side of the grass.

The boys left promptly upon the completion of dinner and the ballgame—a 6-4 Dodger victory. Brad cleared the dishes while Mel rinsed them off and put them in the dish washer. Rather than heading for bed when they were done, Mel grabbed a bottle of red wine and two wine glasses.

Patting the couch gently and smiling, she beckoned Brad to sit down beside her. She poured them both a glass of wine.

"Nice vino," Brad said. "What is it?"

"Buon Ani," she replied. "It's a Sangiovese and Merlot blend. Smooth isn't it?"

Brad nodded. Took another sip and sat back.

Mel took a sip herself and then turned to her husband. "Okay, so what's bugging you?"

"What do you mean?"

"You can hide it from everyone else, but I can tell something is bothering you. Is it your work? Are we going broke again?" Her body tensed as she took shots at the problem.

He stretched across the couch and kissed her gently on the lips. "No, we're not going broke again…I don't think. However, I always reserve the right to worry about it," he said with a wink.

"Then what is it?"

He cleared his throat and turned away from her slightly, staring at the gas fire burning in the fireplace. "Okay, there is something," he began.

"I knew it. Spill the beans, Brad Stephens."

"Well here's the thing. You know I feel awful about losing all our money in Truckee."

"Yes, I do. Now get over it. Does this have something to do with Truckee?"

"In a way, yes." He took another sip of wine and searched for the right words. "The only way I'm going to stabilize our finances is to work like crazy and to take advantage of opportunities when they arise."

"Like John's deal."

"Yes."

She placed her hand on his thigh and smiled. "If you're having problems with John, we can work that out. Maybe it's not a good idea to mix business with close friends."

He shook his head. "That's not the issue. John and I are fine. Something happened on my way home from Las Vegas."

She said nothing, but shrugged to encourage him on.

"It's probably nothing and it probably was just some hick high on meth, but this guy pulled up next to me on the Pear Blossom highway…"

"I hate that fucking road."

"I know you do. I'm not too fond of it anymore myself." He paused, took one final gulp of wine and continued the story. "Anyway, when the guy pulled up next to me, he fired a gun at me."

Mel gasped. "A real gun?"

"Yes, a real gun. What other type is there?"

"I don't know. Maybe a paint ball gun or something."

"I can assure you, this was a real gun with real bullets. Anyway, he missed me but blew out a few of my windows."

"And…."

"And, when he was zeroing in for the kill shot, he didn't pay attention and ran head-on into an oncoming truck."

"Fucking Pear Blossom! I hate that road."

He was silent for a moment. He took a sip of wine and then continued. "The car was obliterated and the guy died at the scene."

"Why didn't you tell me earlier?"

"That's where Truckee comes in. I know we vowed to discuss big things in the future."

"This is a pretty big thing."

"I know," he said nodding his head in agreement. "I called the police but I didn't file a report and I didn't tell you for the same reason: I don't need the complications of police and media hounding me. I thought it was best for me—for us—to keep it under wraps."

"What's changed?"

"I feel like I'm cheating by not sharing such a big

event with you. I don't want to cheat; that's almost more complicated, if you know what I mean."

Again, she said nothing.

He continued. "Anyway the guy is dead. I'm sure it was a stupid L.A. drive-by thing and now I've confessed my sins. Am I forgiven?"

"That's not my job."

"I know, but can you see my point?"

"Yes. In a strange way, I can. It's been a tough several years. But I need you to share with me; it's the only way we're going to make it. No secrets."

He stood up and held out his arms. She rose. They embraced. He kissed her deeply and gently. He guided her towards the bedroom. Rufus rose slowly from his dog bed, suddenly alert and followed them slowly down the hallway.

Suddenly, Mel stopped. "If you thought we were in danger, you'd call the police wouldn't you?"

"If I had reason to believe that you, the boys or… Rufus," he said, glancing at the dog, "were in danger, I'd run to the police so fast it would make your head swim."

"Good," she said and they continued down the hallway.

She stopped again. "Sex, no matter how fulfilling, isn't going to make up for your deception."

"Maybe not, but let's give it a try anyway."

And they did.

19

BRAD AWOKE WEDNESDAY TO A SHARP, clear spring morning. No fog; unusual for this time of year.

He checked the bond market on his computer, sent a few emails and set his schedule for the upcoming day. It was amazing to think how much work could get done before he even showered.

Another miracle of the modern world.

The main reason for going into the office was to meet with clients. The secondary reason was to socialize with his processors and co-agents.

Although a loner in many ways, he definitely enjoyed business interaction. It kept him focused. Working six to eight hours a day from home would drive him crazy. Not to mention that there was constant work to be done living on five acres of land. When boredom set in at the office, he took a walk. If boredom set in at home, he pulled weeds, trimmed the roses or nurtured his fruit trees. The place offered too many distractions.

Besides, where else could he see and hear a lame ass like Jim Johnson, insult a client while selling a loan program? The guy was a classic nut job. Brad thought Johnson might mellow out over the years. He was wrong.

"Listen, Mrs. Smith," he overheard Johnson say into the receiver as he walked into the office that morning. "You've got two kids in high school right? And another bun in the oven, right? Your husband left you when you told him you were pregnant, right? So now you've run out of money but have a ton of equity in your house, right? He's a bum, right? Not paying alimony or child support. You NEED this loan. Don't ask me again about the terms. I'm an expert. I'll get you the money you need."

Johnson semi-listened while Mrs. Smith made some type of reply. His eyes turned from focusing on the file in front of him to Brad standing by the doorway. Without missing a beat, he waved, pointed to the phone, and mouthed "Pain in the Ass" as if Brad would understand. Then he rolled his eyes, shook his head, and made the internationally recognized hand gesture of fingers to thumb indicating the caller was saying, "Blah, blah, blah." Obviously, he thought Brad would appreciate his handling of the call. Johnson smiled as if they shared a common bond. Brad just shook his head and walked upstairs to his office.

"Morning, Stef. Morning everybody," he said as he passed through the processing area. "What have we got on the agenda today?"

"Ruppert docs are in escrow. Lyons closed. John called again. Did you call him back yesterday? And that repugnant Russian real estate agent called at eight thirty sharp. She yelled at me because you weren't in yet. She said that she's in the office every morning at seven thirty and that if you want to do business with 'Nadia', you best do the same."

"It's a good thing for the client that I need the money. Otherwise, I'd pass him over to Jim Johnson. I think Nadia and Johnson were made for each other," Brad joked.

He settled into his chair and called Linden.

"John. Where you at; Pebble or Orlando?" he asked.

"Orlando. And it's beautiful down here today. Not as nice as Pebble Beach, but I already played eighteen this morning. If I wanted, I could play eighteen more."

"Are you meeting with IFPG today?"

"That's what I wanted to talk to you about. Tyler says he can't meet with me until next week. I told him that I'm the client and I made a special trip to discuss my finances. He said I should've called first and that he knows I want to talk to him about financing for my new home purchase. He said he has everything under control. Don't worry about it, he said. Go play golf. Go make more money," Linden said doing his best imitation of the pompous tone used by Tyler Ambrook.

"He's treating you like a seventeen year old rookie."

"Yep. That's the feeling I get. I don't dig it. I'm going over there tomorrow and force a meeting with him or, if that fails, with his father."

"His father? Oh yeah, I remember Stef telling me the old man is back."

"They sent a memo out a few weeks ago saying that he would be returning to full time status until this recession ends. The memo said that the death of Art Smalley came as a big surprise and it would take months before they could train somebody to replace him. So Tyler was going to start handling the major accounts—I guess I'm now a *major* account so don't fuck with me. The memo also said that Steven would handle operations."

"I guess that makes sense. Well good. If Tyler won't talk to you, go to the old man. Explain the situation. I'm sure he'll want what's best for you. He might even appreciate me taking some of the work load off his staff now that Smalley is dead."

"That whole thing with Smalley still bugs me, man. He wasn't depressed. I knew him. He wasn't the kind of guy to commit suicide. I think I'm going to visit his family. Pay my respects. See if they know anymore about why he hung himself."

"Might as well 'kill two birds with one stone' while you're down there," Brad immediately regretted using the death metaphor. "I mean, who would guess that the great John Linden could multi-task like that?" he added quickly, hoping that the joke would cover his faux pas.

"Yeah, I'm a real twentieth century man, ain't I? Anyway, I'll give you a call after I talk to one or both Ambrooks. Have a good day." Linden didn't wait for a response.

Before Brad could attend to the various loan files in front of him, his cell phone rang. "SZ" was calling. Steve Zindo hated cell phones and usually only called when it was something very important. Brad answered.

"Hey Brad, buddy, how you doing?" Zindo asked. And then before Brad could reply, added, "Just calling to say Hi. Want you to know that we're going to kick some butt next time we partner in spades."

"That's it? That's why you called? You never just call to say Hi. What's up?"

"Nothing. Can't I call a buddy without being hassled?"

"Steve…"

"Okay, I did want to ask you a question."

"I'm all ears."

"Do you know my gate code? I seem to have forgotten it and you're the only person I can think of that I gave it to."

"Yeah, hold on for a second, I've got it stored in my cell phone."

The ultra-rich…go figure.

Brad found the code, gave it to Zindo and said good-bye. He smiled when he closed his cell phone and marveled once again how his millionaire buddy got thru the day.

Recently divorced, Zindo was learning new things daily about dating, politics, history, socializing, and maintaining a household. In many ways, he was like a freshman entering college. The world was his oyster.

Now he would know his gate code. He had that going for him. Hopefully, he would have the sense to store it in his own phone.

After a brief respite, he returned to the business at hand. The weekly real estate guide had been distributed via email that morning. No new properties in the four million dollar range. Linden seemed eager to get the house hunting going. Without Johns' financials, however, that could be tricky. Sellers, after all, want to make sure a prospective buyer can get a mortgage.

He was confident that his friend would qualify for the new loan, but he wasn't *absolutely* sure. And given the new, ultra- tight lending standards, it was only prudent to proceed cautiously. John had never indicated that he was prepared to pay cash. So that probably wasn't an option. The loan would be an integral part of the offer and the subsequent negotiations.

Even though he had commissions from both the sale and the loan, he was determined to handle the transaction as if he were only procuring the loan. No conflict of interest that way. He was still concerned that John might not get the financial information from IFPG. Then what?

The bigger question of the day—and one he had been avoiding like the plague—was: If it wasn't a drive by shooting—if Linden was right—then who would want to kill him?

He pulled a legal pad from his desk drawer and started making a list of possible suspects. It seemed like the responsible thing to do. Perry Mason made lists. Andy Griffith, in Matlock, separated his suspects on paper. Colombo always referred to a little notebook before he solved the murder. If you watched any modern detective show, you'd always see a chalk board with pros and cons or cork boards with pictures of suspects. This is what you were *supposed* to do when somebody committed a serious crime.

Wasn't it?

Only problem was, Brad couldn't think of anybody who had cause to hate him—much less kill him. And, of course, he still wasn't even sure he wasn't just a driver in the wrong place at the wrong time.

By no means was Brad Stephens a saint. Look at the people he hung out with: A loose canon golfer, an eccentric multi-millionaire, a headstrong former television executive, and a bevy of foul-mouthed sexist golf buddies. But kill him? It just didn't add up.

He began making his list: 1. Old Fat guy who thought I slept with his wife. 2. Anderson, the contractor from Truckee.

That was it.

He could only think of two—and they were weak suspects to say the least.

The old fat guy (Brad referred to him as "Jaba the Hut") was pissed at the time, but that was years ago. The guy had been irrational, but not homicidal. Besides, he was probably dead by now. Carrying that much weight, a heart attack or stroke seemed more than likely. Brad made a mental note to check on ol' 'Jabba's' status.

Having remembered one person who blatantly hated him, no matter how remote the possibility that this man tried to kill him, made Brad feel better. If it was the jealous husband, then Brad could deal with it quickly and quietly. He'd just tell the guy that his wife was a slut and that she slept with everyone other than him.

Get over it dude and deal with your wife.

'Jaba' was a weak suspect, Brad knew, but he had to start somewhere.

A much stronger suspect was the contractor in Truckee. The guy had built Brad's vacation house improperly and had, in all likelihood, stolen more than three hundred thousand dollars from the project. Brad had sued him, his insurance company and the builder's family. Then he had threatened to pursue criminal charges.

Hostilities had run high as they came face to face during the early arbitration hearings. The process of losing a tremendous amount of money is complex. First comes anger. Then comes frustration. Soon understanding sets in. Followed by capitulation. And, finally, the ultimate revelation: Life ain't fair.

Launching a lengthy lawsuit in an attempt to recapture the lost money, Brad felt confident justice would be served. He'd recapture some of his money and the crook would be thrown in jail.

After ten months and countless hours of depositions, Brad won. The insurance company agreed that the foundation had been poured on non-compacted soil and they agreed to a settlement. The amount they offered barely covered the legal expenses. "Fight us in court," they had said. "You'll probably win. We, on the other hand, are fighting so many of these defective construction suits that we'll probably go out of business before you'll see a red cent from us. You'll have a non-recoverable judgment."

Life ain't fair.

It was a painful lesson in the truth behind our legal system.

Maybe the son of a bitch held a grudge? That had to be it. He was the only person who should really hate him. Feeling confident in his deductive reasoning, Brad proceeded to research his enemy.

"Hello, Glen. It's Brad Stephens in Santa Barbara," he said to the attorney who had represented him in the lawsuit. "I was wondering if you've been able to keep tabs on Butch Anderson, the former contractor?" he asked.

"Hey Brad, how you doing? Sorry we didn't get a larger settlement for you. The good news is that the insurance company did, in fact, go bankrupt. So you did the right thing. As for Mr. Butch Anderson, I guess you haven't heard? He was killed by an angry homeowner several months ago. Anderson did the same thing to him that he did to you except in this case, he stole over a million and ran off with the guys' wife."

"No shit! Dead," was Brad's only reply.

"As a door knob."

"Dead? Damn. There goes that theory," Brad said under his breath.

"Why do you want to know?" the lawyer asked.

"No reason," Brad lied. "I just thought it might be time to harass him again. I was reminded about the whole fiasco today when one of the subs called to inform me that I still owed ten thousand dollars in architectural fees. I tell you Glen that whole mess is like dog poop on the bottom of my shoes. I rub it off, but the stink still follows me wherever I go."

"Yeah, I know what you mean. Hopefully, Anderson's death will give you some closure. When are you coming back up here?" Glen asked. "I'd like to play golf with you again."

"Glen, my friend, don't take this the wrong way but I'd rather stick needles in my eyes than ever visit Truckee again. That place is dead to me. If you ever come down to Santa Barbara, give me a call. I'd be happy to play a local course with you. Take care," Brad said as he hung up.

His prime suspect dead, Brad was forced to think more deeply about the situation. He quickly ruled out Jabba the Hut. He sighed, feeling like he had hit a wall. Maybe it was a random shooting after all. But what about the strange call? And why had the shooter smiled in such a weird way? After several minutes another idea hit him. Could it be Tyler Ambrook? Would he hate him enough to want him dead?

They had had words at the convention center and Ambrook was obviously very upset with him. Tyler could've easily found out where Brad was staying and could've just as easily discovered that he had driven from Santa Barbara. There was only one route back to Santa Barbara. It didn't take a brain surgeon to figure out the most remote—and dangerous—part of the drive was the Pear Blossom Highway. But again, the main question: Why?

Would he really have Brad followed with orders to shoot? Again, it didn't add up. But still, he had to wonder.

Surely Ambrook didn't care about the relatively small commission the loan would generate. He had already conceded the real estate side of the deal. Was Ambrook really that big of an asshole? Brad needed to find out. He went to his refrigerator, took out a Dr. Pepper, sat back in his chair and dialed the phone.

"Hey buddy. Sorry to bother you again. I've been thinking about what you said. I still think the guy on the Pear Blossom was probably a gang-banger or meth head, but I decided to make a list of people who hate me and I could only come up with one person who makes sense. If I'm right, we might have a big problem," Brad said to John Linden.

20

AFTER A BRIEF PAUSE ON THE OTHER end, Linden responded to Brads' unexpected call.

"Glad you called. I think we got a problem too.
Something ain't right down here. I spent the past few
hours with Art Smalley's family. They're absolutely
convinced that he didn't off himself. Every one of them—
his wife, Veronica, his two kids, his brother and his
mother—said he was in good spirits at the time of
his death. His wife even says he was optimistic about the
future. He was drinking too much, but Veronica and
he had talked about it. He was going to try and quit.
If not, he promised he would join AA."

"Huh! Doesn't make sense, does it? So what do you
think happened?"

"I don't know. Maybe he was murdered?"

"That's a big jump, buddy," Brad said.

"I know it is. But after talking to the family, I'm convinced something stinks. Besides, he just had the putting
green mowed."

"So?"

"Why would you keep a putting green absolutely immaculate if you weren't going to be around to use it?"

Brad had to concede the point. He thought for a moment and then said, "I don't know how Art ties in, but I called to tell you that I'm starting to think that if anybody had a motive to send that goon after me, it would be Tyler Ambrook."

"No shit!"

"Yeah, I still have no reason to believe it wasn't a random act of violence, but on the off chance that someone really wanted me dead, I've been racking my brain trying to figure out who it might be. I thought I had it: the contractor from Truckee. But it turns out, he's dead. The only other thing I could think of was that maybe Tyler was so upset that I would confront him— and he obviously has a huge ego—that he decided to punch my ticket. What do you think?"

"I don't know what to think. Talk about big jump."

"Yeah I know. Listen to us. Two amateur detectives." He paused. "Anyway, it's just a thought. If he did have anything to do with it, what was his motivation? You don't send a guy to shoot someone just because you're embarrassed."

Linden hesitated as if trying to wrap his head around Brad's theory. "I don't know Tyler well enough to know if he's that kind of guy. All I know is that he's a USC Fratboy who hasn't worked in the real world. Daddy gave him his first job and then promoted him to top of the class."

"Entitlement issues?"

"Maybe," Linden said. "What do we do, confront him?"

"Tread lightly, my friend. IFPG still represents you and manages all of your money. You don't want to go off half-cocked and ruin that relationship. Why don't you meet with them tomorrow. Discuss only your purchase of this new house. Get a feel for Tyler Ambrook and his relationship with his father. Then give me a call."

"Right on, buddy. I'm still going to snoop around a bit. See what I can find out from Art's other friends. I'll meet with IFPG and get a feel for what's going on over there."

Brad smiled at the thought of the big golfer trying to uncover clues. "Sounds good John; be careful."

Seemingly pleased by the conclusion to the previous conversation, Linden changed subjects. "I'm taking Fabiola out for dinner tonight. Real chic place, 'Anthonys Grotto'. She's excited as hell about moving to Montecito. And like I told you earlier, I'm going to send her out there for a few days? You know, help you hunt for our house."

"Sure. No problem. You realize I haven't met her yet? Does she want to stay with Mel and me? We'd love to have her," Brad offered although he hadn't spoken to Mel about it.

"Believe me, bro, when you meet her, you'll love her. She's warm, outgoing, beautiful, intelligent, and...did I mention this...she loves to do the 'horizontal bop'?" he added with a chuckle.

"Yes, John. You mentioned that several times already. I'm sure we'll love her. 'Mi Casa, Su Casa'. When is she coming?"

"Tomorrow. I'll put her on a flight to L.A. in the morning and she should be in Santa Barbara by three. Have Blake or Scott pick her up. They won't believe that Uncle John has such a hot Latina in love with him. Might make them take up professional golf."

"Naw, they know that boring, anal, assholes play golf competitively. It's a documented fact that the boys do like the ladies, though. And, for some unknown reason, they love you. I'm sure one of them will pick her up. Email me the details in the morning."

"Will do. Now I've got to go take a nap. She's probably going to want to have intense, monkey sex with me tonight. I better be ready. Talk to you later, bro."

Monkey sex? Brad chuckled as he hung up.

Three hours later, Linden found himself salivating over the Lobster Bisque—and his fiancée.

Fabiola, true to her nature had worn a low cut red dress with plenty of room to show off her perfect legs and remarkable figure. The parking attendants, waiters and bus boys, couldn't take their eyes off her.

Linden knew—or at least thought he knew— that he was a good looking guy. But how had he, a Midwest baseball player-turned-golfer, landed a Latina bombshell? The God's Must be Crazy he thought. Then, in a moment of extreme lucidity, he said to himself, "Fuck it. She's with me. Wants to be with me. Digs me. I'm rich. Who am I to question why?"

During dinner, they discussed J-Lo, Oprah, Gay Marriage, Julio Iglesia, and Montecito. Not a major intellectual foray, to be sure. Linden focused on her cleavage and dreamed about the sexual acrobatics soon to follow. Fabiola did nothing to deter those thoughts.

"Juan. I know *juved* got big meetings *manana*. I have to leave early for *tee* airport. Is it *hokay wit ju* if we only make love two or *tree* times tonight?" she asked in her most sincere Hispanic voice.

Linden loved her accent; she had a decent command of the English language, but, it seemed she couldn't lose the slight Charro-like pronunciation of some of her words. Charro had been made famous in the late seventies with her combination of musical talent, butchering of the English language (she was from Spain), and her infamous giggling "Goochie, Goochie" statements when referring to sex.

At least Fabiola left out the "Goochie, Goochie" part —so far. Linden beamed with pride.

Rarely did he pop the little blue pill. If he only had to perform twice, he'd be okay. Three times? That was a stretch. Maybe he should sneak off to the bathroom and take one? Screw it, he decided. Let's throw caution to the wind. If she was going to live with him—hell, marry him—she'd have to take him the way he was. Warts and all. Some nights he could only go twice—and that only after a sufficient period of resting. About time she learned the truth!

The next morning, Fabiola packed three suitcases, crammed them into Linden's SUV and set off for the airport. Lucky for him this was just a short trip to Santa Barbara. On their one official vacation so far, Fabiola had taken five suitcases and various hanging bags. Today, she traveled light. While en route, he called IFPG. Erma informed him that Tyler would be unavailable all day.

"All day?" John exclaimed. "He doesn't have ten minutes to spare for one of his top accounts?"

"I don't see you on the calendar, sir. If he knew you were in town, I'm sure he would've scheduled a meeting with you," Erma responded.

He knows I'm in town, Linden thought. "How 'bout you go ask him—or call him on his cell phone—and ask if he can see me."

"He left strict instructions not to be disturbed. He just returned from Las Vegas and he has a lot to catch up on. I'll send him a text message but I can't guarantee he'll respond," she concluded—sounding as if God himself couldn't gain counsel with the great Tyler Ambrook.

"Thanks. In the meantime, could you put me thru to his father?" John asked.

"Well, this is awkward," she confessed. "He's in the same meeting as Tyler and they both left instructions not to be disturbed. Why don't you let me schedule you with Tyler for Tuesday next week?"

"Too late. I've got a tourney next week. But good try. Go ahead and text them. Tell them that I'm pissed and I'm thinking of moving my account to their main competitor. I'll call back later." He hung up.

"Why am I even doing business with these assholes?" he asked himself. "I'm one of their major clients and I can't even drop in and talk to them? This whole thing stinks." He pulled into the airport and parked by the curb.

"*Adios, mi amor,*" Fabiola sang out as her last bag was loaded on a dolly. "*Ju* keep 'Mr. Twinkle' under wraps while I'm gone. No *messin 'round,*" she joked. She was confident '*Juan*' wouldn't cheat on her. He had nothing to gain.

She was the real deal.

"Believe me, babe, 'Mr. Twinkle' is very tired. You kept him up late last night. He'll appreciate a few days rest. But......he'll be ready for you when you return. Now travel safe."

"I call *ju* when I get to Santa Barbara. Who's picking me up?"

"One of Brads' sons. Probably Blake. He's tall. Blonde hair. You keep your hands to yourself. No playing Cougar in your new home town," he said with a smile and a wink.

"*Ju* are the only man for me. Besides, *Juan*, I am a reverse Cougar. *Ju* are twenty years older than me. What does that make me?" she asked.

A 'gold-digger' John was tempted to answer facetiously. He wasn't sure she'd get the joke. Better to let it lie. Instead he said, "A very smart and lucky woman— that's what. Now go get on that plane and call me when you get there. I'll call Brad and give him your flight details."

21

THE MOVE TO THE NEW LOCATION had gone smoothly—much more smoothly than Von Eisenlow could've possibly imagined.

His remaining men had found the new location comfortable and seemingly safe. Surrounded by thick, dense forest and a rapidly rushing river, the property was comprised of a large residential building, two warehouse structures, a barn and a water silo.

Alongside the smaller of the two warehouses sat a mile long paved landing strip. 'Von Eisenlow didn't know much about flying, however it seemed to him that the landing area was big enough to handle a large plane, perhaps even a jet. It was a mercenaries' dream: access to remote locations via air.

He wondered if the 'whisperer' would provide a plane too?

He assigned his men to the bunk beds in the two warehouse buildings and took the main residence for himself and the cook. "Operations HQ" he told the men.

The outside of the building was nothing spectacular. Red stained siding, a large natural wood front door, a few small porches and a non-descript chimney. However, upon entering the residence, Von Eisenlow was amazed by the opulence of the interior. Large Persian rugs had been placed on beautiful hardwood floors. Expensive leather furniture was arranged around elegant tables in both the great room and the two rooms off to the side. The kitchen was modern and large.

He went upstairs and found the master bedroom at the far end of a long hallway. He had never seen such a big bed. Fit for a king...or a commander, he thought with a smile. While he surveyed the room, his cell phone rang.

"I trust you have found the accommodations suitable," the 'whisperer' began. "This phone line and the property are totally secure. Anything we discuss is private. Do you understand?"

"Yes sir," Von Eisenlow said quickly, feeling as if he should salute the phone.

"Good. Now, like I said before, I do not want to control your operation. But here is some inside information for you: the President, the Speaker of the House and several major politicians will be playing golf together at the Pro-am which precedes the next professional golf tournament. This tournament will be held in Hilton Head, South Carolina, at Harbour Town Golf Links. The Pro-Am will be held next Monday. I would suggest to you that this is an excellent venue for your first attack on the government."

So that's why he said we should be ready by Monday. He knew he was going to deploy us all the time, the shrewd bastard.

The 'whisperer' continued. "The golf course sits alongside the Atlantic Ocean in a very calm inlet. I suggest you form a plan to strike by both land and water. The President, of course, will be heavily protected. I have it on good authority that the Secret Service is not happy about his participation."

"Why is he doing it then?"

"He perceives this socialization with Congress as a positive gesture towards bi-partisan cooperation. Personally, I think he's a fool. Gridlock will undoubtedly continue."

"Of course it will," Von Eisenlow added. "Those criminals can't agree on a single thing."

"Be that as it may, it is a good opportunity to kill two birds with one stone."

"Two birds?"

"Yes, you can make a major statement with your attack on authority and it will create some international chaos which will help me with my immediate needs."

"International chaos? How does that help you?"

The 'whisperer' raised his voice. "You don't need to know. Just come up with a plan and be prepared to attack on Monday. It is imperative that you confirm your timing for me the day before the attack. Do you understand?"

"Yes, I will contact you Sunday evening and confirm all."

"Good. I will contact you shortly with more information, but I want you to begin thinking about how many men you will need. I will come up with a way to breach the President's protection. This is your chance to make history! Do not disappoint me. I will be in touch again soon." He hung up.

The President! Were they ready to go for something this big? Why not? He was just a man and he was as guilty as all the rest. Von Eisenlow settled back on the bed and thought about what the 'whisperer' had just said.

Things were happening quickly. He was confident his men would be ready. He would review the topography maps; he would need a very detailed map of the golf course itself. It sounded like strategically placed snipers might be called for. And bombs. This was good; this is what he'd been waiting for.

His mind was spinning with the possibilities. He lay down and took a nap in his new king size bed.

THE PLANE LANDED PRECISELY AT THREE thirty Pacific Standard Time, Thursday.

The statuesque Latina that exited flight 441 from Orlando made Blake's jaw drop. His father had forced him to pick up friends and run errands before. Blake usually resented it. But not today.

Today, he felt blessed that he had been chosen for this seemingly mundane task. He waved to Fabiola as she approached the terminal. She waved back.

Obviously, Uncle John had given her his description. Hopefully, John had told her about his athletic accomplishments as well. Suddenly, he wanted to impress this woman whom he'd never met.

"Hola. *Ju* must be Blake. I was *tole ju* were very *quapo* —very handsome," she said as she prepared to hug the young man.

"Yes, mam. And you must be Fabiola." He wished he were suave enough to respond with something like: 'I pale in comparison to your beauty, madam'.

But, alas, he wasn't.

"If not, ju've just been hugged by a total stranger and ju *shud* be very proud," she teased.

Uncle John had hit a Grand Slam with this one, he thought. He reached out and took the shopping bag she had hanging from her shoulder and escorted her to the baggage terminal.

"I hope ju drove a big car, Blake," she stated. "I tend to travel a *lil'* heavy. I *jus cudn't* decide between my pink outfit or my cherry red. So I brought *tem* both. And one *ting* leads to another and…next *ting* I know, I *hab* several suitcases. I hope *ju don'* mind." She hooked his free arm in hers and strolled forward confidently.

They drove the fifteen miles to the Stephens house quietly. Blake had put in a Red Hot Chili Peppers CD and Fabiola seemed to like it. She smiled all the way through Californication.

Upon arrival, Blake parked the car and then did something he had only seen in movies—he ran around to the other side and opened the passenger door, extending a hand to Fabiola. He walked in front of her and opened the front door.

Blake Stephens, the ultimate, proper gentleman.

"Mom…Fabiola is here," he yelled as they entered.

Mel appeared from the back of the house. She smiled and walked towards Blake and Fabiola. Throwing her arms around Blake, she planted a big kiss on his cheek.

"Thanks, darling. That was nice of you to pick up our guest," Mel said with a smile.

This time Blake decided to make an attempt at a slick, sophisticated response. "You're welcome, Mom. But, the pleasure was all mine," he said while glancing at Fabiola.

Mel turned her attention to her guest. She hadn't really paid attention when the two entered the room. Now Mel could see that Fabiola was a beautiful woman with wonderful taste in clothing and jewelry. John had outdone himself this time. She wondered how long this one would last before she figured out that John Linden was a self-obsessed, chauvinistic, golf and sports fanatic? A guy's-guy.

When that sunk in, Fabiola would probably abandon ship—like all the others. Oh, well, it was her job to make her feel comfortable; she was the driving force behind John's desire for a home in Montecito.

"Hello, Fabiola. I've heard so much about you. Can I help with your bags?"

"Don't worry, Mom. I've got 'em," Blake assured her.

"It *ees* so nice to meet you, Melanie. Juan has *tole* me so much *bout* you," Fabiola replied. "*Jure* home is beautiful. And *jure* son, he is most *hansome* and most strong. *Ju* must be very proud."

"Thank you. I am. Please call me Mel. I've made up the guest room for your stay. Please follow me."

Rufus approached Fabiola and growled. Not unusual for the protective dog, but not a good sign either. Mel told him to be quiet and go lay down. He did, but not before glancing back at Fabiola as if to say, "I'm watching you. Bitch."

Mel led Fabiola down the hall to a nicely appointed room—complete with its own TV, stereo, and private bath. Blake excused himself and went out to retrieve their guests' suitcases.

"*Juan* tells me that *ju* have two sons. Do they both live here?" Fabiola asked.

"Not any longer. They both live in town. We see them all the time. I thought I was going to die when they left for college. But, I've got to admit, the distance is a good thing—for all of us. You know what they say, 'Absence makes the heart grow fonder'. I've found that to be true with my boys."

"That's nice. I *don tink Juan* and I will ever have children. He's too old and I like my life as it is. How *bout* I adopt *jour* boys when we move here?"

"I'm sure they'd love that," Mel conceded with a chuckle. "Their friends would love to meet Aunt Fabiola."

"*Hokay*. That's settled then," she laughed. "Mel, can I *juse jour* phone? I *tole Juan* I'd call when I arrived. He worries about me so."

Mel escorted her to the kitchen and handed her the phone. She was still deciding if she liked this new addition to their lives. She seemed nice enough. Lord knew, she was beautiful. Her accent was endearing. She seemed to like Blake.

When she and *Juan* moved to Montecito, it would be Mel's job, she was sure, to acquaint Fabiola with her sur-roundings. Nordstrom's downtown; shops on the Upper Village; Saks 5th Avenue downtown. That sort of thing.

Mel decided to withhold final judgment until after they spent more time together.

The first test to their new friendship was about to come.

"Fabiola. Do you watch the Cooking Channel?" Mel asked.

"Oh, *jess*. I watch it *ebry* day."

"Me, too," Mel replied happily as Blake entered the guest room with two suitcases. "I saw the most scrumptious Louisiana Gumbo the other day. I've been dying to make it…"

"Uh, Mom. No!" Blake interjected quickly. "I think Dad said we were going out to the Italian place tonight. He probably forgot to tell you because he's been so busy."

"Going out? We don't go out very often anymore, Blake. But if your Dad wants to, that's all right with me. I love going out. The spinach soup at that restaurant is to die for."

Blake let out a sigh of relief. First night here. Fabiola didn't need to be exposed to his mom's cooking. That could ruin her for life. Make her want to move somewhere else. Best to let them become social friends first. Blake would call his Dad when he wandered out to the SUV to get more bags. His Dad wouldn't like the expense of the dinner, but he would appreciate the food disaster that had just been averted.

"I *lub* Italian food. I've got just *tee* outfit for it," Fabiola gushed. "This will be fun."

Mel said goodbye to Blake. Fabiola planted a big kiss or his left cheek. Blushing, he left the house and headed home.

"That boy is smitten," Mel said with a smile. "I'm sure he's very jealous of his Uncle John right about now."

Fabiola smiled broadly, revealing perfect, white teeth and deep dimples. Her cheekbones and profile were that of a model, her figure, a goddess.

She's fashion model beautiful, Mel thought. She couldn't wait until Brad met the bombshell.

"Let me show you around the house and grounds," she offered. "Then you can call John. After that, if you're up for it, we can sit on the patio with a glass of wine and visit."

Mel gave her the quick, five dollar tour which included a review of the dozens of fruit trees and grape vines on the property.

"Do *ju* grow grapes for *vino*?" Fabiola inquired.

"No, they're just ornamental. Brad struggles with the soil constantly. It's his way of acting like a gentleman farmer," Mel joked.

They went into the kitchen where Mel uncorked a bottle of wine while Fabiola called John.

She returned a few moments later and the two women ventured out to the patio. It was a warm day and the sun shone brightly.

"How is John?" Mel asked.

"He *ees* fine. He *ees* glad Blake met me and *ees* happy *tee* flight went well. He wanted to warn me *bout* all *tee* beautiful homes in Montecito. He *ees* afraid I'll fall in *lub wit someting* too expensive. I *tink*."

"It's easy to do."

"I'm a simple girl. I'll watch *tee* price tag."

Brad arrived while the girls were enjoying their second glass of wine. Glancing out the kitchen window, he could see why his buddy was sexually attracted to this gal. He grabbed a glass from the rack and joined them.

"Mind if I butt in?" he joked.

Fabiola rose and greeted him with a strong hug and a big kiss on the cheek. He glanced at Mel. She shrugged.

"Brad, I am so glad to finally meet *ju*."

"The pleasure is all mine, I'm sure. Please have a seat. Don't let me interrupt."

"We were just discussing the weather; how it's so nice year-round," Mel said.

Addressing Fabiola, Brad said, "We only get eighteen to twenty inches of rain per year. It's sunny most of the time, but rarely humid."

"*Eet* sounds wonderful. Where I was raised in Mexico, *eet* was *bery* hot and very humid. And where I now live in Phoenix, *eet ees* hot all *tee* time." She paused and gazed at the blue ocean in the distance. "I tink I am going to *lub eet* here."

"We hope so. It will be nice to have you and John as neighbors," Brad said.

"We are looking forward to it too. You have a *lubly* home, *eet* must be hard, though, maintaining five acres," she said.

"It has been, but I've got a pretty good system now."

The conversation died for a few moments as the three of them sipped their wine and enjoyed the view. Thin clouds partially obscured the Channel Islands, twenty miles southwest. In the distance, Brad could see a commercial fishing trawler heading back to port.

Feeling like he should drive the conversation, Brad said, "You say you're from Mexico originally. What region?"

"I was born in Mexico City. I lived there until I was sixteen and then we moved to Cabo San Lucas."

"I love Cabo," Mel said.

"Yes, it is a fun place to live and it is not as hot or humid as Mexico City."

"Why did you move?" Brad asked.

"My parents got a good job offer in Cabo. And my father and I love playing golf. They have wonderful courses in Cabo."

"How did you wind up in Phoenix?"

Fabiola straightened her back and stared blankly towards the canyon. "It is not a very nice story."

"If you'd rather not…."

"No, that's okay. It was many years ago. I met a man. I thought we were in *lub*. We moved to Arizona and he helped me learn English and to gain U.S Citizenship."

"I was going to comment on your English," Brad said. "It is very good."

"I still go through times when it is broken, but thank you. I try very hard." She paused and took a sip of wine. "Well, it turned out he was a bum. He left me broke and homeless. I was lucky to get a job and eventually, I ended up in Phoenix."

"That's awful," Mel said. "What is the bum doing now?"

Fabiola smiled slightly, as if remembering a nice event. "He *ees* dead. Was hit by a car in Tucson."

Brad and Mel looked at each other as if to validate that Fabiola's expression didn't fit the story. And what about her accent? It seemed to come and go. Brad decided to let it slide.

"So you play golf? Is that how you met John?" Mel asked.

She smiled and nodded. "I wasn't playing golf, but rather I was watching him play in the tournament in Phoenix."

"He told me the story," Brad said, turning to Mel. "He said when he won he didn't have anybody to hug on camera and then he remembered seeing this ravishing woman in the gallery and asked her to pretend to be his girlfriend."

Fabiola nodded. Mel frowned.

He continued. "So he took her out to dinner and they started dating. Did I get it right Fabiola?"

"*Jess* that is what happened. We *hab* been together for several months now. *Juan ees* wonderful. We will marry soon and we will have a wonderful home here in Montecito."

"It's all happening a bit fast, isn't it?" Mel interjected.

Fabiola shot Mel a quick, nasty glance and then just as quickly, smiled. "No, I don't think so. We are *bery* much in love and we know what we *wan*," she said in a flat voice, abruptly ending the subject.

Convenient accent, Brad thought.

Mel shrugged and rose from the table. "Anyone want a refill? I'm going inside for a few minutes and I can bring another bottle out if you want."

Both declined and Mel excused herself.

"She *ees* a *lubly* woman, Brad. *Ju* are very lucky," Fabiola said when Mel was out of earshot.

Brad smiled proudly. "She's a great person; I hope you two become good friends."

"*Jess*, me too," Fabiola said without enthusiasm.

Changing the subject, Brad asked about her tastes in homes.

"I like all types' *ub casas*," she assured him. "I'm not sure I have a *faborite* style. *Less* look at what's available and go from there."

"Works for me."

Ten minutes later, they finished their wine and went back into the house. Mel took their empty glasses and put them in the dishwasher. "What time is dinner?" she asked.

"Oh that's right, we're going to Italian tonight," Brad said, remembering the panic call he had received from

Blake earlier that day. "What time is it now?" he asked rhetorically while glancing at his watch. "The reservation is for six thirty but we could go earlier if you like."

"No, that will be fine. I need time to shower and fix my hair," Mel said.

"Me too," Fabiola added. "I must look like a mess after the plane ride."

Brad smiled. "You look fine."

Mel frowned. He noticed it. Quickly he added, "You both look fine. Tell you what. I'll go do some work in my office. When it's time to go, I'll let both of you lovely women know."

"What about the boys?" Mel asked.

"We have a system. I call them as we're leaving. That'll give them time to meet us when we arrive."

The dinner, as expected, was wonderful. The restaurant was a typical Montecito 'joint'. Superb food at exorbitant prices being consumed by millionaires—some dressed formally, some wearing flip-flops.

Mel and Fabiola each started with the spinach soup and then split a delicious pasta dish. Blake devoured linguine vongole and Brad and Scott both had salmon. The conversation was relaxed and comfortable. The boys couldn't take their eyes off the Latin bombshell.

"Let's have some dessert and espresso," Brad suggested. "Sofia makes a great tiramisu," he added as if he were required to justify the extra calories.

They all agreed and the order was placed. As they waited for dessert to arrive, Brad said, "Fabiola, would you like a quick tour of Montecito?"

"I'd be happy to come along Dad," Blake offered. "I can point things out while you drive."

Brad appreciated the effort. He wanted to say: "Down Boy! Put that tongue back in your mouth." Instead he said, "Not this time, son. Maybe you and Scott can show Fabiola the U.C. and some of downtown Santa Barbara before she heads back." He gave his son a knowing wink.

The group finished dessert. Brad paid the bill and said goodnight to the restaurant owner, Sofia. "Ciao, Bellos," she called after them.

Everyone was full, happy and smiling. No one noticed when the heavy set guy with the broken nose got up from his table in the back and followed the family out.

23

JOHN LINDEN ROSE EARLY FRIDAY MORNING.

After doing fifty sit ups and various back stretches, he poured a cup of strong coffee and planned his day. He had tentatively scheduled a social round of golf with a few old friends. Not knowing if his meeting with Ambrook—if in fact he did gain access—was going to take ten minutes or two hours, he had warned his playing partners that he might be late. It was decided that he would call when he was on his way to the course.

Apparently, free golf was worth waiting for. At some point today or tomorrow, he should visit Art Smalley's wife again. He made a mental note to call her.

Linden showered and dressed. Opting for a casual, yet serious look, he initially chose khaki slacks, a blue golf shirt and a herringbone tweed jacket. He looked in the mirror, turned from side to side, glancing over his shoulder. Finally, he shook his head and muttered to himself, "Nope, looks too James Garnerish from the damn Rockford Files." He left the jacket behind and headed downtown.

Located in an upscale neighborhood in the middle of downtown Orlando, Investments for Pro Golfers (IFPG) occupied one of Orlando's most distinctive—and expensive—buildings in an area otherwise populated with modern buildings sheathed in glass and stucco.

In keeping with its business plan of working exclusively with professional golfers, IFPG had chosen to construct an almost perfect five thousand square foot replica of the National Clubhouse at Augusta. Cherry wood floors, carved mahogany banisters, and lush green carpet adorned the interior and putting greens, sand traps and azaleas landscaped the exterior.

IFPG's founder, Steven Ambrook, counted on potential clients walking into a duplicate of pro golf's mecca—site of the annual Master's tournament—and picking up the subliminal message loud and clear: "You've arrived. Congratulations."

And that was the message John Linden had received when he signed on with the company more than a decade earlier.

Twenty minutes later, he parked in front of the IFPG building. He checked the notes he had made for himself and remembered Brad's advice to focus on getting the paperwork before turning off the ignition. He got out of the car and walked quickly towards the building. As he approached the entrance, he ran his fingers through his hair, took a deep breath and burst through the large glass front door.

To the left of the entry, a room centered by a fireplace surrounded by comfortable looking leather chairs served as the client waiting area. Photos of famous golfers lined the entryway—each appearing as a studio photo rather than an 'action' shot, giving the impression of past club Presidents rather than an advertisement of their client list.

Very subtle and very impressive.

Various young, pretty women usually occupied the receptionist desk located just outside the waiting area. Obviously, the company's owners realized the value of making a good first impression. This message, too, had not been lost on Linden.

To the right of the reception desk was a walkway full of smaller offices framed by darkly stained French doors. Memorabilia from clients' golfing exploits had been placed in glass cases or secured to the walls. Rather than colorless muzak, sounds of past radio and television broadcasts of major golf tournaments could be heard throughout the building. In any other office, such noise would be a major distraction. But here, in this replica building, it fit like a *golf* glove.

At the end of the hall, positioned in front of what was the largest office suite, sat a bust of the company's founder, Steven Ambrook. The bust was positioned in such a way as to make it seem that Ambrook was staring down the hall; checking on his staff.

IFPG employed fifty young, hungry investment counselors—people who invested player's money in hopes of enhancing the athlete's wealth while making trading profits for IFPG. These investors were joined by several men—and women, for IFPG represented the women's tour as well—who acted directly as managers for current professional golfers. Each had a private secretary which, when added to by mail clerks, receptionists, and secretarial assistants, made the total number of employees well over one hundred.

Overhead was high, but so, too, were the profits.

The business had been founded by Steven Ambrook in the early 1980's. A former touring pro himself, Ambrook had noticed that most pros knew nothing about money. He had been a business major at UCLA and had dabbled in the market on and off since he was twelve years old. The company managed over three hundred touring pros. Up until now, Linden had considered himself lucky to be one of them.

"John Linden to see Tyler Ambrook," Linden announced to the pretty blonde sitting behind the reception table.

"Mr. Ambrook is in a meeting sir. Do you have an appointment?"

Using an authoritative, yet friendly voice, he said, "Yes," he lied. "I told him and his secretary, Erma, that I would be here today and needed a few minutes of his time. Can you point me to Erma? I'd like to discuss this with her."

"She's down this hall," the girl said pointing to her right. "Third door. I'll buzz her and let her know you're coming."

"Thanks darling. You've been quite helpful," he winked and patted her hand—leaning over the desk to get a quick shot down her loose satin top—before heading down the hallway.

He took off down the hall, studying the photos on the wall as he passed. Some he recognized; some he didn't. Ironically, the radio broadcast from last year's U.S. Open came through the speakers. He smiled and entered the open door.

Entering the small office, he extended his hand and introduced himself to a heavy-set woman sitting behind a desk that was too large for the office. She looked like an Erma. Her hair was some type of gray-blue and she wore a gray pants suit with a dark blouse. She stared at him over the top of eyeglasses that rested on the tip of her nose.

"Mr. Linden? A pleasure to meet you." She paused and looked at him sternly. "I thought you discussed a meeting with Mr. Ambrook next week? At least that's what he told me."

Ignoring the schoolmarm tone of her voice, he said, "Yes he did and I told him that was too late. I've got some important business to discuss with either Tyler or Steven. I don't care which. I have a busy day and this meeting should only take a few minutes. Be a doll and buzz one of them, will ya?"

Erma's jaw tensed as she stared at Linden. Finally she drew in a long breath, flashed her tight smile again, pursed her lips, and picked up her phone. Linden had to admit, she did *perturbed* well. "Excuse me, Mr. Ambrook, John Linden just arrived. He has asked for a brief meeting with either you or your father."

Since the conversation was over the phone, Linden couldn't hear the full response but he caught the gist: He wasn't expected until next week! He reached across the desk and grabbed the phone out of Erma's hand. Tyler Ambrook was finishing a sentence. "Tell him I'm in a very important meeting. Please tell him to come back at 10:30. Perhaps I can see him then," the voice from the box said.

Visions of the gate keeper in the Wizard of Oz filled Linden's head. He shook them off and spoke into the phone.

"Tyler. Don't blame Erma. I opted to come earlier. I have a golf outing later this afternoon," he said hinting that this might be a corporate/business affair rather than beer golf with his buddies. "This should only take a few minutes. It is very important to me."

There was no immediate response on the other end. Probably in shock, Linden thought. After a few seconds of silence, he asked Erma impatiently, "Is he in his office?"

Before replying, Erma nervously glanced down the hall to her left and then fixed her gaze on him. "If Mr. Ambrook says he's in an important meeting, I can't disclose the location of that meeting. I'm sure you understand, Mr. Linden. He's a very busy man. It's entirely possible that he's negotiating something for the benefit of his clients—which includes you. You don't want to spoil that, do you?"

"I hear you, Erma," John said as he drifted down the hall, the heavy secretary calling after him.

Walking past two empty offices, Linden stopped when he encountered the third. Through the clear glass inserts of the stained French doors, he could see both the junior *and* senior Ambrook sitting in the room. He waved and then burst through door.

This was better than he thought possible. Two, for the price of one. Like making a double-eagle on a Par 5. Steven Ambrook immediately replaced the frown he had been sporting with a gracious smile and rose to greet his uninvited guest.

The room smelled. Not of sweat per se, but something more primal. Testosterone? Pheromones? Raw and bitter was all Linden could make out. It reminded him of some of the team meetings he had attended during college. Clearly, the conversation between father and son had been heated and intense. John hoped it had nothing to do with him.

"John Linden! As I live and breathe! What brings you to our humble abode?" the elder Ambrook asked, offering Linden a seat next to him in a comfortable looking leather chair.

"Hello, Steven. Long time no see," Linden responded, shaking the older man's hand and taking the seat offered. "I think you know why I'm here. But if not, I can summarize it very quickly. Are you and Tyler really in the middle of an earth-shattering meeting? Or is it just not convenient to see me in person?"

Tyler turned and faced Linden. "I am perfectly willing to meet with you. As a matter of fact, I welcome the opportunity to bring you up to date on your finances and on the opportunities we are working on for you," he said. "I must've misunderstood Erma. I apologize."

"Yeah, whatever. Listen you guys. I've worked with you my entire professional career. You've managed my finances and arranged endorsement deals. I appreciate all you've done and, of course, I want us all to prosper going forward."

Linden paused and took a cleansing breath. That was a lot of talking for him without throwing in a cuss word or a folksy euphemism.

"I made ten million last year and ten the year before that. I intend to make millions in the future…"

"Let me stop you right there, John," Steven Ambrook interrupted. "YOU and your well being are our top concerns. Any indication to the contrary has been an error on our part. We apologize for any miscommunications.

Having said that, this is a very busy time at IFPG. In addition to it being the heart of the professional season, we are dealing with the unfortunate death of Art Smalley. You know how important Art was to our operation."

He continued, "In terms of financial volume, IFPG is a big company but in terms of business size we remain a small, tight knit group of advisors and employees. Arts' death came as a real shock to all of us. And, quite frankly, we just don't have the manpower to replace him immediately. That is why I have stepped back in for a few months. I need to take some of the pressure off Tyler here." He paused and waved an open hand towards his son. He smiled and continued. "I want him to deal with Art's accounts efficiently and effectively," he finished his little speech by walking around the desk and patting his son on the shoulder as he spoke.

"I'm a busy guy too. You know that Steven," Linden said. "I liked Art and I always felt he had my best interests at heart. I'm sure that will continue with Tyler and whoever eventually replaces Art full time. I'm sorry to add to your burdens by dropping in like this. But a situation has come up and I feel like I need to clear the air."

Steven Ambrook acted surprised by Linden's statement—although it was likely he had been fully briefed by his son. Linden knew that a company like IFPG didn't get as big as it was—and a guy like Steven Ambrook didn't become filthy rich off of other people's money—without the top dog knowing what the puppies were doing. But he played along.

"Well, in all the confusion around here lately, I'm sure it just slipped Tyler's mind and he forgot to tell you," he said, using his most humble, business-like voice once again. "I've got a few things going on myself."

When neither Ambrook asked what exactly he had going on, Linden offered, "One, I'm getting married…"

"Married? Again? Congratulations," Steven Ambrook said, interrupting John's speech. "Who's the lucky gal? Do we know her? Tyler make a note, we need to throw John and his fiancée a pre-wedding party. Invite all of our top clients. We can host it here. It will give us a chance to bring everybody up to date on new endorsement deals. Call the Golf Channel. They're so desperate for programming they would probably like to film the whole thing. What else, John?"

"Number two is that Fabiola, that's my fiancée, wants to move to California. Montecito, to be exact."

"Great place. Been there dozens of times. Almost moved there myself. I've got contacts if you need them," he said.

Linden was getting tired of the interruptions. "Let me finish, please. I've got a great contact out there; my best friend, Brad Stephens. He's lived there for thirty years. He's in the real estate business and he's going to help us find the right house. Brad is also a mortgage broker. I want him to arrange the financing for the purchase as well." He paused, silently patting himself on the back for coming across so professionally.

He smiled contritely and then continued. "The problem is that he needs fairly extensive paperwork to get me the loan. And…your office has not been cooperative in providing him with what he needs."

"But John, you don't…." Tyler Ambrook started.

Linden held up his right hand. "Now hold on a minute," he said. "Let me speak my peace. I have hired Brad to perform these services. It is my understanding that Brad went out to Vegas last week and discussed this with you, Tyler." He looked directly at the young man. "And you told him that IFPG would be happy to lend me the money. Brad tells me the terms you offered were no good. He gave you a chance to meet the bank's terms and you refused. You treated him like crap." He raised his voice slightly and sat forward in his seat. He made eye contact with both of them.

"So, here's what I want. I want you to give me the paperwork Brad needs. Today. Right now. I'll send it to Brad myself and we'll inform you when the transaction is complete." Again, he paused. "Are we on the same page here?"

"That's not entirely true," Tyler said defensively, rising from his seat for the first time and coming towards Linden. He had worn a yellow oxford cloth shirt without an undershirt that morning. A bad choice as it turns out. Damp patches of armpit sweat could be seen clearly when he raised his arms. "Your friend, Brad, or whatever his name is, has misled you…."

"Now, Tyler, hold on a minute," Steven Ambrook said sternly to his son. "If John feels his friend has been disrespected by our firm I want you to apologize. Immediately! Of course, John, we'll get you whatever you need. Did you bring a list?"

Tyler looked at Linden. Embarrassment and anger filled his eyes. He stared at this father for a few moments and then slowly gathered himself. He smiled and faced Linden. "I'm sorry if I did anything to insult your friend. It won't happen again." The words came grudgingly and slowly from his lips.

"Make sure it doesn't. He's my best friend. He's had a tough go of it lately. This transaction is important to him and I want to make it as easy as possible for him to do his job." He chuckled to himself while thinking about how hard he had inadvertently made Brad's life. Fabiola was probably dragging him around looking at houses. She was the love of John's life, but that woman could drive you crazy if you let her.

"Okay, I get it," Steven Ambrook said. "It's been nice seeing you; I'm sorry about any misunderstanding." He glanced at his son and then back at Linden. "Is there anything else we can do for you? Any endorsement deals you want to talk about? Any equipment issues? Anything at all?"

"Nope. Just the paperwork so I can move this process forward."

"Good, consider it done."

The three of them shook hands. Steven Ambrook took the list from Linden and pressed the intercom button. "Erma, I'd like you to put together some paperwork for Mr. Linden ASAP." He read the list of items needed and turned to face John. "It will take her a few minutes. Can I get you a cup of coffee while you wait?"

"No thanks. I already had a cup this morning. Don't want to throw off my putting by being jittery," Linden joked.

"From what I've seen lately, nothing can throw your putting off," Steven Ambrook said with a knowing smile. "I'm thinking about going to the claw myself. Any chance we can get in a round before you head out to Hilton Head? I still got some game, you know." At that moment, he sounded—and looked—remarkably like Ted Baxter playing Judge Smails in Caddyshack. Linden expected to hear him say, "Gambling is illegal is this state. And I never slice the ball!" But he didn't.

"That's what I hear. But I doubt we can get in a round before the tourney," Linden replied. He assessed the older man for the first time since walking in. The guy obviously was in good shape, tan and strong. It wouldn't be the worst thing in the world to score some points by playing with the founder of his management company. He begged off, however. "I'm playing this afternoon and then I've got some personal matters to attend to tomorrow. I told the Golf Channel I'd do an in-house interview tomorrow as well. I'm leaving the next day. Let's play the next time I'm in Palm Springs. How does that sound?"

"Just dandy! Have a great round today. Good seeing you John. Keep up the good work. See Erma on your way out. She'll have the papers you need."

Linden turned to leave, smiled to himself and thought, "Now, that's more like it."

== ⊕ ==

While Erma put the tax returns and asset statements together Steven and Tyler Ambrook returned to their seats.

Behind the now closed doors, Tyler scolded his father. "You shouldn't have given in to him. I'm going to trade us out of this mess. But in the meantime, I don't need John *Fucking* Linden and his trusted ally, 'Tonto' Stephens, digging up dirt on us." He sighed and rubbed his chin. "Well at least it's a good thing that I had time to modify the reports. Neither the broker nor the bank will see that he's been taking bigger losses than we've been reporting."

"That was good thinking, son. About time you used your head. I've seen guys like Linden before. He wasn't going to give up."

An hour later, Erma knocked on the door and was waved into the office.

"Tyler. I'm so sorry. I believe that I made a mistake," she said. "I didn't notice the envelope you left for me this morning. Rather than giving Mr. Linden what was in that envelope, I had accounting prepare a new package and gave it to him. I assume it's the same information, but you may want me to call him and confirm that he has what you intended for him to have."

"You gave him fresh data? Where is he now?" Tyler screamed at Erma.

"He left an hour ago. Would you like me to call him? I can explain I gave him the wrong material." She pulled out her cell phone and punched in Linden's number. No answer.

"Should I leave a message and explain I made a minor mistake?"

Tyler looked to his father for guidance.

Steven Ambrook stared at Erma and then at Tyler. He was about to speak. Instead, he sat back, lit a cigar, shook his head and thought to himself, "How can this get any worse? No, this wasn't a *minor* mistake, Erma. It is a *monumental* mistake!"

He had been so proud for a brief few moments. His son had finally done something smart by switching the statements. The expensive USC education seemed to be paying off. Now he felt a deep sense of disappointment. He was surrounded by dumbshits! He shook his head, took a long pull from his cigar and ran his fingers through what remained of his hair.

24

DAVID VON EISENLOW STILL COULDN'T believe the splendor of his new surroundings; the Lord really did work in mysterious ways.

He lay down on the massive bed Friday afternoon, sipped an ice cold beer and turned on the TV.

Finding nothing interesting on commercial television, he went to his back pack and took out a VCR tape of an interview he had conducted a year earlier. He inserted it in the player, increased the volume and laid back down on the bed —large, fluffy pillows supporting his head.

The interviewer, Megan Rich, was the morning host of a local morning show in Atlanta. Strikingly pretty with long blonde hair, a deep tan and an enticing smile, Von Eisenlow immediately took to her. She assured him she was experienced. She had interviewed five religious fundamentalists, two dog breeders and one cock-fighting expert in her short stint at the southern station.

He assumed she'd be intrigued by his exploits.

"So, Mr. Von Eisenlow…."she began.

"That's *Commander* Von Eisenlow," he corrected her.

"Yes, my mistake; *Commander* Von Eisenlow. Why don't you tell our viewers a little about your group, The Sons for Righteous Transition."

"What do you want to know?"

"How did you choose the name; what does it mean?"

"I think the name speaks for itself. I lead a group of men who are fed up with the Federal government interfering in every aspect our daily lives. We seek a transition from the United States government back to the people. Further, we are a religious group; guided by HIS divine grace," he said, looking towards the heavens.

The interview had occurred last year during a time when Von Eisenlow was out recruiting new members. In an attempt to attract new followers and raise fresh money, he had presented his group as peaceful protesters. The local media had lapped up his act.

It would be his one and only media interview.

Shortly after appearing, he was contacted by several men who wanted to join. He took them in and then backed out of the public eye.

Resting his head on a large, down pillow—the huge bed engulfing him—he remembered sharing the stage with this lovely five foot six blonde with absolutely perfect breasts. Her blue eyes sparkled when she laughed. He remembered her smell: musk combined with lavender. He sighed and then returned his attention to the video.

"Transition from what exactly?" she asked.

Flashing a broad smile he said, "Transition from government tyranny to individual freedoms of course.

We want power returned to the people and then, by association, to Jesus Christ, our savior, our lord."

On camera, Megan adjusted her skirt and squirmed in her chair. She appeared to be searching for an appropriate follow-up question.

Von Eisenlow stopped the tape and replayed her actions. She really *was* pretty. Perhaps she'd like to visit his new compound and see how successful he had become? Of course, she'd have to agree to be blindfolded, but he'd bet twenty bucks she'd do it for the scoop now that his group was about to launch a big assault. Of course, he wouldn't tell her that, but he'd hint that something big was going to happen. Soon.

He smiled and turned up the volume.

"How do you intend to accomplish your goals and how did you form the group?" she asked.

"We will protest in Washington until our voice is heard," he lied, knowing full well he intended to bomb, assassinate, and cause havoc. Conjuring up his most sincere expression, he looked straight into the camera. "And if anyone out there wants to join us, please contact me immediately; we got room for more god-fearing Christians." He smiled and then rushed to his next answer as if suddenly remembering the second part of her question.

"And the way we formed, Megan, is that I began traveling around the South picking up where my daddy left off. I preached at carnivals, revival meetings and small gatherings from Atlanta to San Antonio," he began. She nodded her head as if she were really interested, so he continued. "I saw poverty and despair; but more than that, I saw lack of conviction. I talked to folks and

I found out that they loved the Lord and they hated the government. I felt I could help these people with my preaching. But soon, with the Lord's help, I recognized that my calling was more social than it was religious. So I began asking folks at my revival meetings if they wanted to join with me to protest governmental injustices."

"And?"

"And, much to my surprise and delight, I might add, several men joined with me. And here we are today."

"How many are in your group?"

"Currently, we are seven, but I hope to increase those numbers soon."

"All male?"

"Yes. I haven't the resources yet to accommodate female 'soldiers'."

"All white?"

He exhaled and adopted a blank expression. He nodded his head slowly. "Yes, at the present time, my followers are all white men who range in ages from seventeen to fifty five."

"Is your group racist?" He had been told that she wouldn't ask controversial questions, but she just couldn't help herself, he supposed. She was, after all, a trained journalist.

"No, no, not at all. It's just...well, it's just that my message seems to ring true with certain people. So far, neither the black nor Hispanic communities have embraced my teachings," he said. And then looking chagrin, he added, "It is one of my biggest disappointments."

She moved on. "How did you raise your seed capital? I mean, feeding a group of men must cost a few bucks?"

"It does, Megan. But here, again, the Lord has provided for us. I took in donations for our cause at my revival meetings and my followers were able to contribute as well," he had said at the time. Now, he remembered how he conveniently failed to mention the insurance money and small inheritance he had collected at his mother's death. Fortunately, her estate was flush. The fire insurer had paid off her mortgage which had been in foreclosure. When the dust settled, they presented her with a nice chunk of change. Nobody ever discovered that he had burned down her house.

Switching gears, Megan asked, "Is it true you are training these men in the use of weapons and military operations?"

"That is patently false Megan," he said, flashing another sincere smile.

"Then why do they refer to you as 'Commander'?"

Good question, he thought. He took a moment before answering simply, "Because we are soldiers for the Lord, Megan; there is nothing military about us, however."

She checked her notes and then asked about his background.

"I was born in West Virginia. My father, Gordon Von Eisenlow, was a traveling preacher. He instilled the respect—and fear—of God into me at an early age. My mother, Helga, worked for the local furniture factory. I saw how the government and the labor union tried to control her life. It finally led to her death, actually."

"That's awful," Megan said, glancing at her program director off camera. She looked like she was hoping the interview was coming to an end. Apparently, she was told to continue. She looked at her cheat sheet again. "I understand you recently lost the family home to foreclosure."

"Yes and no."

"What do you mean?"

"My mother was in foreclosure and the bank threatened her daily. But before they could complete the process, her house accidentally caught fire and burned down."

"And when did your mother die?"

"About a year ago."

No emotion; no anger. Just, "About a year ago." While watching it more than a year later, he smiled at how smoothly he had handled the issue.

She continued. "Is that part of your protest against the American government?"

"Is what?" he asked.

"The foreclosure, and the fire and, of course, your mother's death." She adjusted her posture and smiled at her guest, awaiting his answer.

He said nothing. If she really knew the depth of his anger at the government and at Wall Street, he thought, she would press him on the military aspects of his group. If she came to realize that the foreclosure and grief over the loss of her home actually killed his mother and that his father was a drunk who abandoned the family, then she might begin to understand why he was going to kill every cheating, lying, scum-sucking politician and banker he could before this war—his war—came to an end.

After a long pause, he shrugged and said, "It is what it is. The Lord will provide for us."

Off screen he remembered the director holding up three fingers, indicating three more minutes. Megan Rich nodded her head solemnly as if she empathized and understood.

"So you followed your father's calling and now you have established a congregation prepared to protest government injustice. Is that it?"

"Yes, I suppose you could say that. I like that... a congregation. Yes."

"That's so fascinating, Commander." She studied her fingernails for a moment and then asked, "Now when you say your members are 'soldiers' for the Lord, does that mean you are willing to fight for your beliefs?"

"No, no, not fight physically," he lied, thinking about the training facility he had established in the foothills. "I mean we're prepared to protest and do sit-ins and stuff like that. You know, the way hippies did in the sixties."

She smiled meekly. She looked towards her director. Von Eisenlow remembered seeing him make the universal slash across the throat indicating it was time to end the interview. She sighed audibly. He hadn't remembered that. Was she bored? Or was she disappointed that the fascinating interview was coming to an end? Maybe he'd call her and find out.

"Thank you for being here today, Commander. Do you have anything else to say to our viewers?"

Von Eisenlow straightened up in his seat and stared into the camera. "The Lord has put us on this earth to flourish. HE did not create the Federal government. Acting through agents such as myself, HE will provide for y'all. Do not let the government control your lives. Support us as we free you from the bonds of tyranny."

He said the last sentence a little too loudly; a little too quickly. He paused and calmed down. "I wish y'all well and I hope you can benefit from our actions. God Bless."

On the screen, Megan rolled her eyes. He hadn't remembered that either.

The station cut to commercial and Von Eisenlow thanked Megan. He made a victory sign with his fingers and walked off the stage.

He remembered thinking at the time, 'Yes, follow me. It might get messy, but I'll lead you to the promised land'. He laid back on the bed and went to sleep dreaming about the sexy female anchor.

25

"Good job, John! I'm looking forward to finally processing your damn loan. How you going to get me the paperwork, Fed Ex?" Brad asked when Linden finally called him back.

"Don't tell Fabby, but I think I'll fly out tomorrow and deliver it by hand. It's amazing. She's only been gone a day or two and I miss her already. So I'm going to surprise her. See you tomorrow." And then before hanging up, he added with a chuckle, "And, hey, Brad, make sure you don't show her anything over four million. Okay."

"Gottcha. Actually, I'm focusing on five properties. All are between three point five and four million. Have a good round today. Say Hi to those knuckleheads for me. Do you need a ride from the airport?"

"Naw. I'll rent a car. We'll need one when I'm out there anyway."

It was only seven thirty pacific time. The sun had just risen but Brad could tell it was going to be a sensational day. Light fog was beginning to burn off, birds were chirping and the temperature had already hit sixty five degrees. Rufus sat by his side, waiting for a morning walk or, better yet, a cookie from his master.

"Rufie, can't take you for a walk this morning," Brad told him while rubbing behind his ears. "Got a busy day ahead. See you tonight." He pet the dog one more time and left the house.

The loan processing could finally begin. Even in the tight credit market, Linden's loan should be a slam dunk approval. He and Stef would be prepared to receive the paperwork from John but until they did, he would focus on house hunting. His job today was to spend the day looking at properties with a beautiful woman.

Tough job. But someone had to do it.

A typical property search in a 'normal' real estate market usually entails sitting down with a motivated buyer and reviewing a whole slew of available properties on paper.

Santa Barbara, California,—more specifically, Montecito—is no normal market. High land value, lack of consistent water supply, restrictive building codes and gorgeous weather made the area pricey and in high demand. Buyers of high end real estate like to touch, taste and feel the property.

Brad had made several appointments to do just that.

By the time he picked up Fabiola to begin their review of properties, he had arranged four private showings. He had made appointments for 10:00, 1:00, 2:30, and 4:30. Four in one day was a lot, but given the new information about John's secret trip out to Santa Barbara tomorrow, it seemed like a good idea to get them all out of the way today.

The first estate they visited was owned by a former child actor. Typecast at an early age, the actor was able to find consistent work until he reached the ripe old age of twenty five. Overnight, it seemed, he became persona non grata in Hollywood. Even his talent agent rarely returned his calls. With no current rolls in front of him and nothing promising in the works, he had made the gut-wrenching decision—according to the listing agent—to sell his Montecito estate and move the family down to Los Angeles. Maybe proximity to the studios would help his fledgling career? His wife, Ashley, didn't agree.

It quickly became obvious to Brad that she was participating in the sale under protest.

The yard was a mess when Brad and Fabiola pulled through the large metal gates. Toys lined the driveway. Bicycles and skateboards sat abandoned and scattered around the pool. Despite the mess, the exterior showed well. The house was a large two story Mediterranean. Not quite salmon and not quite pink, the reddish structure sat behind several large palm trees and was framed by a rich, green lawn. Other than the mess, it looked inviting and comfortable.

They knocked on the handcrafted wood front door and were greeted by a heavyset woman with dark hair wearing what could only be described as a 'Muumuu'.

"Hello. I'm Harriet Windsley. Ashley's mother," the lady said as she extended her hand to Brad. "You must be the people the real estate agent called about."

"We are," Brad said. "I'm Brad Stephens and this is my client, Ms. Fabiola, uh...." It suddenly dawned on Brad that he didn't know Fabiola's last name. It wasn't Linden yet and he hadn't bothered to ask her surname. He looked to Fabiola for some guidance.

"Gonzales. Fabiola Gonzales," she offered. "So good to meet *ju*. *Tee* grounds are *lubly*. *Tank ju* for meeting *wit* us on such short notice."

"I wish I could say it was my pleasure, but the truth of the matter is that my daughter, Ashley, is just sick about the proposed sale. This has been her home for many years. She couldn't stand the thought of showing you around so she asked me to do it; took the kids to the zoo, I think."

"We're awfully sorry about the circumstances. Perhaps it'll help if we go through the property quickly," Brad suggested. "We won't disturb anything or ask too many questions. This is more of a 'get acquainted' trip," Brad said as he made quotation marks in the air with his fingers.

He smiled and then continued, "Fabiola will be looking at several properties today. If she's interested in any of them, I will make arrangements for a more comprehensive showing."

"That's fine. Please make it quick. I apologize for the mess. Ashley refused to clean the house before she left. She said to tell anyone interested that this is how a 'real' home looks. Of course, I think she's trying to jinx the sale. That girl is hard-headed. Always has been. I feel sorry for her husband, Stan. He's a nice man. It's not his fault that Hollywood has forgotten him." The overweight lady shook her head sadly as if talking about the death of a puppy.

She smiled, composed herself and said, "Anyway, as you can see, this is the Great Room and over there is the kitchen and dining room. Why don't you just go ahead and walk around the place. You don't need me telling you that a room with a toilet in it is a bathroom, for goodness sakes. I'll be down here reading the paper. If you have any questions, I'll be happy to attempt to answer them."

With that Brad and Fabiola took off on a non-supervised tour of the property. In general, the house was spacious and open—two traits Fabiola had told Brad she desired.

Fabiola was about to ask Brad a question when the two of them walked into the Master Bathroom. The large vanity mirror sat directly in front of them. On it was scrawled in bold, red lipstick: "Fuck You!!! Leave MY house immediately! Do NOT even Think about buying it!!!"

"She *ees* really pissed, *tis* woman" Fabiola exclaimed, laying on the Charro-like accent. He wondered why? "Can she stop *tee* sale?"

"I don't know. When it comes down to it, she will have to sign the Grant Deed. But that's not our problem. That's his. We just need to decide if we want to do a more serious inspection later. Let's get out of here before the wife comes back and puts some type of voodoo curse on us," Brad responded, shooing Fabiola down the stairs.

They left the house quickly, waving goodbye to the mother and assuring her that they would call the listing agent if they were interested in making an offer. As they drove off, they could see Mrs. Harriet Windsley standing in the front doorway, her pink muumuu flapping in the breeze.

"*Tat* was weird, Brad," Fabiola said exhaling. "I like *tee* house, but *eet* has bad karma I *tink*."

"I agree. Let's move on. I'm sure that will be the strangest showing we ever encounter," Brad assured her.

The next house was presented very nicely. "Casa Serena" was a smaller home with rock facing and natural wood thresholds. The grounds were lush and well kept. Unfortunately, the interior of the home was very dark and the rooms were cut up into a maze of unusable space. Fabiola was getting disappointed and let Brad know it.

"This home is crap!" she said loudly. "I don't want to look at CRAP. You need to do a better job of screening," she insisted. He noticed she had dropped the accent.

"It's not crap; it just doesn't fit your taste. Let's go get a cup of coffee and talk about the types of properties you're going to see in Montecito. It's a whole different world under four million dollars," Brad said in a soothing voice.

"I don't want to talk about it, Brad. I want to buy my dream house! I want large walk-in closets, natural light, open kitchen, large master bedroom…and, above all, I want a large master bathroom with sit down vanity. Is that so hard?"

Brad hesitated for a moment. "Yes, actually, it's going to be hard," Brad hated to admit, thinking that Fabiola's English had become remarkably better the more agitated she got.

"Montecito isn't like Palm Beach or Phoenix," he began, looking for the right tone to proceed with. "These houses are 15-50 years old. They weren't designed with all the 'bells and whistles' that developers throw in these days to entice women to fall in love with them. For four million, you'll be buying location and elements you can live with. To get exactly what you want, you'll have to be prepared to do some remodeling once you move in. That's just the way it is out here."

The fiery Latina was having none of it.

"That's Bull! For four million dollars, I expect to get what I want. If you can't find it for me, then maybe we should get another real estate agent."

Brad held back his anger. He had tried to prepare her for what she was going to see in these older, charming properties. She was the one who insisted on jumping in the car and rushing to the first house before they had a chance to discuss it more thoroughly. Linden had sworn to him that this job would be a piece of cake. Now, he was beginning to wonder.

If he didn't need the commission so badly—and if she weren't so damn pretty—Brad would tell her to go 'pound sand'. As it was, he said, "I understand. Calm down. Let's take a look at the next two houses and if they're no good, we'll sit down and go over a lot of listings to get a better sense of what you like. But you need to understand," he couldn't help but get in a little dig, "What you want may not exist in this area…for the price John will pay. I hope it does, but I can't squeeze blood out of a turnip."

She seemed placated…for the time being.

"Casa de la Luz", the third property they previewed, was closer to what she wanted. Priced at a mere $4.25 million, the home was open, spacious and full of natural light. Fabiola seemed to like the property and asked Brad to do some additional research about the owners and the improvements. The kitchen was too small, she said, but the master bedroom was large and the sit- down vanity was perfect. The closets would have to be enlarged, but she thought that might be easy to do.

As they exited the front door, she locked her arm in Brad's and told him she liked the property much better than the previous one. "I *tink* we might *wan* to make *tee* offer."

Charro again. All goochie-goochie.

Brad breathed a cautious sigh of relief.

The final viewing of the day, "Casita de Oceana y Las Montanas", was postponed an hour. It was a blessing in disguise as both Brad and Fabiola needed a short break from each other. Brad went inside a small coffee shop for a croissant and an iced tea while Fabiola called John. He didn't answer, so she left a short message.

"*Juan. Tees* area is marvelous," she said, reverting to her broken English. "But some *ub tees casas* are horrible. Only one so far *ees* good enough," she said to his voice mailbox. "Tell Brad to find me what I *wan* and only what I *wan*. I'm sure *eets* out there. He *jus* has to look harder. Tell him *eef* he can't find the right house, then we'll get *anudder* agent. *Tere* are mucho agents in *tees* town. I'm sure one would *lub* to work with us. Be firm mi amor. I miss *ju*. Adios."

'Casita de Oceano y Las Montanas' was absolutely beautiful. For once, the property's name described it perfectly. Small house by the ocean and the mountains. The name fit like a glove. Fabiola loved it. Where else on earth could you enjoy the coolness of the ocean and the scenic beauty of the nearby mountains?

Fabiola loved the kitchen. "I *lub* tee master bedroom and *tee* light," she exclaimed as they strolled around the exterior of the property. "I really like *tee* light, Brad. It makes me feel safe and comfortable. I *don* like *tee* landscaping, but we can make a few changes." Like many prospective buyers, her mind was already racing. Fabiola grabbed Brad's arm.

"*Tees ees* it. *Ju* make an offer tonight!" she demanded.

"Fabiola, the house has been on the market for six months. I don't think one day will make a big difference. Let's head back to my house and talk to Mel. You and she can discuss the pros and cons. We should sleep on it tonight and discuss it in the morning."

Fabiola frowned. "If it is not available tomorrow, I'm going to be pissed," she warned. "This is not Mel's decision; it's mine!" she added. A look of competitive fierceness filled her face.

Brad had not seen this before.

What happened to goochie-goochie?

He smiled and assured her he would contact the listing agent that night. He knew that once a buyer showed interest, the poker game began. The seller and the agent would feign no interest. They were likely to mention that some "phantom" buyer from Texas was coming in this weekend. All of this in an attempt to create false competition. In reality, of course, they would be thrilled that someone had finally stepped up to the plate.

On the buyer's end, it was important to have your ducks lined up. Brad still hadn't processed John's loan— hadn't even seen the tax returns yet. The other problem was Fabiola. She was pushing the transaction faster than she should. He needed to talk to John.

He'd do it tomorrow when he came into town.

He was confident that a few days or even a week wasn't going to make a difference with this property. But, again, he had seen only a minor glimpse of Fabiola's fury. He didn't want to see the full Magilla. Best to talk to Linden and process the loan post haste.

26

JOHN LINDEN WAS SET TO ARRIVE in Santa Barbara mid-morning, Saturday.

He had spoken last to Brad for ten minutes Friday night. The conversation had not been very satisfying.

Brad had told him that, in his opinion, it was premature to look at properties with Fabiola. She needed more coaching and without it, she was a little…irritable.

Linden had said, "You mean bitchy, don't you?"

"You said it, I didn't." And then feeling more hospitable, he added, "This process can be quite frustrating."

"Hey, bro. It is what it is. It's going to be her nest. I'll just be a visitor in my own home. You know how it is. If Fabiola's happy than we're all happy and vice versa."

Well visitor or not, it would've been nice to be given a solid head's up that his job description would include showing properties to an emotional—and perhaps hormonal—Latina. If Brad wanted to 'show' properties for a living, he would've become a realtor.

Although licensed by the same department in California, real estate agents and loan agents are as different as night and day. Brad understood the nature of the game; he was willing to play along. It was the only way he knew how to make money.

They decided that he and John would meet for a beer before Linden surprised Fabiola with his presence. They would agree on a strategy to get her to "cool her jets" while Brad answered all the non-property related questions for the lender. Then—and only then—would Brad present an offer to purchase 'Casita de Oceano y Las Montanas'.

Linden's plane landed a few minutes late and the car rental took him longer than expected. All of which made him twenty minutes late for his meeting with Brad. "What's up, buddy?" Linden asked when he finally made it to the bar.

"Same ol' shit. Chasing the almighty dollar," Brad responded with a sly smile. "Pull up a stool. What'll you have? Beer or whiskey?"

Linden sat on the bar stool and ordered a beer. Brad ordered a Jack and soda. When the drinks arrived the two clinked glasses, said 'Cheers' and enjoyed their first sips of the day. After discussing the pains of travel, the conversation turned to house hunting and the loan paperwork.

"I know she can be a pain in the ass," Linden said matter-of-factly, referring to Fabiola. "I didn't tell you in advance because I didn't want to scare you off. I need a new house. You need a healthy commission. She needs to be in control of what she wants. We both need to appease her. It's that simple."

"I get it. And I really appreciate the opportunity. I tried to sit her down and explain that I'm not functioning as a typical real estate agent on this deal. I wanted to make sure that she knew I wasn't the kind of guy who would take her to a property and show her the curtains and comment about the colors." He paused and thanked the bartender as he placed the drink in front of him.

He took a sip, smiled, said, "Aahh, now that's smooth." He took a deep breath and enjoyed the aftertaste for a moment before continuing. Finally he said, "I explained to her that I wasn't going to know the history of the house nor was I up to date on the motivations of the sellers. I'm a 'nuts and bolts guy'."

"Okay, I'm with you so far," Linden said, taking a big gulp of his ice cold beer.

"You said you wanted a nice home for under four million. So, my job is to find you a nice home for under four million," Brad said somewhat defensively. "I never got the chance to discuss it with her. Next thing I knew, we were in the car headed for a long day of property inspections...."

"That's good; that's what she wanted," Linden said.

Brad raised his hand, asking his friend to slow down. "I didn't want to involve her with the loan details so I emphasized that we were just doing preliminary reviews of these properties. And, Bingo, Jingo! She falls in love with the fourth property we see!"

"That's perfect," Linden replied. "I don't see why there's a problem? You found our new house in one day. Sounds like efficient capitalism to me. Let's make the offer and rock and roll."

"That's not the point. We're not ready. I need a few days to process your paperwork. I'm sure everything is in order, but you can't be too careful these days. I want to make sure that we've crossed all the t's and dotted all the i's in advance. Once I know that the lender is going to issue credit approval, I can negotiate a good price for you."

"How long does the approval take?"

"I should know in a few days. Did you bring the tax returns and asset statements? Please say yes. I don't want to make any lame excuses to your fiancée. She's hot to trot on this property."

"I've got the stuff in the car. Let's finish our drinks and I'll give it to you." He raised his glass and took the final swig of his beer.

"Perfect, we can begin it today," Brad said, relieved that he finally had the proper paperwork.

"On a Saturday?"

"I know. It sucks. Ever since this fucking recession hit, we've had to work weekends."

Linden frowned. "Thought we might get another pop, but it sounds like you've got to get to the office."

"Yep. No rest for the weary."

Linden rose from his stool and patted Brad's back and said, "Well the ends will justify the means. You head over to your office and start doing your financial magic. I'll surprise Fabby." He paused as if deep in thought and then grinned. "I can think of a few ways to take her mind off this house—for a few days at least."

"I bet you can," Brad agreed. "Let's 'rock and roll'."

27

LOCATED JUST A FEW BLOCKS FROM THE bar, Brad's office was a short walk.

Linden had given him all the paperwork and now the drudge work was about to begin. Transfer of information to computer formats; verification of reported data; credit reports; mathematical analysis. In other words, 'processing' of the loan.

Approaching his office, he took a deep breath and then entered the front door. The Jack had affected him a little more than he wanted to admit.

He waved to the receptionist, Marge, a middle aged, well-kept, buxom red head. Think Ann Margaret in Grumpy Old Men. A flamboyant dresser normally, she had toned it down today and was wearing a plain, brown pants suit with pink blouse.

"Morning, Brad," she said, looking up from her magazine.

"What's up, Marge? Reading anything interesting?"

She smiled. "Just catching up on my favorite celebrities."

"Let me know if George Clooney has a new girl-friend."

"Well, as a matter of fact…."

Brad stopped her short with a wave of his right hand. "Just kidding. Keep up the good work." He took a few strides and then stopped. "And Marge, thanks for coming in on the weekend."

"No problem. It gives me a chance to catch up on my reading."

He strode by her desk and ascended the stairs more quickly than usual.

Stefanie sat behind her large desk and smiled broadly when Brad entered the room.

"Good morning, Sunshine," she sang out.

He grinned and returned the greeting. In a world full of cynics, naysayers, and hidden agendas, she was almost always freakishly pleasant.

He liked it.

"We finally got John's financials," he announced proudly, holding a thick stack of papers in front of him. "Let's put this on the fast track. I want it organized, punched in, and a full credit report run ASAP. I'll do the initial work-up and give you a laundry list after my review. I want to submit this to United Central Bank first thing Monday."

"Got it," she said, taking the file from him. "Anything special I should be looking for?"

"Nope; should be straight forward," he replied and headed into his office.

He knew Stef liked it when there was work to do. She thrived under pressure. Before the word even exist-ed, she could 'multi-task' with the best of them. She and he had been doing this song and dance daily for over two decades. Like a veteran pilot who still got a rush from the engine's thrust at takeoff, they both felt a shot of adrenaline course through their veins when an important loan application came in.

And this application—to him, at least—was the 'Mother' of all applications.

A few hours later, she brought an organized file into Brad's office and dropped it on his desk. The credit report had come back clean, she informed him.

"Time for you to do the work up, boss," she deadpanned.

He put on his reading glasses, ran his fingers through his hair, cracked his knuckles, smiled and said, "Let the fun begin."

Before they fund loans, mortgage lenders dig deeply into the lives of prospective borrowers. His job was to dig even deeper initially so there would be no surprises at the end.

There were rules about where the borrower lived, how long they had been employed, how many properties they owned, whether they intended to live in the property or not, where their down payment was coming from, and many, many more.

There were rules about the rules. It was silly.

An hour later, after integrating the credit information with the loan application and filling out all the necessary compliance paperwork, he sat back in his chair, took off his glasses, rubbed the bridge of his nose and called Stef into his office.

"I'm going to take a break before I look at the tax returns and asset statements. Want to get a cup of coffee?"

"Sure, I'll walk down to the corner with you."

They grabbed their jackets and headed down the street.

"How does John's file look so far?" Stef asked.

"I only got thru the credit info and cleaned up the loan application, but so far it looks fine. When we get back, I'll dig into the financials and then we'll be ready to submit."

"I'm happy for you. I know this means a lot to you and Mel."

Brad nodded.

They got their coffee and walked back to the office in relative silence, commenting only on the weather and the state of world affairs. Brad asked how she and Tommy were doing and all she said, was "So, so." He let it drop.

Maybe he'd give Tommy a call later and try to help.

When they returned, Brad shed his jacket and rubbed his hands together, indicating he was excited about the next stage.

He raised his hands like a surgeon, breathed deeply and declared, "Okay, I'm going in."

He opened the file and began his financial work up. A few minutes into the process, he looked at Linden's most recent tax returns. His jaw dropped. "What the Fuck! Stef, come in here quick," he shouted.

"What's up?"

"Take a look at his returns." He rubbed his hands through his hair and sat back in his chair as she glanced at the paperwork.

Sitting in front of them were tax returns indicating that Linden's net taxable income was nowhere near what it should be. He had grossed almost six million dollars the previous year, but his bottom line, taxable income, was only two point five. Enough income to qualify for the loan, but way too low for the amount of gross earnings.

"Riddle me this, Batman," he said as much to himself as to Stef. "How does a pro golfer generate three and a half million dollars in legitimate tax write offs?"

She shook her head. "That doesn't make sense. How does he live?"

"It looks like IFPG has gotten very creative with John's tax returns," Brad said.

"Or," she added quickly, "maybe they made rotten investments and lost money like the rest of the world?"

Brad shook his head. He took off his reading glasses, put them on the corner of his desk and turned to his assistant. "Something's not right. I've seen a lot of tax returns in my time and these don't make sense." He paused and then gestured to her to pull up a chair. "I want to go thru these with you page by page; maybe I'm missing something."

It took them another half hour, but buried deep in the return was a schedule indicating that a series of LLC investments Linden was invested in had taken massive losses the past year. Brad grabbed the previous years' returns. Same thing. The names were consistent: IFPG Fund 215, IFPG Fund 216, IFPG Fund 217. The only variance was that last year, a new LLC emerged: Athletes for Change LLC, A Delaware entity. It had accounted for over one million in losses just by itself.

Brad sat back and stared at the returns as if they were a bomb ready to explode and then said quietly, "You know, according to John, Art Smalley was a smart and conservative guy. How did he invest John's money so poorly?"

She shook her head. "Doesn't make sense."

"And, more importantly," he continued, "why hasn't John mentioned these losses? They're pretty big."

"Maybe he doesn't know about them."

"Hardly seems likely."

She shrugged.

He opened the file to the asset section. Presented there were the last two months' statements of liquid and non-liquid assets held in trust by IFPG. Also attached to the general ledger was the year to date income/loss report. Again, Brad was surprised. The most recent asset statement indicated that Linden had one point eight million dollars in cash and net equity of just under one million in all other investments.

"Look at this Stef, his year to date rate of investment return is minus 65%!"

"Minus 65%! You sure?"

"That's what it says here." He paused and then added, "Damn! He thinks he's *making* a positive 8%."

"That's a 73% discrepancy," she added, doing the math quickly in her head.

Glancing at other statements, he could see that Linden retained enough assets for down payment for the loan, but this wasn't the amount of assets one would see for a guy who brought in over fifteen million bucks over the past several years.

Accounting for a high tax bracket, the down stock market and the general shitty economy, Brad estimated that John should still be sitting on eight to ten million. Two point eight was a far cry from that figure and Brad owed it to his buddy to bring it to his attention. It might kill the purchase plans—or force them to downsize—but John should be told as soon as possible.

He'd wait until they were alone; no need for Fabiola to get involved. He'd seen enough of the bitchy side of her for this trip. In the meantime, he would continue his work up and make a laundry list of questions Linden should ask Tyler Ambrook.

Top of that list was: What happened to my money? Followed by, how had you managed it so poorly? And then finishing with, What in the hell is Athletes for Change LLC? Why had John invested (and lost) more than a million in that specific enterprise?

And then of course the final question: What the fuck?

Determined to have a nice dinner with his guests, Brad left the office several hours later.

The drive home was troubling.

On the one hand, Brad had seen some ugly financials in his day. On the other, maybe Linden knew about his and just didn't give a damn. Or, more likely, never looked at his IFPG statements or paid attention to his tax returns.

As long as he had enough money to travel the world and play golf, John Linden probably was a happy camper. Brad knew lots of guys who never balanced their checkbooks or monitored their finances.

That's why they had 'people' who worked for them.

Well John, old buddy, me thinks you've been rat fucked by your 'people', Brad thought as he navigated the car towards the highway.

As he merged his car into the southbound traffic, Brad was hit by a disturbing thought. Art Smalley had committed suicide. Was this because he knew that Linden had lost millions? That wouldn't drive a guy to hang himself, would it? Then again, stock brokers jump out of windows when clients take big losses. Don't they? Maybe it was motivation for him to hang himself. Perhaps this would bring some closure for Art's family.

He drove onward a few miles and suddenly, he had another disturbing thought: Maybe John wasn't the only one who lost 65%? Maybe there were other IFPG clients suffering enormous losses. Perhaps one of them found out and killed Art? Could a golfer possibly lose so much as to lead to murder? "I can't afford my private Jet any longer and I've got to play with old golf clubs because of your bad management; now put your neck in this noose so I can hang you."

Is that what happened?

If there was a deranged golfer roaming around out there, John might want to tread lightly.

And finally, as he reached his driveway, one last thought popped into his head: Why hadn't the mother company, IFPG, said something to John about the losses? Surely they knew. He shook his head and decided he *really* needed to talk to his buddy.

Fabiola and John were waiting for him on the patio when he arrived home. He waved to them and held up his index finger, indicating he'd be with them in a minute. They appeared happy. Fabiola was smiling and making animated gestures as she talked. Linden grinned from ear to ear. Apparently, his surprise visit had been a big hit. Brad was glad for the lovers. He hoped Mel would be caught up in the emotions as well. It would be nice if *everybody* was in a good mood.

Sadly, it was not to be.

"Bradley Stephens!" Mel exclaimed as he walked through the front door.

Putting down the knife she was using to slice some cheese for an appetizer plate, she approached him. "About time you came home. So nice of you to join us. Your best friend has been here since early afternoon."

"I know. I spent some time with him already," he said defensively. "He brought me some important paperwork. I had to analyze it all afternoon. Sorry I couldn't join you sooner."

"You should've called me and let me know he was coming." She wasn't backing down. "I was caught off guard and didn't have any food ready."

"Sorry. It slipped my mind."

"And it's a good thing *she's* been sleeping in the guest room," Mel said, pointing at Fabiola. "I'd feel awful if I hadn't changed the sheets."

"Okay, I get your point. No more surprises."

"That's right," she said, picking up the knife again. She began cutting some salami and French bread. Suddenly she stopped and faced him. "And another thing—before we join them—I've got a question for you: What's up with that woman anyway? She's been hanging around all day talking about this house you guys looked at. She seems to think you didn't do your homework before showing it to her. It was all I could do to bite my tongue."

"There's no doubt she's high maintenance," Brad said, shaking his head slowly and pursing his lips.

"I don't think she's a very nice person. Don't get me wrong, I will tolerate her because she's John's fiancée, but please don't leave me alone with her again. Are you sure

John really wants to marry her?" The questions came at him fast and somewhat furiously—Mel hardly taking a breath in between.

"I'm not sure. He seems infatuated. But it could be the sex. We both know he thinks with his little head sometimes. Let's not cause waves right now. John has some bigger problems to deal with."

"Okay. But I want to be on the record as stating that I think that something is not right with that woman."

"Why? Did she do something or is this your woman's intuition?"

"It's not anything specific. It's her overall attitude. I heard her on the phone earlier today cussing and cursing at a decorator. Sounded like a sailor. Then she walks over and smiles at me like nothing happened."

He had noticed some of the same behavior, turning on and off the Charro accent. Rather than give it any energy, he said, "Fair enough. You've got legitimate reasons it sounds like. Let's try to be pleasant and maybe we'll see another side of her."

Brad poured some Jack Daniels in a glass, topped it with just a splash of club soda and joined the group on the patio. They made small talk for awhile and then prepared to eat dinner outside. It was a beautiful evening. Low 70's. Not a cloud in the sky. The sunset had been outstanding.

Southern California was famous for a consistent weather pattern this time of year: Late night and early morning low clouds, followed by sunshine. In a rare turn of events, there were thousands of stars visible that evening. Brad lit the outdoor fireplace and settled in.

The girls had been determined to cook, but thankfully, Linden had offered to pay for food to be delivered.

Tacos, enchiladas, burritos, rice and beans. Solid Santa Barbara fare.

Brad kept hoping that Mel and Fabiola would excuse themselves for a bathroom break inside. He was dying to talk to John alone.

Fabiola must have the bladder of a giraffe, he thought. She never goes to the bathroom. At one point, he even hinted that Mel and Fabiola should go to the local market and pick up dessert. Mel shook her head assertively.

When they weren't eating, the two lovebirds were inseparable. If he didn't catch an opening tonight, he'd try to wake John up early and go get coffee in the morning. Brad was anxious to discuss his friend's finances— and his new theories—but, if it came down to it, he could wait ten hours.

John and Fabiola had one more drink after dinner and then said goodnight. "It's been a long day of travel, I'm tired," he said with a wink, wrapping an arm around Fabiola's thin waist and leading her towards the guest room.

Mel and Brad cleaned up and retired to their room as well.

A new Stuart Woods novel awaited him. Stone Barrington and Dino were knee deep in the murder of a wealthy New York socialite. Despite his anxieties over Linden's finances, Brad quickly became engrossed in the new book.

Mel took her time before falling asleep. Twenty minutes after they had exchanged goodnights, Mel and Brad heard some muted giggling coming from the guestroom. Five minutes later, the sounds grew louder.

"Aye, Juan! *Jess! Jess!* Aye, *Jess!*" This was followed by a thumping noise against the wall and concluded two minutes later with a mighty groan.

Mel and Brad looked at each other. In a quiet voice Mel said, "Oh God! How long do we have to listen to this?" She rolled over and covered her head with the pillow to muffle the sound.

The noise subsided and Brad put his book aside. Time to turn off the brain and count the sheep.

He began his new nightly mantra: No bad dream. No bad dream.

Mel turned off her light, kissed Brad lightly and rolled over to sleep. Five minutes later, they faced each other again.

The amorous noises began anew. This time, Brad pulled the pillow over *his* head.

28

THEY AROSE SUNDAY MORNING TO A cold mist and a dense fog.

"Damn, Brad," Linden said, walking towards Brad's car. "If I were playing golf, I couldn't see the fairway from the tee box in this shit."

"I think it's the heaviest I've ever seen," Brad agreed.

"Be careful driving, we don't want to rear end a parked car or something."

"Duh! Thanks for the advice."

Rufus jumped in the back seat while Brad started the car, turned on the wipers, and pushed the defrost button. The Rottweiler's breath continued to fog the side window and Brad was forced to roll it down a bit.

"It's cold. You sure you've got to roll the window down?" Linden asked.

"Only if you want me to see."

Linden shrugged.

Making their way slowly, and continuing to comment about the fog, Brad and Linden drove a few miles to Brad's favorite coffee house, Jeromes.

Located on the beach, the views at Jeromes were usually spectacular and peaceful. This morning, however, Brad could barely see the sand much less the surf. Despite this, it was still very comfortable and the two friends settled into large, overstuffed chairs with hot cups of coffee.

Bob Marley played quietly in the background—telling them that 'Buffalo Soldiers were coming to America'.

"Great dinner last night, bud," Linden said as he took his first sip of coffee. "I'm glad you got me up early. That Fabiola is really something, isn't she?" He asked this not so much as a question but more as a statement. Was he fishing? Did he want to see if Brad had heard them go at it last night? Or, maybe he was wondering what Brad and Mel thought of her?

Feeling he should compliment his buddy—because that's what guys do—Brad said, "I thought I heard a little action in the guestroom. And, if I'm not mistaken, it sounded like a two round match."

Linden grinned. "Yeah, well, she always wants to go two rounds…at least. I'm thinking about investing in pace-maker companies. I swear, if we hadn't gotten out of there this morning, she'd be all over me again."

"Oh, what a shame," Brad said in mock sympathy. "No morning bonin' for the U.S. Open Champ? Mr. Twinkle must be tired."

Linden grinned. "Oh, you heard that, huh?"

They both laughed and picked up their coffee cups. Before he could take another sip, Brad turned serious. Putting his cup down, he took a deep breath and began the painful financial discussion with his friend.

"Speaking of investing," he began. "As you know, I reviewed your financial information yesterday...."

"Pretty good, huh?" Linden said with pride. "Your old buddy has done pretty good for himself, hasn't he?"

"Well, that's just the thing. It *is* good. But it's not *great*. I'm not your financial advisor and I'm not privy to all the decisions that you and Art made over the years, but John, you should have more money."

"What do you mean? I didn't make any decisions. Art handled all my money. I never look at that stuff." He put his cup down and turned serious. "When you say more, how much *more* do you mean?"

"Before I answer that, let me ask you this: How much money do you think you have with IFPG?"

"I don't know for sure. I'd say around ten million. That would be my best guess. That's why I feel comfortable looking at four million dollar homes."

"That's what I thought. Well, according to your most recent statements, you have a total of two point eight million. And those funds are losing value as we speak."

"No way!" He pounded his fist on the table, spilling his coffee. "No Fucking way! Art told me my money was safely invested in bonds and conservative shit. He said I should be earning 8% annually after my living expenses. He told me not to worry. He was setting me up for retirement. He always told me that a professional athlete's earning window could slam shut at any moment. You know, injuries or scandals or better players." His face turned red and his voice rose a few decibels.

"I understand. You liked Art. Maybe I'm wrong...but I'm pretty good at reading tax returns and financial statements. Your tax returns for the past several years show massive losses. And your current asset statement reflects a year to date loss of 65%!" He paused, took a sip of his coffee and let the last statement settle in.

"No way; no fucking way," Linden muttered under his breath as if in shock.

"John, the economy is in recession and that could explain some of it, but the stock market has bounced back in the past few years. Anyone who stayed vested made back all of their losses. You've continued to drop. It's not right."

"Okay, okay, okay," Linden repeated while trying to absorb this new information. Wringing his hands and rocking in his chair he continued, "First things first. Do I have enough money to buy Fabiola the home she wants?"

"Yes. But you won't have much left over."

"And I qualify for the loan?"

"Yes. Mathematically you do. But the lender could be concerned by the negative trend in your financials. I'll have to address it and see if I can talk them through it. I'm pretty sure I can. It would help if you could win the next tournament or two."

"Consider it done. What's next?"

"I think you need to talk to Tyler Ambrook and fig- ure out what the fuck is going on."

"Me? How about WE?"

"I'm glad you brought that up. This is something I've been thinking about since last night. *We* need to do this together. I want you to authorize me to instruct IFPG to convert all your holdings to cash. Immediately. Then I want you to leave enough with them to pay your bills for the rest of the year and move what's left to a liquid money market account with a respectable local bank."

"Shouldn't I take it all out?"

"Maybe eventually. IFPG books your tournaments, pays your bills, arranges your travel itinerary and collects data for your taxes. I think they should continue those functions. When you win some more money this year, the purse should be divided between what they need to manage your affairs and what you need to remain liquid."

He paused for a moment and stared at his friend. Linden couldn't have been more distraught. He looked like he had just whiffed a tap in putt to win the Masters. Brad continued. "I know this is a big shock. It was a shock to me. And maybe there's a reasonable explanation. But I say, 'Better Safe than Sorry'."

"I'm with you. If those guys have been cheating me, I want to get to the bottom of it. But man, I've worked so hard for that money. If it's gone…." He suddenly looked pained—as if a devastating thought just occurred to him. "If I can't buy Fabby that home she looked at with you, I'm screwed. I'll never hear the end of it. Hell, I'll probably lose her. Let's get to the bottom of it. Okay?"

"There's another thing," Brad began.

Sighing, Linden said, "What now?"

"Well, I was thinking about this last night. Do you think these losses had anything to do with Art's suicide?"

Linden nodded slowly. "Well, now that you mention it, I guess they could have. But do you think he'd really hang himself over some bad investments?"

"People do strange things for money."

"*Damn!* I wish he'd talked to me about it. I'd have been pissed, but we could've worked it out."

Brad said nothing. He took a sip of coffee and watched his friend process the information he'd just received.

Beyond them, the fog was burning off and morning sunshine was peeking through the clouds. He could now see waves breaking on the sand. Looked like a decent swell.

He took another sip and returned his attention to his friend. Should he hit him with his other thought? Was it too much, too soon? Nope, John was a big boy, he could handle it.

"Here's my other thought." Linden's eyes widened and he stared at Brad. "If Art didn't hang himself, then maybe there is some other golfer who was losing as much or more than you and flipped out."

"And hanged him?"

"Hell, I don't know." Brad sighed and shook his head. "Maybe the guy went over to his house and confronted him and one thing led to another....Hell, I don't know what to think about any of this. All I know is you've got a lot less money to work with than we initially thought...."

"And Art's dead."

"Yep...And Art is dead."

They finished their coffee in silence, paid the bill and rose to leave.

Over the speakers, Bob Marley could be heard confessing that he had 'shot the sheriff' but swore 'he didn't shoot no deputy'.

Brad could tell that John wanted to shoot somebody himself.

29

BRAD AND JOHN REPEATED THE EARLY morning coffee at Jerome's on Monday morning.

They had spent the rest of the day Sunday relaxing. They had decided not to discuss the financial issues around the girls. Linden had taken Fabiola for a drive around Santa Barbara. They had had lunch on the wharf with the other tourists and then ventured up to wine country for some tastings.

Mel and Brad did some light yard work and ate leftovers for lunch.

They all gathered for dinner and hit the sack early. Much to Mel's chagrin, the noises from her guestroom came once again. "Amazing," was all she said this time.

While enjoying a cup of coffee and a bagel, they discussed the losses more thoroughly and mapped out a course of action for the day: Brad would work on the loan paperwork and make the submission to the lender. Linden would call some other players he knew and see how their finances had been handled. He also indicated that he wanted to talk to Veronica Smalley again.

They would pow-wow before John and Fabiola headed back to Orlando later that afternoon.

After finishing their morning meeting, Brad dropped Linden off at the house and then headed into his office.

They had taken longer for coffee than he had intended. It was now eleven o'clock. He usually got in at ten. He'd have to hit the ground running. Feeling good about the overall course of action, he called Linden on his cell phone and reminded him to call IFPG and authorize Brad to move his money to a local bank.

He then called Andy Fuller, the manager of a local bank and informed him that a large wire would be coming in today or tomorrow. A new account in the name of John Linden should be opened. He asked Andy to send him the signature cards and any other mandatory disclosures.

When the conversation ended, Brad, said, "Oh, Andy, by the way, you're welcome. You're going to owe me one." The bank manager chuckled, agreed and hung up.

Business in the 'big' city.

Traveling slowly through downtown Santa Barbara, Brad marveled—not for the first time—at the beautiful combination of Spanish, Victorian, and Craftsman architecture that filled the city of Santa Barbara. The "American Riviera" they called it. And, for once, *they* were right.

As he turned the corner towards his office he was surprised to see that the road had been cordoned off. He drove around the block and found a parking spot. He locked the car and walked a few hundred yards to his office.

He was stopped by a uniformed policeman who stood next to a series of red cones connected by yellow crime scene tape.

"I'm sorry, sir, you can't go in there," the young officer said. The guy was six foot three, had short, neat blonde hair and looked like he spent all his off-duty time in the gym.

"This is my office. I work here. What's going on?" Brad asked.

"I'm not at liberty to discuss it, sir. Please give me your name and I'll inform the sergeant in charge."

"My name is Brad. Brad Stephens." He winced. That didn't come out right; it sounded like he was trying to be Bond, James Bond.

And, lord knew, he was no James Bond.

The officer excused himself and headed towards a heavyset Latino who was standing by the front door with a notebook in his right hand. They talked for a few moments. The uniformed officer kept nodding his head towards Brad. The older Latino approached Brad, his rumpled gray suit matching his prematurely graying hair. He grinned and extended his hand.

"I *thought* this was your office," Sergeant Raoul Espinoza said, putting the notebook in his pocket as he approached Brad. He shook Brad's hand and then pulled him close for a big man hug.

Brad smiled and returned the hug. "Hi, Raoul. What's up?"

"Haven't seen you for awhile. The guys at the golf course miss you. I was just saying the other day that I needed to stop by and say hello. Didn't figure it would be this way—on official police business."

Brad and Raoul Espinoza had been golfing buddies for several years. He was correct, it had been way too long since they last played.

Brad nodded. "Sorry I've been out of touch. I've had some severe financial setbacks lately and it's kept me working long hours. Not much time for golf." Brad stared up at his office window and glanced at the other cops milling around the area. "What the hell's going on?"

"There's been a shooting. One of your co-workers. Let's go over there," the sergeant said pointing towards the large, green, Victorian building that was Brad's office. "I need to ask you a few questions."

"Sure…but who's been shot?" Brad suddenly felt shaky. Could it could be his partner, Donna, or even worse, his assistant, Stefanie?

"I'll get to that in a moment. But first a few questions. Have you been in the building today?"

"No. I'm just getting here."

"Can you tell me where you've been?"

"Sure. Jeromes coffee shop. It's down by the beach. I had a breakfast meeting with John Linden."

The sergeant took notes as Brad talked. What could be so important as to feel compelled to write this information down?

"John's in town?" Espinoza inquired, seemingly surprised by this news. Over the years he had become friendly with Linden, through Brad, as well. Apparently the detail was important, because Espinoza jotted John's name in his notebook.

And underlined it several times.

"He's thinking about buying a house in Montecito and came out with his new girlfriend, Fabiola," Brad said. "Now tell me what happened."

"Fabiola? Latina, eh?" Espinoza said with a grin. "I knew that boy had good taste."

"Wait till you see her," Brad added. "She's a knock-out."

"Can't wait. Maybe the three of us can grab a beer." Returning to the serious business at hand, he said, "Just a few more questions. Do you know anyone who would want to hurt you? Have there been any threats on your life recently? Any strange business dealings? Anything unusual lately?"

Brad sighed, still not understanding the basis of his friend's questions. He hesitated but then said, "Well, yes, there was something weird the other day…." He went on to describe the events on the Pear Blossom and added, "I was going to call the L.A. police today to tell them about it."

Espinoza frowned. "Why didn't you tell them right when it happened?"

"I don't know. I was in shock. I thought it was a drive-by shooting by a meth-head or gang banger trying to earn his stripes. Besides, the guy is dead. The fact is, I'm really busy right now. I don't need further complications in my life."

"Further complications! You were shot at! Seems pretty simple to me. You tell the police the guy fired at you a few times; you didn't know him; you give them your contact information and you're on your way. What's complicated about that?"

"I don't know; sometimes I just do things. I'm over 50 years old and haven't had my prostate checked. Is that a crime?" He glared at his friend. "You know what else? Sometimes I pull the labels off of mattresses. Now stop beating me up, I know it was stupid."

"Yes it was. If you'd come to the police earlier, maybe…."

Oh great, Brad thought, just what I need, more guilt.

"Okay, I know I fucked up. We can talk about it later. What happened here?"

"Anybody else want to hurt you?" Espinoza asked in a direct manner, implying that Brad might be holding out on him.

Brad shook his head. "Nope. And believe me, I've been thinking about it a lot since the Pear Blossom deal."

Espinoza was about to add something when the front door burst open and Stefanie stumbled out. She looked absolutely stunned. Her naturally olive skin had turned pale; her usually immaculate makeup and hair were askew. She moved forward and threw her arms around Brad and sobbed against his chest.

"Oh, Brad. It's awful; just awful. I've never seen anything like it. It's crazy! Why would anyone do this?"

"Do what Stef? Take a deep breath. Calm down. Tell me what happened."

She paused, breathed, pushed away slightly from his chest and looked him in the eye. Trembling slightly, she said, "I was coming out of the rest room when I heard Marge warn me that an angry man was coming up the stairs. I looked down and saw this fat guy with a broken nose in a gray suit coming up. He looked at me with wild eyes as he hit the top of the stairs and asked where your office was. I guess I looked at your doorway because he immediately headed straight towards it. Once he got there, I heard him yell, 'Brad Stephens, you son of a bitch! I know you've been messing around with my Doris Anne! Now you're going to pay!' And then...." She paused for a moment, searching for fresh air.

Brad hugged her tightly, inadvertently rocking from side to side as if he were holding an infant. He really didn't know how to deal with someone in shock.

He assumed human contact was a good thing.

Did she say...*his* office? The sinking feeling in his gut grew. Stefanie sniffled, took a deep breath and continued.

"I saw him pull a gun from his jacket. He fired. He just fucking fired the gun!"

"How many times?" Espinoza asked.

She looked at him, realizing for the first time that he was overhearing her account of events. "Three or four times, I think. It happened real fast. Like, pop, pop, pop, pop. And then, when he came out of the office, the strangest look filled the guy's face. Like he was really confused. He said, 'Oh Shit!' and ran down the stairs and out the front door."

Espinoza looked at Brad. "Why did this guy want to kill you amigo?"

Given Stef's account, it was a fair question.

"I've got no idea," Brad, now ashen-faced and some-what shaken answered. "This whole thing is a shock to me as well. Who got shot?"

Before Espinoza could ask another question, Stefanie quickly responded. "You weren't in on time this morning. Several calls had come in with questions about that new loan program we advertised last week. I put most of them through to your voicemail but the last one insisted on talking to you. He sounded sincere and it sounded like a big loan."

Brad nodded.

"Go on," Espinoza said.

She paused and collected her thoughts. "I couldn't find Donna or Ray so I went downstairs and got Jim Johnson. He was the only loan officer in." She stopped, looked at them, her face as white as a ghost, her eyes growing wide. "Oh, God! I got him killed! Didn't I?"

"No you didn't. Just tell Raoul and me what happened," Brad insisted softly while thinking to himself, "Somebody *really is* trying to kill me. *Damn!*" The thought made him begin to sweat.

"Jim came up to your office to take the call. I could tell he was real proud to come upstairs and sit behind your desk," she began. Turning to Espinoza she added, "We never let the junior loan officers upstairs. Anyway, Jim just glowed. I heard him give the guy a quote and then hang up. It probably was the highlight of his career."

Brad nodded. He knew Johnson. It fit.

"Anyway, he didn't come right out from your office. I figured I'd let him sit behind a real pros' desk. Might do him some good. A few minutes later the fat guy comes up the stairs. Jim must've turned your chair around and was looking out the window. Why else would the shooter not know it was you?"

And with that, she shook her head and said to no-one in particular, "I got him killed! Oh, my God! Oh, my God!"

Espinoza gestured to a female officer to come over and help. Brad looked at Stef; her face was wet and pale. He grabbed her by the shoulders and gently stroked her hair and rubbed her shoulders.

"You didn't kill Jim Johnson, Stef. Some madman killed him. There was nothing you could do. Stop beating yourself up. If anyone's to blame, it's me. I was late for work. I was supposed to be sitting in that chair. I don't know why, but it sounds like the guy was out to get me."

And, although he didn't say it, he thought, *I should've called the police immediately after the Pear Blossom shooting. They might have assigned a guard to me or something.*

She nodded sadly.

Espinoza instructed the officer to take care of Stefanie, but before they left, he asked, "Did you see the guy's face?"

She grimaced. "Yes, I did. I don't think I'll ever forget it."

"Can you describe him for me?"

She wiped away a tear, collected her thoughts and described the killer as a big man, maybe three hundred pounds, wearing a cheap, dark suit and large overcoat. He had a thick beard, wore dark, plastic glasses and limped.

Espinoza thanked her and asked her to see his forensic artist as soon as possible; he'd like to circulate a rendering of the man.

Turning his attention back to Brad, he asked, "What about this Doris Anne?"

"Don't know. The only Doris Anne I've ever met is my wife's aunt."

"Awfully strange. Wouldn't you agree?"

"Yep. Strange and Fucked-Up."

A gurney appeared in the doorway and several medics pushed the lifeless body of Jim Johnson out the front door. Brad looked down at his former colleague.

Shaking his head slowly, while rubbing his chin with his hand, he took a deep breath and fought the urge to breakdown.

Instead, he took a step back and said quietly under his breath, "But for the grace of God, there go I."

30

COMMANDER DAVID VON EISENLOW WAS becoming slightly worried.

His numbers were dwindling and the competence of his men had come into question. Would he lose the support of the 'whisperer'? The failure of the restaurant attack had been his fault; bad planning and bad training.

Nobody could blame him, though, for the first failed attempt on Stephens. His soldier, Mark Hawkins, had been an excellent driver and a crack shot. The crash was an accident; nothing more, nothing less.

He had just been informed that Hollyfield had shot the wrong man in Stephen's office. Again, an unfortunate set of circumstances. But, would the 'whisperer' see it that way?

Thank God Curley had performed well in Orlando. At least he could point to that mission as a complete success.

But, this wasn't the way Von Eisenlow's holy war was supposed to go.

He studied the walnut paneled walls of his new office. Again he was struck by its beauty and elegance. The large mahogany desk gave him a tremendous feeling of power. The rich green Persian rug and large wet bar in the corner added a sense of wealth and financial stability.

He placed his hand on his forehead and then pulled his fingers through his thick hair. How was he going to explain to the remaining men that Hawkins, Sanford and, probably, Hollyfield weren't coming back? He guessed he'd have to come up with some religious justification and then conclude that the group was a 'lean, mean, fighting machine'. "Sell 'em, boy," he heard his father say.

Who the hell were Smalley and Stephens anyway? Why did the 'whisperer' want them dead? The commander had now been asked twice to put a man on close surveillance of Stephens. Twice, the ante had been raised and he had been instructed to have his man take the guy out. Twice they had failed. Would this be a reflection on the Sons of Sovereign Sacrifice? Would it be a reflection on his personal competence? Did these events, so highly removed from the primary mission—his personal holy war aimed at the U.S. government— create a lack of confidence in his operation? His training regimen? His faith?

His mood suddenly brightened when he thought again of the nearly perfect job Curley had done in killing the first target, Art Smalley. The 'whisperer' seemed like a smart man. He would acknowledge how difficult it is to pull these things off without a hitch. He'd appreciate the Smalley operation and he'd understand the frustrations they were having with Stephens.

At least, that is what Von Eisenlow hoped.

His cell phone rang shortly after the national news reported the killing in Santa Barbara. Knowing that it was probably the 'whisperer' and dreading the conversation, Von Eisenlow answered with apprehension.

"Yes," he said.

"You've failed me again, Commander," the 'whisperer' began, not giving Von Eisenlow time for small talk. "This isn't a game. It's not paintball or some video game. This is real life, you idiot! You've been training men for months and you can't even kill one, unarmed, middle-aged businessman. How the fuck are you going to win your holy war?" He let the question hang in the air.

Von Eisenlow said nothing.

The 'whisperer' continued. "I have provided you with food, shelter, training facilities, inside information and…..money. Lots of money. This is how you repay me? Comical displays of incompetence?" His voice began to gain strength. For the first time in their many conversations the whispers turned to true sound.

"I'll fix it. Don't give up on us. We got Smalley didn't we? The car crash was an accident. The shooting was my fault. I take full responsibility," he said, not because he believed it really was his fault, but because he had watched enough television over the years to know that the company leader was always supposed to take the blame.

Silence on the other end.

"Let me make it up to you. I'll send another man out to California this afternoon. I'll have him coordinate with my soldier who is still out there. We'll get him this time. I swear we will." Von Eisenlow finished his plea with a shaky voice.

"You're damn right you will," the 'whisperer' confirmed. "I need this guy dead ASAP or you can forget about any further additional financial or logistical support. Do you understand?"

Von Eisenlow was silent for a few moments, then he cleared his voice to speak. Before he could respond, the caller—with a voice which was now loud and clear—demanded, "Do You Understand?"

"Yes sir. I understand. I'll handle it. You'll have his head on a platter."

"Make it so," the man said and abruptly hung up.

Feeling the beginnings of a little headache before the call, Von Eisenlow could sense it quickly becoming a migraine. Having suffered migraines since childhood, he recognized the symptoms and knew he could be totally incapacitated for several hours. Best to gather his lieutenants now before the pain grew worse.

He walked across the elegant study and stared out the window at the magnificent grounds. To the north, several men were firing pistols at pop up targets. To the south, men were practicing hand to hand combat. These men were ready. They were primed. He needed to turn them loose.

If it took killing one defenseless person in Santa Barbara to insure that he'd have the money and support for the ultimate mission, then so be it.

Before he could assemble his minions, his cell phone rang again. Startled, he cleared his throat and said, "Yes, sir."

"Commander, I want to apologize for my gruff behavior before," the caller began. The soft voice had returned. "You don't need to know why Brad Stephens must die, but please believe me, his death is crucial to the success of your—and my—operation. Unfortunately, it is a necessary evil and one that must happen quickly. I know you understand so I won't belabor the point."

This 'whisperer' was courteous, almost pleasant. Von Eisenlow was impressed. The mark of a true leader he had learned while watching re-runs of Combat as a child, was the ability to inspire your troops and to keep your head while all of those around you lost theirs. Thank goodness for early television; so many important life lessons had been learned.

The 'whisperer' continued, "Let's discuss the status of your plans. Are you ready to begin your war against the government at the golf tournament?"

"Yes, as you suggested, we'll strike when their guard is down."

His headache subsiding, feeling refreshed and invigorated with this latest turn of events, he couldn't hide his enthusiasm. "Thanks to your inside information sir, we are ready. We'll strike while the politicians play golf at Harbour Town."

"Excellent! I will arrange transportation for you and your men whenever you need it. I assume you will need a day to set up?"

"Yes. We will need air transportation to Savannah on Sunday. We'll need ground transportation from the airport. You should rent two large vans for us. And there is some equipment we need." Having regained full confidence, Von Eisenlow was on a roll. The logistics for the final plan had come to him in a dream the night before. He was excited to share some of it with his benefactor.

"We're good on arms and munitions," he assured the caller. "What we need is appropriate clothing and... eight sets of golf clubs."

"Golf clubs? What the hell are you going to do with golf clubs?"

"I did some research. Golfers visit that entire area year round. I will travel with my men disguised as recreational golfers. We can hide weapons in the golf bags and it will make sense that we're out in that area to play some golf."

The 'whisperer' breathed deeply. "I see," he said.

"Can you provide them or should I send a man out to shop?"

"They'll be delivered to you this afternoon. I assume when you say appropriate clothing you mean golfing attire. I'll send over various sizes of shorts, pants, shirts and shoes. Anything else?"

"You'll need to make reservations for us at the resort on the island across from Hilton Head."

"Daufuskie? That island has been hit hard by the recession. I'm sure I can get you two houses to stay in. The owners will be grateful to generate the rent."

"It's all settled, then. I'll take care of Stephens. You take care of transportation, clothing, golf clubs and accommodations. Soon, the world will be a better place," Von Eisenlow declared, trying to sound confident.

"Amen to that," the 'whisperer' concurred and hung up.

The 'whisperer' was a true leader, Von Eisenlow thought. Intimidating during the first call —just as the commander had been when he disciplined young Hawkins for insubordination—and then rational and level-headed. Brilliant!

Von Eisenlow made a mental note to copy this guys' behavior.

The headache completely gone now, Von Eisenlow puffed his chest, lit a cigar and sat down in the large leather chair behind the mahogany desk. Leaning back, he put his boots up on the desk and took a deep long puff from his stogie. Things were falling into place. His benefactor had truly been sent by God. No questioning of the commander's strategy; ample resources and a knowledge of the staging location on Daufuskie Island.

Spreading his arms wide with his palms up-turned, he looked around him and said under his breath, "And, of course, there is all this."

He opened his cell phone and called Lieutenant Simpson. It was time to share his plans for Harbour Town. First, however, he had to keep his benefactor happy.

He would issue new orders: One of his best men would be sent to California to join Hollyfield. The two of them would find and then kill Brad Stephens. The task was clear. The only question: How to do it? He wasn't sure yet, but he would relax and rack his brain for the answer. Maybe it would come to him in a dream again?

No matter what, the lord would provide. All he had to do was maintain his faith…and continue to 'sell' the men.

31

FABIOLA ANSWERED THE PHONE WHEN Brad called.

"Hi, Fabiola, is Mel there?"

"*Jess*, she *ees*. Where are *ju*?"

"I'm at the police department, I'm going to be delayed," he said. "Let me talk to Mel, she will explain everything to you after I speak to her."

Fabiola hesitated a moment and then said, "*Hokay*, but I was hoping we could look at a few more houses before we leave."

Brad sighed. It's all about her, isn't it? "I'm afraid that won't be possible today. There's been a shooting at my office; a co-worker has been killed."

"*Muerto? Aye! Tats* awful," she said, sounding genuinely concerned. "I'll get Mel."

Brad collected his thoughts before Mel came on the line.

"What happened? Fabiola said somebody's been shot," Mel said, breathlessly.

"It's a long story, but, bottom line Jim Johnson was killed…"

"How? Was anybody else injured? Are you okay?"

"I'm fine. Nobody else was hurt, but the police want to ask me a few questions. Might take a while."

"Why would they ask *you* questions?"

He took a sip of water from a bottle Espinoza had provided and explained the situation as calmly as he could.

"And Raoul thinks you may still be in danger?"

"I don't know what he thinks yet. I know he thinks I should've reported the shooting on the Pear Blossom, but other than that, I don't know." He paused, his voice softened. "I think I might've really screwed up this time. Maybe if I'd told them, Jim would still be alive."

There was silence on the other end.

"Mel, you still there?"

After a brief moment, she came back on the line. "I'm still here. I was just thinking about what you said."

"And?"

Her voice strained with emotion, she said, "I'm just glad you're alright. I don't think this is the time to cast blame." She paused and added, "I feel awful about poor Jim. Is there anything I can do?"

Brad thought about it a moment. "Why don't you give Stef a call. She's really shook up."

"Wouldn't you be?"

"Hell, I am; but not as bad as Stef. She saw the whole thing."

"I'll call her and the boys. I'll see you in a while. I love you."

"Love you too."

He hung up the phone and walked into Espinoza's office feeling better, but also knowing that although she didn't say it, Mel felt he should have called the police sooner. He could hear it in the tone of her voice. After thirty years of marriage, sometimes it was things left unsaid that resonated.

If he had called the police right away, maybe this whole mess could've been averted. We all make decisions in life he thought, some good, some bad. Either way, you've got to live with the results and move on. He'd live with this one, but boy he'd sure like to go back in time, back to the Pear Blossom Highway. He'd take a breakfast ball on that one—if offered.

Linden and Fabiola were scheduled to leave later that afternoon and Fabiola was getting antsy.

It was a Monday and the airport shouldn't be crowded, but you never knew these days. Linden had hoped to get to the airport early; Fabiola had hoped to get a few things done before returning the rental car. The murder at Brads' office threw a wrench in both of their plans.

She had intended to make Brad drive them around Montecito for a few hours. She would point out the places that had been previewed and then get a late lunch at one of the local hang outs. While there, she planned on talking loudly about John's money and success. This, she thought, would start the rumors flying and create buzz about the couple's eventual purchase. Areas like Montecito, she knew, worked that way. It was all about the 'buzz' and she longed to be part of it.

Now, with Brad delayed by the police she was stuck. She hated being stuck. It reminded her of the time before she snuck across the border. The people she had hired for the task had treated her like a caged animal.

She swore it would never happen again. And, yet, here she was with no freedom of movement.

Add to this that her fiancé had arrived back after coffee with Brad disturbed and distracted. She had tried to lure him back into bed. But he was having none of it. He said he had a few calls to make and had locked himself in Brads' home office. When word came of the shooting, he had become even more agitated. After a few minutes he had returned to the office and made some more calls.

This period of inattention was going to stop, she decided. Nobody treated Fabiola Gonzales like this! She burst through the office door and confronted John Linden.

"*Juan. Ju* put down *tee* phone. Talk to me. *Que Pasa? Whas goin* on? Why *ju* so quiet? Brad, he *ees hokay. Ju* and I can take a drive around Montecito. I *wanna* show *ju tee* casas."

"Not now, Fabby," he replied. "There's more going on than just the attempt on Brads' life. I need to stay put until I hear back from a few people. Then we can go. Why don't you pack your stuff and go hang out with Mel."

"*Tha* woman. I *don tink* she *like* me. I *tink* she jealous," Fabiola said with a smile as she slowly wiggled her breasts and laid on the Charro accent.

"I doubt that's the case. She may envy your beauty, but Mel doesn't impress me as the jealous type. I think she likes you just fine. You just don't know each other well yet. Give it some time." The phone rang. Linden recognized the area code, but not the number. "Fabby, I've got to take this call. Let's talk later."

Turning her shoulder like a woman jilted by her lover, Fabiola stomped her foot, spun and left the room.

== ⊕ ==

Linden watched her leave. Shaking his head as he turned his attention towards the phone, he wondered what type of future he had with such a self-indulgent woman. She was beautiful and he was pretty sure he loved her. But he had outside responsibilities and she would just have to understand. Golf provided him his income— soon to be *their* income. Golf challenged his competitive nature. Golf completed him.

The world did NOT revolve entirely around Fabiola Gonzales.

Better clear that up sooner rather than later, he thought.

He answered the phone. "Hello."

"Is this John Linden?" the caller asked.

"Yes it is. Who's this?"

"Veronica Smalley. I'm returning your call."

"Oh, yes, thanks. There's been some excitement around here," he explained, "I almost forgot I called you."

The conversation lasted more than thirty minutes. Linden taking notes and asking questions. Art Smalley's widow doing most of the talking. Time and again, she expressed love for her deceased husband and expressed doubts about his suicide. "He just couldn't have killed himself; he loved life," she said more than once.

John agreed and expressed sympathy. Art had been a good agent and, more importantly, a good friend. He told her he was going to do some investigating on his own. Could she provide names and phone numbers of other family friends and contacts?

"You bet I can. Art had tons of friends," she said.

"I'm sure he did; he was that kind of guy."

After providing the names, Veronica asked, "Have you talked to Steven Ambrook yet?"

"Yes, I visited him the other day."

"How did he seem?"

"Real shook up but getting on with business."

"He was like a father figure to Art," she said quietly.

"I know Art respected him."

"Now, Tyler, that was a different story," she said.

"How so?"

"Art felt he wasn't qualified to run the company. They never saw eye to eye."

Linden absorbed this information and made a note to tell Brad about it.

He asked if there was anything else she could tell him.

"Well, I don't know if this is important or not," she began. "But Art kept all sorts of records at home—up in the attic. It seems to me if he did kill himself, it would have something to do with work. Wouldn't it?"

"Makes sense. Did the police ask you about the records?"

"The police, huh," she almost snickered. "They think it's a suicide, end of story. They have no desire to investigate. As far as they're concerned, Art was a depressed drunk who climbed up on a ladder and hung himself. Case closed."

Linden had heard that the local police had given the case very little energy. The suicide note had said it all and, apparently, they were happy. It was a shame, he thought. Art deserved a thorough investigation.

He asked Veronica, "You think I could get my hands on those records?"

"Sure, come on by. I'll have them ready for you."

He reached a point where he had no more questions. Could he call her back if he thought of anything else? She agreed and after thanking him for caring about Art, said goodbye…and then added almost as an after-thought, "Good Luck".

His next call was to Brad's cell phone. The call went directly to voicemail.

"Hey, pards, how you doing? I assume you're still with the police and that's why you can't answer your phone. No worries. I just wanted to let you know that I had a very interesting conversation with Art Smalley's widow, Veronica. She told me that Art had left several boxes of records in the attic. She also said that he had hinted at his job being in jeopardy." He knew he was talking fast—he always did to answering machines and voice mail, but he wanted to get it all in. Brad should know what was happening.

He continued with his message. "She said that he told her the family might have to cut back on spending. Told her that some of his players might have to cut back too. Things like that. She suggested I come by and get the boxes. The police showed no interest in them. She also thought I should call a few other players. She had Art's phone book and gave me their numbers. So that's what I'll be doing the next few hours until it's time to leave. Call me when you're finished with the police."

Linden was no investigator. How was he going to call fellow players and ask them if they'd noticed how much money they had lost recently? He couldn't just call and say, "Hi Jim. How you hitting 'em? Playing next week? Oh, by the way, are you as dumb as me and haven't looked at your tax returns or asset statements in several years?" Nope. That wasn't going to work.

He better tell them why he was calling. He opted for a more direct approach.

For his first call, he chose a young player named Justin Renacker. Justin was an up and coming star. Several top ten finishes the past year. Made lots of money. He was sure to win a major soon. Linden had played dozens of rounds with him. If anyone would be totally honest with him, Renacker would.

"Hello, Justin. It's John Linden. How you doing, buddy? Glad I could catch you. Got a minute for me?"

"Hey John, what's up?"

"I'm out in California looking at real estate and tuning up my game. How 'bout you?"

"Just chilling. Taking some time off; haven't touched the sticks for a few weeks."

Linden smiled, this kid was learning quickly. A golfer's got to rest his body; the professional season can be brutal on the back, neck and legs. "Good thinking. Took me five or six years to figure that out."

"I'm lucky; I've got you old veterans hanging around with your bad backs giving me advice."

Old? He'd show him 'old' at the next tournament when he blew his drives twenty yards past the kid. In the meantime, he'd make nice-nice.

"You dealt with Art Smalley at IFPG, didn't you?" Linden asked.

Renacker hesitated for a moment as if recalling a fond memory. "Yeah, poor guy. He was my manager for the past two years. I guess he was fighting some real nasty demons."

"Yeah it was a real tragedy. He was a good guy." Linden fought the urge to mention his recent conversation with Veronica. There would be ample time for that later. Instead, he continued with the main point of his call. "Hey, listen, the reason I'm calling is that I just found out that I've been losing money on my investments and IFPG never told me. I was wondering if you've checked your statements and tax returns lately?"

"I've got to tell you the truth, John. I don't get statements and I've never seen my tax returns." He paused, as if searching for the right words to justify his negligence. "You know how it is. We travel so much, I have all my mail sent to IFPG. They handle everything for me. All I know is that every time I ask for money, a check appears." He stopped and then asked, "Are you saying I should get more involved?"

"Maybe. Even if nothing's wrong, it's probably a good idea that you and I get more involved in our personal finances. Would you do me a favor and call whoever's managing you now and ask for a copy of your tax returns and a year to date asset statement? Tell them you're organizing your affairs and think it's a good idea to get copies for your personal files. Can you do that for me?

"Seems simple enough. I'll call 'em later," Renacker assured him.

"I hate to be pushy but could you call them right now? And then call me back and tell me what they have to say. I'd consider it a personal favor."

"Okay. I'll call you back in twenty minutes. But, hey, John you're going to owe me a for this."

"You got it. Now make the call. And, Justin...don't mention any of this call to IFPG. Tell them you were motivated by Art's death and thought you should get on top of your personal finances."

"Okay, got it."

"Thanks, Justin." He hung up.

Linden chuckled. The favor I owe him is to teach him the claw grip. Eventually, all the young guys will get the yips. When that happens to Renacker, I'll convince him to go to the claw. It'll save his career. And then we'll be even.

He made two more calls to fellow players. One thought he had seen his tax returns and they were okay. But he couldn't be sure. The other was like Renacker. Never seen them. Never asked about them. He had been assured by Art that his money was safe and secure. The one thing they did confirm was that their accounts were now handled by Tyler Ambrook. Linden decided to wait until he heard back from Justin before requesting that these guys call IFPG as well. A few minutes after finishing his third call, Linden's smart phone buzzed. Renacker's name showed on the display.

"John. It's Justin. I called IFPG. They told me that my account is now managed by Tyler Ambrook," he said. "He would need to authorize it before the information could be sent. He wasn't in but they said he would get back to me later this week. Sorry, man. I know you wanted the info today."

"That's okay. You did what you could. Let me know what Tyler has to say. I'm thinking about making a personal visit there on Tuesday or Wednesday. I'm going to get to the bottom of this. I'd like to know if you've been screwed, too, before I go in."

"Alright, I'll talk to you soon," Renacker said and signed off.

Swiveling around in the brown, leather chair, Linden put his phone down and looked out the window. It had turned into a beautiful afternoon. The morning fog had burned off when he wasn't looking and now the light shone brightly across the tops of avocado trees and danced through the canyon.

A hawk swooped into view—a red tail he surmised. A magnificent creature. Five foot wingspan, piercing eyes. The grace and beauty with which it maneuvered thru the jet stream overshadowed it's vicious, predatory nature. The bird circled, probably looking for lunch. Startled when the bird suddenly dove—undoubtedly, it had spotted some unsuspecting prey—Linden refocused his thoughts on the matter at hand.

It was strange, he thought, that IFPG didn't automatically send out PDF's of information when requested. Brad had led him to believe that all financial companies held scanned records for their clients. Why should they need authorization from the account manager for something so benign?

He looked at the clock. 2:45 p.m., time to take Fabby to the airport. Where was Brad? He wanted—no he *needed*—to discuss his conversations and growing suspicions with him before heading to the airport.

The call from Veronica Smalley had been especially interesting. He couldn't wait to get back to Orlando and go through those boxes.

The fact that the other golfers had been equally hands off with their finances surprised him. What a bunch of knuckleheads they all—including him—were! But the most intriguing thing he had learned was that they all were now managed by Tyler Ambrook.

He wondered if this was standard policy or if Tyler had been the only one available to take over Art's work load?

He was getting that same feeling he got before each of his marriages fell apart. It was the same feeling he got when he discovered that his ball was plugged in a sand trap. No relief. The next shot had to be played. A pit was forming in the bottom of his stomach.

It wasn't just the money.

It wasn't just Art Smalley.

He was a good guy but it was also the attempts on Brad's life. Too much was happening too fast. He needed some help sorting all of it out. He picked up the phone and called Brad again.

"Brad. It's almost three. I've got to leave soon if I'm going to catch the plane back to Orlando. Fabby's pissed at me. That woman is so…needy! Anyway, I've got a corporate outing tomorrow morning. Got to be there. If I don't see you before we leave, I need you to call me as soon as you can. I don't know what's going on, but it involves Tyler Ambrook and I'm going to confront the little prick. I want to talk to you first. Call me." And then as an afterthought he added, "That is if they ever let you go. You're not a suspect are you?" He chuckled at his own joke and hung up. He called out to Fabiola to get her stuff. It was time to go.

"*Juan. Mi* amor. I made a decision while *ju* were on *tee* phone," came the voice from the guest room. "I *wanna* come back here in a few days and do more research on our future home. Brad may not be able to make *tee* offer yet, but I can do my homework. What *ju tink*?"

What Linden really thought was that Fabby would be in the way at the Stephens house. He had told her she was crazy when questioning whether Mel liked her or not. But the fact was he wasn't sure that Mel did.

He had known Mel for several years. She was a stubborn person. She tended to form opinions about other people quickly. Once formed, she hardly ever changed her mind. He had sensed Mel's coldness towards Fabby the night before. He assumed Mel was just having a hard time putting up with houseguests on short notice. But maybe there was something more to it?

He knew Fabby could be difficult.

Maybe he had blinders on. Maybe Mel had seen something he hadn't. He made a mental note to talk to her about Fabiola soon. Couldn't hurt to have some female input, could it? Besides, he hated to thrust his fiancée on his friends and, perhaps, abuse their hospitality. He didn't want to be known as the ugly cousin who visited and then wouldn't leave.

"How about you come back in a few weeks. That will give Brad enough time to get our loan approved and to organize some good showings for you. We've got Hilton Head next week. You'll like the course. Harbour Town is a cool place. It's scenic and the weather should be fantastic," he assured her.

"*Hokay*. As long as I can come back soon. Now, we gotta go. I already put my bags in *tee* car." She smiled a wide, toothy smile.

She'd come back earlier.

Juan just didn't know it yet.

She planned to convince him that evening—after incredible sex. Neither Brad's misfortunes nor a stupid golf tournament were going to slow her down. She wanted her high end home and she wanted it now!

After saying farewell to Mel and the boys, John and Fabiola hopped in the car and drove slowly through the crowd assembled at the bottom of the long drive way. Cameras flashed while a reporter with a microphone in hand attempted to approach the moving vehicle. Linden flipped him off, rolled down the window and told him to move. "The guy must know the police are questioning Brad about the murder," he explained to Fabiola.

He smiled when he heard the reporter yell, "I hope you get the yips, you asshole!"

He stopped the car, rolled down the window and yelled, "Not with the claw, baby. They all go in." He rolled up the window and accelerated down the hill.

Brad had yet to call back.

32

AT FIRST, BRAD THOUGHT IT WAS A blessing that the police station was located immediately across the street from his office. In many ways, Santa Barbara was a quaint town

The drive "downtown" to be interviewed was, in fact, a mere two hundred yard walk across a paved parking lot. He'd go in. Sit down. Talk to his buddy, Espinoza, for a few minutes and be on his way.

At least, that's what he thought.

Four hours later, Espinoza and his supervisor, a female Lieutenant named O'hara, were still asking him pointed questions. O'hara wore cheap looking dark slacks, a green blouse, and black sneakers. All business; she wasn't going to win best dressed cop anytime soon.

Between her and Espinoza, they looked like an advertisement for an upcoming thrift store sale.

Her flaming red hair was cut short and she grinned in a lopsided way, but never smiled. She seemed intent on knowing Brad's every step the past two days. Espinoza tried on several occasions to wrap up the interview only to be shot down by his partner. She seemed to think Brad knew something and, by God, she was going to get it out of him.

She pressed him on business acquaintances and transaction details. She implied that he was involved in illegal activity. Drugs, gambling, prostitution, land swindles—what the hell was he involved in? There had to be a reason for the shooting. O'hara made it clear that she wasn't going to let him go home until she got to the bottom of it. Espinoza apologized several times to Brad when she was out of the room.

"It's okay, Raoul. Sometimes a loan takes longer to work through the bureaucracy as well. It is what it is," Brad said with a knowing frown.

Espinoza began to press him again on the Pear Blossom shooting. "Attempted murder doesn't happen very often in the real world. And when it happens twice in one week it doesn't take a rocket scientist to figure out that somebody wants you dead," Espinoza said in a conciliatory tone.

"You should've called us when it happened," O'hara added; scolding him like a child.

"Hey, I said I was sorry. I've never been shot at before. I didn't know what to do. For all I knew, it was an L.A. drive by shooting," Brad said defensively.

"Yeah, but still…." Espinoza said.

"No, 'but still', Raoul." He stared at his buddy and said, "Please don't treat me like an idiot! I thought it was a drive by. I feel bad about the decision I made and I realize that had I reported it immediately, Jim might still be alive." He paused and then added, "I get it."

"You have to admit, it is kinda strange that a guy gets shot at while driving and then witnesses a horrific accident and doesn't call the police," O'hara interjected.

Brad said nothing; just nodded his head slowly. He didn't really want to explain his rationale all over again.

"Okay, let's start from the beginning," Espinoza suggested. "Why were you in Las Vegas?"

Brad took a deep breath, and told them about the loan issues. He mentioned that Tyler Ambrook wasn't happy with his surprise visit. He went on to describe the subsequent events and then told them about the tax returns and asset statements. Although he hadn't picked up John's latest voice message yet, he included the mysterious death of Art Smalley in his summation.

"So, let me get this straight. They gave you freely, financial statements that showed that Linden had suffered massive losses. But you think they were hiding this information from him before?" O'hara said in a mocking manner. "That doesn't make any sense, Mr. Stephens. Just because something happened on your way back from Vegas doesn't mean it was tied into the events in Vegas. And it's certainly a big stretch to tie this in to a suicide in Orlando, isn't it?"

"I'm just telling you what happened and what John and I suspect, that's all. Take it or leave it." He shrugged.

Espinoza looked at his superior. "What do you think it all means?"

"It means someone tried and is possibly still trying to kill your friend here. But it doesn't necessarily add up that it's someone he just met for the first time in Las Vegas. Nor does it mean that this guy, Smalley, was murdered. Now does it?"

"Maybe the guy on the Pear Blossom followed Brad out to Vegas from here?" Espinoza suggested.

O'hara nodded. "I think we should be looking at local issues before we make this an international conspiracy." Turning to Brad she said, "I want you to go home tonight and wrack your brain for any reason why a local client, realtor, parent, or former friend would want to kill you. You think about it. We'll talk tomorrow."

Brad sighed, nodded and prepared to leave.

"And, oh, Mr. Stephens, if you have any other 'little personal secrets' you want to share with us, the earlier the better. Whoever tried to kill you today may not be done yet," O'hara said.

"What do you mean, 'little secrets'," Brad asked.

"You know. Like, who's Doris Anne? Maybe you've been laying the ol' log to her and now the husband found out? Stuff like that…." she let her voice trail off.

"I already told you, I don't know a Doris Anne. There are no elicit affairs," Brad said, his frustration breaking through. "I'll think about other business issues and past associations and let you know tomorrow. But, I'm telling you, I've already thought about it and the only conclusion I can come to is that it has something to do with the work I'm doing for John. I think this whole mess has something to do with IFPG." He looked at both of them, a bead of sweat beginning to form on his brow. He said quietly, "And I'll tell you another thing, it's beginning to bug the hell out of me!"

"IFPG? In Orlando? Listen to yourself. That company is a billion dollar company. It's located all the way across the frickin country. Why would they risk everything on a small town mortgage broker? Again, it just don't add up," O'hara said sarcastically, glancing from Espinoza to Brad and then back again.

"Still, I think we should send a guard out to Brad's house and provide protection until we figure this thing out."

O'hara nodded.

Brad shrugged.

Brad shook Espinoza's hand, avoided O'hara, collected his things and made the two hundred yard walk back to his office. The medical examiner and police had left hours ago, but yellow crime scene tape still blocked the front door. He had work to do. Under the circumstances, it could wait until Monday.

He called his partner, Donna, and discussed the killing. She was still in shock. She said she gave the whole office a few days off. The police assured her that unless they missed something, she would be able to have his office cleaned and disinfected in a few days. She had already contacted a company that specialized in such things. "How was he?" she asked. He explained the police theory to her.

"Well, we know it's not a past client," she said confidently. "No one has ever filed a grievance against you. Just the opposite. Everywhere I go in town, people compliment me on your performance. So that's not it. What about the other choices?"

"I don't know," he confessed.

Suddenly very tired, he shook his head and continued. "I'm going to head home, hug my wife—and the kids if they're there—pet the dog and try to forget about all this crap for one night. I still think it has something to do with John Linden's management company. But that's just me. The police don't seem to buy it. Anyway, have a good night and let's talk tomorrow. I guess we've got Johnson's funeral to think about."

"And the psychological trauma inflicted on the staff," she added.

"Yeah. That too. Stef was real shaken. I'll call her later. Have a good night…if you can." He pressed the end button and walked around the block to his car. A strange thought occurred to him. What if the killer was still hanging out, waiting for Brad to reappear? Espinoza had even said that the guy might not be done.

He quickened his pace. Arriving at the car without incident, he was about to unlock the front door when another thought popped into his head. What if the killer found the car and planted a bomb under it?

Happened all the time in the movies.

He froze for a moment and looked around. The scene seemed normal. His car was parked tightly between another BMW and a Toyota. He concluded that there was no way a person could get under his car from the front or rear. If the killer had come back and planted a bomb, he would've had to gain access from the street. It was a busy street. Legs dangling out from beneath a car would be noticed.

With minor trepidation, Brad opened the drivers' door. He grimaced as the handle popped.

Nothing happened.

Good.

Passed the first test.

He exhaled.

Now, the next test: Would the car blow up when he started it? Only one way to find out. He put the key in the ignition and turned it clockwise. Flinching as the engine started, he exhaled again. Still in one piece. Patting himself to insure he really *was* still in one piece, he chuckled nervously. "Jesus, I'm getting paranoid…. or, maybe I'm not?" Even paranoids have enemies, don't they?

He put the car in reverse, worked his way onto the road and then into traffic. It would be a fast drive home.

Brad's home was located on a fairly rural stretch of road. It was startling, therefore, to find several cars, vans and trucks parked at the base of his driveway.

The media had arrived and he had not been prepared.

Approaching slowly, Brad rolled down his window, pretended to be an innocent bystander (or by-driver?) and asked the first person he saw what was going on?

"There's been a murder in town. The guy who lives here was the target. We're waiting to interview him," a young woman dressed in a tight fitting black skirt answered. Everything about her said 'hungry for a story'. And her white tennis shoes, completely out of sync with her outfit said, 'I'll hop a fence to get it'.

Brad nodded his head as if agreeing that the reporters were doing a good job, said thanks, and tried to inch past the waiting crew.

"Hey! That's the guy! That's Brad Stephens," a tall reporter with bushy blonde hair and golden tan yelled.

Suddenly, bright lights came on and several dozen bodies surrounded Brad's car.

Shouting questions and holding microphones in front of them like fishing poles, most of the news people asked the same thing: "Mr. Stephens. Why would someone want to kill you?" And, "Do you have any idea who the gunman might be?" Feeling the need to push past them and suddenly remembering what it looked like when Bernie Madoff went to court, Brad yelled at the top of his lungs, "No Comment", rolled up his window, waved the reporters away from his vehicle and drove up the driveway.

Espinoza stood twenty feet further up the driveway, talking to a uniformed officer.

"Thought it might get busy out here," Espinoza said to his startled friend. "I heard from sources that the Los Angeles media had found out you were the actual target. Figured it couldn't hurt to come out and make sure my guy got here before you." He smiled and pointed to the tall, blonde policeman Brad had run into at his office. "This is officer McNabb. McNabb, this is Mr. Stephens." They nodded at each other.

"McNabb will make sure no deranged killer with an AK-47 breaks in to your house while you're snoozing." Espinoza winked at both of them.

"Might keep the press away too," Brad said with a grin. "How come you didn't warn me about the press, Raoul?"

"You left in such a huff, I didn't want to add to your woes and besides until I got here, I wasn't sure there would be so many of them. Anyway, I've got to get home. Have a good night—if you can. McNabb will take good care of you."

Mel greeted Brad with a big kiss and an even bigger glass of Jack Daniels. Rufus ran up to his owner and licked Brad's hand. Brad bent to pet him and, before he knew it, the Rottweiler was licking his face and cleaning his ears.

"Yuk!" Mel exclaimed. "You better go in and wipe that slobber off."

"What, you don't like my slimy ears?"

She smiled and pointed towards the closest restroom.

Upon his return, he settled in with his drink and told Mel about the police interview.

When he finished, she said, "Surely Raoul doesn't think you had anything to do with the shooting, or that we're really in danger?"

"Nah. I don't think so. He's a good cop. He just wants to get to the truth. And I think he needs to avoid showing favoritism. His Lieutenant, O'hara —what a piece of work, by the way—thinks that I pissed somebody off and that person is seeking revenge. She even asked me if I'm having an affair with a woman named Doris Anne?"

"Is there something you want to tell me?" Mel joked, trying to lighten the mood.

He chuckled.

"You keep me busy enough. I can't imagine trying to juggle two women at one time. I told her the only Doris Anne I know is your deceased aunt. She wasn't too happy about that. It would be convenient for O'hara if there was another woman."

"Well, let's not worry about that tonight. John and Fabiola left around four. He wants you to call him. Probably left you a message on your phone. Have you checked?"

"Shit! I meant to pick up those messages earlier."

Brad had seen a few message alerts on his phone before he called Donna. He was about to check them when thoughts of the killer—and the possibility of a bomb in his car—had consumed him. Not wanting to admit to Mel that he was concerned about a follow up attack, he was happy to change the subject.

"I was just about to check," he said. "If there's a message from John, I'd love to hear what he has to say; he was going to make some calls about his finances."

"What's wrong with his finances?" Mel asked.

"It's a long story, but it looks like IFPG has been doing a shitty job with his investments."

"Does he have enough money to buy the house Fabiola wants?"

"I think so, but I'm not sure. That's what we're trying to figure out."

"I hope so. If not, that woman is going to be *really* pissed."

Brad nodded. "Yeah, John said the same thing. Anyway, I'm going to go check the messages. I'll be right back. If it's John, I'm screwed. He'll be in the air another few hours and it will be really late when he lands."

"I can't imagine it's an emergency," Mel said. "If it were that important, he would've cancelled his return trip."

"I suppose you're right. I'll check them anyway." He yawned, rubbed his stomach and said, "I've got a feeling that I'm going to bed early tonight; I'm tired as hell. It's been a long day."

Mel came close to him, gave him a big kiss on the lips and hugged him tight. "I'm so glad you're okay. I don't know what the boys and I would do without you."

"And Rufus. Don't forget the dog." He pointed to the big Rott sleeping peacefully in one of the three beds they kept scattered throughout the house.

She smiled.

"What's for dinner?" he asked.

"I was going to make this great new meatloaf. I saw the recipe on the Food Channel, but now that it's so late, what do you say to a salad, another stiff drink, and some hot sex? You know what they say about facing death, don't you?"

"Enlighten me."

"It heightens the sexual experience," she said with a sly smile.

"For you or for me?"

She grinned. "I've got a good feeling about both of us."

"Terrific. I won't argue with that!" They continued to hug and he added, "You know, technically, someone has tried to kill me twice."

"That's right; well, then this should be twice as good." She pushed away, slapped him on his bottom and strode towards the kitchen.

He watched her leave, admiring her slim, athletic body. He was a lucky man in so many ways; not the least of which was that he had dodged her new concoction for a night: Meatloaf.

His thoughts turned to the phone messages. He took a seat in his home office and listened to both of Linden's calls. His buddy had done good work, he thought. Sounds like Veronica Smalley really opened up.

He called Linden's cell phone and left a message, confirming he received the new information. He said he was really tired and would think about Smalley and the other players tonight. Would call John in the morning. He hung up and took a sip of his Jack.

If Art hadn't killed himself, was his death related to IFPG and John's massive financial losses? He'd have to think about that some more. He'd call John first thing in the morning and go over it. In the meantime, he hoped to sleep soundly tonight; he really didn't want to see the faceless nemesis chasing him in his dreams.

33

No such luck.

He dreamt.

Like so many before, the day was bright and sunny. The type of day you take your son fishing or play catch in the park.

Instead, he was walking in the woods; minding his own business. Not harming a soul. Turning over rocks and stones; searching for lucky four leaf clovers; thinking he really should be fishing on such a fine day. He felt desperate to obtain some good luck and almost obsessed with finding a pot of gold. From behind a nearby tree a figure carrying a rifle emerged.

The figure pointed the gun at him and fired. The first shot winged him in the shoulder. It hurt like hell. He ran, looking back from time to time. He could see the figure moving slowly, methodically after him. No sense of urgency. The dark figure appeared to be pulling currency from his pockets and tossing it into the air; laughing. His car was parked by the end of the trail. If he could make it back to the car without getting shot he was certain he'd be safe. He continued to flee from his pursuer; making a bee line for his car. Thankfully, the parked vehicle came into view.

He quickened his strides, glancing over his shoulder intermittently. The figure was gone. Blood trickled from his wound and he realized once again how badly it hurt. As he approached the parked car, the pain intensified. Fumbling for his keys, he unlocked the driver's side door—still scanning the woods for his pursuer. Failing to see the figure, he breathed a sigh of relief and slid into the driver's seat. The motor turned over but would not start. Panic began to set in.

Pounding the steering wheel, he slowly raised his eyes and glanced into the rearview mirror. Sitting in the back seat, rifle in his hand, sat the faceless figure. The figure raised the gun. He shouted at him, "What the fuck do you want? What have I done to you?" And in a moment of absolute clarity, he realized that his life was over. The gunman pulled the trigger....

Waking with a start, heart palpitating, drenched in sweat, Brad reached for the towel lying on the floor. Wiping his face, he took a deep breath and rolled over and stared at the clock radio sitting on the nightstand beside his bed.

3:30 a.m. *Damn,* same time as last night. And...the night before.

"Shit!" he muttered quietly to himself, his eyes towards the heavens. He shook his head slowly. He raised his left hand and rubbed his reddened eyes. Haven't I been through enough already?

He needed his sleep; he needed this thing to be over with.

It was a dream after all; nocturnal illusion. But based on his recent brush with death, what he was learning about Art Smalley and dealing with Fabiola, maybe the dream had substance?

Hell, maybe this was Truckee catching up with him?

Whatever it was, he vowed then and there to get to the bottom of this mess—even if it killed him.

With that, he calmly rose from the bed, wiped his face again and went in to his study. He turned on the TV, tuned to the Golf Channel and hunkered down to a re-run of Tin Cup.

It was going to be a long night.

34

WAKING GROGGY AND DISHEVELLED Tuesday morning, Brad walked quietly to the kitchen to make a cup of coffee. He really needed the caffeine.

He *really* needed to wake up.

Not only had the bad dream returned, but this time, his tormentor had the beginnings of a face. Much to his amazement, the faceless figure had first appeared as the man Stefanie described to the police—obese with a limp and a heavy beard—and then, by the time he got to the car, the face had morphed into Tyler Ambrook. Maybe it was beginning to make sense?

While the coffee brewed he listened to John's messages again. Checking his watch to confirm that it was, in fact, 7:00 A.M. Pacific Standard Time—10:00 A.M. on the east coast—he called Linden's cell phone. Thankfully, he answered on the third ring.

"Good to hear from you, buddy," Linden said loudly as wind whistled through his phone. "I'm on the course playing in a corporate outing so I've got to keep this short. I told the other players in my group that I was expecting an important call. So they're cool with this one interruption."

He then went on to tell Brad again the details of his talk with Veronica Smalley and about the calls he had made to the other three golfers. He indicated that he was going to get the boxes from her and that he would call Brad if anything jumped out at him. If not, he was going to ship the boxes out to Brad and have him go through them.

Finally, he said he was pretty pissed about his finances. The more he thought about it on the plane ride back to Orlando, the angrier he got. He wasn't going to wait long to confront Tyler Ambrook.

Brad wished him good luck and asked him to keep him in the loop. Before he signed off, Brad warned, "I've been thinking about this a lot too—especially because, apparently, somebody is trying to kill me. You need to be careful. If this is related to IFPG and if they're coming after me, they may come after you too."

He heard a deep exhale on the other end and then Linden replied, "Shit, I hadn't thought of that."

"Just watch your back, that's all I'm saying."

"Gotcha."

Tuesday afternoon was lunch and spades for Brad and his friends. Poor Man's bridge they call it; the favorite game of hardened criminals in prison. At least, if anyone in his group ever got arrested, they'd be able to socialize. Or so the joke went.

Brad found it a great distraction and something he looked forward to all week. They had started the tradition out of need for cheap, competitive camaraderie. Now it was fully ingrained. Like old Italians playing cards around the local Trattoria.

The game had been scheduled for noon at Brad's house. Just because some lunatic killed a co-worker at his office the day before, and just because he was under protective watch, was no reason to cancel the game.

Steve Zindo arrived first.

"Brad, buddy, how you doing?" Zindo asked in a soft voice. He entered the house wearing blue jeans, black tennis shoes, an old, torn sweater and scraggly baseball cap. To the outside world, the multi-millionaire could be a hermit. "I heard there was some trouble at work yesterday. You made the front page," he said with a grin, but with true concern in his voice.

"Glad to hear I'm so popular."

"You've even got your own police protection I see." He pointed to McNabb who was standing on the front lawn conferring with another young officer; probably his shift replacement.

"Go big or go home, I always say," Brad said with gusto.

Brad knew Zindo tended to downplay situations. To him, life was constant theatre. He appreciated it, but he tried to avoid other people's drama. For him to even show minor interest in Brad's situation was a significant thing. "What's up with the two reporters stationed at the bottom of the driveway?" he asked.

"I guess they decided to hover each evening until I give them an exclusive."

"Blood sucking leeches! That's what they are. They're just out for a sensational story. They don't care about the truth. They'll pester you until you confess to killing the guy in your office while wearing Mel's panties! That's the only way they'll be happy! Tell them to get the hell off your property! You want me to go tell them?"

Apparently, Zindo, former multi-national C.E.O. had had a bad experience with the press. Brad was curious about the details, but wouldn't push. Zindo would tell the story in due time. He always did.

Brad assured him that everything was cool. Espinoza had placed a guard down the driveway and Brad had given the press no information. He patted Zindo on the back and suggested that they discuss their strategy for the upcoming Spades match.

"Calm down, pards. I need you focused on cards; we need to beat these guys again. It's time for a Stephens/ Zindo victory."

"You're right; I tend to get worked up," he said with a wry smile. And then added, "I'm Lebanese, what can I say. We run hot."

A few minutes later, their opponents arrived. Erik Bonderman came in first. Heavyset with dark features it was almost as if he were trying to accentuate his ample belly by wearing a white Mexican wedding shirt two sizes too small.

His partner, Ray Tonkling, on the other hand, was fit and firm. A contractor by trade, he usually chose blue jeans and a tee shirt—unless it was a formal occasion, in which case he ditched the tee shirt in favor of an un-tucked button down. He too, was dark complexioned. Taller than Erik by two inches, he had chosen to wear an Oakland Raiders hat for today's match.

Unlike Bonderman who entered the house with a glowing smile, Ray was all business. Spades was a sacred game to him. He was there to win.

He frowned, almost growled, when he shook Brad's hand. "Hope you brought money. We're going to kick your little bitch, asses."

"Bring it on," Brad responded. "I need some good competition. Lord knows you didn't give us any last week." They both grinned.

"What's up with the reporters we had to drive through?" Erik asked.

"Ticks on the butts of society!" Zindo screamed from the front room as he poured himself a glass of wine. "They want to frame Brad for murder. Or, at least, dig up some dirt on him so that the story will be interesting. I'm telling you, before the press is through, Brad Stephens might be perceived as a cross dressing lunatic bent on self-destruction…or some such nonsense!"

"Hey you guys know I've been trying to give up the cross dressing," Brad joked. "It's hard, but I think I've got it licked." He then reached beneath his waistband and pulled out the top of his boxers. "See. Men's underwear! I'm cured!"

They all laughed and pulled four chairs to the card table.

"Seriously, dude. Why are there two reporters down at the bottom of your driveway?" Ray asked again.

"Somebody tried to shoot me yesterday."

"No shit!"

Zindo slapped the table. "Where you been, Ray? Don't you watch the news?"

Shocked, Ray turned to Erik. "Did you hear about this?"

The big man shook his head. "We live in Ventura," he said as if that explained their lack of connection with the media.

"Some asshole waltzed into Brad's office and shot a guy sitting at Brad's desk; thought it was Brad," Zindo said.

"Did they catch the guy?" Erik asked.

Brad shook his head. "Not yet, but they've got a decent description of him and the police are on it."

"Why would they want to shoot you? You're not *that* bad at spades," Ray joked nervously.

"Why shoot me?" Brad shrugged. "I don't know, Ray. I'm working on a few theories, but don't have anything concrete yet."

Zindo's eyes brightened, he raised his eyebrows and grinned. "What theories? Come on. Share. Tell me what you're thinking. Maybe I can help."

"It's no big deal," Brad began. "And since when do you care? You're the guy who says 'Save the Drama for your Mama'."

"No, no, no. You've got me all wrong. I care deeply about my friends. I just don't always show it."

"Besides, he loves violence and intrigue," Erik added. "His favorite show is 'Women Who Kill'."

"Never heard of it," Brad said.

"It's on some obscure cable channel."

"Yeah, and don't forget '50 Ways to Kill Your Lover", I dig that show too." Zindo said, nodding. "Now tell me about your theories."

Brad told the group about Linden's financials, IFPG's stonewalling and Art Smalley's hanging. He tried to skip over the drive-by shooting on the Pear Blossom, but Zindo caught him.

"So this is the second time they tried to kill you? Why didn't you tell me?

"Same reason as the police; I thought it was an isolated incident."

"Interesting," Zindo said. He raised his hands as if praying and touched the forefingers to his chin. "I think you're on the right track. If IFPG has been stealing John's money, they wouldn't want you to find out about it…and if it was too late, and you did find out, that would give them reason to eliminate you."

"Yep. That's what I'm beginning to think."

"But what about the manager?" Zindo said.

"Art Smalley?"

"Yeah, that guy. He probably did hang himself you know. The police don't usually get those things wrong." He took a sip of wine and then continued. "I had a stock broker in Louisiana once who lost so much money he shot himself in the head." Zindo put a finger to his temple and pulled an imaginary trigger.

Brad thought about it for a minute before replying. "Did the guy shoot himself in front of witnesses?"

"Yes."

Brad nodded. "And did he lose his own money as well?"

"Yes. How did you know that?"

He smiled. "I didn't, but I've been thinking about this a lot lately. Being a financial guy myself, I guess I could see committing suicide if I lost all my money too. But I can't see doing it just because your investments up to a certain point were bad. That's part of the risk of investing. If you don't have the stomach for losses, don't get in the business."

Zindo grinned. "You're starting to sound like the detective I saw on TV the other day. This woman murdered her husband…."

They all rolled their eyes as Zindo described an episode from one of his murder shows.

Antsy to play, Ray shuffled the cards loudly and prepared to deal. "I'm glad you're safe Brad; now let's play the game."

"I think Steve's right," Erik said, ignoring Ray. "These folks could still be after you. Do you have protection at the house?"

"Yes. There's a guard around here somewhere and my friend, Sergeant Raoul Espinoza will be coming around from time to time, until this whole thing settles down."

"Good; in that case, I feel safe," Erik said. "Now let's play."

Cards were dealt and play began. An hour later, Brad and Zindo emerged triumphant. Unable to curb his enthusiasm, Zindo rose, slapped the deck on the table and declared, "We own you boys. You're our bitches!"

Mel had been gardening while they played the first game. Taking off her gloves as she entered the room, she greeted the guys.

She allowed Zindo to pour her a glass of wine. She raised it in toast. "Boys, today is a great day," she began as if it were a great oratory. "My husband escaped death yesterday and from what I could hear outside, he has defeated the cross dressing demons that have plagued him for so long." She stopped, waiting to see if her joke hit its mark. It did. "And as an added treat, I have a wonderful new recipe from the Food Channel I cooked for you fine gentlemen. Meatloaf. I made it this morning. I have a fresh spinach salad for you too."

She looked at the men. "This should be the healthiest lunch any of you have had in a long time."

"Beautiful!" Zindo exclaimed. "You might not have noticed Mel but I've lost ten pounds since I saw you last. This new gal I'm dating has me eating healthier and exercising more. It's great. As long as I follow her diet, I get laid!"

"I guarantee this is healthy. You should have some good sex tonight. How 'bout you boys? Does meatloaf and salad sound good to you?" she asked, looking specifically at Ray and Erik.

They both agreed it sounded great. Brad had reservations, but Mel seemed confident, so what the hell. Who cared if it tasted like cardboard? The men would understand. It wasn't as if they were gourmets. These were guys who put ketchup on spaghetti. Food wasn't an event with these guys, it was an inconvenient necessity.

They opened another bottle of wine and enjoyed their lunch outside in the sun. All agreed that the meatloaf was wonderful; moist and flavorful. How did she bake it? Erik and Ray really wanted to know. Brad was duly impressed. Mel explained the recipe point by point as if she were a famous chef. She went into the kitchen to retrieve some of the materials used. She wanted to give them the visual.

"The original recipe called for a full cup of bread crumbs," she explained. "But I didn't have any so I improvised."

Uh,oh! Mel and improvising don't go together well, Brad thought. But the meal was delicious and everyone seemed to enjoy it. Maybe she was becoming a better cook?

"Hey, listen Brad," Zindo said as he gathered his things to leave an hour later. "I'm serious about helping. Just let me know if there's anything I can do." He walked a few steps and then stopped. He turned and said, "And I think you and Linden should be careful. If this guy Tyler Ambrook is as much of an asshole as you say, he could be dangerous."

Brad nodded. "I just hope we get to the bottom of it soon."

"Me too," he said. "Thanks for the food, Mel," he called out, and strode joyfully towards his car. He stopped and waved the fifteen bucks he'd won towards and Erik and Ray. "See you next week, suckers."

"Yeah, enjoy your little victory." Ray said.

"We'll get you next week," Erik added.

They said goodbye to Brad and gave Mel a kiss and then drove away.

== ⊕ ==

Mel threw her arm around Brad's waist. "I love those guys," she said as she sat down on the couch beside her husband.

"They love you too," he said.

"And I'll tell you, after being around Fabiola so much lately, it's nice to have some 'normal' visitors."

Brad gave her comment no energy. Instead he said, "Your meatloaf was a big hit. Everyone enjoyed it."

"I'm so glad. You know I really work hard on these things. This one, though, threw me a curve when it called for so many bread crumbs and so much olive oil."

"Why?"

"It seemed like a lot of olive oil and I didn't have bread crumbs so I used bran flakes," she paused. "Think the boys will notice?"

Brad shook his head and put his hand to his forehead. "I guess time will tell; but that's not a good combination."

She smiled, but slowly, a look of concern came over her. "I hope I didn't overdo it," she said.

"Again, time will tell."

His cell phone rang. He answered it on the third ring.

"Hey, buddy, what's up?" Linden asked on the other end of the line. "I just got done playing golf with three great guys. I'm on my way over to Art Smalley's house. I'm going to pick up those boxes."

"I thought you were doing that tomorrow?" Brad said.

"So did I. But one of the guys I played with today, Mike O'Flaherty, told me he was flying back to L.A. tonight on his private plane. I asked him if he would drop these boxes off for me in Santa Barbara. He said it was a hassle—and would cost him a few thousand bucks in fuel and time—but he would do it if I promised to be his Pro-Am partner at Sherwood in October. I said yes."

"Okay. But are you going to look through them first?"

"You know me. Hey, I'm no financial genius. The more I thought about it, the more I realized that if there's complicated financial data in those boxes, I won't be able to read it. I wouldn't know my ass from a hole in the ground when it comes to that stuff. It'd be like you hitting a fairway in a hurricane."

"Alright, I catch your drift. Where will the boxes be and when can I pick them up?"

"Terminal A. Special Handling. After ten a.m. tomorrow morning. I'll make sure your name is all over them."

"Sounds good. I'll call you tomorrow after I've had a chance to go through them." Then Brad asked the standard golfers question:. "How'd your round go today?"

"Fairways and Greens, pards," Linden replied smugly. "Shot one off the course record. Missed a putt on 16 or would've had it. Anyway it was enough to impress O'Flaherty and get him to do us this favor."

"Sounds like you're on form."

"Yep. My putting is out of this world."

"If you do say so yourself."

"What's your point?"

"Just keep it up; you may need to make a lot of money with that putting soon."

Silence. And then, "Oh yeah, thanks for reminding me. Talk to you later."

Brad hung up, a slight gurgling beginning in his stomach.

Hmmm…bran and olive oil?

35

"WHAT DO YOU MEAN THEY want more information?" Linden shouted as Brad moved the phone away from his ear..

The way he sounded, you'd think Linden just missed a one-foot putt to win the Masters. "We've given them everything I could get from IFPG," Linden said when Brad called him Wednesday morning before heading to the airport to pick up the boxes.

"Sorry buddy, the underwriter wants me to put together a regressive graph of income earned and then collate it with anticipated retention after taxes."

"What the fuck does that mean?"

"It means she questions the consistency of your earning ability and if she's going to approve the loan, she needs some bullshit graph in the file to cover her ass."

Brad could almost hear Linden smile on the other end.

"Lenders always need more information, John," Brad continued. "Always. Don't take it personally. It's their way of proving they did adequate due diligence."

"You know how hard it was just to get my tax returns and other statements. Now they want a breakdown of my earnings, tournament by tournament…what the fuck? How am I supposed to get that?"

"Calm down. I'll talk to the underwriter and find out exactly what she wants. I'm sure we can provide it. Hang in there, we're just beginning the Grand Inquisition."

Loan approval in what was being called the "New Normal" U.S. economy was rarely given without a fight and, like so many things in life, was rarely given unconditionally.

Once granted in this atmosphere, the recipient was expected to appreciate the lenders' decision and move forward. Do whatever the lender wants and get on with it. The ends would justify the means. Solid advice. Sadly, Linden was having none of it.

Brad had taken Johns' loan to a respectable, but unbelievably picky, regional bank. This bank could issue any kind of loan it pleased. It did not rely on the government to purchase the loan after the loan was made. In exchange for this service, the bank was going to make Lindens' life a living hell.

The message from the bank was: "You better really want to borrow this money…and you better really intend to pay it back…because we're going to make you jump through so many hoops, it would be a waste of time unless you really needed the money."

John did, in fact, need the money. Fabiola had made it clear that Linden would see no action unless a new home was purchased. John liked sex, ergo, he wanted a new home.

Repressing his irritation, Linden sighed and said, "Okay, I get it; they're going to make me suffer before making the loan. What can I do to help?"

"Get me a list of all the tournaments you played in the past two years," Brad began. "Indicate how much money you collected at the end of each tournament—minus travel, management expenses, food and accommodations."

"My tax returns should show that," he said, his blood beginning to boil once again.

"I know. I know. Let me break it down for the underwriter and explain how your arrangement with IFPG works. Okay?"

"Don't tell them about my losses. They'll think I don't follow my money."

"You don't."

"*I* know that. And *you* know that, but *they* don't know that."

"They're going to see your losses, John. It's all over your tax returns and asset statements. The point is, however, despite those losses, you are still earning more than enough money to qualify. We just have to play their game."

Lending is predicated on four basic tenets, income, assets, credit and collateral. Residential lenders had done a good job throughout the 1980's and 1990's keeping these elements in balance. Suddenly, beginning in 2000, the formula fell out of whack.

For various reasons, standards became very lax. Millions of borrowers received loans they shouldn't have and the world's economies were now suffering under the weight of massive foreclosures and bankruptcies.

To Brad, lending was easy. Start with character and then apply the other elements. J.P. Morgan had said it best: "A man I do not trust could not get money from me on all the bonds of Christendom."

CHARACTER! Where was it in today's lending system? It certainly wasn't encased in some Geek's credit score formula.

Character was the couple whose home value was upside down but they still made the payments. Character was the guy who lost his job but still tried to make good all his debts. Character was the working single mother who cared for and nourished her children.

Character could not be bought; it was possessed.

And no computer model could ever adequately assess its existence. That's why guy's like Brad used to exist; to be advocates for the borrower's character.

Today, people with solid ethics and good character were being treated like criminals and being denied loans because their credit scores were too low. In its zest to weed out bad borrowers and predatory lenders, the system had taken a wrong turn.

Mr. J.P. Morgan would roll over in his grave if he witnessed these current atrocities.

"You think I'll be okay?" Linden Asked

"Look, they've already given you conditional approval. At some level, they know you're good for the loan. The underwriter probably plays golf. He knows you always finish in the top ten and have many good years ahead of you. He just needs to fill the file with statistical information to justify his existence and reinforce his basic beliefs. Don't worry about it," Brad said. "But do get me the spread sheet ASAP."

"I'll have Hank work on it. He was at all the tourneys. He knows what I made because he made 10% of my gross." Brad could hear him exhale. "Man, I thought this was going to be a slam dunk."

"I know. Don't stress out. Take a deep breath. We'll get you thru this process. Why do you think Stef calls me the 'magician'?"

"Yeah, yeah, I know, you pull rabbits out of your hat. But I'll tell you what, buddy. If I don't get approved for this loan and if I can't buy Fabby the house she wants…you'll be a whole different kind of magician."

"How's that?"

"Fail and Fabiola will leave me. And then my damn sex life will disappear."

"We wouldn't want that," Brad said with a nervous chuckle, beginning to feel some pressure for the first time. "Okay! Got your point. Now send me that income analysis and I'll do my abracadabra thing."

36

SOLDIER, FIRST CLASS, KEN HOLLYFIELD had slept fitfully Tuesday night.

Consistent with Stefanie's description, Hollyfield was, indeed, a big man. Not necessarily fat, but big boned and heavy-set. Contrary to what she described to the forensic artist, however, he did not have a beard and although heavy, was not obese. He had discarded the fake beard and had removed the additional padding from under his shirt shortly after leaving Brad's office. Despite his bulk, Hollyfield was fairly agile. The limp had been faked as well.

Sleep—even in the best of times—had always been difficult for him. The restlessness he experienced last night, however, had little to do with normal issues. He had been contacted by Von Eisenlow early in the evening.

The conversation had not gone well.

Von Eisenlow had informed him that another soldier would arrive Wednesday morning. Hollyfield was to pick him up, discuss local logistics and develop a plan to kill

Stephens. Failure was not an option. The commander had made that very clear.

Hollyfield had been following Stephens for several days. He had seen the reporters who had been stationed at the bottom of the driveway for the past few days and he now knew that Stephens had around-the-clock police protection. Getting to him a second time wasn't going to be easy.

"I have faith in you, Ken," Von Eisenlow had said. "We have come too far and we are too close to our destiny. We need the support of our benefactor to accomplish our goals. And for whatever reason, he wants Stephens dead."

"Yes sir," was all Hollyfield could say.

On the one hand, he was glad that the commander was sending a partner. On the other, it was obvious that he had utterly failed his mission. This would affect his standing in the Sons for Sovereign Sacrifice. This would affect his self esteem. Most importantly, however, if left unchecked, this would affect his final pay check!

He had screwed up. Sure. But it was an understandable mistake. Wasn't it? How was he supposed to know that some other guy would be sitting at Stephen's desk?

As far as Hollyfield was concerned, he had carried out the assignment as instructed. He shot the guy sitting in Brad Stephen's chair; in Brad Stephen's office; at the designated time that Brad Stephens was supposed to be there. Hollyfield resolved to argue his case vigorously before Von Eisenlow cut his share.

He showered, read the local paper—not surprisingly, Johnson's murder was still the front page headline—and drove to the airport to pick up his new partner.

He watched the plane land, and with renewed confidence, approached his new ally, Bobby "One Eye" McCoy.

Standing six foot two and weighing a mere hundred and seventy pounds, McCoy had come about his nickname the old fashioned way, *He Earned It*. While hunting birds as a young man, McCoy had tripped and shot himself in the eye.

Now, fifteen years later, he wore a black patch over the dead socket. To him, it was a badge of valor. Hollyfield recognized him immediately.

"Hey, 'one eye', how you doing?" Hollyfield said, extending his hand.

"Not bad, not bad at all," McCoy mumbled, shaking his friends' hand. "What's going on, Ken? I was rousted in the middle of training and told to high-tail my ass out to Santa Barbara and join you in an operation."

Hollyfield sighed, rubbed his face and stared McCoy directly in his good eye. "I was sent out here to neutralize a threat to our organization. I failed and now the target will be harder to get."

"Who is he?"

"That's not important right now; I'll tell you when we get in the car," he said, looking around to make sure nobody was overhearing their conversation.

"Do you have a plan?"

"Yep."

"Good, let's get this done and get the hell out of here." McCoy looked around the airport and the parking lot. "I can tell I'm not going to like it here; everything's too neat." He smiled and punched Hollyfield in the shoulder

Hollyfield informed McCoy of his plan when the two of them got into his rented sedan. "It's pretty simple," he began. "I went over to Kinko's and had some business cards printed up for you and me. They're official looking and they say we're detectives from Ventura."

"Ventura? I thought we was in Santa Barbara?" McCoy said.

"We are. But I thought it would be better to make us come from out of the district. Ventura is thirty or forty miles south of here and I think it would make sense that two detectives from that neck of the woods joined the investigation. By the time anyone figures it out, Stephens will be dead."

McCoy chuckled. "I always knew you were the smart one."

Hollyfield took the compliment with a smile and nodded smugly. "I got these fake badges too. Look real, don't they?" He opened his jacket and showed McCoy a brass shield that said 'Detective'. It hung over his inside pocket. "Found them at the army surplus store in town."

"You've been busy."

"Yep. The commander wants this guy dead. I messed up the other day," he said with a shrug as if it were no big deal. "Anyway, here's your business card and shield, Detective McCoy."

"I feel so ooh-ficial."

"Let's head over to my hotel room, get you cleaned up and dressed properly and go get us Brad Stephens."

"Amen, brother."

He put the car in gear and headed for the hotel. Hollyfield had pasted a picture of Brad Stephens to the dashboard. There would be no mistaken identity this time.

At nine thirty, Hollyfield and McCoy took off for the Stephens house. Given the events of Monday, Hollyfield assumed there would be a policeman posted at the property. Rather than going straight to the house, he drove to a nearby ridge and parked the car. Across the canyon, he could see the driveway and the front of the house.

"What are we doing over here, boss?" McCoy asked.

"Reconnaissance. We need to see what's going on at the enemy's camp before we strike," Hollyfield said with a wink. He brought out a pair of cheap binoculars and focused them on the house.

After a few moments, he turned to his partner. "Well, I've got good news and bad news. The good news is that Stephens' BMW is parked in the driveway."

"What's the bad news?"

"A police cruiser is right next to it."

"Damn!" McCoy exclaimed. "What now?"

"We wait and see if anything changes."

== ⊕ ==

They didn't have to wait long. Ten minutes later, a young officer exited the house, got in the cruiser and backed down the driveway.

"Hell, it might be our lucky day," Hollyfield said, handing McCoy the binoculars. "Take a look at that."

McCoy held the apparatus to his one good eye and stared at the departing cruiser.

"Where's he going?"

"I don't know. Getting donuts, maybe?" Hollyfield said.

"Or maybe it's a change in shifts?"

The big man shrugged. "You know, ol one eye, you might be right. I bet that kid was guarding the house all night long and now his time is up. Quick, let's get over there before the new guard arrives."

They drove the short distance to the house, checked it out again from above. No sign of a new cop; Stephens' BMW still in place.

Hollyfield glanced at this partner. "All systems 'Go'," he said, giving the thumbs up sign. "Check your gun; make sure the silencer is in place."

McCoy pulled the Beretta 9mm from its holster. "Snug as a bug in a rug," he said, screwing the suppressor a bit tighter. "You sure Stephens is here?" he asked.

"Why would his car be parked out front if he wasn't there? Now remember, if anybody in the house gives us any trouble, don't hesitate to take them out. The commander says we are to use extreme prejudice."

McCoy grinned. "Got it. About time we did some military shit."

37

INSIDE THE HOUSE, MEL STOOD IN the kitchen, a mug of strong coffee in her hands.

She knew Brad wasn't home, that was no surprise. She was surprised, however, when Officer McNabb had informed her that his watch was over and that a new officer would replace him shortly. Her surprise turned to concern when he answered his radio and then turned to address her.

"There's been a major traffic accident in town, mam," he began. "All units have been instructed to respond. My replacement won't be here for a while."

She blew on her coffee and sighed. Suddenly feeling disappointed and vulnerable, she asked McNabb if he could stay until his replacement arrived.

The officer shook his head. "Sorry, mam. I've been instructed to get back to the station and sign myself out. With the current budget problems, they don't want any of us working overtime."

"But...."

"Don't worry, I'm sure you guys will be okay. Mr. Stephens is with sergeant Espinoza and there have been no signs of trouble here at the house."

"Brad's with Raoul?"

"Yes. The sergeant volunteered to watch Mr. Stephens today. He went with him to the airport."

Call it woman's intuition, but she had a bad feeling in her gut. She didn't know if it was because McNabb was leaving or because Brad had gone to the airport. She only knew that she wished Brad—and Raoul— was here with her.

"I'll tell you what, Mrs. Stephens. If I get back to the station and they haven't sent a man out here yet, I'll change into my civvies and come back out. I'll stay with you until my replacement arrives."

"That's very nice of you Officer McNabb."

"Call me Randy, mam."

"Well Randy, please call me Mel. No need for the 'mam'. Makes me feel so old."

"Yes, ma…Mel," he said with a grin, catching himself.

As he walked towards his cruiser, he stopped and turned. "You might want to keep Rufus close," he yelled back at the kitchen window. "He should keep you safe until my replacement arrives."

She smiled and waved good-bye. "Come back soon," she said under her breath. She took a sip of coffee and beckoned the dog to stand by her side.

"Man's best friend," she said, rubbing his ears.

Fifteen minutes later, Mel heard a car coming up the driveway. Good, she thought, Randy's replacement.

She watched from the kitchen window as a gray sedan parked outside the fence. Two men dressed in ill-fitting suits emerged. She watched as they looked around, spit on her flowers and headed for the front door.

Rufus barked as the front door bell rang. She put a leash on him and then cautiously approached the front door.

"Yes," she said, opening the door only enough for her voice to be heard; Rufus barked and tugged at his leash.

"Whoa there big boy," Hollyfield said peering through the opening and seeing the large Rottweiler salivating alongside the woman. "I'm Detective Hollyfield and this is Detective McCoy," he said, nodding towards his partner.

Mel had a bad feeling about these two. Not only were they comically mismatched, but they hadn't made an appointment in advance. Brad had made no mention of a scheduled interview. He wouldn't have left so early if this had been planned, would he? And, it was obvious, the dog didn't like them.

Go with your gut, Mel.

"Can I see some identification please," she asked.

Slowly the two detectives produced business cards and handed them to her.

"What about badges?"

Hollyfield opened his jacket so she could see his shield.

"You?" she said, indicating McCoy.

He opened his coat as well.

"Mind if we come in mam?" The heavy man asked.

Again with the 'mam'. She must look exceptionally old this morning.

"We only have a few questions. It won't take but a minute," the skinny one said.

Mel closed the door, unchained it, secured a tight grip on the dog's leash and opened the door. She still had a bad feeling but seeing their credentials quieted some of it; and having Rufus made her feel safe. Only an idiot would attack a woman with a hundred pound Rottweiler at her side, she thought.

"Sorry to be so cautious, but as you know, someone is trying to kill my husband. We've had guards at the house round the clock. One is around here somewhere," she lied. "I had no idea you guys were coming by."

"I totally understand," Hollyfield said. "We didn't know we were coming by until a few hours ago."

Mel escorted them into the front room, offered coffee and asked them to sit down.

Gripping the leash, she poured them both a cup of coffee and then joined them. Rufus, still clearly agitated, sat on his haunches in front of her.

Protecting his master.

"You say you didn't know about this meeting until a few hours ago. Why is that?" she asked.

McCoy began to answer but Hollyfield extended his hand to stop his partner. When he devised his plan, he had thought of various contingencies and this situation fit one of them. "We had a similar thing happen in Ventura a few months ago," he began. "A real estate agent was killed. We're still looking for the killer. Our captain told us to come up here and talk to the local police and to Mr. Stephens, specifically. You know, see if the victim ever did business with Mr. Stephens or if they had common friends. Stuff like that."

Mel nodded. "And you think the cases could be related?"

"Well, you never know. We got to check all leads," Hollyfield said confidently, trying to sound like Joe Friday in Dragnet.

"I'm sorry to disappoint you gentlemen, but Brad isn't here. He left about an hour ago and I'm not sure when he'll be back," she said, continuing to restrain Rufus.

"But his car's here," McCoy said quickly, glancing nervously at the dog.

"How do you know what his car looks like?"

Another contingency for Hollyfield. "We were given some background on Mr. Stephens. We know he's a mortgage broker; we know what he looks like; and we know he drives a silver BMW."

She gripped the dog's leash even tighter. None of this was making sense. She hesitated and then said, "Well, anyway he took my car this morning." Noticing the skinny man's concern with the dog, she added, "I don't know what's wrong with Rufus. He usually warms up to people once they're in the house."

The skinny guy's hand shook slightly as he put his cup down. She noticed his good eye focus on the table as if he might misplace the cup if his attention wandered.

"Maybe he's just hungry," Hollyfield offered, pointing at the menacing dog.

"Perhaps, but I'd say he doesn't like one or both of you. Maybe it's the eye patch," she said, pointing to McCoy. "Whatever it is, I wouldn't make any sudden movements. I'm not sure I could hold him back if he lunged."

"Do you know where your husband went, mam?" McCoy asked in his most professional, detective-like voice.

"I have no idea," she lied. "I have your cards; I'll have him call you when he gets back. Maybe you can conclude your business over the phone."

Hollyfield hadn't thought of this contingency, so he winged it. "We've got to run into town and meet with some local detectives. How 'bout we stop by on our way back home? It should be early afternoon."

"That's fine with me," Mel said in an agreeable tone, hopeful that McNabb's replacement would be there soon. "I can't promise Brad will be back. If you want to call first, I'll give you our home number. I'd hate for you to waste your time again." She rose, took the dog with her into the kitchen.

The two men followed her. Rufus growled as she handed the skinny man a piece of paper with the home phone number on it.

Hollyfield's eyes swept around the kitchen and settled on a large object in a glass baking pan sitting on the stove.

"Is that Meatloaf I see?" he asked.

"Why yes it is," she said. "I learned a new way to cook it recently. I served it to some of my husband's friends. It was a big hit."

"Hot damn! I thought I smelled hamburger or steak when we entered the house," Hollyfield said with a satisfied nod.

"You obviously have a great sense of smell. I was about to send it over to my boy's house but they called and told me they had gone fishing today," she lied. "It's such a shame. I hate to waste it. Would you gentlemen like me to make you a few sandwiches for the road?"

Without missing a beat, they both responded affirmatively. Hollyfield asked if she could spare a Coke or Dr. Pepper.

"You bet," she said. "I think we've got a few cokes around here somewhere."

She found the sodas and put them in lunch bags along with the sandwiches she had made.

"Here you boys go," she announced, handing them the bags. "Hope you enjoy the recipe." Thinking the day old meatloaf may be too dry, she put extra olive oil on the sandwiches. Might give the 'detectives' the trots? Oh, well. She smiled.

Looking somewhat disappointed, they thanked her and departed. She waved good bye, unleashed the dog, watched them get into the gray car and then picked up the phone. She dialed Brad's cell phone. Espinoza and he should know about the surprise visit.

The two 'detectives' sat in the car a moment before Hollyfield started the engine. McCoy scratched his head, adjusted his eye patch and stared straight ahead with his good eye. "Damn, Ken, did you see the teeth on that Rott?"

"Hell yes, the goddamn thing almost bit me."

McCoy pulled out the Beretta from its holster and caressed the gun. "Maybe we should go back in there and shoot the dog and kidnap the woman? Make Stephens come to us."

Hollyfield shook his head. This guy really was back woods, he thought. Too stupid to know there was a time and a place for killing. Clearly, this wasn't either.

"Don't worry about it 'one eye'. I've got a Plan B. Let's go eat these sandwiches and I'll tell you how we're going to get this guy."

McCoy grudgingly agreed and they drove off.

38

BRAD WAS SURPRISED TO HEAR FROM MEL.

He figured she would sleep until at least ten thirty. It was that kind of morning. Hazy, not too warm; birds intermittently chirping. The only other sound coming from the canyon below had been a slight humming made by fog caressing the power lines. On days like this, Mel was known to sleep late.

"What are you doing up so early? I thought you might sleep till noon today."

"Very funny. Be quiet and listen," she insisted.

He listened to her account of events. The phone was on a Bluetooth speaker. His passenger, Raoul Espinoza could hear every word.

"Mel," Espinoza said. "You say they showed you badges and said they were from Ventura. Is that correct?"

"Yes. I've got their business cards right here." She reached across the desk and picked up the cards.

"Describe the cards to me," he said.

"They look very official. They have a Ventura County seal up in the left hand corner and various phone numbers and an address typed along the bottom."

He looked at Brad and shook his head. "That's not what Ventura Police business cards look like," he said loud enough so that Mel could hear him.

"Then who are they?" she asked.

"I don't know, but I'm going to try and find out," Espinoza said calmly. "Describe their appearance to me."

She did and he took notes.

"The heavy guy doesn't fit Stefanie's description," Espinoza said.

"He could've been in disguise at the office," Brad said.

"Yeah, that's what I'm beginning to think. The skinny guy could be an accomplice. Maybe he drove the get- away car or something?"

"Or maybe they were reporters, trying to get an inside story?" Mel suggested.

"Did you see a gun on either of them?" Espinoza asked.

Mel hesitated for a moment, straining to remember, she said, "Well, yes, now that you mention it, I saw a bulge under the skinny one's right arm pit."

"There you go," Espinoza muttered.

Brad took a deep breath and spoke to both Raoul and Mel. "I think that until we know differently, we have to assume that these guys are the killers and that they both came here to finish the job."

He stared at Espinoza. Raoul nodded.

"Why wasn't McNabb at the house?" Brad asked Espinoza.

Before Espinoza could answer, Mel responded. "His shift ended and a replacement guard was on his way, but there was an emergency in town. Randy said he'd come back out in his civilian clothes if the replacement was tied up too long."

"Randy? Since when are we on a first name basis?"

"Oh, get over it. I was tired of him calling me mam and we decided to use first names."

"Okay. What else happened?"

"Nothing really. I told them you weren't here; they seemed disappointed, but not devastated. I made them a couple of meatloaf sandwiches and sent them on their way."

Brad thought of his own upset stomach; wondered again if it was caused by Mel's mystery meatloaf or the stress of recent events? "It sounds like you handled it pretty well. I'm sorry the guard wasn't posted. We'll make sure that doesn't happen again…won't we Raoul?" he said, looking to his right.

Espinoza nodded and then said, "Yep. I'll make sure someone is posted 24/7."

"That would make me feel better." She let out an audible sigh of relief. "I had Rufus—and I can tell you, that dog did not like those guys—so I felt safe. But even a Rottweiler is no defense against a gun."

"He'd get a few bites in," Brad predicted.

"Well anyway, I'm glad they're gone and I'm glad Raoul is with you." She paused for a moment and then said, "Oh, here comes a police cruiser. Randy's replacement finally made it."

"That's great dear. Tell the officer everything that happened. Describe the two men to him and make sure he has Raoul and my cell phone numbers."

She assured him she would and said goodbye and hung up.

"That's a brave wife, you've got there, Brad," Espinoza said.

"Yep."

"Why did you cringe a little when she told you about the sandwiches she made for the men?"

"Well, she's a brave woman but a mediocre cook. I've got a feeling those guys aren't going to like her sandwiches as much as they thought they would."

Espinoza grinned as if he understood.

Suddenly it felt to Brad like the stakes had been raised. Events were accelerating. The killer or killers had visited his home. He'd better review the contents of the boxes quickly. Hopefully, the information would provide clues as to what was going on.

39

THEY REACHED THE SPECIAL HANDLING bay at exactly ten a.m.

Brad was pleased to see three large, white boxes stacked neatly by the door. The facility appeared empty.

"You think we can just take the boxes?" he asked Espinoza.

"Doubt it."

As they approached the packages, a large Samoan-looking guy, standing six feet tall, weighing at least three hundred pounds appeared. His long, dark hair was braided neatly under his company cap.

"Wonder where he came from?" Brad said under his breath to Espinoza.

"Beats me. He's too big to hide. But I sure didn't see him when we came in." Acting as if he intended to solicit help all along, Brad flagged down the Samoan.

"How's it, Bruddah?" the huge man asked, making the 'hang loose' sign with his thumb and little finger. His name tag read, Izzy, and yes it indicated that his home country was, indeed, Samoa.

"Just trying to pick up my cargo," Brad replied, hoping the Samoan was an official baggage handler and not a killer in disguise.

His new- found paranoia knew no bounds.

Espinoza seemed to be reading his thoughts. Brad noticed his hand slide inside his jacket pocket.

"What's the procedure for claiming my boxes?" Brad asked.

"No worries. You got to clear it thru a supervisor first," Izzy said as he came to a lazy stop just a few feet away from Brad and Espinoza. "Show your driver's license for I.D. and the supervisor will check it against the manifest. Then you done Bruddah."

Ten minutes later an older man with short, perfectly coiffed gray hair, and wearing an immaculately pressed blue suit approached them. He shook Brad's hand and then Espinoza's.

"Is the cargo dangerous?" he asked.

"No. Why would you ask?" Brad said.

The man cleared his throat, straightened his tie and said, "It's not every day I deal with a policeman in our sleepy little special handling department, that's all," he said nodding towards Espinoza.

"How did you know I was a cop?" Espinoza asked. Impressed.

"I saw your picture in the paper the other day. You were interviewed about that shooting downtown...." He stopped and stared at Brad. "And *your* picture wasn't in the paper, but your name was mentioned, Brad Stephens. *You* were the intended victim!"

Brad nodded.

The group grew quiet.

After a few uncomfortable moments, the man checked Brad's I.D. against the manifest and released the boxes into his custody.

Brad paid Izzy ten bucks to cart the boxes over to the S.U.V. and load them. When accomplished, Brad thanked the big Samoan who promptly slapped Brad on the back, knocking the wind out of him.

"Stay cool, Izzy. And thanks for the help," Brad sputtered, trying to regain his breath.

"Drive safe, Bruddah."

Brad smiled and gave him the 'hang loose' sign.

Once clear of the airport, boxes securely stashed in the back of the S.U.V., Brad called Mel. "We're leaving the airport now. We should be home in thirty minutes. Is the new guard in place?"

"Thomas is here protecting us."

"Thomas?"

"Yes, Brad, from now on, I'm on a first name basis with all of our protectors."

"Okay, fair enough"

"Has he walked the perimeter?" Espinoza asked.

"Not yet. He's eating some of my meatloaf first."

Brad rolled his eyes at Espinoza as the sergeant chuckled. "Okay, just make sure he inspects the whole property when he's done."

"I will. And another thing, the dog loves him. The more I think about it, the more I'm sure that Rufus knew those two fake detectives were bad guys. He's such a good dog; he was trying to warn me."

"Dogs have an incredible way of knowing these things," Brad said.

It seemed such an obvious statement, nobody responded.

"Make sure Thomas knows that the men said they
would stop by again on their way out of town."

"Will do. See you in a little while."

Brad looked over at his friend. Espinoza was busy
texting something to someone. His face revealed nothing
but his strong keystrokes indicated he was agitated.

"Who you texting?"

"O'hara."

"What are you telling her?"

"I'm telling her you and Mel need better protection.
I don't care if the department doesn't have it in the
budget. These guys aren't kidding around. There should-
n't be gaps between shifts."

They rode in silence for the next ten minutes.
Espinoza's phone pinged. He swiped the screen and read
the incoming message.

"I'll be damned!" he said.

"What is it? Did the wicked witch fire you?"

He rubbed his chin and shook his head. "No. She
said funds were no problem now. An anonymous donor
called the station a few hours ago and said he'd pay for
your constant surveillance. The donor wants two guards;
one at your home and one at your office."

"Anonymous?"

"Yeah, got any idea who it is?"

Brad shrugged. "As you know, I'm friends with lots of
rich people."

"You think it was Linden?"

"I doubt it."

"Zindo?" Espinoza offered.

"Maybe."

This *was* a typical Zindo move. He'd pretend he didn't really care but then would do something behind the scenes. Brad made a note to thank his wealthy friend although he doubted Steve would take the credit.

He was suddenly remorseful that Mel's meatloaf might have given Zindo slight dysentery.

Intent on inspecting the boxes, he made it home twenty minutes later. He and Espinoza unloaded the boxes in the garage. The boxes had clear packing tape wrapped around their exteriors and each box was carefully labeled by year. One read 2009, the next, 2010 and the final one 2011. The unsuspecting observer would assume that the files contained very boring, technical records. Brad hoped the contents would be anything but.

He was not to be disappointed.

He opened all the boxes. The only thing they contained were legal-sized manila folders.

Each file he pulled had a different player's name on it and a different colored label helping differentiate it from the others. The third file he came to simply said, Linden 2009. The label was pink. Very feminine. John would just love that.

Espinoza had hung around while Brad performed his inspection. "Find anything interesting yet?" he asked.

Holding up the folder with the pink label, Brad confirmed that it was Linden's file from 2009. "It doesn't take a forensic genius to see that Smalley separated John's finances into two categories: 1. Investments that should be made, and, 2. Investments and use of funds that were actually made. Smalley was running two sets of books."

"Why?"

"Don't know, but look at this." He pointed to the first category: Investments that should've been made.

The page was full of stock and bond references. "I'm not an expert, but I recognize the companies listed and the Treasury bond references. These were very safe; very liquid; very conservative investments."

"And the other category?"

Brad shook his head, the meaning of the notations slowly sinking in. "I'm not sure, but it looks like John's money actually went into very risky investments like Pork Belly futures, Treasury Futures and...." he paused. "Holy shit! Mortgage Backed Security derivatives."

"What's wrong with those? Are they illegal?"

"No, not at all. But here's the thing Raoul, Linden was in no position to gamble his entire fortune on market driven risky investments—especially when the economy was melting down in 2009. These things—mortgage backed securities—led to the downfall of Bear/Stearns and Lehman Brothers and much of our banking system."

"No shit?"

"No shit."

"What was Smalley doing gambling with his money?"

"I don't know." Brad scratched his head and dug deeper.

"The investments that should've been made showed a steady 4% rate of return and modest growth."

"4% is good, isn't it? I haven't seen 4% on any of my investment statements in a long time," Espinoza said.

"Yes, it is good—given the rotten economy," Brad concurred. He stuck another page in front of Espinoza. "Now take a look at this. The investments that were actually made all tanked." He pointed to the page in front of them. Somebody had made notations in the margins.

7/14. Dow at 13,450. MBS off 10 pts.
7/18. Dow at 12,140. MBS off 15 pts.
8/13. Dow at 10,450. MBS off 25 pts.

"Who did those and what do they mean?" Espinoza asked.

"I assume Art did. But, hell, I'm not sure. They seem to chronicle how the investment economy was collapsing while the bad investments were made. He used the Dow as his baseline. See here." He pointed to the first notation.

"Dow at 13,450. That's the Dow Jones Industrials. They were at 13,450 on 7/14," Brad said.

"What's the MBS mean?"

"Mortgage Backed Securities. When the Dow was at 13,450, mortgage backed security futures must've tanked. According to this, they were off ten points."

"Again, I ask, what does that mean, amigo?" Espinoza asked.

Brad read on before answering. A few moments later, he put the file down and said, "It looks like IFPG—or Art—engaged in contrarian trading."

"Huh?"

"You really don't get this stuff do you?"

"I'm a simple police sergeant working on his retirement. I'm just hoping to have something left in my IRA."

"You and the rest of the world."

They both nodded sadly. Then Brad continued. "In simple terms, it means that when the Dow went down, they bet it was going to go up the next day. So they went long and then went it went up, they reversed course and went short."

"Is that legal."

"Unfortunately for the small guy, yes. But it is extremely risky."

"Gambling?"

"Without the free drinks."

"I bet whoever made these moves consumed plenty of alcohol when they saw the outcome," Brad said as he inspected another set of documents.

He stopped for a moment and turned to face Espinoza. "The real danger with these investments is not only the loss in value, but the possibility that these losses triggered margin calls."

"Okay, amigo, now you're losing me."

"Sorry about that. Believe me, you don't want to see a margin call. It means you've lost a ton of imaginary dough and now you got to pay up."

"Ouch," Espinoza said, appearing to catch on.

He looked in the next two boxes. Same thing. Linden 2010. Green label this time. Linden Year to Date, 2011. White label. Same results. He checked some of the other files. Same separation of investments for each player.

It appeared that Art had been chronicling Linden's portfolio as if he didn't control the investment strategy any longer. Slowly, but surely, Brad began to understand. "I think Art Smalley had been stripped of actual investment control some time in 2008 or 2009."

"Maybe he fought the decision? Maybe Smalley wanted someone to know that these trades weren't his decision?" Espinoza said.

"Don't know. All I can say is that it appears that behind the scenes, Smalley created a spreadsheet that showed the investments that John—and the others under his management—might have made had he still been in charge."

The other file documents the actual usage of funds. Huge amounts of cash were transferred from Linden's primary money market account into what was labeled IFPG Bond Fund #1."

Excited by the discoveries, Brad pushed forward. It helped his understanding to articulate these things to Raoul. He was glad his friend was there.

"Jesus! The losses are staggering!" he exclaimed.

"How much?"

"Millions…maybe tens of millions. Shit, maybe hundreds of millions!"

"Lots of financial firms lost money during the recession, didn't they?" Espinoza asked.

"Yes, banks and investment banks did, but IFPG is neither. Their job is to safeguard players' money. If it means taking less yield, then so be it."

Brad traced the paperwork from 2008 to 2011. The Bond Fund investment entries had ended several months before Smalley's death. The final one was labeled IFPG Bond Fund #107.

107 bond funds? An outfit like IFPG would usually only invest in a few funds per year. Under normal circumstances, there wouldn't be a need for so much diversification. It looked to Brad like somebody at IFPG had bet big in 2008-2009.

And lost.

That's why there were so many independent funds.

No wonder John only had two point eight million dollars left. If Smalley's notes could be believed and if Brad's interpretation of them was correct, IFPG had lied to its clients.

IFPG wasn't making safe, long term investments. They had tried to hit Grand Slam homeruns.

And struck out.

Rather than face the music, they hid the truth. It was the same old gambler's story. "If I just roll the dice one more time…." Well, whoever orchestrated this scam rolled the dice like a crazed gambler.

And they came up Snake Eyes.

Brad was about to wrap it up when his eye fell onto a separate, small file tucked deep inside Linden's records. He wouldn't have noticed it but for the unusual label: Black, with white print. He pulled out the file. It was only a few weeks old. He noticed the full name written on the label: Athletes for Change, LLC/S.S.S.

"I remember that name, Athletes for Change. It came up when I looked at John's tax returns."

"What is it?"

"I don't know. I saw it but dismissed it; it was not a big item."

"What does S.S.S. mean?"

"Not sure. Let's read on."

The next page they came to was labeled: Sons for Sovereign Sacrifice.

S.S.S.

"Think we found our answer," Brad said, handing Espinoza the sheet.

Smalley had written the name David Von Eisenlow and had jotted down a phone number. He provided a brief overview of the group and then he wrote, *"Wish I had never found Von Eisenlow. He's a terrorist in the making!"*

"IFPG and a terrorist group?" Brad said.

"Probably more like a home grown group of extremists," Espinoza said.

"But still…."

Espinoza shrugged.

They read on.

The rest of the file contained various accounting categories for income and expenses dating back several years. Behind the financials, a one page document had been stapled to the back of the folder. It contained a series of questions written in block print.

A date just six weeks before Smalley's death had been written in long hand next to the sentences. Brad read the page aloud:

SUMMARY and QUESTIONS

- Losses Mounting. No End in Sight.
- Is Athletes for Change, LLC: A legitimate entity?
- Have any players been notified?
- If this affects all our players, and not just the forty I manage, the losses would be…over a billion!
- What role is S.S.S. playing?
- Why is more money going into A.F.C. account?

In the margin Smalley had written in long hand:

Who authorized all this? Tyler?

The last question was hi-lighted in yellow and then the file ended.

No more entries.

No more questions.

Art Smalley would never get the opportunity to hear the answers.

Or, maybe he had?

And they got him killed?

Always the cop, Espinoza had a few questions of his own. "Who's Tyler? You think Smalley confronted this guy? Do you think Smalley really didn't know about these investments?"

Brad shrugged. "I've got a feeling we opened a hornet's nest." He paused and then said, "And why would IFPG be involved with this S.S.S. group?"

"I don't know, but I'm sure as hell going to look into it," Espinoza said, taking out his notebook.

40

ONCE THE HAZE HAD BURNED OFF, the temperature had become unseasonably warm.

Perfect day for golf with a buddy. Crappy day to be holed up in the garage sorting through paperwork.

Brad put the files back in their respective boxes and suggested they go inside to grab a beer; he was thirsty and the garage had become hot and stuffy.

He took a seat on the countertop; Espinoza rested his ample rear end against the sink. After taking one long chug from the bottle, Brad began answering Espinoza's other questions. "Tyler is Tyler Ambrook, the guy who runs IFPG. He's the guy I had words with out in Las Vegas. He's a little prick."

"Looks like Smalley might've thought so too," Espinoza said, finishing his first beer and asking for another.

Brad pointed to the refrigerator and said, "Help yourself."

Espinoza grabbed another beer, moved his large frame to a nearby chair and settled in to listen to his buddy's theories.

Brad continued. "Do I think Smalley confronted him about the bad investments? Don't know. What do you think?"

"Guy's losing millions of clients' dollars. Smalley feels loyal to his players. Tyler won't let him disclose the losses. Tells him to keep his mouth shut. Removes him from handling the actual investments. Smalley calls him on the carpet. Soon after, Smalley's hanging from his study's ceiling."

"Or, perhaps Smalley had been required to go along with the investment losses if he wanted to keep his job but then when he found out about the involvement of S.S.S. he drew the line at the unauthorized support of a subversive group?" Brad theorized.

"Could be. Let's get back to Tyler Ambrook," Espinoza said in between gulps.

Brad thought about it for a moment. He did the math in his head. "It makes perfect sense. Smalley's dual files start shortly after Tyler Ambrook took over control of IFPG in 2008. According to John, Tyler's father, Steven Ambrook, retired and made his inexperienced son the president of the company."

"Not a smart move, eh amigo?"

Brad continued. "The guy probably was a young, brash, college graduate who hadn't yet been humbled by the stock market. He might've looked at a conservative investment strategy generating 3-5% and conclude that he could make the company much greater profits. *He* could beat the market. All it took was capital and an aggressive trading platform."

"He had both."

"And a USC education."

"Those frat boys think they can conquer the world, don't they?"

"Look at Wall St.," Brad said. "Trades are made by a bunch of young, cocky Ivy Leaguers high on caffeine; low on experience. Maybe Tyler figured he could use his west coast education and beat those guys."

"Or join them?"

"Yeah, if you can't beat 'em, join 'em."

Brad grabbed another beer himself. Rather than open it immediately, he held the ice cold bottle to his forehead. A slight headache was coming on.

"Anything else you deduce from those records?" Espinoza asked.

Brad moved the bottle back and forth across his forehead, closed his eyes for a moment and sighed. "I don't know Raoul; it's so much to take in and I really don't know the cast of characters. I only met Ambrook in Las Vegas and I hardly knew Smalley."

"Since that's the case, you need to contact the one person who knows them both—John Linden."

"I agree. I'll call him in a little while. Let me think about the numbers for a few minutes."

"Okay amigo, but if you're right about this stuff, maybe it would be best to turn the whole thing over to the Feds."

"I will once I have more substance. For now, it's just you, me and Mr. Coors here speculating."

"Let me just add one thing," Espinoza said. "And let me make this perfectly clear." He did his best Richard Nixon. "If Tyler had Smalley killed to keep him from exposing the losses, then he's extremely dangerous. Catch my drift?"

Brad breathed deeply once again. He still hadn't taken a sip from the new beer. "If that's true then once it became obvious that John wasn't going to go along with the IFPG loan offer, Tyler panicked. He knew that an extensive review of John's asset statements and tax returns would reveal the losses."

Espinoza nodded, finished his beer and rose from his seat. "People have killed for less."

"Kill the loan officer before he can tell John about the losses; do the loan for John; keep him happy. Presumably, John would be so distraught at my death he would turn to his only other long term ally, IFPG." He looked at Espinoza for validation.

"That's how I'm beginning to see it."

A clammy chill slid down Brad's spine. He flinched. He finally got it. Johnson was dead because of *him*. And that crazy driver with a gun on the Pear Blossom—it wasn't random after all.

He'd bet anything that the visit to Mel this morning by those fake cops really was another attempt on his life. They'd left her alone because he wasn't there. Probably didn't hurt that she had Rufus by her side either. It made sense.

Brad needed to stop Linden before he confronted Tyler Ambrook. The guy might be dangerous. John should be warned.

Out of the corner of his eye, Brad noticed Espinoza gather his things and prepare to leave. He approached his friend and thanked him for the protection and the brainstorming session.

"No problem, amigo. I'm glad I was able to take the morning and afternoon off. I'll make a few phone calls and make sure you got protection at the house and at the office. I can't cover you in transit, but once you get to where you're going, my men will protect you."

"Thanks, buddy. That makes me feel better. Have a good rest of the day."

"I'm going home and take a nap. Me and the old lady haven't been getting along too good lately. Maybe I'll take her to a movie tonight? You know, try to smooth things out."

Brad opened the door, slapped his friend on the back, wished him good luck with Rosa and stared at the brilliant sunshine outside. "Hell, Raoul, we should've been playing golf on such a glorious day—not dealing with all this crap."

"Concur, amigo," the big man said while getting into his car. "See you soon." He drove off.

Brad opened his cell phone and dialed Linden's number. No answer. It went to voicemail.

"John. It's Brad," he began. "Raoul and I have made some interesting discoveries. You were right. The boxes contained important information. You might also be right about Art Smalley. I don't think he killed himself. Give me a call ASAP. And, this is *very* important, TALK TO ME BEFORE MEETING AGAIN WITH TYLER AMBROOK!!!"

He practically shouted that last line. He didn't know any other way to emphasize it.

He wasn't sure if Linden had advanced to text messaging yet, but in case he had, Brad sent him a text with the same message.

While waiting for a call back, Brad looked at the Athletes for Change, LLC paperwork and Smalley's comments again. John's tax return indicated that his total investment over the past several years in Athletes for Change was over $1,000,000. Where did that money go? How much had been taken from the other players?

Seemed like there might be several reasons to bring in the Feds.

Millions of reasons, actually.

He would wait, though, until he talked to John.

41

LINDEN CALLED BACK AT FIVE THIRTY.

Slurring his words slightly, he explained that he had taken Fabiola out to a fancy lunch. They had returned home, made love and gone out to a fancy dinner. Under the circumstances, he had turned his phone off.

Brad understood. Some things trump murder and financial ruin.

"So what's all this business about not meeting with Tyler?" Linden asked.

"It's kinda complicated, but I think Tyler Ambrook made tens of millions—maybe hundreds of millions—of bad bond trades on Wall St. Apparently, he diverted much of the player's monies to various funds without their consent. It looks like Art Smalley threatened to expose him, or tell his father, or tried to blackmail him for a raise—I'm not exactly sure what happened with Art—but I think he fouled his nest; and I think Tyler may have had him killed."

"No Fuckin' way! Tyler Ambrook killed his best account manager?"

"That's my theory."

"That little piss ant. I'll kill *him*!"

Brad could just imagine his friend getting worked up on the other end of the line.

"That's one option," Brad said calmly. "The other is that we call the FBI and discuss the situation with them. There are three more elements to consider." He made a number one gesture with his finger in the air—he talked with his hands a lot, even when on the phone. "First, I think Tyler has put out a hit on me. The driver in the desert was the first 'hit man'. Then I think he sent two goons out here to kill me. They got Johnson by mistake. We think they visited the house today while I was picking up the boxes."

"No Shit. What happened?"

"Mel did a great job with them. I'll tell you about it later."

"But everybody's okay?"

"Yes, for the time being." He paused and then raised a second finger. "The second thing is that IFPG might be tied up with a white supremacy organization called Sons for Sovereign Sacrifice. IFPG may've donated millions to the group. I just don't know."

"No shit!" Apparently, this had become Linden's favorite new expression.

"Looks that way,"

"Finally," he said, popping up another finger, "It appears that Smalley had concerns about two things: unauthorized risky investments and money funneling through a Limited Liability Corporation called, Athletes for Change. Know anything about it?"

"Art mentioned it several years ago, I think. He said it was a foundation or something like that and that all the players put a few bucks into it each year. It would be a good tax deduction is what he said."

"Well, I think it became more than that. Did he mention how it started?"

"Something to do with Steven or Tyler Ambrook, I can't remember."

"That's what I thought," Brad said, rolling his left fingers into a ball and tightening his grip on the phone with his right. "And the unauthorized investments are what led to your, personal, massive losses."

"How could they do that without someone catching it?"

"Apparently, as you found out from your calls to the other golfers, you guys don't tend to check your tax returns. And IFPG apparently never provided asset statements. Or if they did, and I don't know this for sure, maybe they doctored them?"

"No shit!" There it was again. Despite the circumstances, Brad had to smile.

"Next time I tell you something earth shattering, I need you to come up with a different expression buddy," he joked.

Linden chuckled slightly. "Yeah, I guess I sound like a broken record."

"And the Athletes for Change, LLC would've looked to you like any other investment if, by chance you actually reviewed your tax returns." Brad paused for a moment and then added, "I don't think we need to be too concerned about the LLC losses for now. Let's focus on the risky trades."

"Holy Moley!"

"What?"

"You told me not to say 'no shit', so this is my new expression. Holy Moley."

Brad chuckled.

After a few moments, Linden said, "Okay, listen, I follow you." He was sobering up in a hurry. "Where do we go from here? Should I follow up with our original plan and take all my money out?"

"I think you leave your money in for the time being. Let me talk to the local police. Espinoza went thru the material with me, maybe he's thought about it and come up with a different angle?"

"Alright, I'm pissed, but I'll wait until I hear from you before doing anything. In the meantime, Fabiola is coming out there again on Thursday. She just sprung it on me, I couldn't stop her. I haven't told her a thing about my finances. Don't say anything," he said, almost begging.

"I won't."

"Thanks. Last thing I need is her ragging my ass. Show her a few more houses or focus on the one she really likes. Just keep her busy if you can."

"I'll try, but she's a handful."

"Yeah, she's cool isn't she?"

Brad wanted to tell him that 'cool' is *not* what he had in mind, but he bit his tongue. "She is that," was all he said.

"I'm going to think about my future relationship with IFPG and then I've got a big tournament coming up at Hilton Head. The way it looks, I better win the damn thing and pocket the money," Linden said.

"Yep, winning cures all ills, or so they say. Now get back to dinner, I've kept you long enough. Have a good night. Call me with Fabiola's flight info. I'm sure I can talk Blake into picking her up again." He began to press end, when he heard Linden's voice still coming through.

"One last request, buddy. Is there any way you can convince Mel to be nice to Fabby? She seems to think that Mel doesn't like her. It would mean the world to me if they could be friends."

"You know I can't control Mel. I'll make a few suggestions. But I can't promise anything."

"Just try. Okay?"

"I will," Brad said, knowing damn well it was a lost cause. Mel would never accept Fabiola as a true friend. "Fabiola may not have to worry about Mel, though. I'm trying to convince her to visit her folks. Let's see what happens."

"That means you would be alone with my fiancée in your comfortable house?"

"Not alone. I have an armed guard at the house 24/7 and a big Rottweiler," Brad pointed out.

"That Rufus is one big dog, I'll give you that. Is he trained to attack?"

"Naw, but the bad guys don't know that."

He chuckled. "Hope they don't find out."

After a brief pause, Linden said, "Talk to you soon."

At least they seemed to have gotten to the bottom of Linden's missing money, Brad thought. IFPG—or Art Smalley—had been making risky investments. That much was clear.

The protection issue seemed to be solved as well. The police were guarding Brad and Mel around the clock. Hopefully, it was just a matter of time before the bad guys would be caught. But something bugged Brad. How did The Sons for Sovereign Sacrifice figure in to this mess? He wished he had talked to John about it. Maybe Linden could shed some light on the outfit?

In the meantime, he'd Google the group.

Before he had a chance to turn on his computer, Mel announced that dinner was served.

"It's not meatloaf is it?" Brad asked.

"Nope. While you were going through those boxes, I went out to the video store and rented a few movies for us. Did you know there's a Taco Bell right next door to the rental store?"

Did he know?

He shook his head and lied. "First I heard of it."

She continued. "Me too. So I bought us a bunch of tacos and burritos. I figure we'll scarf out and chase it with a few cold beers."

"Fantastic! Which movies did you rent?"

"A suspense thriller staring that guy from the Bourne movies and a comedy with Adam Sandler."

"Let's skip the thriller. I'm not in the mood."

"Okay. I'll watch the thriller tomorrow…by myself. I've got a boring day planned. This will give me something to look forward to."

He grabbed her around the waist and planted a big kiss on her lips.

"You got something else in mind sailor?"

"Naw…well, maybe, but that's not the thing," he said awkwardly. "I just want you to know I love you and I'm proud of you. That's all."

"What brought that on?"

"The way you handled those fake cops today and the way you're handling this whole thing, actually."

"Thanks, but what other choice do I have?"

"Well, you could go down to your parent's house until this all blows over," he said, knowing she would resist the suggestion.

"Nope." She pulled away and shook her head. "You're not going to get rid of me that easily. We're in this together."

Brad cringed as he realized that Mel wasn't going to visit her parents. More importantly, he hadn't told her that Fabiola was coming back into town tomorrow. Sparks might fly. He better look for an opening during the comedy.

Mel would be upset by her visit but she'd calm down. On the other hand, she'd be downright pissed if he just sprung it on her tomorrow. *Damn!* He didn't need to watch a Hollywood thriller, his whole life had suddenly become one big drama.

Hopefully, tomorrow would be a mellow day. He ate his dinner and settled in with Mel just as Adam Sandler was taking a pie in the face.

Now *that's* real comedy, Brad thought as he laughed for the first time that day.

42

BLAKE SAT IN HIS NEWLY WASHED surfer wagon Thursday afternoon searching for a place to park along the curb.

Prepared for the lovely Fabiola this time, he had cleaned his car, thrown away the junk in the backseat, hung a brand new fresh scent tree from his rear view mirror—Coconut—and rehearsed suave lines to use if the opportunity arose.

Hopefully, the coconut smell would make her think of sunshine and the beach. He could imagine her on the beach in a skimpy thong bikini. The thought made him grin.

Hell, the thought made him horny.

Arriving on time, the private jet Linden had booked for her landed smoothly and taxied to its parking spot. Fabiola departed the plane, stopped at the bottom of the stairs and thanked the captain and the flight attendant.

"*Ju* made the flight so nice and easy," she said. "I didn't know it could only take four hours to get here from Florida."

The captain sucked in his gut and replied, "This plane flies at fifty thousand feet, mam. Our airspeed averaged over six hundred miles per hour."

She smiled, laid on the charm. "*Ju* are such a good captain, I *wan* Juan to hire *ju* all *tee* time."

"I'd like that," he said. He looked like he meant it.

Feeling well rested —even after a four hour flight— she strode towards the exit and greeted Blake. "*Tanks* for picking me up, *hansome*," she said, giving him a long, wet peck on the cheek.

He blushed and smiled.

Nirvana.

As they waited for her bags to be removed from the plane, Fabiola walked around the holding area, stretched her long legs, puffed her hair, checked her makeup and discreetly adjusted her bra. She made sure Blake noticed every move.

The drive home was uneventful. They discussed Santa Barbara, Montecito, shopping and Blake's girlfriends, but no further opportunity presented itself for Blake to say something like, "The pleasure is all mine" or "I believe you have me at a disadvantage" or "It's nothing, I always keep my car clean."

== ⊕ ==

"*Hola amigos*," Fabiola sang out as she entered the Stephens house twenty minutes later.

"Hello Fabiola," Brad replied, coming out of his office to greet his house guest. "Welcome back. How was your flight?"

"Hola, Brad. My flight was marvelous; only took four hours."

"Four hours, what did you do, fly at the speed of sound?"

She smiled. "I talked to the captain after we landed. He explained that the plane flies very fast because it flies very high." She paused, looked around the house as if inspecting the premises. "*Ees* Mel here?"

"She had to step out for a few minutes. She's really looking forward to seeing you again," he lied. He chastised himself; he'd have to stop lying.

"And, I want to see her."

Brad couldn't tell if she was being honest or just polite.

"Well I'm glad your flight went well. Was Blake on time to pick you up?"

"Oh, *jess*, he *ees* a dream."

"He's a good guy. I'm glad he was on time. Why don't you settle in and then we can talk business."

Blake came through the front door lugging a few suitcases and Fabiola asked him to take them to the guest room. She went into the kitchen, opened the refrigerator door, found an open bottle of wine and poured herself a glass.

"*Tis ees* good wine, Brad. *Ju* and Mel have good taste."

Again he noticed she seemed to reduce the Charro-like accent when John wasn't around. "Thanks. We try," he said.

They sat on the living room couch and chatted for fifteen minutes. Fabiola describing the features she hoped to see in any new listings, Brad defensively explaining why she might not see them.

Fabiola finished her wine, took the glass to the kitchen and announced that she was ready to visit some more houses.

"Already? You just got here."

"I *don wanna* waste time. Let's go look at a few places. *Ju* do have some showings lined up *don ju*?

"Do you really want to look at new properties? Or do you want to only revisit Oceanos y las Montanas? I know you loved that house. I've put them on alert that we might drop by today or tomorrow and I've made a tentative appointment to preview one other house." He paused then added, "You tell me."

"Have you seen this house, Brad? Is it up to my standards? I don't want to waste my time, you know." Her tone was formal and, suddenly, more serious; not even a hint of Charro.

"I think you'll like one of them. It is located up in the foothills; has 180 degree views and wonderful grounds. Very open. Very spacious. I think it's as good as Oceanos y las Montanas. It's listed for three hundred thousand dollars less," he added quickly, as if the price might influence her. He knew it would John.

"*Ju* know, Brad," she said returning to a slight accent. "Money *ees* no object. I *don* care *eef* it *ees tree* hundred more…*eef* it *ees* better."

Brad knew money *was* an object now but didn't let on.

"In that case, I'll make an appointment at the new property and we can go by Oceanos y Las Montanas on the way. How does that sound?"

"*Bueno*. I *go* tinkle first and *ten* we go. *Hokay*? When does Mel come home?"

"She had to run an errand, it could take a while. We'll see her at dinner. I'll be waiting in the car," he said, desperately wanting to avoid the relationship issue between the two women.

Having not found an appropriate gap in the movie the night before, he had told Mel only that morning that Fabiola would be coming. "She will only stay for a day or two," he had said when she gave him the evil eye.

"Listen. I know John is your best friend. I know you—we—need the commissions. I'll try to be…tolerant. But I don't like her," Mel had said. He knew he was walking on eggshells, so he didn't stop her. "Call it woman's intuition, but I think she's got bad intentions. I think she looks down on us. Maybe I'm overly defensive due to our recent financial reversals? I just don't know," she had grudgingly admitted.

Again he assured her it was only for a day or two and that this would be better for John.

"Why the hell can't she stay at the Inn?"

He shrugged.

She continued. "Why do we have to entertain her? I think she's just using John for his money. Look at her. She exudes sex! She could get any of you weak ass males to think exclusively with your dicks. It's obnoxious."

"How can you say that?" Brad responded, sensing that most of what Mel said was true. "You've only known her a few days. We've all been under stress. Let's give her a chance. John seems to really like her."

"Pssh! Poor Fool! I'm just telling ya, I just feel it in my gut. I don't like her nor do I want to be confronted by those bolt-on boobs and botox lips. I just don't think there's anything 'real' about that woman."

Brad shook his head and took a deep breath. Mel was usually right but he didn't need her to be unpleasant to Fabiola. They weren't going to be best friends. That much was clear. As long as they could establish a cordial relationship, things would be okay. The truest part of her little tirade was obvious to Brad: They needed the commission income.

And needed it badly.

Dressed in tee shirts, baggy shorts and sandals—hoping to fit in as typical tourists—Hollyfield and McCoy sat in the blue Honda they had stolen that morning. Both still a bit squeamish from the stomach cramps they had experienced the day before, they were determined to finish the job today without expending too much energy

"You ready to finish this thing, 'one eye'?" Hollyfield asked McCoy.

"Hell yes, I want to get the hell out of here."

Hollyfield sighed. He liked it in Santa Barbara. But he knew the time had come to fish or cut bait.

"Okay, follow my lead and, hopefully, we can get this over with quick."

Having been at the house the day before, they knew there was really only one way in and one way out of the Stephens property. If Brad's car came down the hill, they would see it and either bag him while he drove—that was Hollyfield's plan 'A'—or follow him and wait for the right moment. That was his plan 'B'.

The police guard made it impossible to return to the house. And that dog would probably go berserk if they tried to break in anyway. It was too bad, he thought.

If time and circumstances permitted, he'd like to take care of that bitch too. He was positive Mel had poisoned the sandwiches.

He wasn't sure if the guard would follow Stephens when he drove. He assumed the police department could only afford so much protection. He had called Von Eisenlow the night before.

"Follow him every time he leaves," Von Eisenlow had instructed. "You'll see if he has a tail. If he doesn't, waste the son of a bitch."

Hollyfield had agreed. "I'll let you know when he's dead."

Now he watched from a distance as the BMW came into view. Brad was driving, that much was clear. He had a passenger. His wife? He couldn't tell. He fumbled for his gun and told McCoy to be ready.

"Take out the driver first," Hollyfield said. "If you hit the passenger, then so be it."

Before he could fire, McCoy saw the police unit pull in behind Brad. He put the gun down and watched as the two cars passed.

Hollyfield put the car into gear and slowly pulled away from the curb. He nearly hit the patrol car, swore and continued slowly.

After a moment, he accelerated and followed Brad and the police cruiser onto the freeway. They travelled north for a few minutes and then took the frontage road exit.

"What we gonna do now, Ken?" McCoy asked.

"Don't worry about it. We're going to follow Stephens and figure out when we can get him."

"What about the cop?"

"What about him?"

"Do we waste him?"

"Looks like we're going to have to, doesn't it?" Hollyfield rolled his eyes. How did he get stuck with such a dumb shit partner?

The driver of the brown sedan trailed behind the three cars, monitoring events from a discreet distance.

First stop for Brad and Fabiola was the estate known as "Oceanos y Las Montanas". As Brad opened the gate using the code the owners had left, Fabiola let out a gasp. "Oh, Brad. I *lub tis* place. *Eet* feels like home. *Ees* the house empty or will we run into *tee* owners? I *don wan* any problems."

"It's empty. They told me to take our time." He pulled forward slowly. "Their only request was to lock up and close the gate when we left." He paused, looked at his cell phone and said, "I'll call them when we leave and let them know the showing's over."

Behind him, he noticed the police cruiser putting on its red lights. He motioned to the officer to roll his window down.

"Trouble?" Brad asked.

"There's been a traffic accident up the road, sir. I'm the only squad car in the vicinity."

Brad got out of his car and approached the police unit. "Does Espinoza know?"

"I have a call into him. I'll return when I can. Will you be okay?"

Brad nodded as he surveyed his surroundings. Things looked mellow enough. He took a deep breath, nodded and returned to his car. The cruiser sped away.

"*Eef ju don* feel safe, we can return to your house," Fabiola said. She smiled coyly as if challenging his courage. "But I'll tell *ju tis*, I need an agent who *ees* flexible. Maybe *ju* can't do *tis* job right now?" she added.

"I'm okay, let's go in and take a look." He stopped the car, opened the door for Fabiola and the two of them walked up the pathway.

She strode into the front room, her head high, shoulders back.

The Queen inspecting her castle. She began to rattle off changes she would make. Itemizing furniture she would purchase.

Constantly reminding Brad that she wanted to make a full price offer soon, she exhaled loudly and questioned him extensively. Why couldn't they buy it today? Why were they waiting so long? If someone slipped in front of them, there would be Hell to pay! Brad bit his tongue and smiled.

The perfect sales agent.

She instructed Brad to walk with her and take notes. "I'm going to find every imperfection so the owners will either have to fix the problem or give us credit," she said. "Make sure *ju* take meticulous notes. And, if *ju hab* a camera on that phone of *jours*, take pictures."

He nodded and removed the phone from his pocket. They ascended a large spiral staircase made of mahogany railing and marble steps.

The pecking order had been established: Fabiola the Matriarch led Brad her trained and soon-to-be humble servant up the stairs.

== ⊕ ==

Neither of them heard the blue Honda come through the gate and park under the large pepper tree located along the side of the house.

Hollyfield couldn't believe his luck. Thinking he would have to follow Stephens for hours and then set up an elaborate scheme to neutralize the policeman assigned to him, he was pleasantly surprised when the cop turned on his lights and accelerated down the road. The Lord, truly, did work in mysterious ways. Just as Commander Dave had preached.

Watching from a distance, he had given it five minutes and then approached the house.

Confident that the guard wasn't returning soon, but anxious nevertheless to get this over with, he drove through the open gate.

Hollyfield and McCoy sat stone still as they listened for activity and watched for movement in the house and in the yard. Failing to see or hear anything, they slowly got out of the car and advanced towards the house. It was time to put their commando training to the test.

"How we going to do it? You want me to stand watch out here?" McCoy whispered.

"Nope. There's two of them. It will take two of us."

"What about the guard?"

"He's long gone. Must've been an emergency or something. Once we get them isolated, it should only take us a few minutes. We'll be out of here by the time he comes back."

"What if he returns?"

"Shoot him."

They walked quickly but quietly towards the back door.

== ⊕ ==

"You see *tee* nail holes along *tis* wall?" Fabiola said, pointing to an area in the upstairs hallway where, obviously, pictures had once hung. "*Tees* must be patched and painted. *Tee* paint must match perfectly."

"They probably had pictures hung there," Brad said pointing to a spot above her head. "Maybe they took them down for the showing?"

"I *don* care. *Tere* will be holes in *tee* wall when they leave and we must make *tem* pay for *tee* work."

It continued like this for the next fifteen minutes. Fabiola noticing rather small blemishes and then making a big deal out of them. Fabiola bossing Brad around like a paid man-servant. So many, "I *wans*", "I *needs*", and "I, I, I". No wonder Mel was so cold to her.

He wondered if John had seen this side of her?

"I *wan tees* wall painted orange. Make a note, Brad," she said pointing to a perfectly good neutral brown surface in the hallway. They walked past a sitting room and entered a small study. "I need *tat* rusty hinge replaced. And *tees* cabinets! *Tee* knobs must be re-set. *Tey* must be *sactly* level. Are *ju* writing *tis* down Brad? Brad?"

Hearing no response from her faithful secretary for the day, she whirled around, tongue ready to lash out at her servant.

Suddenly, she froze.

THREE O'CLOCK THURSDAY AFTERNOON. LINDEN was getting antsy.

He hadn't heard from Brad today. He knew that Fabby had landed safely and he was pretty sure that Brad and she were looking at houses together. He was beginning to think that he couldn't afford the four million dollar spread.

The thought made him mad.

And somewhat embarrassed.

He had worked hard for that money. He had trusted IFPG. If it was a fight they wanted, then by God, he'd give 'em one.

Brad had warned him to not meet with Tyler. But, fuck it. That just wasn't his style. Golf fans knew Linden was a swash buckler on the course, going for every par five in two.

He stopped and considered the pros and cons: On the pro side, it was time to fight for his money. These guys should explain to him how they lost 65% of his dough.

On the con side, they might get pissed, drop him from their management team and blackball him with sponsors.

After kicking it around for a few minutes, Linden decided to go for broke. He'd pay a little surprise visit on Tyler Ambrook. Soften him up a bit. It was time the little piece of shit found out who he was messing with!

Quickly dressing in his best power suit—an Armani, dark blue with thin pin stripes and red tie—he combed his hair once more, checked himself in the mirror and began his journey to IFPG Headquarters.

Strange things happen to a person when they've had a significant amount of money stolen. Some become violent, almost homicidal. Some become depressed and despondent. Some just accept their fate.

Linden opted for a fourth option: controlled anger. Maybe there was a valid excuse? Maybe the whole thing was blown out of proportion? He'd leave that door open, or at least, slightly ajar. Brad would be proud of him.

He left his condo, got in his car, put it in gear and checked his cell phone. "Damn, suddenly nobody wants to talk to me," he muttered under his breath. He merged into traffic, took a cleansing breath to relax and thought about his situation.

He had missed two foot putts in his career that had cost him hundreds of thousands of dollars; lost large sums gambling; even had small amounts stolen by scamming associates but he had never felt anger like he was experiencing now. Maybe it was Art's death; maybe it was Fabiola?

Whatever.

He was pissed.

He took another deep breath. "Calm down," he said to himself. "Breath like you do before an important shot. It's just a surprise visit. Don't lose your cool."

Arriving at IFPG thirty minutes later, he purposely parked his car behind Tyler Ambrook's gold BMW. Worse case, he would block the son of a bitch from leaving the premises. Or, better yet, ram the little preppy asshole if he made a run for it. Linden opened the car door, slammed it shut and approached the building—determined to make this the most important meeting of his economic life.

It was late afternoon and the IFPG building was framed magnificently by the setting sun. Rays of light danced off the office windows and shadows crept from around the corner of the building. Linden looked around, the parking lot and grounds seemed awfully empty, maybe it was a holiday and he hadn't gotten the memo. He shrugged and opened the front door.

"Mr. Linden. What a privilege to see you again," the hot blonde receptionist he had seen the other day said, putting down her nail file, rising from her desk and extending her hand.

"Great to see you again," he replied. And he meant it. Her blonde hair was shorter today. And, her legs! He hadn't noticed her long, tan legs before. They were marvelous. What an asset. Today, she wore a yellow skirt with turquoise top. Her three inch stilettos accentuated the tone in her calves.

His mind wandered as he imagined getting her in the sack.

Fighting back the urge to flirt with her and remembering why he had burst in, he politely asked to see Tyler Ambrook.

"Mr. Ambrook is in, but…." she began.

"Listen, darling. Don't give me no bullshit. I'm here and he WILL see me. I know it's your job to protect these guys from unwanted visitors, and I assume you do your job beautifully, I might add, but I'm going to see him— or his dad—one way or another. So please call his secretary. What's her name? Erma? Tell her I'm coming back and that I'll need at least thirty minutes."

Apparently impressed by his forcefulness and seemingly unprepared for his appearance, the receptionist sat back down, picked up the phone and called Erma.

As he began to walk away, Linden caught himself. Where were his manners? He turned back to the girl, grabbed her left hand and lightly but confidently kissed the top of it.

"My dear, I greatly appreciate both your beauty and your efficiency. Maybe we can have a drink sometime?"

A regular Rhett Butler was he.

She smiled. "I don't usually have drinks with older men."

"Well, maybe this time you'll make an exception. Here's my number." He handed her one of his business cards.

She stared at it a minute, placed it in her purse and said, "Maybe." She returned to filing her nails.

Still got it, he thought. If things go south with Fabby, he'd give this gal a call. Always have a Plan B, his old pappy used to say. He turned, threw his shoulders back and sauntered down the hall.

== ⊕ ==

"Mr. Linden. How nice to see you again," Erma said. Clearly, she was caught off guard but her job was to be courteous as well as competent.

"Cut the crap, Erma. You hate seeing me. I'm sorry to be so blunt. I'm sure you're a very nice person. But this really is very important. Is the little shithead in his office? Or do I have to search the building to find him?"

"I don't know why you insist on being so disrespectful to Mr. Ambrook?"

"I can give you about ten million reasons," he replied. "Now, is he in or not?"

"Yes, but…"

Linden didn't wait for her to finish the sentence. He went straight to Tyler's door and yanked it open, his financial—and maybe professional—destiny on the line.

Tyler had his feet propped on the desk, phone in hand, his usual self-satisfied smirk plastered on his face as he talked. His eyes darted up at the sight of Linden and he stopped mid-sentence.

Behind him a big screen television was tuned to CNBC. The Dow was up 128 pts.

At least some investor was having a good day.

"Hang up the phone Tyler. We've got a lot to talk about."

Tyler stared at Linden for a moment then turned away as he swung his legs off the desk. "Hey, listen, something's come up, can I call you back a little later? Great." He replaced the receiver and took a deep breath. "John, you seem to be making a habit of unscheduled visits." He managed a tight smile. "To what do I owe the honor this time?"

Linden grabbed the remote control sitting on the corner of the desk and clicked the T.V. off. "You're going to want to give me your FULL attention," he said roughly, grabbing a chair and planting himself at the edge of it, ready to pounce. The 'controlled' part of his anger beginning to wane.

"I've been reviewing my tax returns and financial statements. I'm not happy. Care to explain?"

"I'm afraid you have me at a disadvantage. I haven't seen your financials. Give me a minute and I'll have Erma send in your file."

"Quit stalling. You know damn well what my assets look like. Instead of ten million liquid, I'm down to two point eight."

"And you think it's my fault?"

"Damn right!" he said, slamming his fist on the desk. The anger had taken the better of him. "And you're going to give me some answers or I'll have the Feds in here going over your books by tomorrow."

That got Tyler's attention. He adjusted his tie, rubbed his chin and looked Linden directly in the eye.

"Calm down. Let's discuss this like men," Tyler said. It looked to Linden as if the young man's brain was straining, trying to come up with something to say to calm him down, maybe some lie to defuse his anger. His eyes twitched and he fiddled with a pencil.

Linden hesitated a moment, and then pulled the brown leather chair closer. Tyler took another deep breath and continued. "It's very complicated, John. Over the past three years, IFPG has taken terrible losses in the Stock and Bond markets. 2008 and 2009 were unusually difficult years due to the recession. They're calling it the 'Great Recession', you know."

Linden nodded.

"Companies cancelled many endorsement deals, tournaments lost sponsors, yields on dormant capital plummeted. I'm sure you know all of this."

"Of course. I don't live under a rock. Go on."

"Well, due to the economic conditions I just described, IFPG decided to diversify the investments made on your—the players—behalf. We…"

"You got greedy and you fucked up."

"No, that's not true! The investments were a bit more aggressive than in the past but we made good position plays. The economy conspired against us."

"Okay," he said, prompting the young man to continue. Tyler was sweating by this time. Linden didn't want to let him off the hook. "Continue. Who is 'WE'?"

Before Tyler could answer the last question, the office door swung open. Linden heard movement behind him. He turned in his chair to see who it was.

"Hello John," came the booming voice of Steven Ambrook. "Erma told me you were meeting with Tyler. I thought I'd stop by and say hello. See if there is anything I can add to your discussion with my son."

The older man entered the room with a flurry, took Linden's hand in his and shook it vigorously. He sat down and pulled his chair towards Linden's.

John smiled. He hadn't expected to see both Ambrooks. "Good to see you, Steve."

Steven Ambrook nodded. He raised his forefinger as if indicating there was one more thing and said, "Oh, and before I forget, I've got a favor to ask of you. Please remind me to ask before you leave. So, what's going on?"

Tyler explained that Linden was concerned about his current liquidity. Tyler further relayed to his father that Linden was quite upset and wanted answers. He was in the middle of explaining the situation when the company's founder had joined the meeting.

"Continue, then," the father instructed calmly, looking steadily at his son. "Might as well get it all out."

The elder Ambrook, dressed in tan golf slacks, black golf shirt and tasseled loafers, pulled a leather chair close to John and sat down. He placed his left arm on the arm rest, sat back and raised his hand to his chin, forefinger pressed against the tip of his nose.

He wasn't an expert on reading body language—reading putts was more his style—but Linden thought the movements indicated deep concern. The frown behind the palm was easier to read.

Disgust.

At him or at Tyler?

Linden pressed forward. "Yeah, Sonny-boy here has been telling me that basically, you guys lost most of my money due to the shitty economy and some bad investments."

Tyler interjected quickly, "*I* was telling John, that in an effort to hedge against the economic downturn, and in an attempt to generate more yield on cash for our clients, we became a bit more aggressive in the market." He stopped and stared at his father.

"Go on," his father said.

"Well, as can happen to any active trader, our moves backfired. We sustained substantial losses. But our capital base remained strong." He smiled at Linden as if seeking validation.

When Linden said nothing, he continued. "There was no reason to alarm you. We were—we are—in position to cover your expenses without missing a beat."

Linden thought about it for a minute. Absorbing not just *what* the guy sitting across the desk said, but *how* he was saying it. So smug; so confident when describing how strong the company was.

Yet slightly troubled while describing the losses.

If he was lying, he deserved an Academy Award. The question in Linden's mind was: Is it a Best Actor in a Leading Role, or in a Supporting Role? He looked from Tyler to Steven and then back at Tyler again. Who was pulling the strings around here? He decided to press on.

"So, you got tagged...."

"IFPG got tagged," Tyler corrected.

"Okay. IFPG got tagged by the markets. How much? How many clients have been affected? And what are you going to do about it? The whole thing smacks of unauthorized trading to me." Brad had given him that term; told him to use it only if he needed an ace-up-his-sleeve.

"Now hold on there, John," Steven Ambrook chimed in. "I agree that the company's trading policy became too risky. I'm not happy about the losses. But, 'unauthorized trading' is a big allegation." He stared at Linden, his face turning red for the first time.

"That might be, but what would you call it, Steven?"

"Your contract with us contains several stipulations concerning the management of your money. One of which is the power to act on your behalf in matters concerning the Stock and Bond markets. It's called 'Power of Attorney'. We have done that for you and many of your peers over the years. Very successfully, I might add. Unfortunately, this time, like Tyler said, the economy conspired against us."

Linden turned his attention away from Tyler and towards the older man. He pulled some notes he had made after talking to Brad out of his back pocket, glanced at them and then continued. "I understand I gave IFPG certain powers. But I also signed up with your management company based upon certain very specific assurances. One of which was that you would maintain a very conservative investment strategy, seeking a decent rate of return. Another was that I would be informed if more 'unique' investment opportunities presented themselves." He glanced at both Ambrooks. They appeared to be listening intently.

There was a knock on the door, Erma stuck her head in. "Mr. Ambrook," she said, directing her comments to Steven. "There's a very important call for you on line...."

"Not now Erma. Tell them I'll call them back," he said, "And Erma please hold all calls for both Tyler and me until Mr. Linden leaves."

John poured himself a glass of water from a pitcher Tyler had sitting on the desk. He looked at both men and asked if they wanted a glass. Both declined.

He took a sip from his glass, remembered what he was talking about and continued. "My understanding is that each player would choose *if* they wanted to expose themselves to more risk and *how* much they would invest. I never gave you carte blanche to play Monopoly with my money."

Tyler took up the defense. "We didn't feel the investments were that unique. The money was invested in U.S. Bonds and Mortgage Backed Securities. These are hardly 'unique' in nature." Tyler snickered, sounding like George W. Bush discussing Hussein's weapons of mass destruction. "It's not like they were Bolivian Gold Mines or Venture Capital. Those would be unique."

Steven Ambrook added, "And IFPG would have consulted with you in advance on those types of investments."

His son nodded his head in agreement. "Listen John, there is no violation here. The fact is we sought higher rates of return from a very conventional market."

"Again with the 'WE' Tyler." Linden turned to face him. "Who is the 'WE'? Is it you and your father? Is it a group of advisors? Who is it?" Linden demanded.

Tyler turned to his father and spread his arms as if deferring the answer to Steven.

"John, this will be difficult for you to understand. I know you liked him a lot. I didn't want to tarnish his reputation with you or any of his clients. Tyler here has been protecting him by saying the company made bad investments. That's just not true. But you leave me no choice." Steven Ambrook rose from his chair, positioned himself on the edge of the desk and looked Linden straight in the eye.

"What are you saying?"

"The main culprit, if you will, in this unfortunate scenario was," he paused for dramatic affect…"Art Smalley."

Linden stared back at Ambrook. For once, the golfer who couldn't shut up while playing had no words. If this information was correct it could be a game changer. If it was a lie, then what did that have to say about IFPG?

He needed to get some more information out of these guys, finish up this meeting and talk to Brad ASAP. It was time to compare notes.

Briefly, he wondered how Brad's day was going, and then he refocused his attention on Tyler and Steven Ambrook.

He still had work to do here.

Why hadn't he heard from Brad?

44

TWO MEN DRESSED IN TACKY tourist clothes were standing in the doorway.

The fat one had his gun pointed at Brad. The other one, skinny with a black eye patch stood proudly with a shit-eating grin on his face. And a revolver in his hand.

"Who the fuck…Who are these men, Brad?" Fabiola was just as imperious as she'd been a moment before, but Brad noticed the cute, Charro accent had disappeared entirely.

"Unless I miss my guess, these men are here to kill me," Brad said staring down the barrel of the fat man's gun.

Brad could hardly believe those words had come out of his mouth so calmly. He waited for a jolt of fear to rip through him, but none came. Was he getting used to this? For some reason, he was facing his death without blatant fear. An interesting, but worthless insight—given his current plight. It appeared he was still going to die, frightened or not.

"The fat guy killed Jim Johnson by mistake," Brad said, pointing to Hollyfield. "Am I right?"

"Yep. We're going to kill the Mexican bitch too. Now that she's seen our faces," the skinny guy said, waving his gun at Fabiola.

"Shut up, McCoy," Hollyfield said forcefully.

"Why, Brad? What did you do to them?" Fabiola asked in perfect English.

"You might as well know. Seeing as we're going to die," Brad confessed in a shaky voice, beginning to feel the fear that had eluded him earlier. "I found out that IFPG—specifically, Tyler Ambrook—has been stealing money from John. They killed his manager because he knew about it and they tried to keep me from finding out. But I did find out. Apparently, I'm a threat to IFPG. I'm sure Tyler Ambrook sent these goons in hopes that he could keep a lid on it. Ain't that right boys?"

"I don't know what the hell you're talking about," Hollyfield said. "Me and McCoy here work for Commander David von Eisenlow. We represent The Sons for Sovereign Sacrifice. We don't know who the fuck Tyler Ambush, or whatever, is. I've never heard of IFPG."

"Sounds like some type of political shit...IFPG... I'm For Pregnant Grandmas," the skinny guy said and began chortling.

"Sons for Sovereign Sacrifice?" Brad repeated slowly. There it was again. "I've heard of your group." He rubbed his chin. Smalley had mentioned them in his notes. Why would this group want him dead? Was he wrong about Tyler? Were these fanatics somehow manipulating IFPG? Maybe Tyler was a member?

Then it made sense. Tyler Ambrook was paying these thugs thru the Athletes for Change LLC. They were on the pay roll. But why?

Before Brad could ask any follow up questions, the fat man grabbed his arm roughly and pushed him towards the study's door and out into the hallway.

"Money? When *ju* say money, how much *ju* talking about?" Fabiola asked, obviously not interested in their captor's murderous intent, her accent returning.

"Almost all of his money," Brad replied looking back over his shoulder.

"*Ju* mean *Juan ees* broke?"

"Not broke exactly. But if he buys this house, he'll be close."

"I *don* believe *ju*. *Gib* me *jur* cell phone. I *gonna* call *Juan*."

"Ain't nobody calling nobody," McCoy said, grabbing Brad's cell phone and putting it in his pocket. "Now move."

"Does the money matter that much?" Brad asked Fabiola.

"Are *ju* crazy? *Ub* course *tee* money matters, *ju* idiot," she spat at him defiantly. And before she could stop herself, she added, "Why else *wud* I marry an *estupido* professional golfer? He's boring and dull. Look at me. I *cud hab* any man."

"She's right," McCoy chimed in.

"Shut up, 'one eye', keep them moving," Hollyfield said.

Brad grinned and shook his head. "I'll be damned, Mel was right again," he said quietly under his breath.

"It ain't going to matter to either one of you pretty soon," Hollyfield said impatiently. "Now move out the door and stop your squabbling."

"Yeah, what he said," McCoy added, waving the gun again as if he couldn't focus on just one target.

Brad stared at Fabiola and shook his head. His buddy had made a bad choice in women again. Only this time, the girl would be dead and John would mourn her loss without knowing that she was using him only for his money and fame.

"Well, there it is then. Good to know your true colors and true motives before we die."

She frowned and then shrugged.

"Come on, McCoy, push the girl faster. We'll take them downstairs and create a convenient way for them to die. Maybe we can make it look like murder/suicide?" Hollyfield said.

"Why not do it up here?"

Hollyfield looked around. "I know this sounds crazy under the circumstances, but this is a nice house; I don't want to get it all bloody and shit."

"Really? You're one strange dude, you know that?"

"Maybe, but I'm in charge and I say we take 'em out back and arrange it like he killed her and then shot himself."

"What would be my motivation?" Brad asked, interrupting the big man's train of thought.

"Hell I don't know. Maybe you was jealous of your friend. She is awfully sexy," he said, turning to Fabiola and giving a wink. "And if you couldn't have her, nobody was going to have her."

"Maybe she just bitched him to death," McCoy added, chuckling. "Dude couldn't take being bossed around no more."

== ⊕ ==

McCoy grabbed Fabiola by the arm roughly and said, "Come on, muchacha. Let's go."

Fabiola stared at him, made as if to follow his instructions but suddenly turned and spit in his face. "Fuck *ju*!" she shouted.

McCoy raised his hand to his face, wiped the spittle from his cheek and grinned. "Why…. ain't you the fireball? I'm going to have some fun with you before we kill you." Without warning, he hit her with the back of his hand.

She had felt worse slaps. She buckled, but did not fall. The first rule of survival she had learned when young: "Don't let them see fear." Righting herself and rubbing her cheek, she tossed her head back and laughed.

"*Ju heet* like a *lil'* girl," she said between clinched teeth. "I bet *ju* like lil' boys…*don' ju*?"

"Hell. I'm ALL man. Bitch!" McCoy said, grabbing his crotch. "I'm gonna show you just how much man I am when I get you downstairs."

"No you ain't, 'One Eye'," Hollyfield said, the voice of reason. "We got one job to do. Kill them and get the hell out of here."

"Wouldn't it help set the scene if the police found evidence of a rape?" McCoy asked coyly. "I know I should do the job and get the hell out but, damn, if she ain't sexy. Gives me a hard on just thinking about doing her."

"Not with your DNA. Don't you remember what we learned in camp? They test for those things these days. So just keep your dick in your pants and let's get this done."

McCoy sighed. "Shit, okay, but it's such a waste," he said, pouting.

As they moved out of the study, Brad's eyes darted about. No weapons to grab. Nothing to throw. No diversion to make. He saw no obvious way out of this jam. He silently wished Rufus was here to rescue him. He chuckled at the thought.

"What you laughing at, slick?" Hollyfield asked.

"Nothing; you wouldn't understand. Had to be there."

They continued forward.

Funny the things you take solace in before you're going to die, he thought.

He had told John about the financial records and had told him to stay away from Tyler Ambrook. And at least this was happening away from his home. He hadn't been able to convince Mel to move to a safe location. Once they killed him, the fat guy said they would be done. Mel and the boys would be safe.

Small comfort in the face of death but comfort nonetheless.

They reached the stairs and began the long descent. Contrary to his agnostic leanings, Brad said a silent prayer.

45

THE TRIP DOWN THE SPIRAL staircase seemed to take forever.

Brad hadn't remembered it being so long on the way up.

Walking down these stairs with a gunman pushing him from behind, created an almost surreal mental time delay. It was as if time were, in fact, standing still. The most interesting part, however, was that he felt an extremely heightened sense of the here and now. His vision was crisp, his hearing precise.

And his sense of smell seemed unusually sharp. He smelt Fabiola's expensive perfume. He took a whiff of McCoys' body odor. And...something else caught his attention. What was it?

In an effort to postpone the inevitable, Brad turned his head and said over his shoulder, "You know, Mr.... What's your name again?"

"Hollyfield, Lieutenant First Class, Hollyfield to you."

"Mr. Hollyfield," Brad said, refusing to acknowledge the man's fake rank. "You're never going to get away with this."

"Oh, yeah, why's that?"

Brad thought for a moment. He really didn't have a true reason; was just stalling. He took another step and replied, "Well, first of all, the police have a description of you and your sidekick, there," he said, indicating McCoy.

"Second, Sergeant Raoul Espinoza is doing research on your group the Sons for Religious Sacrifice. It won't be long before he brings in the Feds and shuts you guys down."

"Sovereign."

Brad chuckled nervously. "What?"

"The group is Sons for SOVEREIGN Sacrifice. You dipshit. Not *religious* sacrifice."

"I said sovereign."

"No you didn't. Nothing wrong with my ears. You said religious."

"Yeah, I heard it too," McCoy added.

Fabiola nodded in agreement with her captors.

Nice ally.

"Whatever. The point is Raoul knows about your group and it won't take long for him to connect the pieces. If I were you, I'd put the guns down and get the hell out of here."

Hollyfield let go a deep belly laugh. "Nice try, pretty boy. We ain't going nowhere. We got orders to kill you and that's what we're going to do."

Oh well, he had given it the old college try. Hollyfield nudged him and he continued his descent, taking the next marble step slowly.

"Keep moving," Hollyfield commanded. "I want to get you two outside, and get it over with." He paused for a moment and then added, "Believe me you'll thank me for making it quick."

Oh, gee, thanks, Brad thought.

Behind him, Fabiola was being forced down the stairs as well.

McCoy had made her put her hands in front of her, wrapped them in duct tape and was grabbing her long dark hair from behind. His gun securely tucked in its holster, he pulled back on her hair with his right hand—making her wince in pain.

He placed his left hand inside her skirt, resting it firmly on her left butt cheek.

Cheap feel.

"Damn! Muchacha," McCoy exclaimed. "That other wetback with a beautiful ass, what's her name? J-Lo? Got nothing on you. You've got the most perfect butt I've ever seen. Or, felt," he added with a snicker.

"I bet *ju* felt many nice asses in *jur* time—all *ub tem* on *lil'* boys, *ju hoto*," she hissed.

He yanked her hair harder. Brad glanced back. It looked like she might pass out. Her body swayed and her eyes rolled up into her head for a second, but then she regained her footing.

"Are you okay, Fabiola?" Brad asked.

"No I'm not okay. This *hoto* is pulling my hair so hard, it feels like he's going to scalp me."

Hollyfield frowned. "Damnit, 'one eye', quit that. We don't want her to look abused when they find her.

Remember, we're going to stage this as a murder/suicide. If the police see patches of hair torn out, they're going to question it."

"Come on, Ken. Let me stick it to this bitch," McCoy pleaded, his pitch growing higher with anticipation. "She's got me hot and she deserves to feel a real white man in her before she dies. Nobody will know. I'll wear a rubber."

Hollyfield, his left hand tightly gripping the back of Brad's collar, turned to address his comrade. "Leave it be, One Eye. We'll drive down to Mexico when this is all done. If you really want some Mexican pussy, you can have as many ten dollar Mexican whores as you want. But right now, we got this job to do and your continued belly-aching ain't helping matters none."

The two continued bickering as the group neared the bottom floor landing. Something felt—actually, smelt—different to Brad. What was it? Cologne? After shave? Definitely something he hadn't smelt earlier. It seemed to fill the entire space. He turned his nose towards Hollyfield and sniffed.

"What the fuck you doing?" the big man asked.

"Just smelling your fear."

"*My* fear? *You're* the one what's going to die."

"Maybe. But I can tell you and McCoy are amateurs. You're afraid too."

Hollyfield shook his head and pushed Brad forward.

The scent he had noticed several steps earlier grew stronger. After sniffing behind him, he was sure the scent came from neither of his captors. Then, what was it?

Maybe his senses were now so heightened that perhaps he was smelling something he had missed earlier?

He hoped that wasn't the case.

He swiveled his head, moving it from left to right and breathed deeply. Suddenly, Brad recognized the scent. He had spent several hours recently locked in an interrogation room with that same smell.

Glancing to his left he saw faint shadows streaming thru a nearby door. Understanding that they might not be alone in the house after all, Brad's pulse began to race.

Was he wrong and maybe these were the owners returning early? No they are wealthy people. The husband wouldn't wear the after shave he was now smelling.

He stopped before reaching the bottom. "Are you sure there's nothing I can say, no money I can offer you to forget this madness?" he asked Hollyfield.

"Nope. We gotta do this. Now keep moving."

Brad glanced at the shadows. They were still there but not moving.

Keep these two assholes bickering. Give the shadows a chance.

"You know, Ken. Can I call you Ken?" he began. "I think ol' 'one eye' there is right. You're going to kill us anyway. No matter what you do, nobody's going to believe I killed my best friends' fiancée. Let him have his way with her. It's obvious he will never get an opportunity like this again in his pathetic life. Give him his fifteen seconds of pleasure."

Fabiola gazed at Brad, daggers exploding from her eyes.

"You stay out of this," the fat man responded. "I've got enough responsibility on my shoulders without making this type of decision." He was fully turned towards Fabiola and McCoy now. Brad felt the big man's hand come loose from his collar. He turned his head slightly. He could see that McCoy liked what Brad had to say. The skinny man was grinning.

Brad decided to act.

Spinning quickly, Brad pushed the fat man as hard as he could. Hollyfield lost his balance for a moment and stumbled to the side. Brad grabbed Fabiola by her wrists and pulled her forward.

From the corner of his eye, Brad could see McCoy's left hand slide free from the inside of Fabiola's skirt. He tried to grab his gun but Fabiola pushed against him with her shoulder. McCoy appeared startled and slipped on the next step.

Brad and Fabiola darted forward—towards the door to their left. Praying that his heightened senses were correct, Brad yelled, "We're clear!"

Hollyfield regained his balance quickly. "I don't know who the fuck you're yelling at, Stephens; nobody can hear you." Hollyfield said. "I'm tired of your bullshit, I'm going to kill you right here, right now."

Brad watched in horror as Hollyfield raised his gun to fire. He closed his eyes anticipating the worst.

46

THE SHOT ECHOED THROUGHOUT THE HOUSE.

Brad opened his eyes and watched in amazement as the gun fell from Hollyfield's hand, clanking heavily on the marble stair below him.

The big man sat down on the step and stared back at McCoy as if his partner had shot him from behind. A small red daisy-patterned stain formed on Hollyfield's shirt; just below his collarbone. After a few seconds the stain began to spread.

For his part, McCoy stood frozen. He pointed towards the top of the stairs, said, "Oh, shit!" and raised his hands in surrender.

"Don't shoot," he yelled.

"Throw down your weapon," the shooter demanded.

McCoy reached for his Beretta.

"Slowly. Two fingers. Don't be a hero," the voice said.

McCoy did as instructed.

"Good. Now go sit down by your friend."

McCoy did as instructed; a look of pain, anger and embarrassment covering his bony face.

"Hey, Brad, you okay, buddy?" Raoul Espinoza asked while pointing his still smoking .38 caliber pistol at Hollyfield and McCoy.

"I made sure to only hit the big man," Espinoza said as he descended the stairs.

Wheezing from the exertion and terrified from the experience, Brad looked at Espinoza, bent over, exhaled and gave the thumbs up sign.

Espinoza walked down the stairs as the two policemen whose shadows Brad had seen from the stairs burst through the partially opened door and took Hollyfield and McCoy into custody.

Espinoza stuck his service revolver back in his holster and placed a toothpick in his mouth. He approached Brad apologetically.

"I'm sorry I let it go on so long," he began. "But you were never truly in danger….."

Brad stared at him. "How do you define 'danger' Raoul?"

Espinoza smiled. "Fair enough. I'll admit you might have been in slight danger, but I was in the upstairs bathroom adjacent to the Master the whole time. My men were downstairs. If either of these bozos cocked the hammer on their revolvers, we would've been on them like 'white on rice'."

"How did you know?" were the only words Brad could squeeze through his dry lips.

"My man, Thompson. He followed you this morning. He noticed that the Honda had pulled in behind him."

Brad turned towards Thompson who now had McCoy in his grasp, nodded and said, "Thanks."

The officer tipped his hat.

"Anyways," Espinoza said, "I was following back several cars. I noticed the same thing but he had a better view. When they followed you down the road towards this house, he called me and we compared notes." He paused as if he were Columbo dissecting a crime.

"And?" Brad prompted him.

Looking annoyed at Brad's lack of appreciation for his pregnant pause, Espinoza continued. "We decided to send him past with lights flashing. We hoped they would think he had deserted you." He stopped forward, looked around and flashed his big, toothy smile again. "It seems to have worked. Obviously, they thought they were in the clear and decided to ambush you inside the residence."

"Obviously. Go on."

"That's when it got dicey. I didn't want to expose you to harm, understand, but I wanted to hear if they said anything incriminating."

Brad shook his head. Exhaled, but said nothing.

"You did a great job prodding him, by the way. I have the whole thing recorded."

Brad stared at him dumbfounded. "Did a great job doing what?"

"Getting them to confirm that they're working for that stupid extremist group. Don't you see it? Sons for Sovereign Sacrifice is behind Johnson's murder and your attempted murder."

"And Art Smalley?"

"Hey, I don't know about that," Espinoza said now standing just a few feet away from Brad. "I'll have to compare notes with the Orlando police department. But if they killed Smalley, we'll get 'em." He winked and continued his explanation.

"Thompson doubled back and met me out on the street. We made sure to remain hidden from view while we waited for these two assholes to enter the house," he pointed towards the now handcuffed killers, "I called for backup." He indicated the stocky officer helping Thompson.

"You could only get one other guy?" Brad joked, half serious.

"Busy day; turns out there *really* was a bad car crash a few miles away." He shrugged. "Go figure. Anyway, we followed the two goons into the house. I wanted to take them right away, but I couldn't find them. Thompson and I waited downstairs until Irving over there arrived."

"How did you get upstairs without us seeing you?" Brad asked.

"When all four of you went upstairs, I knew I should try to get behind you and have my men down here out in front of you. I found an alternate stairway in the kitchen that led to the upper west wing—this is really a nice house, don't you think?"

"Yeah, yeah, it's a real gem. Go on."

"From there, I made my way to the adjoining bathroom and watched as events unfolded. I was prepared to take action at any moment—if the situation got violent." Again he shrugged.

Just another day in the life of a police sergeant.

Brad said, "Again, I want to talk to you later about your definitions of 'danger' and 'violence'."

"I almost intervened when McCoy hit the girl but decided to hold off because I didn't see a weapon."

"Still no violence as far as *you* were concerned?"

"Nope. But when he raised the gun...."

"Violence?"

"Extreme," Espinoza said nodding, flashing the toothy grin.

Brad stared at his buddy. He couldn't decide whether to be happy or pissed.

Espinoza had left them exposed to two killers far longer than Brad thought reasonable. What if they finished the job before Raoul got there?

Oh, what the hell. Dizzy with exertion but giddy with relief, he smiled and approached his buddy, right hand extended.

They shook and then embraced.

"I don't care what the logistics were, Raoul, I'm just glad you got here when you did. These guys were going to kill us. Ol' 'One Eye' over there may have raped Fabiola before everything was said and done. I'm a little pissed that you allowed us to be exposed as long as you did, but I'm glad you got these shitheads and I'm ecstatic that you heard the part about the Sons for Sovereign Sacrifice."

"Like I said, you were never in serious danger," Espinoza reiterated slapping Brad on the back and leading him towards the kitchen.

Brad nodded. "I get it. I'm happy to be alive. Let's get out of here. I'm anxious to see my family." Brad paused, "And hey, Raoul. Thanks for wearing that heavy cologne. What brand is it anyway?"

"Old Spice, my friend; five ninety nine on sale at the drug store. Can't afford the expensive stuff on a cop's salary."

"Well, it's now my new favorite fragrance," Brad said with a grin.

== ⊕ ==

Fabiola had stayed crouched in the corner. Her head down, her chest heaving while officers cut the duct tape from her wrists and checked her for injuries.

They seemed happy to give her the full review.

She rose to her feet and sidled up next to Brad. She adjusted her breasts, rubbed his arm and looked him in the eye.

The affect was dazzling.

"*Ju* know, Brad. *Anyting* I said during *tees* ordeal, was said in *tee* heat *ub* battle. I trust *ju* will keep *tat* in mind. As my realtor, who *goin* to make *mucho* commissions, I '*spect ju* to keep our conversations confidential." Charro almost purred.

"Fabiola, you don't have to worry about me breaching confidentiality," Brad said. "I am no longer your agent. I quit."

He watched her blink rapidly, apparently surprised by this revelation. She regained her composure quickly and changed gears. "Good. Since I *don* like to mix business *wit* pleasure," she said softly as she slid next to him and rubbed her hand up and down his left arm. She whispered in his ear, "*Ju* are a *bery* sexy man, Brad Stephens. *Ju* saved my life. *Ju* make me hot. I *cud* show *ju* *tings* in bed, *ju* never dreamed *ub*. We *cud hab* a *bery* close relationship. *Juan* and Mel *don* need to know. Do *ju unnerstand*?"

Wow! Where did that come from?

Brad hesitated before responding. He felt the slightest bit of temptation—he *was* a man after all and she *was* a beautiful, sexy woman. Every guy's fantasy.

What was he thinking?

"You're amazing," he said, shaking his head slowly.

She smiled as if it were a compliment.

"How could you think I would place my financial profit, or my dick, in front of my friendship with John? He frowned. "I suggest you tell John the truth and get on with your life. If you don't do it, I will."

"Fuck you, Brad Stephens! Who died and made *ju* God?" Fabiola hissed quietly, making sure Espinoza didn't overhear the full conversation. "And Fuck John Linden! He lied to me. He said he was rich. I wasted time on that loser."

Brad noticed that her cute, quaint, Charro-like accent had given way to perfect English. Another indication that she had been playing Linden for a sucker all along.

What else had she lied about?

"That's another difference between us," Brad said boldly. "My decision was a no brainer. You, with your almighty sense of self-importance would sell out your own mother. Me. I'm loyal to my family and friends. Might seem quaint; but that's the way it is."

Fabiola sighed, put a hand on her hip and pursed her lips. "You're an old man and an idiot."

"And you're a money grubbing gold-digger." He paused, thinking of something else brilliant to say. "I prefer my position to yours."

She frowned, checked her fingernails and then flipped him off.

He had to grin. "Listen, Fabiola. I think its best if you tell John you can't take all the publicity that goes along with being married to a celebrity. You're so shaken over this near death experience that you need to move on. Do you catch my drift?"

She smiled. Maybe she did; maybe she didn't. Didn't matter. Either way, he made certain she knew he would protect his friend from emotional harm—if he could.

"Go find another man. Make sure he has money—real money—this time." he said.

With a look that could kill, she told him she'd stay around Montecito for a while. "Did he have a problem with that?" He shrugged. "Just leave John alone."

"Who?" she said coyly.

"Already forgot him, how convenient."

"Whatever." She stared at Brad for a moment and then began to walk off, stopped and turned to him, "You know, I really did like him at first. Make sure he knows that. If he still had money, we'd be together forever. I'm sure you know how it works." She strode off, grabbing a startled Raoul Espinoza by the arm and asking him for a ride to Brad's house. "I will pack my things and be gone before you come back," she said over her shoulder.

Brad stared at her and then at his friend. Espinoza grinned from ear to ear.

What a weird day, Brad thought. He almost gets killed. Then he almost gets…well, a chance to have wild sex with a 30 year old bombshell, one of the most incredibly hot women he'd ever encountered.

And then he turns the fantasy down flat.

Unbelievable.

He thought of the night John and Fabiola had been going at it in the guest bedroom. Then his mind wandered to the idea of Fabiola in his bed and lingered there. *What would it be like…?*

Whoa! He suddenly pulled hard on the reins, forcing his mind back from the path it was galloping down. God knows he loved Mel.

But sometimes it was hard being a man.

Then he grinned.

He'd rather go home to Mel than hang out with this imperious, bitch. He'd celebrate life tonight with his family. Maybe when he went to sleep, he wouldn't have that crappy nightmare? His pursuers had been captured. The police had a handle on who had sent them.

He'd call Linden tomorrow. He had quite a story to tell.

Maybe he'd leave out a few parts?

ACROSS THE DESK, TYLER AMBROOK could hardly conceal his surprise.

He had fully expected his father to throw him under the bus. Blaming the losses on Smalley was a stroke of brilliance. He had been ready to fess up; take his medicine; throw himself on the mercy of the court; and explain to Linden how he was going to 'trade' them back into the black.

Now he joined his father's lead.

"Of course, IFPG stands behind all of its employees. We didn't want to soil the reputation of an otherwise good man," he said, a patronizing smile, full of false sympathy breaking out on his face.

Like a mortician, expressing concern for the loved ones, while internally counting the profits brought about by death, Tyler added, "Besides he's dead. Why put his wife and kids through the drama?"

"So, you're telling me that Art orchestrated a bunch of unauthorized trades; lost a shit load of money and then hung himself because he couldn't face me or his family?"

Tyler nodded. Steven spoke, "I know you liked him. I did too, but the facts are the facts, John."

Linden listened to both father and son intently. Rising from his chair when Tyler finished speaking, he ran his hands through his hair.

Realizing that he could get pissed and confront this story head on or could argue that Art was happy in general, but concerned with the company's investments, he had a decision to make.

If he opted to defend Art, he could point to the separate set of books as evidence that something more sinister was going on.

Hell, he could walk around the big desk and grab the little turd by the throat and squeeze until Tyler admitted to killing Smalley.

Instead, he decided to treat this information like it was a golf match. Patience usually paid off. Let the other guy make a mistake. Just play your game. In this case, he felt the more he encouraged them to talk—the more rope he gave them—the more they were likely to hang themselves.

He grimaced at the thought of Smalley dangling from the ceiling.

"I guess this makes sense," Linden said.

Feed them more rope.

"He *did* stop communicating a while ago. And there *was* some feedback from co-workers that he had been drinking heavily."

They took the bait.

"Once he sustained the trading losses in a few accounts—yours being one of them—Art panicked," Tyler said quickly.

Too quickly.

"He began 'doubling up to catch up'. It's sad, really. He had been such a good account manager…in the past," Tyler said.

"Yes. Sad," Steven Ambrook said nodding. "It's the main reason I came back into the daily management of the business. Tyler here feels confident he can make a few low risk trades in the current market and recoup all your losses. I think we owe it to Art—and to you—to let Tyler try."

"Why didn't you make me aware of the losses? It's my money, you know."

"I apologize for that. We should have informed all our players the minute we discovered it. Obviously, that was a mistake on my part." Steven Ambrook sighed. Held his hands in front of him as if surrendering. "I plead guilty."

Linden watched the father and son closely as they delivered their lines. They hadn't known he was coming to confront them in advance so he had to conclude that this little dog and pony show was totally impromptu. Not bad, he thought. They're both fine actors.

Maybe they could do a two man show in prison.

La Cage aux Folles, perhaps?

"So, where do we go from here?" Linden asked in the most sincere voice he could muster.

"I'm glad you asked," Steven Ambrook said. He stared across the desk at his son. "Since we don't want to drag Smalley's name through the mud, I suggest we keep this information contained between the three of us. Tyler will make a few trades and in a short while, your account will be restored to its rightful balance."

He paused looking very satisfied with himself. He smiled at Linden and continued. "In the big picture, the losses were rather small and the damage to our client's accounts limited to a small circle of players. From what I've seen so far, your account was one of the hardest hit. Art must've really felt secure in using your money."

Taking the queue from his father, Tyler added, "I think Art liked you the best, John. He wanted you to prosper the most from his aggressive trades." He put on the phony smile again. "Remember, he intended to make money for his accounts. He didn't intend for these investments to go sideways. There wasn't enough commission in it for him to be motivated by personal profit."

"Well, I'm a grown man. I understand shit happens," Linden said looking at Tyler and winking. "So what you're telling me is that if I'm patient, keep my mouth shut, give you enough time to do your thing, I should be able to withdraw over ten million dollars from my IFPG account in a few weeks?"

Tyler's eyes shifted to his father, pleading for validation. When it didn't come, he responded. "As you know, John, my father has always been quite the optimist. I know it's true that we can restore your account, I don't know if I can do it so quickly. Let's say a few months. I think that's more realistic."

"Steven," Linden barked, turning towards the father. "Which is it? A little while or a few months? I'm in the process of buying an expensive home. If I'm going to keep my mouth shut and allow your plan to proceed, I need some assurances."

This business talk was coming fairly easily to him now. He was glad he'd slipped the voice activated tape recorder into his coat pocket. He had seen McGyver do this a few times. Brad was going to love hearing this crap.

He'd be impressed.

"I'll make it happen more quickly, John," Tyler said. "But you need to promise me that you'll keep a lid on this thing. And that you'll keep your money with us. Are we agreed?"

Linden decided to play along. He had no intention of keeping a lid on this *thing*.

If Art Smalley's records were correct, the losses suffered by IFPG were in the hundreds of millions. The other players should know about their finances. And, if he and Brad were right, Art had been killed because of those losses.

Ambrook was correct about one thing—Linden owed his former manager. Art had been his friend. If John could help restore Art's reputation, albeit posthumously, and bring some closure for his family then that was what he was going to do.

Other than Art's books—and his personal losses—he had no tangible evidence of wrong doing. They didn't point a finger at anybody in particular. A shrewd lawyer could argue that Art had kept the dual set of records out of personal guilt. Or perhaps there was some way he could use them to cover his tracks.

If he played along with these two slick operators, perhaps he could catch them in a lie.

"Okay. I agree," he lied. "In the meantime, except for what you need to pay my expenses, I want to withdraw all of my remaining money. My buddy, Brad Stephens, will contact Erma in the morning and give her wiring instructions for a bank in Santa Barbara; any problem with that?"

"No, no problem," Steven Ambrook said while staring at his son and nodding slightly. "If that makes you feel better and as long as you promise not to go public with this 'little indiscretion', I have no problem with that."

Tyler quickly added two additional stipulations. "And…the money we make you goes back into your IFPG account…and…you sign a new five year contract with us."

"I can live with that. Anything else?" Linden asked as he approached the men to shake their hands.

Tyler Ambrook shook his head, no. Looking relieved, he took a deep breath and sat back in his chair. If he was concerned about earning the money back, Linden couldn't tell from looking at him.

Steven Ambrook spoke. "I'm glad we were able to work this out as men and as business partners. Thanks for the opportunity to win your trust, John. I hope we can bury this episode in the past."

I bet you do. Ain't going to happen old man. Tyler is involved in this up to his preppy little neck. He probably had Art killed and he tried to have Brad killed. I've got the tape recording from this meeting. I've got Smalley's files. I've got you acknowledging that unauthorized trades occurred. Most likely, Brad and I will take what we know to the Feds. I've just got to talk to him first.

"Now, John, about that favor I mentioned earlier," the now exceedingly gracious senior Ambrook said. "The President, the Speaker of the House, and several key Congressional members are scheduled to play golf together on Monday at Harbour Town. It's a charity promotion for a local children's hospital. More importantly it's an opportunity for the politicians to show the nation how well they all get along." He winked at Linden as if this were an inside joke.

Linden shrugged. "Bi-Partisanship and all I suppose," he said.

"Yes, that's it. Well anyway, I just got word this morning that the President can't make it. Apparently something has come up in Syria. He needs to make a trip to the Middle East. Rather than cancel the event, the organizers of the tournament thought it would be fun if you, the reigning U.S. Open Champ, filled his spot. I'm sure the Speaker would be thrilled. He's a five handicap, you know. What do you say?"

Linden had to start practicing for the upcoming tournament anyway. What could it hurt? Might score him some brownie points with the public?

He quickly agreed.

"Wonderful. I'll let the tournament organizers know immediately. We can arrange a minor add campaign around this. Probably get you a few more endorsements." He spoke directly to his son. "Tyler, let's schedule a meeting with the marketing department this afternoon. I'll be playing in the foursome behind John. It should be a great day for IFPG."

"Oh, and John," he continued. "About that *other* matter. Are you sure nobody else knows about Smalley's activities?"

"You know, now that you mention it, there is one other person who knows about the losses. My buddy, Brad Stephens out in California. I discussed it with him before coming here this morning. If I ask him though,

I'm sure he'll keep quiet," Linden lied. He was getting good at this, he thought.

"You sure he'll keep his mouth shut if we meet your terms?"

"I'm sure."

"Good," Ambrook said.

"Well, guys this has been fun but I gotta run. Glad we had this talk." He shook both Steven and Tyler Ambrook's hands, turned and walked quickly from the room.

He was anxious to call Brad.

== ⊕ ==

Steven Ambrook had listened to the first part of Linden's response without really hearing it, his mind wandered.

So many moving parts.

He had calls to make and information to share. He had to confirm Monday's events with that idiot, Von Eisenlow.

He'd have to tell the guy that the President had backed out. Security wouldn't be as tight.

It was more important for him to know, however, that there was a new, specific target.

The new target would be playing in the first group, along with the Speaker of the House.

He, the 'whisperer' would be in the second group— at least a hole behind.

Von Eisenlow should be extra diligent. He had to kill the entire first group but take care not to let his men shoot at the second group.

Ambrook had gotten what he had wanted from the meeting—a few more days to save his company.

It was time to fill Tyler in on his plan. He would share all the unsavory details. The boy would probably think less of his father, but screw him. He caused this mess in the first place.

The company was all that mattered.

His focus returned as Linden spoke the last few words. He thought to himself, *I'm absolutely sure Mr. Stephens will keep his mouth shut. And, sadly, after Monday, you will too.*

Permanently.

48

FINANCIAL MARKETS, ALTHOUGH VOLATILE BY nature, tend to act predictably in times of crisis—they panic.

They run for the high ground; the safe ground.

The 'whisperer' knew this very well.

An hour after Linden had left the building, Steven Ambrook paced back and forth in his office suite. Brilliant slivers of light from the setting sun shone through the partially closed blinds.

He took this as a sign of enlightenment.

It was time to explain how markets work to his son.

"Erma," he said into the intercom, "Please find Tyler and send him to my office ASAP."

Ten minutes later, Tyler arrived, sweaty, a white towel wrapped around his neck.

"What the hell have you been doing?" his father asked.

"Working out in the company gym. You should try it some time."

Ambrook frowned. They were in the midst of a financial crisis—the company he built at stake—and his kid was working out in the gym. He shook his head as he said, "I don't have time to 'work out'." He made quotation marks with his fingers for emphasis.

"Somebody's got to navigate us through this cluster-fuck you got us involved in."

Tyler smiled. "No worries, pops. I got it under control. I've mapped out some trades for this week and after we close them, I'll use the profits to pyramid our way back to solvency."

Again Ambrook shook his head. "You don't get it, do you?"

"What?"

"You can't make back as much money as you lost with a relatively stable market; the reason you lost so much was because the market was incredibly volatile the last few years. Bears gained traction and then Bulls tried to fight back. You got caught up in the gunfire."

Tyler rolled his eyes. "Dad, I understand the markets. Have a little faith in me, will you."

"It's not you I'm worried about—although you've proven to be an incredible failure so far—it's the markets. We need volatility; we need uncertainty; we need the markets shook up." He slapped the table in front of him.

"Okay, okay I get it. I'll watch it closely and then consult you before I act. Does that make you happy?"

"No, it doesn't." He sighed, rose from his chair, walked around his desk and sat down facing his son. "Have a seat Tyler, I want to give you a little history lesson."

Tyler hesitated, rolled his eyes again and sighed like a sixteen year old teenager being scolded by his obvious-ly stupid parent.

"I said, SIT DOWN!"

This time Tyler did as instructed.

Steven Ambrook straightened his tie, rolled his neck like a boxer before a fight, crossed his legs and began his dissertation. "You see, son opportunities only exist when the market is taken by surprise. Domestic crisis, foreign crisis, it doesn't matter. As long as it's an unforeseeable, immediate event that affects a country's economy, the market is going to either go up or down. It won't hold steady.""Stability is the death of Wall Street traders."

Interrupting his father, Tyler said, "Yeah, I get it. We just went over this."

"Shut up and listen."

Tyler slumped in his chair.

"I learned a few lessons about the markets over the years—though none of them as costly as the one you've exposed us to." He paused and let the statement sink in.

When he was sure he had his son's full attention, he continued. "When Chernobyl melted down in Russia, threatening the world with its first 'China Syndrome', investors panicked. They sold nuclear energy stocks; hoarded gold; sought safe haven in U.S. Treasury notes; and dumped the Dow."

"When was that?"

"1987."

Tyler grinned. "The world has changed a lot since 1987, Dad. The market is more sophisticated and the New York Stock Exchange has more control these days."

"Bullshit. The market has a mind of its own. Never forget that."

He slammed the desk with his hand to emphasize the point. "And super-fast, high tech velocity trading can make it even more volatile," he said, referring to the super computers located in close proximity to the NYSE floor. These computers could make billions of trades in a split second.

Amazing technology.

Unfair to the average trader.

"I think you're being overly-dramatic; but I get your point. Anything else," Tyler said, making as if to get up from his chair.

"Oh, I've got a lot more for you, boy. Sit down and shut up."

Tyler stayed put and pursed his lips. He gestured with a sitting semi-bow, indicating that he was ready for his father to continue.

"When Reagan was shot, investors 'rallied around the flag' and bought U.S. Treasuries and U.S. stocks. It was viewed as patriotic."

Tyler gave a bored nod.

"The pattern has been the same over the years. When Tsunamis hit Japan, earthquakes rock Kuwait or, god forbid, terrorist planes fly into U.S. buildings, the market knee-jerks."

"But all of those events were unpredictable," Tyler said.

Ambrook smiled. "Yes they were. So my point is this: For you to make back the billion you lost, we need a 'predictable' crisis—something the market will either buy or sell off of."

Tyler looked puzzled. "It's impossible to know about a crisis in advance."

It was Ambrook's turn to grin. "No it's not, Tyler. Sometimes crises can be influenced. Do you understand?"

"I've got to be honest….No, I don't."

Steven Ambrook rose from his chair and walked towards the window. With his back turned to his son, he continued. "Tyler, you're a nice kid, but awfully dense sometimes. It's time for you to wake up and smell the roses."

Tyler rose and walked over next to his father. "Okay, I'm all ears."

Ambrook turned and faced his son. Placing his hands on Tyler's shoulders, he looked the young man directly in the eye, leaned forward and whispered in his ear. "Don't worry son; as always, your old man is coming to the rescue."

49

"**LET ME SPELL IT OUT FOR YOU,**" Steven Ambrook said, sitting down in his high-back leather chair once again.

"I'm going to create an event that the market will respond to. You're going to place orders in advance of that event. We're going to make the money back very quickly. And then, you're never going to take a major risk again. Got it?"

Tyler sat down in a nearby chair, curiosity replaced the smirk he had been wearing. "What have you done, Dad?"

Ambrook took a cigar out of a mahogany box sitting on top of his desk. He snipped the end, struck a match and lit it. Taking a long first drag, he looked through the cloud of smoke at his son. "When I learned of the losses caused by your foolish trading, I immediately knew you couldn't make the money back—legitimately. Just doesn't happen that way." He blew a smoke ring from his mouth and watched it curl upward.

"Sure you can. Hedge fund traders make billions," Tyler said defiantly.

"You're not a hedge fund trader, Tyler. You're a cocky young man who lacks the sense God gave a rock."

"But…."

"Don't interrupt me, let me finish. Anyway, I decided to make the money back myself."

"How?" Tyler asked, not being able to stop himself.

Ambrook stared at him and then smiled. "You see son, like Las Vegas, Wall Street is full of ghosts of investors past—men like you who chased 'can't miss locks' of the century. I'm not one of those guys; I stack the cards in my favor."

It was time to inform his son.

He needed Tyler's help with the final logistical steps and, in a way, it was a form of poetic justice—despite what they say, the son *should* suffer the sins of his father…especially when the goddamned son caused the goddamned problems in the first place.

"Listen up, son. I've got a few things to go over with you. Some you will like; some you won't."

He began describing the events of the past few weeks. He explained that his immediate reaction to the news of the tremendous trading losses was one of profound disappointment in his son.

After thinking about it for a few days, he had decided that the only way to make back such a huge sum of money was to engage in additional unauthorized trades.

Tyler concurred, confirming for his father, that he, too, had come to the same conclusion.

"No son. You may've come to the same conclusion, but you did not create the proper course of action." The young man looked offended, then curious. "You see, Tyler, your reaction to this mess was the same as a blackjack player in Vegas. You were determined to place one more major bet and then use those winnings to bankroll many smaller bets."

Tyler nodded his head in agreement. "But the trades I'm going to make will have downside protection. If I'm wrong, we'll get stopped-out early and live to play another day."

"The problem with your trades is that they will be relying on events beyond your control. As is the case with many Wall Street traders, you may be absolutely correct in your assumptions, but your timing may be off. You can lose even when you're right. I can't have that. The company can't have that."

"That's what happened the past few years," Tyler quickly agreed. "I invested in Collateralized Debt Obligations, Mortgage Backed Securities, and Treasuries, only to lose in the short term but be right in the long run. It sucks!"

"Yes it does. But that's the nature of financial markets —they need winners and losers. And believe me, if you're not an insider, you *will* lose."

"What's your solution, then? Do we fess up to our clients and risk a Federal probe? You know, Dad, I could go to jail. *YOU* could go to jail," he said nervously.

"I understand. That's why I have chosen a more drastic course of action. My plan will save IFPG. It will refill our coffers and, most importantly, if all goes correctly, nobody will be the wiser."

Intrigued, Tyler said nothing; just stared at his father anxiously.

"Sit back and follow me. I'm going to take you through this slowly. Don't ask any questions. Just process the information and then help me prepare for our next course of action—hopefully, our final course of action."

Tyler did as his father requested. He sat back and listened as Steven Ambrook recounted the events he had put in motion.

"Initially, I wanted to protect you from any further wrong doing, so I enlisted the aid of Art Smalley. Art understood the necessity of saving the company's name. Hell he worked for me for more than twenty years."

His phone buzzed and Erma's voice boomed from the speaker. "I'm leaving for the night, Mr. Ambrook, do you need anything else?"

Thinking what he needed from her was to go back in time and have her *not* give Brad Stephens those fucking tax returns and those fucking real asset statements, he breathed deeply and then said calmly, "No Erma. We're all good. You have a nice night dear."

He turned back to Tyler and continued his story. "It turns out that Art was extremely upset about the trading losses. Of course, he noticed them when he got the annual reports. He stayed mum though."

Tyler shrugged. "He was still making good money."

"It wasn't about the money, you idiot. It was about the company. Art loved IFPG, he figured the losses would subside. He wasn't sure if you were making the trades or me or some outside firm we had hired."

"Art Smalley was a jerk."

Steven Ambrook slapped the table again. "No he wasn't. He was a decent man who got caught in the wrong place at the wrong time." He rubbed his face and continued. "Anyway, after I talked to him about the losses, I enticed him to help me."

"How did you do that? Art was a straight shooter."

"By promising him your job."

"My job!"

Watching his son's shock and then outrage and controlling his own anger, Ambrook took another long drag on his cigar. He exhaled and looked at the son he had raised to do great things; the son he had spent a fortune to feed, educate and then train to take over the business.

Tyler looked smaller somehow.

He certainly hadn't done great things. "Don't get your panties in a wad," Steve Ambrook said. "I would've found something useful for you to do."

"Why didn't you tell me?"

"I already told you I didn't want to get you in deeper. Besides, the fact is, son, you have proven to be a major fuck up." Ambrook let that sentence hang in the air as he blew another smoke ring.

Tyler's face reddened. "But you need my help now, don't you."

"I do. Smalley's not here any longer and I'm just about ready to make up all your losses but I need you to do a few things."

"What?"

"Shut up and I'll tell you."

Silence.

Ambrook put his cigar down, took a deep breath and continued. "As I said, Art already knew about your trading losses. I'm not sure he understood the full magnitude, but he knew they were big." He paused, brushed an ash that had fallen on his shirt to the floor and grinned. "He thought you were a fuck up, too, by the way."

No response.

"I told him I had a plan to make the money back but I needed him to help me. He swore he would and I was happy. He helped me begin to divert more money into a slush fund. And…."

Tyler interrupted him. "Wait a minute. Why would you need more money?"

Ambrook frowned. "You really don't get it, do you son? Money is power. I knew I needed to hire some people to do some things—some very bad things. The only way to get them was to bribe them. For that, I needed money—hopefully, untraceable money." He paused and stared at his son, almost willing him to nod his head in understanding.

When Tyler didn't, he frowned and then continued. "Smalley had heard of a small right wing group in the south. Saw them on TV or something. And unlike so many other religious extremists, their leader, David Von Eisenlow, came across as fairly dynamic, Art said. He did some background research and discovered that Von Eisenlow was training a few men in the Georgian hills."

"So, he's your basic nut job," Tyler said.

"Not quite," Ambrook said. "An insider told Art that Von Eisenlow hated the government and was training his followers in military actions. After a few phone calls, Art came up with Von Eisenlow's contact information."

"And he called this idiot?"

"Yes he did, but then, I think, he came to regret it. At some point, unfortunately, Smalley had an attack of conscience. He confronted me and told me that he would go to the authorities with what he knew about your unauthorized trading if you weren't removed immediately."

"That asshole," Tyler spit out.

"Yes, quite," Ambrook said, dejectedly. "He told me he would stay quiet about the money if I abandoned my plans to use Von Eisenlow."

He rose from his seat again and walked over to the large, picture window. The sun had set and the lights from the city could be seen in the distance. "This really is a wonderful area," he said under his breath.

"What happened next, Dad?" Tyler asked, apparently anxious to put the pieces together.

Ambrook turned to face him. "He told me that he and I would figure out how to make the money back legitimately." He shook his head sadly. "I've already told you that wasn't going to work; you don't make a billion dollars back in a short period of time without insider information."

Tyler nodded.

"You're starting to get it. Good." And then in a soft voice, he said, "Art left me no choice."

Tyler's eyes widened. He immediately grasped the implication. "Dad, you didn't? What did you do?"

"I eliminated the threat to you and to our company, Tyler," the old man shrugged. He looked like he had aged several years since the meeting began.

"I contacted Von Eisenlow myself. I promised tremendous financial support to him and his organization. It amounted to just a few million—nothing that would go noticed in the LLC fund. In exchange, he was going to have to perform some duties for me. The first of which, he performed admirably. He sent his best man to Art Smalley's house...you know the rest. Made it look like a suicide. No further questions were asked."

"Oh Shit! Shit! Shit! Shit!" Tyler exclaimed as he rose from his seat, put his face in his hands and began walking in circles.

"Calm down. What's done is done. Now sit down," he pointed to Tyler's chair. "I encouraged Von Eisenlow to pursue his personal agenda; told him we supported him."

"Through Athletes for Change?"

"No I never mentioned my name or the foundation. As a matter of fact, whenever I talked to him, I whispered. I'm sure he wouldn't even recognize my voice in person."

"Okay so what's the plan?"

He went on to explain that his plan almost blew apart when the Sons for Sovereign Sacrifice was implicated in the failed assassination attempt at a popular restaurant in D.C..

"Yeah, I remember reading something about that. A banker and a Senator almost got whacked."

Ambrook nodded. "By that time, I was fully committed to my plan to rebuild our finances. I provided more money and transportation to the group and relocated them to an empty farmhouse in West Virginia."

He explained that he had planted the seed for a convenient time and location for the extremist group to make its statement: The upcoming Monday in Hilton Head, South Carolina. "The President wanted to show bi-partisanship so he arranged for many governmental dignitaries to play in a charity event prior to the tournament. This would be like shooting ducks in a barrel, I told him."

"Did he take the bait?"

"Yes. And that just about brings us up to date."

"I still don't get it, what's your plan? Have these guys kill politicians?"

"Not just kill politicians; start a domestic crisis," he slapped an open hand on his desk. "You see, Tyler, it doesn't matter whether this idiot, Von Eisenlow, succeeds or not. Just the threat of violence to the heads of government will make the markets move. And, this time, we will be ready in advance."

Tyler frowned.

Had Steven Ambrook misjudged his son? Would the spoiled little brat have an attack of conscience, just like Art?

Slowly, Tyler said, "I get it. We *know* the crisis is coming and we position ourselves appropriately in the market." He paused for a moment, ran his hands through his hair and stared at his father. "I have to admit, it's brilliant!"

"Yes, I know," Ambrook said in a quiet voice—almost a whisper.

50

WE'VE ONLY GOT ONE OTHER PROBLEM, as I see it,"
Ambrook said, putting his cigar out in a nearby ashtray.

"What's that?"

"Linden and his mortgage buddy, Brad Stephens."

Tyler took a deep breath and rubbed his forehead.
There was a lot of forehead rubbing going on. "I knew
I shouldn't have given them those financials."

His father shook his head. "We had to give them
something. I needed more time. Of course, it would've
been better, however, if they had been the doctored
ones."

Tyler nodded.

"Well, water under the bridge as they say. Let's move
forward."

"What about Linden and Stephens?"

"I've made arrangements to dispose of Mr.
Stephens. I had Von Einsenlow's men attack him twice
already. They failed, but I'm sure the third time will be
the charm."

Again with the frown, again with the forehead rubbing.

Tyler seemed for the first time to fully understand all that was happening. "And John?" he asked nervously.

"And John...well, let's just say that John unfortunately will be collateral damage; killed by those religious fanatics when they assail the golf course Monday."

"No shit? You'd kill the goose that laid the golden egg?"

"Sad, but true," Ambrook said. "I'm going to miss him, in many ways he was like a son to me." He took a puff and blew the smoke directly at Tyler.

"Damn. That's cold."

Apparently all this talk of death didn't sit well with Tyler. He looked like he wanted to vomit. His tan face was ashen. His palms sweated profusely. He wiped them on his pants and looked directly at his father. "My first question is: What the fuck? Murder? Dad, now we're murderers? I lost a lot of money. I didn't kill anybody. Have you gone mad?"

"You're in this up to your ass, so drop the act," Ambrook said aggressively. He took a cleansing breath and then continued. "Look son, desperate times call for desperate measures. How do you think I built this business? It's not all glitz and glamour. There were agents and coaches I had to bribe. There were wives I had to wine and dine. And, I didn't want you to ever know this, but there were golf matches I had to rig. I did this all for you. For our family legacy." He raised his hands in an all-encompassing gesture.

Tyler sat mesmerized by the man he thought he knew so well. The smart businessman; the incredible golfer; the social mixer.

Not a murderer.

Steven Ambrook continued. "And I'll be fucked if I'm going to let a second rate touring pro who got lucky to win a Major Championship and his shit-eating buddy take us down." He raised his voice a few decibels. "I'll grant you your moment of moral and ethical conflict. But what's done is done and you've got to accept it and move forward. Are you with me?"

Shaken by his father's bluntness, the son who had mistakenly thought he was in total control acquiesced, "Yes sir. I'm with you. What can I do to help?"

"Good boy. I need you to inform your traders that we will be positioning our client's money in several investments Sunday evening," he began. "We should be able to establish some positions on International markets without too much notice. Once the market opens Monday morning, we will increase those positions." He smiled. "Now, grab a pen and a piece of paper."

Tyler did as requested.

"Write this down: Go long a hundred thousand treasury contracts. Spread them between 2 Yr. to 30 Yr. notes. That'll cost us thirty five million dollars. Buy fifty million in gold futures. Short the S&P. Wait thirty minutes and then place another fifty million dollars in shorts on the S&P." He paused and made a steeple out of his fingers.

He stared at his hands for a few seconds as if they were disconnected from his body before continuing. "Finally, I want whatever remains of our client's money, and it should be around fifty million, invested in hard tack businesses—Taser companies, Kevlar vests, security services."

"How am I going to know which ones to invest in?" Tyler asked.

"Tell your guys to find the top companies in these areas and buy their stock; it's easy." He gave his son an uncomfortable glare. After a brief pause he continued. "Place puts at reasonable values and, in general, bet that they are going to go up in value. If the Sons for Sovereign Sacrifice are successful, we will see panic in the streets. This could be the equivalent to Katrina in New Orleans. Let's get on the good side of these bets."

"What about John Linden? Anything I can do to help with him?"

"Let me take care of Linden. You focus on Wall Street. Mask our trades the best you can. Make sure that the international trades are placed by noon Sunday and the domestic trades first thing Monday morning."

"Why the split trade?"

"It will look like we're following up on reasonable trades rather than stockpiling on insider information."

"Got it," Tyler said with a deep sigh as if he'd just run a fifty yard sprint. "Can I ask one more question?"

"Go ahead."

"Were you really going to give Smalley my job?"

Steven Ambrook sighed. He stared at his son for a long second and then smiled. It was a bittersweet smile. "You bet your sweet ass I was."

Tyler's eyes widened.

"Hey, don't look at me that way. You fucked up. You put the entire company at risk. You potentially ruined my life's work. If Art had done what I asked him to do, he would be sitting in that chair now. Not you."

Ambrook rose and walked around his desk until he hovered above the still sitting Tyler. He placed his hand on his son's shoulder, drew the boy close and whispered in his ear, "I love you son, but business is business."

51

JOHN LINDEN AWOKE ON FRIDAY morning to brilliant Florida sunshine, a beeping cell phone, and a slight hangover.

After leaving Ambrook's office he had visited the Golf Channel and given a rather quick interview. He then stopped off at one of his favorite local watering holes, Jimbos.

Many a golfer in the area had drowned their sorrows inside the musty walls of the fifty year old bar. Pictures of Jack, Arnie, Floyd, Trevino, Player, Snead, Hogan and Nelson adorned the wall behind the well-worn bar. Tiger and the young guns hung on the wall back by the bathroom. Apparently, they hadn't made the first string cut.

Yet.

He was pleasantly surprised to see the blonde receptionist from IFPG sitting on a stool at the bar. Thinking he might make time with this blonde, he turned off his cell phone and settled in next to her.

At first he thought that she might be a spy for the company. After a few drinks and some racy small talk, he was convinced that the meeting was purely coincidental.

Her name was Mary. She liked Pina Coladas, long walks on the beach and, fortunately, for Linden, success-ful professional golfers. The flirting was fun, but he was an engaged man. When it came time for the customary 'hook up' he demurred.

"Mary, you're a babe; I'd love to go home with you, but I can't," he had said while downing his last beer of the evening.

"Is there a problem, Johnny?"

Johnny? How long had it been since someone called him Johnny? He shook his head and tried to explain. "I'm engaged to a beautiful woman. She loves me and trusts me." He paused. Looked at her long legs and sighed. "Do you understand?" he asked.

"Is she in Orlando?"

"No she's out in California."

Mary snuggled closer. "Then she'll never know, will she?" She smiled and put her right hand on his thigh.

He hesitated for a moment and then brushed it away and stood up. He pulled his wallet out of his back pocket and put forty bucks on the counter. "Man, you are one hot woman, and normally I'd love to spend some time with you. But I just can't." He looked pained. Like a kid who just said no to a second serving of dessert. He turned and left the bar.

As he reached the front door, he could see Mary's reflection in the large glass window. She was shaking her head and smiling as if this had never happened to her before.

He stopped briefly before exiting and said to himself, "I can't believe I just did that. But Fabby's worth it." He opened the door and walked towards his car, gaining confidence with each stride. He had done the right thing; the chivalrous thing. He had felt good.

Despite the hangover, he still felt good about his decision the next day.

Maybe he was a changed man?

He checked his cell phone and saw that the last call had been received at eight a.m. that morning. Squinting to see the caller I.D., he silently prayed that the caller wasn't Fabiola. He didn't want to explain to her where he had been the night before.

His prayers were answered. The phone number displayed belonged to Brad.

Yawning, he walked to the kitchen with cell phone wedged between his shoulder and ear. He called his voice mail and listened to the message: "John. It's Brad. What did you do, turn off your cell phone last night? I had a hell of a day yesterday. I want to fill you in. Give me a call. We need to talk."

He opened the refrigerator and stared at a carton of orange juice. He checked the date. Three weeks old. He shrugged, reached down and opened the carton. The smell made him yank his head in disgust.

Note to self: throw away the fucking orange juice before it turns rancid.

He really wasn't a very good bachelor. Further evidence that he needed a woman in his life.

He went to the sink, poured out the orange juice, and dabbed his face with a wet cloth. After scratching himself several times, he sat at the kitchen table and called Brad.

"Hey, buddy. What's up?"

"John. Thank God you called. You're never going to believe what happened. Man, *do* I have a lot to tell you," Brad said.

"No worries, sorry I didn't get back to you sooner."

"You sound groggy. Everything okay?"

Linden grinned at the thought of the previous night. "I'm fine. Had a few too many beers. It's no big deal. What's up?"

Brad told him about the killers and his narrow escape. "Fabiola is fine," he assured him, "but you might want to give her a call when you get a chance."

"Holy Moley! And these guys are part of that Sons for Sovereign Sacrifice group Art mentioned?"

"Looks that way. They swear they never heard of Art Smalley or IFPG or Tyler Ambrook though."

On his end, Linden shook his head slowly. "What do you think is going on?"

"I don't know John, I really don't," Brad began. "But it seems obvious to me that these men are merely puppets. We got to find out who's pulling their strings."

"I'll bet its Tyler."

"Me too, but we don't have any real evidence." Brad hesitated as if deep in thought and then continued. "I think this all revolves around those books we found at Smalley's and all the unauthorized trades IFPG made."

Linden rubbed his chin and nodded as Brad spoke. Apparently, he had underestimated Tyler.

That little fucker would stop at nothing to protect his secret financial dealings. He had sat there smugly in his chair while his daddy had explained that it was Art who had lost all the IFPG money.

Now, he had sent some goons after Brad.

This was bullshit.

Linden made a split second decision.

"Listen Brad, I had an interesting day too," he began. "I want to tell you all about it, but I think it's better if we talk face to face."

"You met with Ambrook didn't you?"

"Yes I did. Both of them. I just couldn't wait."

"And you were confrontational."

"Yes I was," Linden said. And then added quickly, "But only when the situation called for it."

"And?"

"And given what happened to you and what they told me, I think we may want to bring the Feds in sooner rather than later."

"To investigate murder and attempted murder? We have no firm evidence," Brad said.

"Okay, maybe not murder, but financial fraud or some shit like that."

"I don't know about that. Those are major allegations. The only thing we have is Art's notes."

"And my losses," Linden added.

"That's the thing; without solid evidence, they're going to think you're out for revenge." Brad sneezed.

"Gazoontight," Linden said.

"Thanks." Brad sniffled. "Damn, hope I'm not coming down with a cold."

"Probably allergies."

"Yeah, probably. Anyway, Espinoza's got the two guys who tried to kill me in custody. He's not releasing information to the press about the attempted murder. He wants to bleed these guys as long as he can before they clam up or lawyer up."

"How long can he hold them without counsel?"

"I guess it depends." Brad sneezed again. "Damn! Hold on, I've got to get a Kleenex."

Linden could hear Brad rummage through a few drawers. Then he heard him blow his nose. After a few minutes, Brad came back on the line. "Much better. I think I'll increase my daily dosage of Vitamin C."

"Good idea. You'll live longer."

"Anyway, as I was saying, maybe Espinoza can get some information out of these guys to connect them to Smalley or IFPG."

"Have you told Espinoza about our suspicions?"

"Yeah, I did this morning. He's skeptical, but at the same time, he acknowledges something must be going on. Why else would two hillbillies try to kill Fabiola and me?"

"It's all really weird, isn't it?"

"You can say that again."

"If Raoul gets information out of them, will he go to the Feds?"

"Yes and they'll believe *him*," Brad said, emphasizing how much more credibility Espinoza would have than the two of them.

"Okay, I can live with that. Does he think you're still in trouble?"

"He thinks that if the killers knew that their boys failed, they might send someone out again. After all, they've tried three times already."

"But they won't know if Espinoza doesn't release the story."

"That's what he's betting on," Brad said. He blew his nose again and then added, "He's also betting that they don't understand their Miranda rights and that he and O'hara can convince them not to use a low level public defender."

"And he'll keep this away from the press?"

"Raoul says they're all afraid of O'hara—she's a real ball buster, I'll give her that—and if she says to keep it quiet, they will."

"Well good, it sounds like you can relax then."

"Hey, from your lips to God's ears," Brad said, silently praying his friend was right. He'd like to get a good night's sleep.

"Since it sounds like you're not in immediate danger, this brings me to my next point of business," Linden said, sounding like the chairman of the board at a stock holder's conference. "Can you fly out to Savannah later today?" he asked.

"A little last minute to get a ticket wouldn't you say?"

"I can arrange a private plane; I've got sponsor's money to spend. IFPG can't take that away from me," Linden said confidently. "I really want to tell you all about my meeting with the Ambrooks. It was really strange."

"How so?"

"I'll tell you when I see you," Linden said. He excused himself for a minute and grabbed a glass of water. The hangover was subsiding, but he felt dehydrated.

After downing the water he continued speaking. "I'm scheduled to play in a Charity Pro-Am Monday. Hank can't caddy for me. It was a last minute thing and he's not scheduled to come out until Wednesday. I thought you might want to carry my bag. We can discuss our next moves and you can enjoy a relaxing atmosphere—for a change."

Flattered by the offer, yet concerned about the urgency in John's voice, Brad quickly agreed...on two conditions. "One. Mel has to agree to let me go and, two, Raoul has to accompany me."

This thing was coming to a head. He could feel it. At the very least, they were going to involve the FBI or the Securities and Exchange Commission, or somebody, in the unauthorized trades at IFPG.

He was probably out of danger while whoever was behind this thought the two killers had matters in hand, but what if he wasn't? Espinoza would make him feel safe.

"You think Raoul will come all the way out to the east coast?"

"Sure. He loves golf and I think he'd want to continue protecting me until he's caught all the bad guys."

"I hope so. Think Mel will agree?"

"I think so. She'll argue with me but when I tell her what we think is going on with your financials and that we want to present some information to federal authorities, she'll understand," he said, hoping reason would prevail. "And she'll realize I'm taking precautions by having Raoul come with me. Hell, I can't just hole up in a cave."

"I hear you."

"And I'll have Raoul Espinoza, my Knight in White Shining Armor," Brad said with a chuckle. Turning serious, he said, "I'll bring some copies of Smalley's notes. If the Feds decide to take this seriously, they will want to see what he wrote."

And he said to himself Mel would understand that it would certainly be better if Brad was around when Fabiola called John to break it off. The poor son of a bitch would be devastated. He'd need his best friend's support.

He told Linden he'd call him back in a few minutes and went to find Mel.

52

"Shoot. I don't know... I think it's insane," Mel said when Brad told her about the trip.

"Calm down. Just hear me out."

"You and John aren't trained in this. You're not Starskey and Hutch you know." Her voice was shaky.

"I know, I know," he said as he lightly massaged her shoulders.

She shrugged him off and moved away. "There's some lunatic out there who wants you dead...."

"And he thinks I *am* dead or soon will be."

"Well that might be, but do you really think you should be traveling?"

"I've got to talk to John face to face. He may not even know it, but he may have found out something in his meeting with the Ambrooks that we can use against them."

"Why face to face?"

"We have some minor evidence of financial wrong doing. We can press that issue." He paused, ran his hand thru his hair and sighed. He was suddenly very tired.

"And If I'm right and IFPG is somehow behind these attempts on my life, I think now is the time to force the issue—while they think I'm dead."

She shook her head.

"Don't you see? It's a break in the action. Maybe I can move more freely and then when Raoul and I go down to Orlando to confront them, they'll be surprised to see me. Maybe they'll panic."

"Then what?"

"Hell, I don't know, but it feels right to me." He paused and then added, "Besides, John's going to need a friend around when Fabiola breaks up with him."

She sighed. "I don't like it, but as long as you're taking Raoul with you, I guess you'll be as safe there as you would be here."

He nodded. Said nothing.

"Can you promise me one thing?"

"Maybe. What is it?"

"Promise me that you'll hire some extra security guys to help Raoul. I want you well protected."

Brad nodded. "I think that's a good idea. I know John and I can't handle this by ourselves. That's not the point."

"What is the point then?" she asked seriously.

"The point is that we don't have enough evidence yet to go to the Feds and have these guys arrested. We *think* Tyler Ambrook may have had Art Smalley killed. We *think* he might be after me because I know they made unauthorized trades." He paused and then sighed. "But financial crimes are a far cry from murder. And *thinking* ain't *knowing*."

Nice twist of phrase, he thought.

Mel rolled her eyes.

He grinned and then continued. "Maybe we can put enough pressure on Tyler that he'll run or, better yet, break down and confess."

"From what you tell me about him, that seems unlikely."

"He is a spoiled, arrogant prick; that much is true." He took her hand in his and stared into her eyes. "But you know what Mel, sometimes those are the guys who just can't keep their mouths shut and the next thing you know, they've said something to incriminate themselves."

"I hope so. What am I going to do with you?" Her eyes softened and her cheeks grew rosy.

Brad remembered for about the millionth time why he loved this woman.

Finally, she shrugged and said, "Okay, you've got my blessing, but please watch your back. This whole thing sucks. There still might be someone out there who wants you dead."

"I know. I'll be careful." He paused and then added, "And I want you to know that I don't *want* to be back there. I just think the time has come to confront these guys."

"This stuff has to stop," she agreed.

"It doesn't seem to matter that we're on the West Coast. They send thugs out here anyway." He took her in his arms and held her tight. After a moment, he said in a soft voice, "I just want to end this thing and get back to a normal life."

"All right." She kissed him and started to walk off. Turning, she pointed a finger at him and said, "And, Brad Stephens, I will never forgive you if you get yourself killed."

Fair enough, he thought. He'd hate to die with a guilty conscience.

He went into his study and called Espinoza.

He answered on the fourth ring.

"Raoul, I'm about to make you an offer you can't refuse."

"I'm all ears."

"But first, have those two morons said anything useful?"

"Not yet. The big one has gone back in the hospital and the little weasel, McCoy, claims he doesn't know anything."

"Damn. I was hoping they would roll over like greased pigs by now."

"They still may. I'm bringing O'hara in to question McCoy next. Hollyfield will be out of it for a few days but then we can squeeze him," Espinoza said. "So what's up? What's this offer I can't refuse?"

"You are going to accompany me to Savannah, Georgia, and then on to Harbour Town Golf Links in Hilton Head, North Carolina," Brad said doing his best nasally game show accent.

"No shit? What's up?"

Brad returned to his normal voice. "Linden is playing in a Pro-Am on Monday and wants me to caddie for him."

"What's that got to do with me?"

"You're my protector. You've got to keep the bad guys away; like you did today."

Espinoza hesitated. The line went silent.

"Raoul, you still there?"

"Yeah, I'm here. I'm just trying to figure out how I'm going to finagle this with the boss."

"O'hara?"

"Rosa."

Brad chuckled slightly, thinking of Espinoza's wife. He had only seen her once. She was a short gal with long black hair, deep brown eyes, and from what Raoul had said a temper that could scare a lion. "She's that tough, huh?"

Espinoza didn't laugh. "We've been having some problems lately. I was supposed to take her to Palm Springs this weekend."

"How about next weekend? If things go right, Linden will pay for your whole trip to the desert."

Espinoza's spirits lifted. "You think so?"

"Yes I do. And here's the best part…we're flying on a private jet coming and going."

"First class, eh amigo? Okay, count me in. I'll figure out some way to sell it to Rosa."

53

LINDEN'S SPONSOR HAD GONE ALL OUT.

A midsize Citation X was waiting for Brad and Raoul on the tarmac in Santa Barbara. Brown with slight camouflage overlay, the plane looked like it was combat ready.

Brad hoped there would be no air fights on this trip.

As the plane ascended with Brad and Espinoza its only passengers, Brad became curious as to why the pilots hadn't gone over basic safety rules. When they leveled off, Brad approached the co-pilot.

He was a young guy named Arnie according to his official name tag. Tan and thin with distinctive angles to his face, his crew cut hair reminded Brad of a young Clint Eastwood in "Dirty Harry".

"Sorry to bug you, Arnie. Is there anything I need to know in case of an emergency? You know, like when will oxygen masks deploy? Or how to use the emergency exit."

"No sir. FAA regulations only stipulate that you need to be seated with seat belt securely fastened during take-off and landing."

"What about oxygen masks and flotation devices?" Brad asked again.

"Well, sir, we're not supposed to share this information with passengers but here's the truth....The fact is that we are now flying at fifty thousand feet. Our airspeed is slightly higher than six hundred miles per hour. We will arrive in Savannah faster than you thought possible. The downside is this: If we lose oxygen or pressure at fifty thousand feet, you will be dead before a mask deploys." He snapped his fingers to emphasize his point. "So, I wouldn't worry about it. Just sit back, enjoy the ride. We'll be there in a few hours."

Oh, good. Trained killers couldn't get him, but a sudden drop in pressure might.

Beautiful. Just beautiful.

Startled by Arnie's honesty, Brad straddled back to his seat. Then he chuckled and thought it would've been fitting given his current circumstances if the pilot would've looked him straight in the eye and responded like Dirty Harry, "Oxygen Mask? Feeling Lucky? Are You? Well, Are You, Punk?"

Amazingly, and contrary to recent events, Brad *was* feeling lucky. He had no idea why. Maybe it was because he had survived three attempts on his life? Or maybe it was because he felt so close to solving this thing? He sat back and enjoyed the ride.

The landing was smooth. Linden was there to greet them. They hopped in a Porsche Cayenne and began the thirty minute journey to Hilton Head.

"Nice ride," Espinoza commented.

"It's not mine; it's provided by the tournament sponsor. Don't scratch it."

Espinoza smiled. "I knew they spoiled you professional golfers, but a Porsche? Don't you think that's a bit over the top?"

Linden shrugged. "We get brand new Lexus's in Los Angeles, brand new BMWs in Atlanta, and brand new Cadillac's in Palm Springs. It's standard practice."

Changing the subject, Espinoza asked, "How many golf courses are located between Hilton Head and Savannah anyway?" He was staring out the window and pointing towards an opulent stone gatehouse on his right.

"I'm not sure," Linden said. "But there's a shitload of them. And they're all good courses with a lot of character."

"I played one the last time I was out here," Brad said. "There was a 625 yard par five with water along both sides of the fairway."

"I played there too. What's the name of that course?" Linden said, raising his eyebrows and thinking hard.

"It started with a 'B'...BallyComin, I believe," Brad said after thinking about it for a moment.

"Yep, that's it. I think it's coming up on our left."

Espinoza shook his head. "Damn, a guy could play a different course out here every day and never get bored."

"That's assuming you can get on the course," Brad said. "Most are private."

Espinoza smiled. "Hell, I can get on any course I want." He reached forward and patted Linden's shoulder. "I know one of the best professional golfers in the world."

They laughed.

It felt good.

It felt natural.

Linden pushed the accelerator and the Porsche immediately responded. They passed lush woods lined with small creeks and ragged brush. Every few miles there was a break in the foliage and another ostentatious gatehouse materialized.

Linden was anxious to describe his meeting with the Ambrook family. First he wanted to make sure Brad was okay and then, of course, confirm that Fabby had been unhurt. Brad assured him that she was fine.

"Bruised, bloodied, and battered…but still breathing," Brad said, doing his best Vin Scully impersonation.

A regular Rich Little.

Linden turned and stared at him. "That's the best Vin Scully I've ever heard."

"Thanks. Been listening to him forever."

"What do you think Raoul?"

"I've heard better."

Linden shook his head and then told them about his surprise visit to Tyler Ambrook, making sure to begin with, "I know you told me to wait for further instructions but I got fired up and figured, now or never. You know how I am. It's why I could never hit a curve ball. Patience is not my greatest virtue."

He looked at Brad for some form of validation.

Brad stared back. "What? Why are you looking at me that way?"

"Well, you know. Are you pissed?"

"I'm pissed they stole your money. I'm pissed they tried to kill me. Let me rephrase that…are probably still trying to kill me. But I can't be pissed that you confronted Tyler. That took balls."

Linden straightened his shoulders and grinned. "Yeah it did, didn't it? I've got balls of steel." He cupped his groin as if Brad didn't know where his balls were and then continued. "Having said that, I will confess I was nervous as crap the whole time."

They all shared a good laugh. This wasn't a game— but in a way, it was. They had to win and that meant someone had to lose.

The stakes were high.

He and John had to win

No other choice.

He thought about it some more. On the one hand, they had what they thought was solid evidence from Smalley's files about the unauthorized trading at IFPG but, on the other hand, this might not be enough to entice the Feds to act quickly.

Hopefully, Tyler might become desperate. The challenge on this trip, therefore, was clear…get more evidence that Tyler stole the money and, if possible, convince the Feds that he was a murderer.

But how?

Espinoza suddenly focused on the conversation and made a suggestion. "Given what you've said about your meeting and the way they tried to blame Smalley for the unauthorized trading, maybe I should just call the FBI in Orlando and meet with them ASAP. Maybe they know about this Sons for Sovereign Sacrifice outfit? I could bring up the murder attempts and Smalley's suicide without claiming we have any real evidence. You know, see what they think."

"You're supposed to be guarding me," Brad said.

"Do you really think you need protection on a world famous golf course? What could possibly happen?"

"He makes a good point, Brad," Linden said. "Besides

with all those politicians playing, there should be tons of security on the course."

Brad thought about it for a few minutes and then reluctantly agreed. "You're probably right. And the FBI will be much more likely to listen to you than to a pro golfer and a mortgage broker."

Espinoza nodded.

Linden said, "Yep."

"Just please, for the love of God, don't let Mel know you weren't by my side twenty four hours a day."

"Will do. And you make sure I get an all-expense paid trip to La Quinta," Espinoza added.

"Oh, yeah, I like La Quinta," Linden said. "How can you afford to go there during peak season?"

"We'll talk about it later," Brad said quickly.

Linden stared at Brad for a moment, pursed his lips and nodded. He understood. "You got it Raoul, amigo. Just keep Brad safe and help us solve this thing."

"Can do."

Brad took out a small pad of paper and started making notes. After ten minutes, he stopped, put the pen down and asked for both of his friend's attention. "Okay, here's how I see it. It's four o'clock now, still plenty of time to do some work."

He studied their faces. They were all ears –as if he were laying out plans for robbing Fort Knox. "John can stretch his back, hit some balls, do whatever pro golfers do before a tournament. Raoul, you do whatever cops do when they think something's fishy."

"That's it? That's your plan?" They both said in unison.

Brad grinned. "Hold on; don't shoot the messenger." He held both hands in front of him as if to stop the onslaught. "My overall plan is this: We do the pro-am on Monday. While we play, Raoul drives down to Orlando and contacts the local FBI regarding the unauthorized trades. See what they suggest."

He continued. "I will caddie for John. And then on Tuesday, I'll join Raoul down in Orlando. Hopefully, by that time, the Feds will be ready to take us seriously. And then we'll figure out how to confront Tyler."

"Won't he be at the tournament?" Raoul asked.

"I don't know. I hope not. What do you think John?"

"I know the old man will be here. He's playing in the pro-am. But the son isn't much of a golfer. So, your guess is as good as mine."

"Let's assume Tyler remains in Orlando," Brad said. "Is everyone agreed on our course of action?"

No complaints. Brad took that as a good sign.

They rode in silence another five minutes and then Linden pulled the Cayenne into the hotel parking lot.

As they departed the car, Brad looked at Linden. "What does a pro do before a tournament anyway?"

"He goes to the putting green," Linden said grinning. "I need to 'claw' a few hundred putts so that I don't make a fool out of myself Monday. You're my caddie. You can return all the balls to me and heap praise upon my technique. And if you want, you can do it while drinking a Jack."

"What about me?" Espinoza asked. "I can't go down to Orlando until Monday."

"You're here to protect me," Brad said, winking. "So bring your gun and look tough."

"So I just stand around while he putts?"

"I'll get you a putter. You can hit a few too."

"Alright, that's more like it."

"What about Sunday? Can we get a round in some-where?"

"Probably," Linden said. "Let me look into it."

That made both Brad and Raoul smile. A round of golf was just what the doctor ordered.

"Great. I need to contact my office first; find out if there's anything new with Hollyfield or McCoy. I'll join you at the putting green in a few minutes."

"That's the spirit," Linden said.

"Sounds good," Brad said. "Maybe hitting a few putts will take our minds off this IFPG crap for a day." And then as an afterthought, he asked Linden, "Who are you playing with on Monday anyway?"

"The Speaker of the House. I think his name is Wilson. The Treasury Secretary. Don't know his name. And some top-dog Senator, named Ellings. I guess he's a Democrat from Georgia. They're all pretty good golfers from what I hear. Might be interesting."

"More like boring as hell. But should be a good warm up for the tourney. You can work on shaping your shots and get a feel for the Greens."

They hustled to the room to change. Linden grabbed his putter; Brad grabbed a bag of balls; and Espinoza hopped on his cell phone.

It was a nice afternoon. Mid-70's, slight breeze off the waterway. The sun would be up for another few hours. They'd make the most of it.

And the next day, he'd relax with his buddies, flogging a little white ball around a beautiful golf course.

What could be better?

54

COMMANDER DAVID VON EISENLOW KNEW what he'd be doing before the Pro-Am too.

He had arrived on Daufuskie Island late Saturday afternoon. He and his men dressed, talked and tried to act like golfers. Two of them had actually played the game before so they dominated the conversation when other people were around. They were just eight guys out on a golfing trip.

Standard for this resort island.

During its hay day, the island had boasted three decent golf courses. Now, due to the recession, the golf courses were in disrepair; the island, bankrupt. Wild vines grew around and through two of the abandoned clubhouses. What once were neatly kept quarters looked like something out of Jurassic Park. Locals still swore the island was viable, but like most vacation areas its heart was barely beating.

The name, Daufuskie, actually referenced the fact that the small island was 'Da First Key'—the first of many little islands that dotted the inter-continental waterway.

Situated a few miles off the harbor at Hilton Head, the island takes twenty minutes to get to by ferry. Under normal conditions, ferries ran every hour on the hour. Now, locals had to plan their excursions around a morning, afternoon and evening schedule.

Von Eisenlow had used the time since arrival for reconnaissance; and some deep thinking. There were two goals behind this mission he concluded: death to government officials and continued financial support from the 'whisperer'.

The second reason, however, far outweighed the first. Sure he wanted to destroy the government, but realistically, his efforts would take money. His anonymous donor had promised him tremendous financial support if he performed this mission.

He must not fail again.

Not only would he be embarrassed, but he was sure his funding would be pulled.

He rose from the bed of his rented house and changed out of his golf shorts and back into his army fatigues. Donning his special hat with the hawk heading towards Heaven with an AK47 in its beak, he felt like the commander of an army once again. He called his men together to lay out the plan.

"Men, before we discuss our plan of attack, I want to thank you for your hard work and dedication to the cause," he began. "Some of you might not make it back after this attack. I want you to know that your heroism will not be in vain. You will be rewarded by God himself. Let us pray." He bowed his head and snuck a peek at the men. They were actually joining him in prayer.

Amazing.

"Oh, Heavenly Father, give us strength. Deliver us from our enemies. Allow our arrows to fly true and straight," he began. He surveyed his crew. The men stood still, heads bowed, listening to his every word. He continued. "Provide us with the courage to smite Satan's evil messengers for they have wreaked havoc upon this nation."

At this point, he closed his eyes and raised his arms towards the sky. "Thank you, oh Lord, for providing us with information, tools and equipment to perform your work. And, finally, we pray that you deliver any of your fallen soldiers to eternal salvation." He opened his eyes for a moment and studied his troops.

They looked a bit more nervous than before.

Perhaps he should tone down the talk of potential death for the cause?

The men's demeanor reminded him to procure more rum for the evening.

"Amen," he said. The other men followed in unison with "Amen". Having dispensed with the religious stuff, Von Eisenlow could now continue describing his scheme.

"Men. You've all heard of Paul Revere I trust. He of the 'One if By Land, Two if By Sea' fame. Well, we're going to steal a page out of his playbook. We're going to hit the sinners from land and sea." He smiled and looked around the room.

He pulled out a map of the island. It included details about the channel which separated Harbour Town from Daufuskie Island—Calibogue Sound. He then laid out a map of the golf course next to it. Without missing a beat, he used a golf club to identify various points of attack.

When he finished, he smiled but added firmly, "Our main goal is the destruction of lying, cheating, politicians, however, we have been given a specific target by our main financial benefactor."

A few of the men shuffled their feet but, in general, everyone was listening to their commander. "He has required that all of the players participating in the first group of golfers be exterminated before anyone else." Using the golf club, he pointed to the map of the golf course. "The first group should be here on the eighteenth Green when we attack. Do not, I repeat, do not fire on the group behind them. Our benefactor will be in that group."

The men nodded.

Von Eisenlow smiled. "If we do this properly, I have been assured that our funding will continue so that we may proceed to bigger and better targets in the future." He paused and then added, "It is imperative we take the first group of golfers out entirely. No survivors."

He tapped the eighteenth Green with the club. "I will coordinate the action from here," he said, pointing to the famous Harbour Town Lighthouse, sitting several hundred feet from the back of the eighteenth Green.

"Remember, men, with God's help—and our bene-factor's money—we will succeed. Lieutenant Simpson will go over your specific assignments later this evening," he said, indicating his second in command. "Any questions?"

Mullaby, a tall, lanky soldier with crooked teeth, yellowed from years of chewing tobacco, stepped forward. "I have a question sir."

"Yes, what is it, Mullaby?"

"Do we get paid before or after the assault?"

"Why does it matter to you?"

"Well…It's just the men and me been talking," he paused, swiveling his head from side to side, looking for an empty cup. Finding one, he quickly spit—like chewers do—and then continued. "We'd like to know that our families back home get the money we're due if something happens to us."

Von Eisenlow smiled. He walked over to Mullaby and put a caring arm around his shoulder. "Why that's a fine notion and I can promise each and every one of you that if, God forbid, something happens to you, your families will be duly compensated." He paused and turned his attention to Simpson. "Lieutenant, make a note of this promise please."

The men all nodded. Mullaby said thanks and one by one, they shuffled out of Von Eisenlow's building.

Watching them leave, he knew that as long as he convinced them that there would be a future they would continue with confidence. And the promise of compensation made it even more solid. Of course, he knew, the odds that any of the foot soldiers would make it out alive were slim to none.

And, unfortunately for them, slim had left town.

55

MONDAY MORNING STARTED WITH A BANG —literally.

The fog horn inside the famous Harbour Town light-house went off at precisely 6:00 a.m. causing Brad to fall out of bed. Walking to the window, he looked out and could see that it was a pea soup, foggy morning. It didn't really matter, though. The only negative might be some slight discomfort from the humidity and the chance that the ball wouldn't fly quite as far. Other than that, Brad was ready for a good walk around the course.

He turned to wake Linden and discovered that the bed was empty. Had John gotten up early, he wondered? Where the hell was he? He picked up his cell phone to call but before he could dial the number, Linden came walking through the door.

"Where have you been?" Brad asked.

"Sssh. Don't wake the neighbors. It's okay. I just went for a walk."

"You're going to be walking all day. What's up?"

"If you must know, I got a call from Fabiola last night."

Dreading the worst, Brad rose from the bed and said tentatively, "Everything okay?"

"I don't think so. She said we should talk when the tournament is over."

Brad exhaled. At least he didn't have to comfort his buddy...yet. He really wasn't good at all the touchy feely stuff.

"You know, Brad, there are days I wish I never got involved with Fabby."

Believe me, I get it.

He nodded.

"I really love that woman, but sometimes, she can be so...needy. Do you know what I mean?"

Knowing that it was over between them but not wanting to be the one to tell John, Brad walked into the bathroom. When he returned, Linden was lying face down on the bed.

"God, I'm tired," he said.

"You okay?"

"Yeah, I just didn't like the tone of her voice."

"I think the matter will resolve itself," Brad said.

Dear Abby, he wasn't.

"I hope you're right, pards."

Brad stared out the window. The fog was lifting and the wind had picked up slightly. It looked like it would be a nice day. "I suggest you focus on golf and call her after you've won the tournament."

Linden smiled. "From your lips to God's ears. Let me grab a shower and then let's head over to the course. I got a good feeling about my swing today. I'm not going to worry about Fabby." He walked towards the bathroom but suddenly stopped. "Do you think this has something to do with you guys almost being killed the other day?"

Brad shrugged. "Funny things happen when you're looking down the barrel of a gun."

"Damn! I feel like a louse. I've been so caught up in my own financial deal and Art's death, I never really asked you about the incident."

Brad walked over to him, patted him on the shoulder and assured him that everything was okay. "It was surreal while it was happening, I can tell you that. Maybe Fabiola is more shaken up than me?"

"Yeah, that must be it."

"Go take your shower and let's play some golf."

Officially known as the Harbour Town Golf Links, the regal harbor side golf course has been the home to many memorable professional golfing events.

The front nine features tight, tree lined fairways and spectacular Greens. Like most Carolina golf courses, natural hazards like water moccasins and alligators are present, but unlike so many other courses, they seem to keep to themselves.

The front nine is wonderful golf but pales in comparison to the back nine. Beginning with the Par 3, 14th, the course really becomes interesting.

Water to the right and out of bounds to the left frame the 180 yard Par 3, 14th. A slight miscue and the ball swims with the fish—or alligators in this neck of the woods. A well placed shot and the player has a chance at par.

Rarely does anyone birdie the 14th.

Sand dunes, water and trees frame the rest of the finishing holes. None is more spectacular, however, than the world famous 18th—the Lighthouse hole.

From the tee, the nervous golfer sees nothing but trouble. A decent tee shot still leaves a long iron which must carry the Green. Or you can bail out to the right.

Neither option is appealing.

The Lighthouse is not only picturesque but is also strategically placed. Sitting in the distance directly behind the 18th Green, the golfer must aim for it with his tee shot and his approach shot.

Even the putts seem to break towards the building.

Brad had viewed the lighthouse earlier that morning from the clubhouse lawn. The site made him remember the first time he visited Harbour Town.

A local caddie had been assigned to him. A guy named 'Moose'. The guy was a bit of a history nut. He wouldn't shut up about that damn lighthouse.

"Did you know that the Harbour Town Light—that's what we locals call it—was built in 1969 using private money raised by investors who wanted a unique look for the Harbour Town Marina?"

Brad remembered being surprised that the lighthouse was only thirty five years old. Due to the annual coverage of the Heritage golf tournament, he had come to assume that the lighthouse was an older structure, full of history and culture. Maybe even a story or two about saving wayward ships during the Civil War. But Moose had destroyed that fantasy.

Another fantasy destroyed.

"The group who built it had petitioned the state and federal governments to underwrite a lighthouse to aid navigation, but they were told to pound sand." Brad remembered the caddie chuckling at that point in the story. "A local developer took it as a personal affront and he pushed the project through. Some say he painted it like a candy cane to get back at the government bureaucrats."

Brad had stared at the lighthouse for a long time that day. The colors made sense, he thought. Very distinctive. It kinda ruined it for him to know the whole thing was done by a real estate developer, though. Oh, well, it was a great course and the lighthouse was an extremely distinctive and memorable feature.

To the left and off the point, recreational boats, wind-surfers and jet-skiers typically occupy the calm waters of the Calibogue Sound.

When the official starter notified him it was time for Linden's group to tee off, Brad walked from the practice Green to the first tee. He had played Harbour Town several times in the past, but never caddied the course.

He was excited by the prospect and happy to have a day sure to be full of relaxation and camaraderie.

The other players joined him and John at the first tee.

"Good to meet you," Linden said as he shook hands with his playing partners.

Wilson, the Speaker of the House, was a rotund man, standing five foot eight. He smoked a long cigar and looked eager to make a speech. He stared Linden directly in the eye and asked about the golfer's political leanings.

Linden shook his head. "Mr. Speaker, I'm a golfer. My daddy always told me to keep my politics and religion to myself; my eye on the ball; and, when the time was right, hit the damn ball."

The Speaker chuckled. He looked around at the group, making sure they were all paying attention and said, "Your daddy was a smart man. I hope you don't mind if I tell you that you hit the ball like a Democrat."

"How's that, sir?"

"Long and straight, but with flair and finesse."

"You can tell that all from watching me play."

"You bet."

"And how does a Republican hit the ball."

The Speaker had set the hook and now went in for the kill. "Short back swing. Twisted face, and very conservative with his club selection."

He waited for the gallery to laugh. After a few moments they did. Linden looked at Brad and sighed.

Brad tossed Linden a new Titleist ProV, winked and told him, "Fairways and Greens all day, big man. Give it a rip."

And Linden did. Three hundred yards right down the middle.

The Speaker smiled. "See. Flair and finesse." The foursome took off down the fairway

== ⊕ ==

As the round progressed, it became obvious that the politicians could actually play the game. Wilson, the Speaker of the House, sported a true five handicap. Blowhards like him were famous for reverse 'sand bagging'—saying they were better than they actually were—but in his case, surprisingly, the five actually fit. The same for the other two players. They got to their balls quickly, took a few practice swings and, in general, hit pretty good shots. Brad was impressed.

The day continued to warm up. The fog had totally lifted by the turn at the 9th hole. A warm Carolina breeze blew thru the pine trees that lined most of the fairways and a faint smell of sea water and sea weed filled Brad's senses.

As was his custom, John had been talking non-stop since his tee shot on the first hole. His nickname, after all, was 'flappy'. Unlike many of his peers, the politicians seemed to enjoy his bantering.

The conversation was casual; the Speaker had given up on political chatter and was now discussing California wines. Linden had made the mistake of telling him he was moving to Montecito.

"That Seasmoke Pinot Noir is absolutely fantastic," Wilson said.

"I'm partial to the Foxen Chardonnay," said Ellings, the Senator from Georgia.

Wilson took a puff on his cigar and said, "I should've known…a chardonnay drinker." He rolled his eyes.

Security was present, but not obvious. Brad knew that's how they do it when politicians attend these things. He relaxed, knowing he could tell Mel honestly that he had been given additional security. It was comforting to know that some of the 'spectators' were actually protective guards from the Secret Service and Capitol Police.

To commemorate the occasion, Linden had worn an outfit comprised of blue shoes, white pants and a red shirt. Even his hat had an imprinted American flag on the brim.

John Linden, ultra-Patriot.

It had been Steven Ambrook's idea. Would be good for his image, Ambrook had said. Knowing how lucky John was, Brad figured it would be good for another million or two in sponsorships.

In America, the rich get richer after all.

As the group approached the 14th hole, the challenging Par 3 with water on the right, Brad's phone vibrated in his pocket. He knew he should've turned it off, but the way things were going, he didn't feel comfortable being completely out of touch. Caller I.D. displayed the one name Brad had been hoping to see: Raoul Espinoza.

"Is this a convenient time to talk?" Espinoza asked.

"Not really," Brad whispered as Linden teed his ball. "Can you text me a message?"

"Yeah. I'll do that. It'll take me a few minutes because I don't type too good. But you'll want to read what I have to say."

"Great. I'll confirm receipt."

"Nice Shot!" Speaker of the House Wilson remarked as Linden's ball landed in the middle of the Green. Teeing up his own ball, the Speaker took a balanced swing and pushed it slightly into the bunker. "At least it's still dry," he said hoping to coax a chuckle from his playing partners.

The other two players—Treasury Secretary Willis and Senator Ellings—both put their balls in the water. Not the first balls to go to a watery grave on that hole. And certainly not the last.

Brad followed the group to the Green slowly, waiting for Espinoza's text. He had already given Linden his putter. His phone rang. Pulling the cell phone from his pocket, he opened it and read the message from Espinoza.

"McCoy gave up some interesting information to O'hara. He said that the group's leader, Von Eisenlow, was talking about taking the group to Hilton Head. He didn't know the dates, time or targets. Said they all had been taking extra shooting practice. It seems a helluva coincidence that the tourney is in Hilton Head this week. Don't you think?"

Brad typed, "Oh Shit! Sounds like they're planning something connected with the tournament. What do you think?"

Two minutes later Brad's phone buzzed. Linden was lining up his birdie putt when Brad opened his phone and viewed the message.

"They'd be crazy to do something there today. Security is too tight."

Brad typed. "Yeah, but I think they are kinda crazy. Don't you think?"

"Good point. The more I think about it, the more I think those crazy sons of bitches might be planning on killing some politicians...TODAY! If I were you, I'd get the hell out of there. I'm calling the local police and the Feds."

"Where are you?"

"Orlando."

Shit! If the terrorists didn't kill him, Mel would. He should have never let Espinoza leave his side. He felt his pulse race. A heightened sense of alert overtook him.

Not again. Please not again.

A million thoughts raced through his head: Why did I come out here? Mel was right...again. Why hadn't he hired extra security?

Anxious to reveal what Espinoza had just told him, he searched the gallery, looking for the most obvious federal agent.

Easier said than done. He couldn't tell who was Secret Service and who was an innocent spectator.

There were more than fifty candidates. All men dressed in shorts, golf shirts and various hats, sweaters, or vests. Typical golfing crowd. Not one guy in a gray suit with an obvious earpiece. John made his birdie putt. For an instant, Brad's thoughts focused on the present. Speaker Wilson stepped up and tapped in for a bogey.

Behind him, on the 13th Green the crowd exploded in a roar. Brad asked a spectator what was happening.

"That old dude from IFPG just sunk a bomb!" a young man dressed in Nike's latest golfing attire said. "He's nine under par; same as your boy, Linden. They're both flirting with the course record."

Brad wished he could be happy for both Linden and Ambrook. He knew from reading pre-tournament literature that the course record was eleven under; held by John Huston, a journeyman pro now playing on the Senior Tour. Instead, one thought danced through his head: Shit! What have I gotten into?

The first group moved towards hole number 15.

Linden was in a giddy mood. "Did you see that putt I just hit, pards? If I keep rolling 'em in, nobody's going to challenge me this weekend. And who knows, I might set a new course record today."

"I wasn't really watching to tell you the truth. But you've been putting great all day. Listen, John…."

"This is a good group isn't it," John 'flappy' Linden said before Brad could finish. "They're decent golfers and they got a good sense of humor. The Treasury Secretary came up to me a few holes ago and asked me to watch his swing. He wanted to know why his ball consistently drifted to the right. I told him, listen to this, I swear

I made it up on the fly. I told him that he was gripping the club too tight. The golf swing needed to be like money during Quantitative Easing: Free Flowing and Loose." He smiled at Brad and punched him on the shoulder. "Get it? The Treasury's got to release that money back into the economy, just like a golfer's got to release his club when he swings."

"Yeah, I get it. You're a regular Sheky Green. But seriously, listen to what I've got to say…." Brad told him about the message from Espinoza.

"What do we do?" Linden asked, his mood turning darker. "I've got a great round going. I could shoot the course record. I can't have some terrorists screw it up."

"Calm down," he said, handing Linden his next club.

"As we walk down the fairway, I'm going to ask the Speaker to point out his security team to me. Once I know who they are, I'll have a talk with one of them and tell him what Espinoza said. I think it's safe to assume that we're in no imminent danger while playing on the golf course." He paused and looked around. It seemed quiet enough. "If they're planning on assassinating some politicians, it would make more sense to wait until the awards ceremony afterwards. All of those guys love making speeches. Politicians always stick around for the free press."

"Okay. Makes sense…I guess," Linden said. "I've got to be honest with you, though. This whole thing has gotten really, really weird. I mean, since when aren't we safe on a goddamned golf course?"

As they strode down the fairway, following another perfect shot by Linden, Brad noticed that Flappy wasn't talking and Sheky wasn't smiling any longer.

56

THE MORNING FOG HAD PROVIDED A nice cover for Von Eisenlow and his men.

Rising early on Daufuskie Island, he had given each man his personal assignment to supplement what Lieutenant Simpson had told them the night before.

Five were to commandeer the jet skis he had reserved at the resort. Armed with AK47s, they were to ride around in the channel until he radioed them to strike. Two of the men were to ride over to Harbour Town on the ferry with him.

Once there, they were to position themselves by the entrance to the golf course. Both of the men were rigged with dynamite vests and each carried a marksman's rifle. Their instructions were simple: Position themselves near the entrance and be prepared. He would signal them when the final group came to the 18th Green. Target as many government-looking people as possible.

Do maximum damage.

"If visual contact expires, walk onto the course and detonate your vests as close to the players as possible," he had told them calmly.

"What the fuck?" Mullaby had said. Quickly becoming Von Eisenlow's least favorite martyr for the cause.

"You've got a problem, soldier?"

Mullaby had looked at his comrades uncomfortably and then returned his stare to their leader. "I was under the understanding that we were attacking the enemy, sir."

"We are. What's your point?"

"You just called for a suicide bombing. We don't do that shit. That's what ragheads do." He had spit tobacco on the floor in a defiant manner.

"Not today. Today you are mercenaries for God. If it is HIS will that you detonate your vests, who are you to argue?"

The other soldiers had looked around, shuffled their feet and made non-committal shrugs.

"And our families get paid?" Mullaby finally asked.

"Every penny."

The group had fallen silent.

For the final twist in his plan, Von Eisenlow told the men that he would enter the base of the Lighthouse via a special entrance. The popular tourist attraction had been closed for this event, but he would gain entry. His benefactor, the 'whisperer', had called yesterday and told him how to get in.

Von Eisenlow resolved to place himself in the Lighthouse, sniper rifle at the ready. If all else failed, he would shoot some of the assholes as they settled on the 18th Green. Best case, his water warriors attacking from the east would take out dozens before being neutralized; his suicide bombers coming from the west would inflict serious damage.

He knew his men weren't going to make it out alive, but that was the price they would have to pay for justice.

If all went well, when the dust settled, he'd retreat and mingle in with the chaotic crowd.

He would live to play another day.

In the early hours of the morning, when the fog was still thick, Von Eisenlow set up his 'observation' post on the top floor of the lighthouse. It had been remarkably easy, really.

Disguising his weapon as a Driver with a big furry head cover, he had carried his golf bag off the ferry and proceeded through the gathering group of spectators unnoticed.

Located exactly where his caller had indicated, the entrance was easy to find. It was small by contemporary standards but big enough for him to drag the entire golf bag through. Once inside, he pulled out his rifle and the fatigues he had stuffed in the bags' longest pouch. Changing quickly downstairs he then climbed the stairs to the top floor.

Once there, he secured a perfect view of the 18th Green. Pulling up a wooden box and using it as a chair, he placed his weapon on the window sill and waited.

== ⊕ ==

Several hours later, Brad and the first group of golfers strode down the 15th fairway. Hundreds of spectators had gathered outside the ropes.

Linden, of course, was the longest and straightest driver of the group. He would hit last. The wait gave Brad a chance to discreetly approach the Speaker of the House.

The Speaker was still sucking on the cigar he had fired up on the first hole. His outfit—khaki pants and blue golf shirt—went well with his leathery tan and full mane of silver hair. A bulbous nose and many broken blood vessels on his swollen face provided evidence of a busy life full of heavy drinking and rich food.

It had been an easy walk today, yet the Speaker was sweating profusely. Brad caught up to him immediately after the Speaker lofted a well struck five iron a hundred and sixty five yards onto the Green.

"Can I ask you a question, sir?" Brad asked in a quiet voice, his eyes focused straight ahead.

"Of course you can, son. Nice shot I hit, huh?" the Speaker asked in a manner that required validation.

"Great shot. Hope you make the putt."

The Speaker smiled. "We didn't really meet earlier; we just shook hands on the first tee. I'm Thorngood Wilson. You can call me Thorny," the Speaker said, extending his hand to Brad.

"Brad Stephens," he replied. And then feeling compelled to explain, he quickly added, "I'm not John's usual caddie. I'm a very close friend and he asked me to stand in for his caddie today."

"Yes. I remember hearing something about that. Well you're doing a great job. Your boy is playing wonderfully. I can't remember the last time I saw so many perfect approach irons. He's really throwing darts today."

"He's a fine player," Brad agreed quickly, needing to wrap up the conversation in order to provide John with the appropriate mid-iron for his next shot. "Can you do me a favor and point out your security detail? I don't have time to explain right now, but I've just been contacted by a police sergeant from California. His people are interrogating some suspected murderers and terrorists. They've found out that there's a chance that a right wing extremist group may be planning some type of terrorist action here today."

Startled, the lawmaker stopped dead in his tracks. "Are you an officer of the law son?"

"No sir, I'm not. I'm a mortgage broker." Brad shrugged and then continued. "But I have been the target of three failed assassination attempts over the past few days. The police have determined that this right wing group, The Sons for Sovereign Sacrifice, has been behind the attempts."

"Why? What have you done to garner such wrath?"

"I'll be happy to explain later. Maybe over a drink. But for now, I'd like to alert your men to the possibility of an attack. I doubt the bad guys can do anything while we're on the course, but..... who knows?"

The Congressman's mood changed from startled to perturbed. "If you're the target, why the hell did they let you caddie today? Weren't you vetted properly? I'm going to look into this. If security let down because the President bailed, heads will roll." His large jowls flapped for emphasis.

"I can assure you, I was fully reviewed sir. They don't think I'm a target. Nobody knows that the last attempt on my life in California failed. Details haven't been released to the media yet. Whoever sent the killers probably thinks I'm dead."

He hesitated for a moment. Why were these things happening to him? He exhaled and then continued. "Most likely, it's you and your political peers they're after. It's just a fluke that I happen to be here. Now, who's your chief of security?"

Wilson pointed out a large, middle-aged guy standing by the cart path. The agent was wearing blue shorts and a white polo shirt. To the naked eye, he looked like every other white, middle-class golf enthusiast. The Taylor Made hat and rolled-up program he held in his right hand completed the ensemble. Upon closer inspection, the only indication of his true nature was the polo shirt. It was made from thicker material than a golfer would wear. And it was un-tucked. Probably concealed a handgun stuck in the back of his waistband.

Very stealth.

"His name is Krnich, Jim Krnich," Wilson added and began walking towards the Green.

Linden hit his shot; another perfect iron on to the middle of an undulating Green. Brad approached the guard. "Agent Krnich. Brad Stephens," he said, extending his right hand.

Brad briefed the agent on the Sons for Sovereign Sacrifice. Krnich smiled and assured him that the entire area was fortified. "Nobody can get in or out without our knowledge. I've got Capitol Police, Secret Service and even some Homeland Security here today. Don't worry, you're in good hands Mr. Stephens. Enjoy the rest of your game, sir." He patted Brad on the back and pointed him back to his group.

Enjoy the rest of your game?

He thinks I'm crazy.

He dismissed me like a six year old who wet his pants.

Well, maybe I am crazy? Maybe these attempts on my life have put me on edge? Maybe Espinoza misunderstood? That guy, McCoy, didn't seem too bright. He's not the kind of guy the leader gives details to. Krnich seems competent. Take a deep breath. Let's get through this round and get the hell out of here.

Brad had never been so focused.

The 16th and 17th were routine holes. Linden made birdies on both of them. He was now eleven under for the round. He had tied the course record. Approaching the 18th tee, he looked at Brad, requested his 3-Wood and asked him if everything was copacetic.

"Yeah. I think everything is 'copacetic'," Brad said with a chuckle. He hadn't used that word since seventh grade. "You're eleven under. A birdie here and you set the course record. Somebody told me that Steven Ambrook is now ten under behind us. You sure you want to hit 3-Wood and not Driver?"

"I've been crushing my 3-Wood all day. If I hit a good one, it'll leave me two hundred in. I can put a 5-Iron on the Green. A Driver gets me twenty yards closer but brings the reeds and water into play. Let's stick with the 3-Wood."

He was right.

A perfect drive with the 3-Wood left him a hundred and ninety six yards to the middle of the Green. Wilson hit Driver into the reeds and the other players hit feeble shots which required a layup to the front of the Green.

After taking the obligatory drop, Wilson approached Brad. "Was Krnich any help?" he asked.

"Yes Sir. I feel much better knowing he's on the job."

"Good. I really don't think we are in danger. Krnich is a good man. He takes his job very seriously. If a threat materialized, he would take care of it," Wilson said.

"I'm sure he's very competent, but still...."

Wilson patted him on the arm, smiled and said, "Let's finish this hole and do the press conference. I'm hoping you and John will join me and the little lady for dinner tonight?" He winked as if it were an inside joke.

It wasn't everyday Brad was invited to dinner with one of the most influential men in the world. He quickly said yes. He glanced at Linden, hoping his friend hadn't made plans for the evening. If so, he'd just have to break them. When the Speaker of the House asks you to dinner, you don't say, "Thanks for the invite, but I've got to go call my fiancée and catch up."

You said yes.

Linden was last to hit. Lofting a majestic 5-Iron high into the air, he twirled the club in his hand and began walking down the fairway. "I dead-nutted that one pards," he boasted to Brad. "Let's go set the record."

Behind them, the crowd roared again. Brad inquired about its source.

Another birdie for Steven Ambrook.

The old man was now ten under. They both had one hole to play—the course record within each golfer's reach.

"Damn! That old man is one helluva player," John exclaimed. "Too bad he's got such a shithead for a son. Maybe I'll let him tie me. Might be better in the long run?"

"Fuck that. You're John Linden. Son, you don't play for no tie!" Brad reminded him. "One more birdie and you've got the course record. And, by the way, did you see that 'shithead' was caddying for the old man today?"

"I hadn't noticed, to tell you the truth, but I'm glad he's here. It will be nice to rub it in his little, preppy face." He grabbed his putter and strode towards the hole. "Let's make the birdie and force Steven to be aggressive."

"That's the John Linden I know and, sometimes, love."

The sound of jet skis reverberated from the waterway to their left.

Two, maybe three, were headed their way. Brad assumed they were recreational skiers frolicking in the sun; having a good time.

He smiled, remembering the trip he and Mel had taken to Cancun before the economy tanked. The Jet Skis had been the best part of the trip. He made a mental note to purchase one in the future…if he ever got financially solvent again.

As they walked to the Green, the jet skis grew louder. Linden marked his ball and tossed the dirty Titleist to Brad.

"Those damn jet skis are pretty close, aren't they?" Linden said.

"They're just kids out having fun," Brad said. "You know hang-gliders fly pretty close to Torrey Pines when the pros play there too. It's common on the tour."

"Yeah, but they don't make so much noise. I think I'll talk to the tournament organizers about it. Can't have them coming so close when the real tournament is under way."

Suddenly, to the right of them and several hundred yards away, explosions shattered the afternoon air. The whole group turned towards the sounds. Seconds later, gunshots came from the left side of the fairway. Brad spun around and saw two jet skis idling off the shore, no more than a hundred feet away. The riders sat high in their saddles; guns pointed towards the golfers on the 18th Green.

Dropping the golf bag he was carrying, Brad ran towards Linden and tackled him just as he stroked his final putt. They rolled behind a small knoll which provided them temporary shelter.

It wouldn't take long for the riders to adjust their aim.

"What the fuck!" Linden exclaimed.

"Stay down, those bullets are meant for us," Brad said, as the turf around him exploded.

Behind them, Krnich yelled for assistance.

Brad saw a tall guy dressed in Khaki pants, green golf shirt and white baseball hat run down the fairway towards the Green, weapon drawn. His heart stopped for a moment, hoping the man wasn't one of the bad guys. He breathed a sigh of relief when Krnich waved to the guy and pointed towards the shooters.

Surprisingly, although the shooters could clearly see the two agents, they didn't change their aim; bullets continued to tear at the soil around Brad and John. One almost caught Brad in the leg.

Krnich and the other agent knelt side by side and fired.

The riders went down.

Gingerly, Brad rose and surveyed the damage. There were bullet holes in Linden's golf bag and the Green had been torn up, but nobody seemed to be dead or dying. Thankfully, the shots had come in too low.

He pulled Linden up, dusted him off and asked him if he was okay?

"I think so," he said, inspecting himself for injuries. "Just a little scrape on my elbow." He showed Brad his left arm. "How about you?"

Shaken, trembling slightly, Brad bent over and exhaled deeply. He, too, checked his body for injury and then reported that he was fine. "Just a little shook up from all the commotion."

Linden used the pinky finger on his right hand to remove debris from his ears. He looked at Brad and smiled. He tilted his head from side to side like a swimmer trying to drain water from inside his head. "Damn! Those guns sure make a lot of noise."

Brilliant insight.

Brad walked towards the Green. "Looks like the shooters on the jet skis didn't account for the subtle wakes along the shoreline. They shot too low."

Linden nodded.

Brad's focus turned to the group around him. The bag he had dropped was full of bullet holes. The Green was a mess and the Treasury Secretary sat several hundred feet away holding his leg. Apparently, one round had found its way into his left thigh. It would be sore, Brad thought, but he should live.

Brad turned towards the beach.

Two jet skis floated impotently in the water, their pilots bobbing harmlessly with the tide. Bullet holes filled each rider's chest. Reddish brown water surrounded the fallen terrorists. "Hah! Deader than a duck hook," Brad muttered under his breath. Rising to his feet, he swiveled his head from side to side.

Behind him, he detected frantic motion coming from Steven Ambrook's foursome on the 18th tee box. Although it was several hundred yards away, Brad could clearly see a figure beginning to run towards him.

Was it another gunman?

The guy couldn't possibly get past Krnich. But still, Brad braced for the worst.

57

STEVEN AMBROOK RUSHED DOWN THE 18th fairway.

He wanted to see John Linden's dead body with his own two eyes.

As he drew closer, he saw Linden standing on the Green, dusting himself off and shaking his head from side to side. He cursed and then continued forward.

He stopped when Krnich raised his gun and demanded identification.

"I'm Steven Ambrook," he said. "I'm John Linden's manager." He pointed towards the 18th Green. "I want to make sure he's okay."

Krnich approached him, gun still drawn. "Let me see your I.D. please, sir" Krnich asked.

Ambrook removed his wallet and presented his driver's license. While Krnich called it in to an unknown authority, Ambrook stared at the group on the Green. Was that Stephens up there with Linden? He hadn't noticed it earlier, but the guy seemed to be caddying for John. And, obviously, they both were still alive.

"Goddammit," he muttered under his breath.

Krnich handed Ambrook back his license and offered to escort him to the Green. The shooting had stopped but they still had to be careful, the agent said. "There might be more gunmen hiding around the course."

"No, that's okay. It's only a little ways. I'll grab John and then we will get the hell off the course."

Krnich nodded and let the older man pass.

As he continued his walk towards the Green, Ambrook thought about the situation. It had been a perfect golfing day; ten under par going into the historic 18th hole—a chance to either tie the existing record or establish a new one. It would be the crowning achievement of his golfing career.

He looked at the now empty jet skis floating in the channel. The killers had been perfectly positioned to take out Linden and his pesky caddie, Stephens. Everything should have been perfect! What went wrong?

He stopped, shook his head and said under his breath, "They're just fucking incompetent. I should've known it."

He checked his watch. The disturbance had started exactly at 12:45 p.m. That much was good. The markets were still open. Once they got word of the attack, the financial markets would have panicked. IFPG's investments should have sky rocketed.

At least that part of his plan had come together.

The only setback, as far as he could tell, was that Linden and Stephens were still alive. How many lives did that guy Stephens have anyway?

Why wouldn't that moron just die?

Time for an executive management decision.

In one respect, he had achieved the chaos he needed for the market to move. Major politicians' lives' were in jeopardy. Democracy was threatened. Better to take his winnings off the table.

Time to cut his losses.

He had become good at that recently.

He would deal with the golfer and his mortgage buddy later. It was time to cover his tracks; time to go to a plan 'B'.

He picked up his pace and then began running towards the group, waving his arms and pointing. He yelled to no one specifically but everyone in general. "Look out! Look Out! He's got a gun!"

He pointed towards the Lighthouse behind the 18th Green.

== ⊕ ==

From his vantage point, high atop the Lighthouse, Von Eisenlow stared down at the action.

He used the scope on his rifle to focus on the golf course below. What he saw stunned and confused him.

If all five jet-skiers had come through, surely there would have been more people dead. He had seen two of his men approach the shore. He'd waited as long as he could for the other three to show up before finally giving the signal to attack. He had radioed both the jet-skiers and the snipers to commence the moment he saw the first group of golfers approach the 18th Green.

And where were his bomb-strapped soldiers?

He'd heard only a few shots, but no explosions. He had to face the fact that a number of his men had abandoned the mission; deserted the cause.

His two men in the water were down and security was already swarming the place. Well, dammit, he'd just

have to take care of this himself he decided while load-
ing his rifle.

Much to his surprise, he had noticed Brad Stephens
standing next to John Linden. His soldiers in Santa
Barbara must've failed their mission again. "God help
them if I survive this fight; there will be hell to pay," he
said under his breath. Checking that the safety was off on
his rifle, he made a few quick decisions.

First, he'd knock off that cockroach Stephens and
then that golfer, Linden. Perhaps the 'whisperer' would
still pay for their heads. The next shots would be saved
for the politicians huddled around the front of the Green.

As he bent his head down to get a good sight on
Stephens, he noticed someone on the course who
seemed agitated. Looked like the guy was screaming,
practically running towards one of the security guys
down there.

He suddenly realized that the guy was pointing at the
Lighthouse.

At him.

He racked his brain for a few moments trying to figure out who knew he was positioned in the Lighthouse?
He hadn't fired a shot yet. Nobody other than his soldiers
would know he was watching the fight.

Then, in a moment of absolute clarity, he figured it
out: The 'whisperer'. He was the only other person who
had known he was in the tower.

It made sense.

But why?

He thought about it for a moment and, when no
rational answer came to him, shook his head. Well, fuck
it, he thought. I'm not going to let that bastard keep

me from completing this mission. We've come too far. "It's time to make them all pay," he muttered quietly.

Returning his focus to the scope on the rifle, he prepared for his first shot. Exhaling slowly, just as the mercenaries had taught him, his finger tightened on the trigger and he fired.

Twice.

Around the course, players, politicians and spectators could be seen running for the clubhouse or taking cover behind trees and rocks.

Brad and John stood by the 18th Green, taking in the commotion. In the distance, sirens could be heard approaching the golf course and the paramedics who had arrived quickly positioned themselves on the side of the fairway, waiting for secret service agents to escort them to the fallen Secretary of the Treasury.

Security personnel could be seen herding players to safety, checking I.D.'s and reassuring spectators that everything was alright.

To his right, Brad saw an older woman lying on the ground. He didn't see any blood on her clothing or any obvious evidence of injury. He surmised she had fainted; or, had a heart attack. Paramedics looked as if they were waiting to treat her as well.

"We should be getting out of here John," Brad said forcefully.

Linden stood still, grinding a pinky in his ear. "What did you say?"

Brad drew closer to him and said loudly, "We should vamanose, amigo." He grabbed Linden's arm and made to go.

Before they could move, however, Krnich and the other agent in Khakis ran past them yelling at them to get down.

"What now?" Brad screamed back.

"The Lighthouse," Krnich yelled. "There's another shooter up there." He pointed towards a window at the top of the candy-striped building.

Without further warning, two shots filled the air.

Brad grabbed Linden and forced him into a nearby sand bunker, twisting his knee as he fell.

The shots flew over their heads, the bullets whistling as they passed. He had heard the noise before—when the maniac had tried to shoot him on the Pear Blossom highway. It was not a sound he cherished.

He hoped to never hear it again.

The depth and lip of the greenside bunker provided protection from additional shots fired from the Lighthouse. Brad relaxed slightly and thought about the situation. If the shots had been meant for he and John, the guy was an awful shot; the bullets had traveled well over their heads.

If not them, then who were the shots meant for?

He made sure John was okay and then rolled on to his side in order to gain a view of the fairway.

Behind them, maybe twenty yards or so, Steven Ambrook lay on the ground, clutching his chest. One of the rounds had caught him flush.

Brad watched as the old man reached up with his right hand and felt the hole where the bullet had entered. Even from this distance, Brad could tell that Ambrooks' blood flowed freely and he could see a look of confusion and despair on the man's face.

His first instinct was to run to the fallen man; see if he could administer a compress to the wound or blow life back into the man's lungs.

Do something.

Save him.

He remembered Krnich's orders, however, and stayed down. He rolled back over and looked at Linden.

John's face was covered with fine white sand, his head creeping up towards the lip of the trap. "What do you think? Should we make a dash for it?" Linden asked.

Brad spit some sand from his mouth and shook his head. "Krnich said to get down. To me that means there may be additional shots fired." He wiped his mouth on his shirt sleeve and then spit out some more sand. "I don't think this thing is over."

Linden peeked over the lip again. "Seems pretty quiet to me."

Brad shrugged. Remembering what he had just seen, he told Linden, "Steven Ambrook has been hit. I think those last two shots were meant for him."

"Steven! Why?"

"Don't know."

"Does it look serious?"

"If you call bleeding out serious, then, yeah, it looks really serious." Brad spit more sand from his mouth and turned his head back towards where Steven Ambrook lay.

He watched as Tyler ran at full speed and dropped to his father's side.

== ⊕ ==

"Dad. Dad. Oh, Shit. No Dad. This wasn't supposed to happen! No...." Tyler said, falling to his knees and cradling his father's head in his hands.

The elder looked at his son. A slight grin came to his lips. He asked Tyler to come closer. He had something to tell him.

"Don't worry about me, son. I had a good run. Every golfer wants to die on the golf course with his spikes on." He wheezed, blood and air expelling from the opening in his chest. "The important thing is that my company should be solvent again. That's all that matters."

All that matters? What about family?

Tyler flinched as his father grabbed him by the back of the head and pulled him even closer. Rather than delivering one last father to son embrace, Steven Ambrook whispered, "You can't let Linden and Stephens leave here alive."

Tyler stared at his dying father. "What do you mean? What can I do?"

His father wheezed again, taking in air like a fish floundering on the rocks. "I've got a gun in my golf bag. Finish the job boy. Make the religious kook kill them if you can." He pointed towards the Lighthouse.

"Who, that guy Von Eisenlow? How?"

"He's in the Lighthouse. He's got a rifle."

Ambrook grimaced, began to speak, but all that came out was a small trickle of blood. Tyler watched, transfixed, as his father's eyes focused on him. A look of profound confusion came across the old man's face and then, in an instant, the eyes glassed over and Steven Ambrook went silent.

Tyler shook his father, kneeled down to check his pulse, began C.P.R. but realized it was too late. His father was dead. He stared at the body for a few moments and then rose.

He walked slowly towards his father's golf bag, surveying the scene around him. Once he was sure nobody was watching, he reached in to his father's bag and found the semi-automatic weapon wrapped in a towel in the side pouch. He took it out; stared at it for a moment.

He walked towards the 18th Green.

He hesitated. Was he a killer too? Did it run in the family genes? Anger and fear enveloped him. He had never been truly close to his father, but by God, he would avenge his death. He would grant his father's last wish. He would kill those meddling assholes.

Picking up his pace, he walked towards Brad Stephens and John Linden.

58

VON EISENLOW BEGAN TO RELOAD HIS weapon. The rifle only held two bullets at a time.

He paused and wondered what had gone wrong?

He supposed that any plan begotten with the help of Satan was bound to fail. He had been weak. He had bought into it hook, line and sinker.

The 'whisperer' had provided money, weapons, transportation and logistical planning. In retrospect, it had all been too easy. Now his benefactor lay in a pool of blood, several hundred yards away in the middle of the 18th fairway.

"Good," Von Eisenlow muttered and then sighed. "I hope he burns in hell."

Refocusing his attention on the present threat, he considered his options. He could try to sneak out of the tower and blend with the crowd. He could surrender. He could stay and fight.

He liked the last option.

If this was to be his last stand—and he could sense it would be—he'd go down in a flame of glory. The whole world would know about the Sons for Sovereign Sacrifice after today.

Searching for Stephens, he raised his gun and leveled the sights. "At least I can finally take care of that asshole," he muttered while scanning the Green and fairway below.

He watched as two security personnel raced towards the tower. He cussed under his breath as he failed to pinpoint Stephens or Linden. He found two more bullets in his left pocket; loaded his weapon and assessed his alternate targets.

The fat politician lay flat on his stomach in a deep greenside bunker, head buried in the sand, hands covering his silvery mane.

He would be the target of the next two shots.

Von Eisenlow pulled the trigger.

The first shot missed the Speaker.

He wouldn't miss again.

== ⊕ ==

Special Agent Krnich used the distraction of Ambrook being shot to rush the Lighthouse.

Taking aim, he fired several shots from his service revolver at the window in the tower and then ducked behind a nearby tree. The revolver held only six shots. How many had he fired? Checking his pockets, he remembered he had not packed additional ammunition. It was a golf tournament, after all. Not war.

He instructed his associate, Kingston, the agent in the khakis, to cover him. Counting to ten, he took a deep breath and ran towards the front door of the Lighthouse. No shots followed him.

Forcing the door open, he entered, looked around for the main control panel and found it after a few seconds. He opened the panel's cover and located the switch labeled "Fog Horn".

He returned to the front door and waved his associate forward.

Kingston ran towards the front door, dove through it and rolled towards Krnich. He got up, dusted himself off and asked what the plan was.

"When I yell, flip this switch," Krnich said, indicating the fog horn toggle.

"You got it."

Krnich began to climb the stairs, but suddenly stopped. "How many bullets do you have left?"

The agent shook his head. "Got one in the chamber. That's it."

Krnich nodded and continued his assent.

== ⊕ ==

Above him, Von Eisenlow leveled the rifle, spotted his target again and pulled the trigger.

The shot grazed the Speaker's arm. "Damn!" he muttered. The fat politician had rolled to his right just as the shot had been fired.

Von Eisenlow began reloading the weapon but stopped when he heard footsteps coming up the metal staircase.

"Who goes there?" he yelled.

"Secret Service. Put your weapon down and come out with your hands up."

"Never."

"Give it up; you'll never make it out alive."

"Too late for that. I have to complete my mission."

Krnich rounded a sharp, metallic corner and saw the terrorist kneeling with a rifle held firmly in front of him.

"Now!" he yelled back down the stairs.

He put his fingers in his ears.

The loud roar of the massive building's fog horn filled the air.

The horn had been used many times to warn wayward ships of potential danger. This time, however, Krnich hoped it would throw his adversary off.

It worked. Von Eisenlow shook his head and dropped the bullets he held in his hands.

Krnich rushed into the room, gun drawn.

"Put down your weapon," he said again, pointing his service revolver directly at Von Eisenlow.

He hoped to God he had counted his shots correctly.

"The Lord is my savior," the assassin mumbled. "I shall not want. you are the sinner, not I. My cause is righteous You must put down your weapon, sir. Not I."

When Krnich refused to drop his gun, Von Eisenlow raised the rifle.

There were two simultaneous sounds: a bang and the "click" of an empty weapon.

59

SENSING A LULL IN THE ACTION—no new shots had been fired in their direction for several minutes—Brad rose to his feet in the sand trap and grabbed John.

"I think we can run for it now," he told Linden.

The Speaker, still lying in the sand trap, held his grazed arm, but smiled and gave them a 'thumbs up' sign. Some of the other golfers and their caddies had taken refuge in the reeds and muddy waters along the fairway. They rose slowly, one by one, as security agents pulled them to their feet and towards safety.

The paramedics finally came forward and administered to the Treasury Secretary and the unconscious woman.

"Come on, John, let's get out of here," Brad insisted.

Putter in hand, Linden rose and dusted himself off.

Throughout the fiasco, he never took his eyes off the twenty foot putt he had put in motion before the shooting began. The ball had stopped millimeters short. It hung on the edge of the cup, teasing the hole.

Even after all the commotion, the ball refused to drop in the white cup. He had to conclude it was short. The course record was intact.

He had made a par.

"Shit, Brad. Did you see that?"

"What do you mean, did I see *that*? Of course I saw it. Those gunmen could've killed us. It looks like they got Steven Ambrook, though, and the Treasury Secretary has been hit." Brad looked at the paramedics administering care to the fallen politician.

"No, not *that*," Linden responded testily, pointing to the ball hanging on the lip. "My putt. Did you see my putt stop right on the lip? It was dead in the heart. Man, I thought I had the course record."

"Are you serious? We almost get killed and you're worried about the course record. What the hell?"

"What about Ambrook? What did you say?" Linden asked as if coming out of a deep dream.

"I think he's dead?"

Brad grabbed Linden's shoulder and began to push him towards the woods.

"Damn! I liked that guy. Why couldn't they have shot his son?"

"Speaking of the little puke, here he comes. And he doesn't look too happy."

== ⊕ ==

Tyler Ambrook ambled forward, the gun still wrapped neatly in a green golf towel, the barrel only slightly visible. Sorrow and anger filled his eyes. His head swiveled from side to side—making sure no security personnel had seen the gun.

He stopped a few feet short of Brad and John. He surveyed the area for police one more time. When he was sure he was clear, he grabbed Linden by the arm and pulled him closer.

"My Dad's dead. It's your fault. You and this asshole here," he said in a low growl, discreetly waving the hidden gun towards Brad.

Brad saw the gun barrel sticking out from under the towel.

Oh, no, not again!

"Put the gun down, Tyler. Let's talk about this calmly," Brad suggested.

"All he ever wanted was a strong, well respected company. And, YOU...you took that from him." Tyler motioned to Brad to stand next to Linden.

"No. *You* took that from him," Brad said. It was the third or fourth time—depending on how one kept count—in the past few days his life had been in peril.

Brad was getting good at facing his own mortality.

He hoped he wouldn't get any more practice.

"And if we don't move off this Green, we're all sitting ducks for whoever shot your father," he added.

'We're not going anywhere," Tyler said, pushing the barrel of the gun into Linden's side.

"You stole the money from your clients. You killed Art Smalley. You tried to have me killed several times. You brought disgrace upon your family," Brad said.

"You don't get it, do you?" Tyler snickered. "I never stole money from our clients. I never killed anybody. I didn't try to kill you. I made some...er...bad investments during a very volatile market." He moved the gun from Linden's side, shoving the towel forward into Brad's face. "I was going to correct them. If you'd just kept your nose out of my books, I would've had it fixed in a few months."

"Bad Investments. Stole. Whatever. You screwed the pooch and now your father is dead."

"And, even worse," Linden interjected, "Art Smalley is dead."

"Jim Johnson too," Brad said.

"I was just trying to make money for the company. I had it all under control and then *he* had to butt in." He pointed towards the body of his fallen father.

"Bullshit! You wanted total control of IFPG." Brad was giving no quarter. What the heck, he thought, if you're going to go out, go out swinging. "You figured with your dad retired and Art Smalley out of the way you could use the company as your own personal casino. Art found out and threatened to expose you. So you killed him. Made it look like suicide."

Brad was really on a roll now, so he continued. "When I demanded John's financials, you panicked. I had become a threat. You hoped to kill me before I had a chance to confirm my suspicions and tell anyone else. The only thing I don't get...is why such an extravagant ruse? Couldn't you figure out something more subtle?"

"You just don't get it do you? The attack wasn't geared exclusively for you. Don't be so pompous. You're not that important," Tyler spat back. "My father planned these events. It took many months and lots of money to win the support of the idiot extremists who carried out this attack."

"Your father?" Brad replied not quite grasping the implications.

"Yes, my father. You think you're so fucking smart!" He laughed nervously, his eyes darting about like a meth addict looking for a fix. "Well, you're an idiot. When I told my father about the company's losses, he formed his own plan to regain the money and restore dignity to IFPG."

"What about Art?" Linden asked.

Tyler smiled. "My dad tried to get Smalley's help but the son of a bitch betrayed him. Dad had Smalley killed. No big loss. He was a real prick anyway."

"Fuck you," Linden hissed. "He was twice the man you will ever be."

Tyler glared at him and shoved the barrel of the gun back in Linden's side. For a brief moment, it appeared he was ready to pull the trigger.

"Okay, okay. Calm down," Brad said in a soft voice, both hands out in front of him, pushing towards the ground; the international symbol for slowing down. "What about the 'idiot extremists'?" Brad asked.

Tyler grinned, pulled the gun away from Linden's side, pointed it at both of them and stared at Brad. Was he enjoying this?

After a moment, he continued. "Dad funneled money through the Athlete's for Change LLC and provided funding for them. His plan was to create a national emergency —one that the various markets would respond to. He had me purchase certain stocks and bonds. You two were just collateral damage."

He stopped for a second and looked at his watch. "The markets should've reacted by now. Our trades, I'm sure, have been very successful." He turned his attention to Linden. "Too bad you're going to be shot by the terrorists. You're probably a rich man once again."

"Fuck you, I don't want your blood money," Linden spat back.

Sensing that Tyler was about to shove the gun in John's side again, Brad quickly interjected, "And you helped him along the way. You're as guilty as he, Tyler. They'll never let you run the company. You're done."

"That might be true. But not before I take you two clowns out." He waved his free arm in a grand sweeping motion. "Nobody else knows about all this. The IFPG accounts will be in the black tomorrow. None of the players will be the wiser."

He turned towards the lighthouse. "Enough talk," he said. "It's time to end this." Tyler thrust both Brad and John forward several feet in front of him.

Suddenly, they had heard the fog horn go off.

And then a single gunshot.

And then all was quiet.

"Hey asshole! You up there," Tyler shouted towards the tower. "Here are your two main targets. Take them out. Finish the job my father paid you to do."

Above them, a figure could be seen moving around in the window. The face was hidden by shadow. The barrel of a rifle appeared through the opening.

Brad and John looked at each other. "Now I know why people who think they're going to die pee all over themselves," Brad said, feeling sudden pressure in his bladder.

"Don't I know it," Linden said, the color draining from his face, making him whiter than a brand new golf ball.

The rifle appeared to steady; the figure clearly aiming at the group. Brad closed his eyes and thought of Mel and the boys.

Again, like in the stairwell with Hollyfield, he found comfort in the knowledge that his family would be safe. One way or another, this thing would be over soon.

He opened his eyes, turned his head and looked at Linden.

"It's been a good ride, pards."

"Sorry I got you involved in this buddy," Linden replied.

"Hey, not your fault. It's his," Brad said pointing his thumb over his shoulder.

"Shut up, both of you," Tyler shouted.

He looked up to the tower again. The figure hadn't moved. The gun barrel still appeared in the opening. "Are you going to shoot them, or what?" he screamed.

"Now why would he want to harm those nice boys?" the agent in khaki pants said as he approached the group, gun drawn. "Put whatever you have hidden under that towel down," he demanded.

Startled, Tyler took a few steps closer to Brad and raised the gun. His head swiveled as he focused on the lighthouse. What had happened to the sniper in the tower?

"He's got his sights set on *your* chest buddy," the agent said, tilting his head towards the window at the top. "And agent Krnich is a very, very good shot. Now put the gun down and drop to the ground. Hands behind your head."

Tyler blinked his eyes rapidly and raised the gun to Brad's temple, the towel now slipping to the ground.

Brad felt the cold steel of the barrel press against the side of his head. His body grew tense and a thick bead of sweat ran down his forehead. For a moment, he thought his bladder was really going to explode.

"You don't understand," Tyler said to no one in particular, his eyes flickering even faster, his tongue licking his lips like a parched hiker in the desert. "My father was a great man. These guys got him killed." His voice drifted in the afternoon breeze.

The agent was not impressed. "We'll sort it out later, sir. For now put the gun down and back away from them."

"But…"

"Do it now!"

Tyler froze; no sign of surrender in his face or in his body language. Brad tensed for the shot to his head.

He took a deep breath, began to close his eyes, and then suddenly stopped.

From the corner of his eye he watched, amazed, as Linden raised the putter he still held and, in one quick chopping motion, knocked the gun out of Tyler's hand. It fell impotently to the ground.

Brad collected himself, spun around and tackled Tyler.

"Fuck you, asshole," he said, straddling his assailant's chest, prepared to beat him to a pulp if he put up any resistance.

Tyler lay there motionless.

Sobbing.

Defeated.

Linden approached them. He raised the putter as if to perform the coup de gras, but Brad rose and grabbed his arm. "It's over, buddy. We won."

Looking disappointed, Linden dropped the putter to his side. "Okay. I'm okay," he said, raising his free hand in mock surrender. He took a step towards Tyler, spat on him and then, in a move that would have impressed Bruce Lee, kicked him in the ribs.

Hard.

"That's for Art Smalley." Before Brad could stop him, Linden kicked again. "And that's for Brad, you piece of shit."

Rolling his body into a defensive ball position to protect from further assaults, Tyler winced in pain as the agent in Khakis approached him. He reached down and rolled Tyler on his stomach, cuffed him, and then lifted him off the ground.

He stopped for a moment and looked at Brad. "We've got it now, sir. You guys did a great job. It's over."

Brad nodded to the officer, bent over, put his hands on his knees and exhaled. After a moment, he straightened up, looked towards the tower and waved to Krnich.

The agent waved back. "Glad it was you up there," Brad mumbled under his breath.

He turned to face Linden. His buddy was holding the putter by his side. The club head rested comfortably on the grass. It was as if the long steel shaft had morphed from peaceful club to violent weapon to peaceful club again all in a span of a few minutes. A wizard's stick?

Brad grinned and asked, "Was that the 'saw' or 'claw' grip?"

Linden laughed. "Neither. I use the conventional grip when stroking really long putts or…when I'm mad as hell and beat the crap out of my golf bag. Under the circumstances, I felt the conventional grip was the correct choice. "

Brad chuckled, shook his head. "Damn, you've got to teach me that move sometime."

Before he could respond to the comment, Linden punched Brad in the shoulder. "Look buddy! My putt...." He didn't finish his sentence as the ball he had stroked before all the action began started to wobble. Slowly, gently, the ball fell into the hole.

"I wonder if that counts?" Linden asked.

"It does in my book pards," Brad said with a smile. "It was good by me."

60

BETWEEN THE SECRET SERVICE, CAPITOL Police, local police, paramedics and fire department, order had been restored rather quickly at the golf course.

But for the gunmen who had been killed and, of course, Steven Ambrook, injuries had been limited to the woman who had suffered a minor coronary, the Treasury Secretary and a few other spectators who hurt themselves while seeking cover.

Tyler had a broken rib or two, but he didn't count.

After assurances from the Secret Service and Homeland Security that the site had been swept and no further threats had been found, the tournament organizers decided to move forward with the regularly scheduled tournament beginning Thursday.

Damage to the course had been minimal. Amazing how little damage bullets do to grass and sand. A few well-placed cut and paste jobs followed by smooth sanding would fix most of the damage to the 18th Green and Fairway.

It wasn't pretty, but it would be playable.

Espinoza arrived late Monday evening. He joined his friends in the clubhouse bar.

"I leave for one day and all hell breaks loose! What gives? Couldn't you guys wait for me?"

Brad raised his half-full glass of Jack Daniels. "Have a seat, my friend. John and I were just discussing how you conveniently missed all the action."

Turning serious, Espinoza frowned. "Sorry about that, amigo." He sighed. "I was supposed to protect you and instead I was chasing bureaucrats in Orlando."

Brad patted him on the back. Before he could tell him not to worry about it, a voice came from behind the group. "Don't be too hard on yourself; you called in the threat," agent Krnich proclaimed, joining the group at the bar. "Can I buy you guys a drink?" He motioned to the bartender for another round.

Krnich ordered a Jack. Neat.

"Man after my own tastes," Brad said, raising his glass in toast.

The group sat silent for a moment, enjoying their drinks.

Finally the silence was broken when Krnich turned to face Brad. "Sorry I didn't take your warning more seriously." He shook his head. "We get so many cranks…."

"I understand. It must be tough separating fantasy from reality."

Krnich nodded slowly; said nothing.

"Hey, I'm just glad you acted as quickly as you did," Linden said.

The group toasted their new friend, agent Jim Krnich.

"What's going to happen now?" Espinoza asked.

"Well, we've already done a thorough search of the area. Found a few pretty expensive sniper rifles and two unexploded bomb-vests in a dumpster behind the parking lot."

"Any other terrorists?"

"Nope."

"What's up with the vests?" Linden asked.

"We're not sure, but it looks like Von Eisenlow had planned for a few men to attack from the west. He probably stationed them out by the parking lot and gave them orders to start shooting when the action started."

"And the vests?" Linden prodded.

"Oh yeah, the vests. Well, again, this is only speculation—we may never know—but I'd guess he told his men to commit a suicide bombing if they got caught or if they had a chance to take out a big-time politician."

"And the guys abandoned their mission?" Brad said.

"Looks that way."

Krnich raised the glass to his lips; took a long sip; put the glass down and shook his head slowly. "Suicide-bombing is not an easy sell this side of the Persian Gulf. Von Eisenlow's guys probably chickened out and ran for safety." He shrugged. "The FBI has a team out looking for them now. They'll find them if they're still in the State."

The sun had set several hours earlier and the night had turned cool and crisp. "How 'bout one last round on me?" Linden offered. "I don't have to play until Wednesday and I need a little more aiming fluid."

"Don't get too drunk," Krnich warned. "All the agencies want to debrief you guys tomorrow. It could be a long day."

"Good luck. I don't know shit," Linden said with a grin.

"That's not true, John," Brad said. "We discovered the financial mis-dealings at IFPG and we developed the theory that Art Smalley had been killed."

"Oh yeah, that."

"And Espinoza called me to warn us about a possible terrorist action. So I think they're pretty confident we know quite a lot about this actually."

"And he called it in to the local FBI, too," Krnich added. "They took it seriously enough to inform Homeland Security, but not serious enough to warn on-course personnel."

Linden nodded, accepting Brad and Krnich's logic. "And I guess there *were* the attempts on Brad's life."

The group nodded in unison. The final round of drinks was set before them. "On me," the bartended said with a wink.

Linden smiled. The rich get richer.

Turning to Krnich, Brad asked. "So we know what you think about the men outside the golf course, but what's your theory about the rest of it?"

"I really shouldn't speculate," he began. He looked around the room, searching for other agents, and then smiled. "Oh, what the hell! They're all pissed at me for not providing adequate security at the course anyway." He shook his head. "How the fuck was I supposed to know they'd send armed jet skiers? They're a bunch of assholes—these bureaucrats."

The Jack was kicking in.

He continued in a lower voice, beckoning the group to come in closer. "I think Von Eisenlow planned to attack from land, sea and the tower. For some reason, he seemed intent on having you guys killed and then who knows how much other damage he could've inflicted?" His voice drifted off as he took another sip of his cocktail.

He grinned. "Man that stuff's smooth," he said, and then continued. "It looks like he sent five guys out on jet skis and, like I said, positioned at least two men outside the parking lot."

"But I only saw two jet skis?" Brad said.

"Yeah, I know. We found two skis returned to the rental Harbour on Daufuskie Island and the Coast Guard found one floating around in the middle of the channel. Fortunately for us, his 'soldiers' weren't very good."

"What happened in the tower?" Linden asked.

Krnich rubbed his left hand over his face while reaching for his drink with his right. He suddenly looked very tired. He sighed. "I entered the bottom floor of the lighthouse and found the control panel with the fog horn master switch. I figured if the guy was armed and organized, I'd need a big distraction to have any chance of getting a jump on him."

"And the other agent—the guy in khakis—flipped the switch?" Brad said.

"Yep. I yelled down to Kingston—that's his name by the way; you guys might want to thank him when you get a chance—to push the button when I got to the top of the stairs. He did and Von Eisenlow was startled. I was able to enter the alcove during the commotion and when he turned around, we faced off."

"Shit!" Espinoza muttered.

"My thoughts exactly," Krnich said. "And…I didn't know if I even had any bullets left."

"Shit!" They all said this time.

"Yeah, well anyway, I guess I caught him in the middle of re-loading his weapon and he, for sure, didn't have any bullets in his rifle."

"And you did," Brad said.

"Yep. Had at least one."

The group fell silent again. The events of the day settling in and the booze mellowing their spirits.

Krnich finished his drink, rose to leave and then stopped suddenly. He turned to face Brad. "Let me ask *you* a question, now."

"Go ahead."

"Why did this lunatic, Von Eisenlow, want you dead so badly?"

"Tyler Ambrook told us that his father had hired him to kill Art Smalley and then when I became a threat, added me to the list."

"And Linden?"

"He was along for the ride. John and I found financial records that indicated someone had made massive unauthorized trades at IFPG. We thought it was Tyler."

"So you had to die."

"Apparently."

"Damn!" He shook his head as if taking in the inhumanity of it all.

"See you in the morning?" Brad asked.

"If I still got a job." He turned up his collar, put his hands in his pocket and exited into the cool evening.

The men watched him leave. They raised their glasses in one final salute to the man who saved John and Brad's lives.

"That is one good hombre," Espinoza said.

"Concur," Brad said. "Hope he still has his job."

Changing the subject, Espinoza asked, "Have you guys talked to Mel and Fabiola yet?"

Brad cringed. He quickly said, "Yep."

"And?"

"I told her I was okay. She cried. I cried. We kept it short. She assured me she'd have a lot more to say when I got home."

"Ouch!"

"I know. I'm in trouble. But she'll get over it."

"You hope," Linden joked.

"What about Fabiola?" Espinoza asked.

"She hasn't answered any of my calls," Linden said, puzzled.

"I'm sure she'll get back in touch with you soon." He pointed to the television set above the bar. "It's all over the news."

Brad wasn't so sure, but this wasn't the time to let his friend know about his soon-to-be former fiancée.

The running banner under the scene of crime tape and Ambrook's fallen body on the TV caught Brad's eye: President resting comfortably after assassination attempt in Syria. "What the fuck? Did you guys see that? They tried to kill the President in Syria."

"Didn't you know that?" Espinoza asked truly surprised. "It's been the lead story all afternoon. You guys and Hilton Head have played second fiddle."

Brad and Linden both shook their heads. "Had no idea," Linden said.

"Well, anyway, a guy fired a shot while the President was coming down the stairs on Air Force One. The Secret Service killed the shooter instantly. Turns out he was Al Queda."

"Big day for the Secret Service," Brad said.

The group focused their attention on the television screen. A beautiful, dark-haired, female reporter came on the screen and announced that the financial markets had tumbled when news of the shooting was released. "The Dow Jones industrials dropped over eight hundred points today to finish at ten thousand two hundred and thirty." She pointed at the big board behind her. "And in the bond market, as could be expected, the benchmark Ten Year Treasury rallied two full points in a flight by investors to safety; its yield falling to one point sixty five percent."

Brad wondered if these were the events Ambrook had bet on to make his company solvent again? There was no way Steven Ambrook could know about the assassination attempt in Syria...could he? Was he that well connected?

He shook off the notion, took a slow, steady swallow of his Jack and shrugged. No sense in speculating, he thought. He made a mental note to ask Krnich about it later.

"Well, hells bells, there probably goes the rest of my money," Linden said, shaking his head. He gulped the remainder of his drink.

"Maybe not," Brad said.

"What?"

"Never mind. We'll talk about it later."

Changing the focus back to golf, Brad asked, "What's your plan for this tournament?"

"Hank's coming in Wednesday to caddie for me. Looks like he and I got to win this thing." He paused and then chuckled nervously. "If I'm really broke, Fabby is going to be pissed at me."

Brad frowned; said nothing.

They finished their drinks, said goodnight to each other and headed to their rooms for the evening.

Brad's head hadn't hit the pillow for more than a few seconds when he suddenly realized that he might—finally—enjoy a restful night's sleep.

The face in his dream had been filled in. It was Steven Ambrook.

Ambrook had been the mastermind behind this whole fiasco. He was now dead; his son in custody; the terrorists, either dead or being tracked down by the authorities.

Brad didn't die at the end of the dream after all.

He took a deep, cleansing breath and drifted into a sound, peaceful sleep.

THE FOLLOWING DAY WAS A BLUR, full of de-briefings and media questions.

Brad and John answered questions for the various intelligence agencies all morning.

Amazing how they could all ask the same questions, didn't they compare notes?

Local journalists swamped them with questions during an impromptu news conference while the national news channels pushed for exclusive interviews.

Brad deferred to Linden. The professional golfer had experience dealing with the press. "We'll be happy to do interviews next week. Just give us a few days, okay. For now, I've got a tournament to win," Linden said, dismissing the requests with unusual diplomacy.

Another hidden talent?

Brad and Raoul prepared to leave for the airport to board the private plane back to Santa Barbara Wednesday morning. When saying goodbye, Linden grabbed Brad and gave him a big man hug.

"Thanks for everything."

"Good luck in the tournament, buddy," Brad said.

"Yeah, good luck," Espinoza added.

"Don't need luck, pards. Got the claw grip."

Typical Linden.

"See you in SB soon?" Brad asked tentatively.

"Be there as soon as I win this bad boy." He went to join his regular caddie, Hank, on the putting green and then stopped abruptly. He turned to face Brad and said, "Still haven't heard from Fabby. If she's still out there, tell her I'll see her on Monday."

"I will."

"And Brad...tell her I love her, okay."

Brad nodded. This breakup might be harder than he thought.

As the plane maneuvered for its final landing, Brad stared out the small round window to his right. Several thousand feet below lay the Pacific Ocean where waves broke gently along the shore. He wasn't positive, but it looked like a pod of dolphin swam immediately below the plane. Either that or seaweed was moving rapidly in the afternoon tide.

It was good to be back home. He belonged on the West Coast.

The plane landed ten minutes later and a few minutes after that Brad and Raoul departed to a beautiful combination of sunshine and clean, crisp, California air.

He remembered immediately why he loved this area so much.

He looked across the tarmac and saw Mel standing with the boys, her thin arms wrapped around both of their waists. Stef was there too. Rufus was on a leash by her side.

"I'm going to let you enjoy your family reunion," Espinoza said, patting his friend on the back and waving to the group.

"Thanks, buddy. Hope you enjoy Palm Springs."

"I got a feeling we're going to have a great time." He shook Brad's hand, gave him a quick hug and increased his pace to exit the tarmac.

Mel rushed forward. She gave Espinoza a big kiss on the cheek. And then a hug. "Thanks."

Enough said.

He blushed and shrugged.

All in a day's work.

He pecked her on the cheek and told her he'd see her soon.

Rufus broke free from Stef's grip and raced towards his master, leash dragging on the asphalt, tongue flopping from side to side. Older Rottweiler's do not run gracefully, they lumber at a fast pace. Brad bent to pet his dog and when it became obvious that Rufus wanted a kiss, bent down further and let the big dog lick his face and ears.

Man's best friend.

"Glad to see you're in one piece, you big idiot," Mel said, punching him on the shoulder, tears flowing. He smiled. They embraced and shared a long, hard kiss.

He pulled away slightly, brushed a few strands of hair off her face and stared into her beautiful green eyes. "Good to see you too, honey. Anything exciting happen while I was away?"

"Very funny. We can talk about it later. As a matter of fact, I've got a few things to talk to you about."

"Great. Looking forward to it." He rolled his eyes.

He gathered the dog's leash and, together, they moved towards the exit. When he got there, he hugged the boys and Stef. The whole group jumped into Mel's S.U.V. "I feel like Dorothy at the end of the Wizard of Oz," he said. "I'm just so happy to see all of you again."

"And, Rufus, too?" Stef joked.

"Yes, and Rufus too."

They drove a few miles in silence.

As they approached downtown Santa Barbara, Brad's thoughts drifted to his day job. "Hey Stef, how are things going at the office?"

"You've only been gone a few days Brad. Not much has happened since you left."

"I'm thinking about moving my office downstairs. I'm not sure I can concentrate in that room where Johnson died."

She shook her head. "No, don't do that. The corner office is *your* office. You've earned it after so many years of hard work. Don't let the crooks win by chasing you out."

He nodded and grinned. "Okay, okay. I didn't know you felt so strongly about it. I'll stay put." He paused and then added, "Sorry I haven't been around that much lately. Has the paperwork stacked up?"

"I stayed on top of most of it, but you have a few calls to return." It was her turn to pause now. The dog had positioned himself so he was leaning over her shoulder, drooling slightly. She pet him and wiped his mouth with a Kleenex she pulled from her purse.

"Sorry about the dog," Mel said. "He's just so excited to see everybody."

Stef smiled. "No problem. You know I love Rufie." She pet him again and then turned her attention to the front of the car. "I do have some news."

"Do tell," Mel said.

"Tommy and I are splitting."

"Divorce?"

"Yes, I think so."

Hoping he hadn't done anything to hasten the split, Brad asked tentatively, "Why? What happened?"

Reading him like a twenty foot downhill putt, Stef smiled and said, "Don't worry boss, you didn't have anything to do with it. I know you called him a few days ago. But this has been building up for a while."

Phew, dodged another bullet.

"Anything specific?" Mel asked. "Did he hit you or something?" Her face suddenly became more concerned as if the thought had real merit.

"No, no, nothing like that. It's just that I've come to see his real side. He's been mean, vindictive, and surly since his latest injury. And, he's become jealous and possessive as hell."

Mel nodded. She understood.

Brad said nothing.

Stef continued. "Anyway, I decided life is too short for all that bullshit. The kids are grown. They'll be okay. So I'm moving on." She pet the dog's head again and asked almost as an afterthought, "Got any rich, handsome, single friends for me to meet?"

"And nice. Don't forget nice," Mel added.

Brad smiled. "Maybe."

== ⊕ ==

John Linden arrived at Brad's house late Monday afternoon. No trophy in hand.

A wad of cash in his pocket.

"I didn't get a chance to watch the whole tournament," Brad said as he greeted his friend, "but I did see that you finished second."

"Yeah, I had a chance to win it on the final hole, but the putt didn't fall this time." He pursed his lips and shrugged. "I guess even with the claw I can't make them all."

"You're going to make your fair share, don't worry. Second place ain't too shabby you know."

Linden reluctantly agreed and continued into the house, stopping to rub Rufus' belly and calling out for Mel. "Lucy, I *hone*," he said, doing his best Desi Arnez.

Mel came down the hallway and smiled when she saw Linden. "Brad says you had a good tourney," she said as she gave him a warm hug.

"It was okay, I guess. But I really wanted to win."

Brad knew his friend. He knew that John would've shaken hands, done the necessary press interviews and said the right things, but...second place was unacceptable in his world. He was a competitor. He might talk a lot on the course to relieve tension and he might appear extremely easy going, but John Linden coveted winning.

Brad knew.

It's what separated him from the pack. Second place finishes paid the bills; but they didn't satisfy the ego. He'd redouble his practice sessions and increase his focus. He'd be back on top soon.

Or die trying.

Brad draped his arm over his buddy's shoulder and escorted him out to the patio. "Mel, could you get that bottle of Dom Perignon I have chilling in the refrigerator?"

Startled by the request, Mel stared at her husband and asked, "What's the occasion? He finished second. We don't usually celebrate second place do we?"

"Yeah, buddy. I appreciate it, but it's no big deal," Linden added. "Nobody remembers who took second place."

Brad kept his arm around Linden's shoulder and continued to guide him outside. "I know you wanted to win, but six hundred and fifty thousand dollars ain't chopped liver."

"That's true. I do need the money."

"Yes you do," Brad said, taking the bottle from Mel. He pointed the neck towards the canyon below and popped the cork. He poured each of them a tall glass. "But not as much as you did this morning."

Linden and Mel looked at each other as if Brad had gone crazy. What was he talking about?

"I can see from the look on your faces, you're confused."

They both nodded.

"Well, in that case, I'd like to raise a toast to my new multi-millionaire friend, Mr. John Linden."

"*Splain*," Mel said, now doing *her* best Desi.

"I got a call from Jim Krnich this morning. He told me three things: One, Tyler Ambrook has lawyered up, so we may never know more about what happened other than what he disclosed to us out there on the golf course."

Linden shrugged.

"Two, the FBI caught the two would-be suicide bombers. He says they've got the combined IQ of a golf ball, but they did say something about a compound in Virginia. The feds are hoping to launch an assault on the place later today."

"That's good," Mel said. "I hope they get all those guys. I don't want one of them thinking he has to finish the job, if you know what I mean."

"Highly unlikely," Brad assured her. "Without their leader, a group like the Sons for Sovereign Sacrifice can't function. If there are any of them left, they've probably disbanded by now and have gone home."

"That's all well and good. What's the third thing?" Linden asked.

Brad frowned; exhaled and shook his head. "Well, here's the thing." He took another deep breath. He paused, rubbed the back of his neck as if conflicted.

Eat your heart out Al Pacino.

After a moment he faced Linden and said, "Krnich said the FBI and the Treasury Department have concluded their investigation into IFPG's books."

Linden's expression remained neutral. "And?"

"He said that after our de-briefing the other day, they were curious and decided to do a quick, forensic audit of the current accounts at IFPG." Brad paused, took a sip of the champagne. He was enjoying this moment and wanted to stretch it out as long as possible.

"And?"

Lots of 'ands' suddenly.

"And...it turns out that Tyler Ambrook was definitely a little shit, but apparently his father was a genius. His investments were well placed and proved to be highly profitable."

"But they were illegal," Linden said. "Even *I* know you can't keep monies earned from illegal activities."

"Well, here's the thing." Brad picked up a nearby stone and flung it in the canyon, took a sip of champagne and turned to face his friend; a small grin beginning to form at the corners of his mouth. "The market moved *before* the shooting started in Hilton Head."

"Before?"

Brad nodded.

Time to abandon the charade.

"Apparently, the market focused on the assassination attempt on the President. By the time the Speaker was shot, the market had lost over a thousand points. Since the market recovered a few hundred points before the close, the authorities have been forced to admit that the events at Harbour Town didn't cause the market volatility. Therefore, the trades by IFPG have been deemed legal and final."

Brad raised his glass in toast. "You, my friend, have recaptured all your money—and then some—and you will be allowed to keep it all."

"Holy shit! That's great news!" Linden screamed, doing a little Irish Jig. He slugged down his glass of champagne, asked for another, chugged it and then hugged Brad.

"I'll drink to that," Mel added and clinked glasses with both Brad and John.

62

A FEW HOURS LATER, THEY gathered their things and drove into Montecito for dinner.

Linden's treat.

Barneys, the local steak house, made two boasts: The best in-bone sirloin in town and the stiffest cocktail for miles around.

The group decided to test both claims.

While waiting for their dinners to be served, Brad decided to address the proverbial thousand pound elephant in the room. "Have you heard from Fabiola?" he asked.

"No, I haven't. It's the strangest thing. I'm almost thinking I should call the police."

"I'd hold off if I were you."

"Why? Do you know something I don't?"

Brad took a deep breath. Under the table, Mel kicked his shin. He glanced at her and frowned. "I think she's okay. I have a feeling she's just overwhelmed and needs her own space right now."

Mel smiled.

Dodged another bullet.

"Her own space? Now that I have all my money back, we can buy a really big house. She'll have plenty of space."

As he finished the last sentence, almost on cue, a familiar voice drifted from the bar located twenty feet away across an open patio.

"Aren't *ju tee* gentleman," the Latina voice said.

Brad turned his head and saw Fabiola being ushered on to a stool at the bar. He glanced at Mel. She winced. He stared at John, hoping his friend hadn't seen her.

Too late.

Damn! Didn't dodge that bullet.

Linden was already rising from his seat before Brad could stop him.

"That's Fabiola," Linden exclaimed. "I'd recognize that voice anywhere." He stopped, looked at Brad and Mel quizzically. "Excuse me," he said, putting his napkin down on the table.

He moved quickly towards the bar.

Brad and Mel exchanged knowing glances. Nothing needed to be said. This wasn't going to go well. Should they have warned John? How do you tell a friend his lover no longer loves him (and maybe never did)?

Brad watched as Linden approached Fabiola and tried to give her a kiss. She rose and gave him a slight hug and then sat back down. They exchanged words for a few minutes. Linden waved his arms around a few times as if swatting at flies. Fabiola continued to shake her head. Brad grinned as John reached into his wallet and pulled out five crisp hundred dollar bills and threw them in her face.

Linden turned and strode towards the table. His mood had darkened and his shoulders slumped.

"Fabby dumped me. Said she couldn't handle the pressure that came from being married to a famous athlete." He paused, looked from Brad and then to Mel, his eyes sad and moist. "Can you believe that? Can't handle the pressure. What kind of horseshit is that?"

Mel reached across and touched his arm. "I'm so sorry John. I know you loved her."

Brad pursed his lips, nodded.

It's what guys do when they have no words. They nod.

Linden called the waiter over and ordered another round of drinks for the table. After a few moments, he sighed, sat back and said, "Well, fuck it. She doesn't know what she's missing."

"That's the spirit," Brad said.

It's the other thing guys do. They validate their buddies.

"I really loved that girl, you know, but I've got to tell you the truth. You probably never noticed it, but she could get…moody."

"*Moody*?" Mel said.

"Okay…bitchy. But it's only because of her hot, Latin blood."

"If you say so," Mel said.

"You doing okay?" Brad asked.

It's the final thing guys do. They ask innocuous questions, rather than explore feelings.

"I think so. Let's eat dinner and get out of here. I've got some thinking to do."

They finished up their steaks, unable to rate them appropriately due to the circumstances. But based on Mel's slurring of words and Linden's blood-shot eyes, Brad could confirm that Barney's did, in fact, pour one mean cocktail.

The next morning, Brad arose to a slight hangover and, fortunately, the smell of freshly brewed coffee. He stumbled in to the kitchen and found John and Mel sipping coffee and chatting quietly.

"Hey Brad, hope we didn't wake you?" Linden said.

"No, you didn't. How are you doing this morning?" Brad asked, reaching for a cup of coffee.

"Fabulous," Linden said.

"Really? You didn't look too fabulous last night."

"Last night hit me like a triple bogey, but I'm okay now. As a matter of fact, I'm fabulous!"

"Glad to see you bounce back."

Linden blew on his coffee then took a big sip. He nodded towards Mel. "Your wife is a great woman, did you know that?"

Brad nodded.

"We've been talking all morning. She's helped me come to grips with it. Fabby was fantastic in bed and a real live wire—don't get me wrong. I like those things. But, she was needy. And in retrospect, I'm not sure she ever really loved me. I was beginning to think I'd have to walk on egg shells around that woman. Now, I'm a free man."

"And this is what my wife helped you decide?"

"It is."

Brad glanced at Mel. She was making a big deal out of blowing on her coffee, her eyes fixed on the brown liquid in her cup. He waited her out. After a few moments, she raised her eyes, met his and shrugged.

He grinned.

Linden continued. "My game is tight. My friend's are safe. I'm rich again. Life is good."

"What's your next move, big man?" Brad asked.

"Funny you should ask. I've been thinking about my life a lot since last night."

"Wonder why?" Mel said facetiously. "You've only gone broke, had a friend nearly killed and were almost killed yourself. And now you lost the 'love' of your life."

"Yeah, bullets flying will get you thinking about things," he agreed.

Linden took of a sip of coffee, stared out the kitchen window at the canyon below and then continued. "Here's the thing. I want to live in Montecito. It should be my home base. It just feels right. You guys are my family. I want to be close to y'all. I don't give a damn if Fabby is in town. She can screw all the dorks she wants. Doesn't matter to me. I hope she finds happiness. Me, I want to live in this wonderful place." He spread his arms wide. "So, first thing, Brad you got to find me a nice comfortable house. Let's not make it as grandiose as Fabby wanted. Okay?"

"No problem; I've got a few in mind."

"Second, and I won't take NO for an answer, I want you to become my personal agent. IFPG is out. I got a feeling they'll probably go out of business by year's end anyway."

The offer took Brad by surprise. IFPG was big—until a few days ago, too big to fail.

IFPG had been the undisputed super-agent for the entire tour. Surely there were enough experienced agents left at the company to reform the business.

"I don't know how to represent you, John. I'm a mortgage guy."

"You didn't know how to investigate fraud and murder either. But you did it. And did it well, I might add." He smiled, blew on his coffee and took another sip.

"Think of this as just another challenge. I'm really pretty easy. Just keep me in cash, book my travel, pay the tourney fees, and handle all my finances. What could be easier?"

"I know you think it *sounds* easy on paper, but…." Brad didn't finish the thought. He let it hang in the air. He stared at his friend.

Linden shrugged. "But what?" he asked.

"But….nothing. I think I can do it. I want to keep originating mortgages though. Can't quit the core business." He paused, looked at Mel and smiled. He returned his attention to Linden and said, "And I've got to be able to put Stef on the payroll…."

"Demands. Already?" Linden professed mock surprise. "Tell you what. Let's set up the bank accounts and work up my calendar and then we can talk about logistics. Who knows, play your cards right, maybe I can talk a few other guys into using your services."

This was better than anything he could've imagined. The slight change in job would be good for his pocket book and invigorating for his soul.

He hmmed and hawed for a few minutes, brought up a few more issues—not the least of which was business between friends—but eventually agreed.

They shook on it.

"I think this is going to be a match made in heaven," Mel said.

"Just stay focused on my shit, and you'll be okay," Linden said.

His shit. This is what Brad was worried about. Was it always going to be about John?

He guessed time would tell.

In the meantime he *was* focused. He wouldn't lose sight of anything this time around. It felt good to get a second chance at financial success.

He almost wanted to pound his chest like a Gorilla and declare that he was the king of his domain.

Zindo would be proud of him.

"Hey pards" Brad said.

"Yeah."

"Thanks for giving me a chance to earn my way back. You don't know what this means to me."

It was a new thing guys might say to each other coming out of this shitty recession.

The two friends exchanged knowing looks. Linden winked.

He moved closer to Brad. Taking him by the arm, he told Mel he had some immediate business to do with his new agent and it involved the internet. They needed to go into Brad's home office.

Mel waved them off and turned her attention to the beautiful morning. The sun was shining brilliantly and the ocean was as calm as a freshwater lake. She grinned as she watched Rufus chase a bunny rabbit across the front lawn.

They entered Brad's office and sat down, Linden sprawling out in a large leather chair and Brad sitting behind his desk, next to his computer. "So what's so important I got to look it up on the internet?"

"Oh that? I was just making an excuse so we could get away from Mel." He rose and closed the office door.

"Why?"

Linden cleared his throat. "Well, Mel told me this morning that Stef is getting a divorce."

"Yeah, so what?"

"So I always thought she was smokin' hot. Think she'd like the company of a boring, rich, professional golfer?"

There it was. Just like that. Fabiola had just dumped him. He had just fallen off the horse and already he wanted to get back in the saddle and ride.

Well, not with *his* Stefanie—at least not without conditions.

"Before I answer that, let me tell you a few things. One, Stef is very vulnerable right now. She just broke up with Tommy. Two, if, and I say *IF*, I give this my blessing, you have to promise me you won't break her heart." Brad stared at Linden, letting the statement really settle in.

Linden raised his hands in front of his face as if warding off a vicious blow. "Hey, I'm just asking. If you don't want me to date her, just tell me. I'll respect your wishes."

Brad thought about it for a few minutes. He wished for his friends to be happy. Who was he to stand in their way? But he didn't want to lose either one of them as a friend because of a stupid, rebound romance.

A conundrum. He hadn't one of those in, oh, forty eight hours or so.

"Let's play it one hole at a time. Let me think about it while we find you a new house. Maybe I can feel Stef out a little and see if she would have any interest in dating you."

"Fair enough. I've got nothing but time."

Brad said nothing.

They say opposites attract. Maybe Linden and Stef would hit it off. Who knew?

Look at him and Mel. Ying and Yang.

It had worked for three decades.

Brad sat back in his chair and watched as Linden stepped in front of a long mirror affixed to his office wall. He began rehearsing his back swing, phantom club gripped in his hands. He checked the position of his wrists every foot or so.

A golf thing.

A truly addicted golfer can practice his swing anywhere, anytime. But when you put them in front of a mirror—giving them automatic feedback—they almost squirm with delight. Linden was in hog heaven.

"I think you're lifting the club too quickly," Brad said.

Linden stared at him, suddenly, deadly serious. "You think so? I was thinking the same thing. See here, my right hand is taking control too soon." He pointed to his right hand and insisted that Brad come around the desk and force him to push the imaginary club back more with the palm of his left hand.

Watching the joy Linden felt in correcting his imaginary swing with his imaginary club, Brad suddenly thought, "Hell, it might actually be fun managing this guy?"

He left Linden standing in front of the mirror and joined Mel in the kitchen. He put his arms around her waist and kissed the back of her neck gently.

"What's that for?" she asked.

"Nothing special. Just because."

"I like 'just because'." She smiled and sighed. "You can do it again if you like," she said quietly.

He did.

They stood like that for several moments and then he broke the silence. "Mel do you believe in righteous retribution?"

"You mean, Karma? What goes around comes around?"

"Yeah, something like that I guess."

"I do. I believe in it strongly."

He smiled. "I do too. Now," he said. "I think we've got some good Karma going for us. And I want you to know I'm not going to screw it up this time around."

"What on earth are you talking about, Brad Stephens?"

"In golf, they call it the "Post Birdie Fuck Up"— a bogey is likely to follow a birdie."

"So, what does that have to do with us?"

"Don't you see? This opportunity John has given me is like making a birdie in life—it's a second chance at financial success. I'm not going to fuck up this time. I'm going to, at least, make par on the next hole."

She turned and stared at him. "Well, if you're going to continue to use golf metaphors for life, then I'm going to do so as well."

He feigned shock. "You know golfing metaphors? I'm impressed."

"I've lived with you for thirty years. Of course I know golf metaphors."

"Okay. Hit me with your best shot." He jutted his chin forward.

She paused, took his hand in hers and said, "Don't we all deserve a second chance? You see it in golf after hitting a bad first shot out of bounds. Your friends tell you to tee it up again."

She smiled, impressed with her metaphor. Emboldened, she continued. "They're telling you: No worries buddy, you weren't warmed up...No harm, no foul. Go ahead, hit another one: we'll give you a Breakfast Ball."

Read on for an excerpt from

J.A. Maloney's next

Brad Stephens Novel:

DEATH AT THE HIGH END.

Available from JM Publishing
on Amazon.

December, 2013

HE AWOKE EARLY, *around six a.m.. A distasteful job and ironically, baseball, on his mind.*

After doing his customary hundred push ups and two hundred crunches, he turned on the television just in time to catch the local weather report. The announcer, a geeky looking guy in bow tie and cheap gray suit with a flower in the lapel, announced that San Diegans would experience another summer day of 'early morning low clouds giving way to sunshine around eleven thirty' along the coast.

How boring.

He didn't like predictability. The nature of his business required him to plan his movements meticulously —but do so without establishing a repetitive pattern. Today, for instance, he would visit the pool and Jacuzzi early. He would take a good book with him and order breakfast by the pool. Yesterday, he ate in the café. The day before, he ventured out.

Unpredictable.

If the hired help was asked questions about the man in room 227, they would have to confirm that he acted like any other normal tourist.

Nothing special.

No unusual characteristics.

Just another 'ordinary guy'.

Tonight, he hoped the fog would stay offshore until late evening. He was going to the ballgame and wanted to dress light.

As he ventured poolside, he took great pains to ask the front desk and bell men for directions to the ballpark. It was important that they know he intended to go to the game downtown. It started at five p.m. and would take him at least an hour to get there from the coastal hotel. The time line should provide him adequate coverage for the afternoon's activities.

He wondered if he'd really ever need a true 'alibi'. After all, he had been performing his duties on this specific assignment for several weeks. Neither the local police from San Francisco to San Diego to Palm Springs nor the FBI—or whatever special Federal task force they used these days—appeared close to catching him.

Hell, they hadn't even discovered a plausible motivation behind his crimes.

The 'experts' seemed fully content labeling him a "Serial Killer" with a pent up grudge against people in a certain profession. In this case, real estate agents. Obviously, they concluded, the killer either had 'mommy issues' or had been burned by the recession and was now 'acting out'.

He was sure that law enforcement spent hours –if not days—researching local real estate transactions that had gone awry; death threats that had been made to local realtors; or digging for any violent connection to the local real estate communities in which the murders had occurred.

What idiots.

As long as those bozos continued barking up the wrong tree, he wouldn't need an alibi. They'd never question him. However, since he was a professional and since he prided himself on his preparation as well as his performance, it was imperative that he continue to back-fill his actions and make certain that the hotel staff see him daily. If some smart cop expanded the search criteria to suspicious visitors or persons of interest noticed around the crime scene, he would be prepared. His alibi—if needed— would be airtight.

He finished his morning swim, Jacuzzi, breakfast and reading session around eight thirty. After showering and shaving, he packed a few items in a day bag and announced to the front desk and the valet that he was going site seeing in the North County. Did they have any suggestions?

After exchanging ideas about his proposed itinerary, he hopped into his non-descript gray Chevy Nova, waved goodbye, and told the parking attendant he'd see him in a few hours. He headed towards the freeway. Ever the stickler for details, he entered the I-5 going north. He continued for a few miles and then, abruptly, took the next off ramp doubled back, and headed south.

The day was unfolding just as the geeky weather guy had predicted. By the time he reached his destination, Coronado Island, the sun was clearly burning through the clouds. Driving around the island he noticed several 'For Sale' signs in front of various styles of homes.

There were Spanish homes for sale. There were older Tudors, older Craftsman, and one unique Victorian. Coronado had originally been established as an Air and Naval support area. Sections were filled with military housing, condos and apartments.

Along the water, however, high end real estate averaged well over a million dollars in value. Base commanders and other political dignitaries had built and established their homes on the island. These were of higher quality and larger size than the homes occupied by average military families.

His target—his soon to be latest victim—that warm afternoon, would be found in the older, 'unique' Victorian.

He drove slowly around the neighborhood, casing the house while acquainting himself with the various driveways, alleyways and walkways around and adjacent to the property.

Satisfied with his early recognizance, he allowed himself a quick trip over to the famous Coronado Hotel. His favorite movie of all time, "Some Like it Hot", with Tony Curtis and Marilyn Monroe, had shot many memorable scenes at the elegant hotel.

He laughed at the irony. The gangster in the movie, George Rath, would be proud of his current role—the hired professional killer. The Rath character would understand and appreciate the killer's main motivation: Money. The stately hotel looked smaller in person. And really, really old.

Disappointed, he exited the island via the bridge and found the nearest on ramp for I-5 North. Time to truly visit a site or two in the North County, grab lunch and make the return to his hotel obvious to all.

Along the way, he opened the disposable cell phone he had purchased while driving through Los Angeles. Searching for the number on the newspaper ad, he quickly found it and made the call.

"This is Anna Marie Gustapo," the female voice on the other end said.

Hello, Anna Marie. Do you mind if I call you Anna Marie?" he asked confidently, knowing full well she preferred the two name moniker. Her advertisements—which could be found in any local real estate rag, the local newspaper, and on shopping carts all around upper-end communities in San Diego—declared, "There's only ONE Anna Marie!"

Now he was speaking to her.

"That's fine, Mr..."

"John. John Feinstein."

"Well John, what can I do for you?"

"I'd like to preview the listing you have in Coronado. 14752 Island View Way," he said.

The older Victorian? It's a lovely house. Good bones. Well worth the $1.8 million the owner is asking. It was recently remodeled and the views are to die for!"

That's exactly what I'm looking for, Anna Marie," he said with a grin, recognizing the irony of her last statement. "Can you meet me there at oh, say, four p.m.?"

"I'm not sure I can make it, but I can have one of my assistants open it for you and your agent."

That's the thing. I don't have an agent. I was hoping to see the house, meet you and discuss *you* representing me," he said in a calm yet assertive manner. "After all, there's only ONE Anna Marie," he added.

Motivated by the notion of 'double ending' the commission—making money from both the seller and buyer—Anna Marie Gustapo quickly agreed to meet Mr. Feinstein at 4:00 p.m. sharp.

She had one final question, "Have you been prequalified for an appropriate loan?"

Won't need one I'm an all cash buyer. See you at 4:00." Knowing she was feeling smug, he said goodbye and hung up.

Oh Anna Marie, he thought. 'How quickly the moth comes to the flame.'

He opened his glove compartment and caressed the butcher knife wrapped tightly inside a San Francisco street map. Lying next to the knife was a ticket for the Padre game that evening.

She had better be prompt, he thought. If the bitch made him miss the first pitch, he'd be pissed.

Right now this was a professional hit. A cold, calculated murder. Done properly — although this one would be the bloodiest yet—she wouldn't feel much pain. The first thrust of the knife would be directly to her heart. His training in this matter had been precise. She'd be dead before she hit the floor. Once dead, he'd cut her up. Make it look like a crime of passion.

But, if he missed part of the ball game due to her tardiness or some other unforeseen delay it would become personal.

Believe me, Anna Marie, my ONE and only," he said to himself, "You Bitch! You do *not* want me to make this personal!"